TRAVELER

BOOKS BY ARWEN ELYS DAYTON

Seeker
Traveler

TRAVELER

ARWEN ELYS DAYTON

CORGI

CORGI BOOKS

UK | USA | Canada | Ireland | Australia
India | New Zealand | South Africa

Corgi Books is part of the Penguin Random House group of companies
whose addresses can be found at global.penguinrandomhouse.com.

www.penguin.co.uk
www.puffin.co.uk
www.ladybird.co.uk

Penguin
Random House
UK

First published 2016

001

Printed and bound by CPI Group (UK) Ltd, Croydon, CR0 4YY

A CIP catalogue record for this book is available from the British Library

ISBN: 978 0 552 57056 5

All correspondence to:
Corgi Books
Penguin Random House Children's
80 Strand, London WC2R 0RL

Penguin Random House is committed to a sustainable future for our business, our readers
and our planet. This book is made from Forest Stewardship Council® certified paper.

To my Tolkien-loving mother and father, for,
many years ago, treating me like an adult but giving
me all the time I needed to be a child.

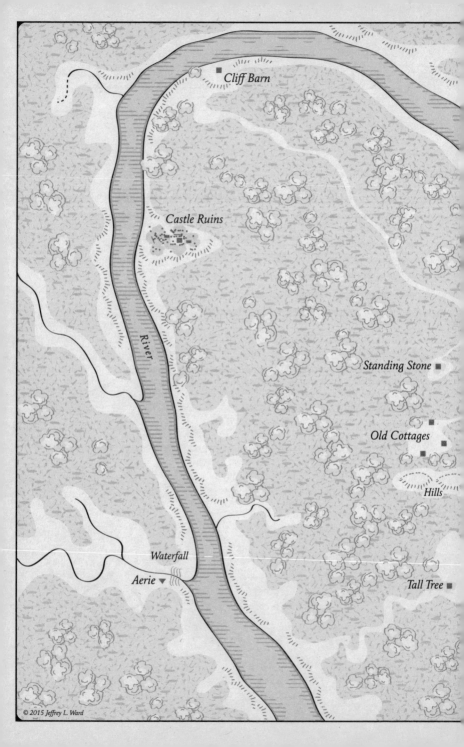

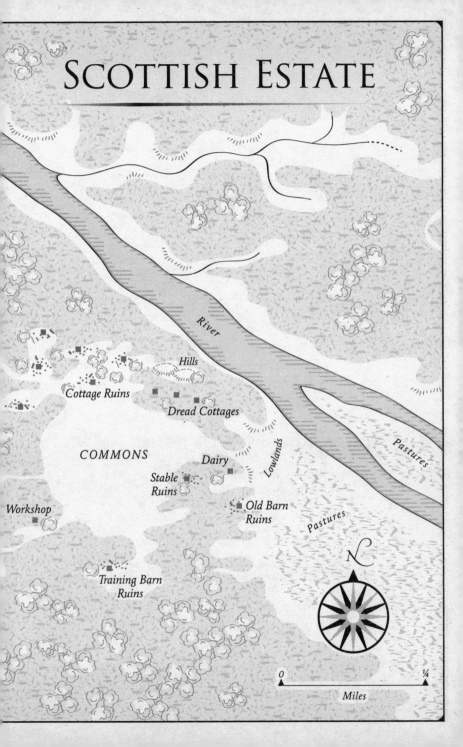

TRAVELER

CHAPTER 1

QUIN

"Shinobu?" Quin asked when she saw him stirring. "Are you awake?"

"I think so," he answered slowly.

Shinobu MacBain's voice was thick and groggy, but he raised his head to look for her. It was the first time he'd moved in several hours, and Quin was relieved to see him conscious.

She carefully tucked the leather book she'd been clutching into her jacket pocket and crossed the darkened hospital room to where Shinobu lay, in a bed that looked too short for someone so tall.

Even in the dim light, she could make out the burns on both of his cheeks. They were mostly healed, and his head was now covered with a thick, even growth of dark red hair—but she was stuck with the memory of the singed and blood-caked hair the nurses had shaved off when he was admitted for surgery.

"Hey," she said, crouching next to the bed. "It's good to see you awake."

He tried to smile, but it ended up as a grimace. "It's good to be awake . . . except for every part of my body hurting."

"Well, you don't do anything halfway, now, do you?" she asked, letting her chin rest on the bed's railing. "You'll help me even if it means throwing yourself off a building, crashing an airship, and getting cut in half."

"You jumped off that building with me," he pointed out, his voice still thick with sleep.

"We were tied together, so I didn't have a choice." She managed a smile, though the memory of that jump was terrifying.

Shinobu had been in the London hospital for two weeks. He'd arrived close to death—Quin had brought him by ambulance after their fight on *Traveler* and the airship's crash into Hyde Park. She'd been in this room, walking restlessly and sitting and sleeping in its uncomfortable chair, ever since. She had, in fact, turned seventeen several nights previously, while pacing between his bed and the window at midnight.

Behind Shinobu, the hospital's monitors beeped and whirred, glowing lights traveling across their screens in shifting patterns as they measured his vital signs. They were the familiar backdrop of Quin's days.

She lifted his shirt to look at the deep wound along the right side of his abdomen. The nearly fatal gash he'd received from her father, Briac Kincaid, had healed into a tender purple line, seven inches long. It had been sewn up so neatly, the doctors said the scar might disappear altogether, but at the moment the wound was still swollen and, judging from Shinobu's expression, terrifically painful whenever he moved.

Aside from that injury and the burns on his face, he'd entered the hospital with a badly broken leg and several crushed ribs. The doctors had bathed the wounds liberally with cellular reconstructors, which were forcing him to heal at an accelerated rate. There was one drawback: the process was rather excruciating.

Quin brushed her fingers over a lump beneath his skin near the sword wound, and Shinobu caught her hand.

"Don't make it drug me, Quin. I want the doctor to take those things out. I'm sleeping too much."

To help with the quick-mending wounds, he'd been implanted with painkiller reservoirs near his worst injuries. If the pain became too intense, or if he moved too vigorously, or if someone pushed on the reservoirs directly, they released a flood of drugs, which usually knocked him out. That was why he'd been mostly unconscious for the past two weeks. This brief conversation was already one of the longest periods awake he'd had in days, and Quin took it as a very good sign. The doctors had told her his recovery would happen this way—slowly at first, and then accelerating unexpectedly.

"You're refusing drugs now?" she asked him archly. Shinobu had been on very friendly terms with illicit substances back in Hong Kong, a habit he'd only recently broken. "You're full of surprises tonight, Shinobu MacBain."

He didn't laugh, probably because that would have hurt, but he pulled her closer with the hand that didn't have an IV running into it. Quin eased herself onto the narrow bed, and her gaze instinctively swept the chamber. The room was large, but bare of furnishings except for the bed, the medical machinery, and the chair in which Quin had been living. Her eyes stopped on the large window above the chair. They were on a high floor of the hospital, and through the glass was a panoramic view of nighttime London. Hyde Park was visible in the distance, emergency lights still erected over the broken bulk of *Traveler*.

Shinobu pushed his shoulder into hers on the bed, bringing her back to him. Her mind went to the journal in her pocket. Perhaps he was awake enough to see it.

He whispered, "There are things to say, Quin, now that I'm awake. You kissed me on the ship."

"I thought you kissed *me*," she responded, teasing him lightly.

"I did," he whispered seriously.

That kiss . . . she'd replayed it in her mind hundreds of times. They'd kissed and held each other during the nightmare, whirling crash of *Traveler,* and it had been *right.* They had been so close as children. They'd remained close during all of their Seeker training, even when John came to the estate and altered the dynamics of their lives. But it was not until they'd met again in Hong Kong, changed and older, that she'd seen him for what he was—not just her oldest friend but the other half of her.

"Is it too strange, the two of us?" she asked before she could stop herself. She wasn't sure of her footing in this new and unfamiliar territory of intimacy.

"It's *so* strange," he replied immediately. Quin didn't like that answer at all, but Shinobu drew her hand up to his chest before she could respond, kissed the palm, and whispered, "I've wanted to be with you for so long, and now here you are."

The words and the weight of his hand filled her with warmth. "But . . . all those girls from Corrickmore . . ." she said. There had always been lots of girls in Shinobu's life. He'd never once given the impression he was waiting around for her.

"I expected those girls to make you jealous, but you never noticed," he told her. He didn't say it bitterly; he was simply opening his heart. "All you cared about was John."

She responded softly, "You took care of me anyway. When John attacked the estate . . . and in Hong Kong . . . on *Traveler* . . . You're always taking care of me."

"Because you're mine," he whispered back.

She glanced at his face and saw a sleepy smile appearing. He moved her hand closer to his heart, held it there. She turned toward him on the bed, thinking it might be time to kiss him again—

"Ow!" he gasped.

"What happened? Did I—"

"It's—at your hip."

"Sorry! That's the athame."

Quin scooted away from him and drew the stone dagger from its concealed location at her waistband, where it had just been crushed into Shinobu's hip bone.

"Oh, there it is," he said, and he took the ancient implement from her hands. "I've been thinking about it a lot while I've been lying here half-asleep—or dreaming about it, maybe."

The athame was about as long as her forearm and quite dull despite its dagger shape. Its handgrip was made up of many stacked circular dials, all of the same pale stone. This particular athame belonged to the Dreads. The Young Dread had handed it to Quin after the crash of *Traveler,* and it was somewhat different from the other athames she and Shinobu had seen during their Seeker training, more delicate and also more complicated.

Shinobu shifted the stone dagger's dials with practiced ease, his IV tube bobbing as it trailed off his left hand. "It has more dials, so you can get to more specific locations than you can with other athames, don't you think?"

Quin nodded. She'd spent hours in the quiet of the hospital room examining this athame. As on all athames, a series of symbols was carved on each dial. By rotating the dials, you could line up seemingly endless iterations of those symbols. Each combination was a set of coordinates, a place a Seeker could go using the ancient tool. The additional dials on this particular dagger meant one could choose locations with much greater precision. During their fight on *Traveler*, the Dreads had used it to enter the moving airship. It was a feat that would have been impossible with any other athame. None but the athame of the Dreads could access a moving location.

Watching Shinobu study the dagger so intently and rotate the dials so nimbly, Quin decided that there was no reason to wait; he was alert enough to hear more. She pulled the leather book from her jacket and held it out to him.

"Is that . . . ?" he asked.

"It arrived this afternoon."

It was a copy of the journal that had belonged to John's mother, Catherine. Quin had had the real journal with her when she and Shinobu had parachuted onto *Traveler* during that crazy night two weeks ago, but she'd lost it—or rather, John had found it and taken it during the frenzied confrontation on the airship.

What Quin was holding was a copy—a copy she'd made back in Hong Kong weeks ago, before they came to London. Her mother, Fiona, had been with them on *Traveler* during the crash, and then in the hospital. Fiona had returned to Hong Kong a few days prior, and the first thing she'd done upon arriving was send the copied journal to Quin. She'd even bound the pages in leather, turning them into a new journal in their own right, an accurate copy of Catherine's original in size and shape.

Quin flipped through it, with Shinobu watching over her shoulder.

"Some of it is so old, I can't read it well, but the parts I can read are about the different Seeker families."

"Families besides ours?"

"Yes, but our own families too," she answered.

While Quin and Shinobu were growing up on the Scottish estate, they'd understood—theoretically—that there had once been many other Seeker families. But they'd only ever met members of their own two houses—Quin's, the house with a ram for its emblem, and Shinobu's, the house of the eagle. They knew that John came from another Seeker house. But John's family had already fallen apart and mostly disappeared before his generation, and she and Shinobu hadn't given his ancestors, or anyone else's, much thought. Quin's father, Briac, had even removed the insignia of other houses from the estate.

Other Seeker families had felt like distant history. They were part of the old tales Shinobu's father had told them as kids, about Seekers who had unseated terrible kings, hunted killers, driven criminals out of medieval lands, and been the force of much good in history. *If . . .* , Quin thought angrily, *any of that was true.* They'd grown up believing that Seekers were noble, but Briac had changed their world. He'd used their ancient tools and once-honorable abilities to turn Seekers into little more than hired assassins, collecting money and trading on power, and Quin couldn't help but wonder: *How long has it been like this?*

"We know Catherine and John belonged to the house of the fox," she said, turning pages until she reached one with a simple, elegant drawing of a fox at the top. Beneath this picture were paragraphs in small, neat, girlish writing, which continued for several pages. "These notes are about older members of the house of the fox," Quin explained, running her finger down a list of names and dates and locations. "Catherine was writing about her grandparents and ancestors. She's trying to account for where everyone was, and where they all went."

" 'She.' You mean John's mother, Catherine?" Shinobu asked.

Quin nodded. "This is her writing. See?"

She flipped to the very beginning of the journal. Beneath the front cover, on an otherwise blank page, was a small inscription in the same hand:

"A traveler?"

"That's what she says. Her handwriting is everywhere in the journal. Though there's also writing from a lot of other people in the earlier entries."

"So . . . you get this book a few hours ago, and the first thing you check is John's family?" he asked, his head bumping softly into hers on the pillow to take the sting out of his words.

She rolled her eyes and poked him gently with her elbow. "It's because I'm still in love with him. Obviously."

"I knew it," he whispered.

He pulled her closer. Quin thought about closing the book, but Shinobu was looking at it intently, and she wanted him to see it while his mind was sharp, before he drifted off again.

"I read about John's family first because his mother took the best notes on her own house," she explained, trying to ignore, for the moment, each place where her leg and arm and shoulder were touching Shinobu's. "But it looks as though Catherine was trying to keep track of all the Seeker families for a long while. She wanted to know where they'd all gone."

"And where did they go?" Shinobu asked.

"That's still the question." Quin fanned through the journal. "When I've read all of this, maybe we'll get some answers."

"Quin."

Shinobu struggled to sit up a bit, then gave up and lay back on the bed. He took her hand again and looked at her seriously.

"Quin, what are you doing?" he asked.

She glanced down at the journal, closed it. "I thought we should follow—"

"We aren't Seeker apprentices anymore," he told her. "We've gotten away from your father and from John. When I get out of the hospital, we don't have to be anything. We could go somewhere together and just *be*."

Quin was quiet for a time, thinking about this. That simple future sounded lovely when Shinobu offered it. He had set the athame on his chest, with his left hand over it, protectively. Quin put her own hand on it as well, feeling the cool stone and the warmth of his hand. Why couldn't they go off somewhere and just live—live as ordinary people? Their life as Seekers would never be the life they'd expected as children; that future had been a lie. So why not become something else?

But she knew the answer already.

"The Young Dread gave this athame into my keeping—for a while at least," she told him. "She wanted me to have it."

"That doesn't mean we have to use it," he responded gently.

"I think maybe it does."

He regarded her for a long moment, then asked, "What is it you want to do, Quin?"

Shinobu looked tired, but his eyes held that intensity that was particular to him. Quin understood that whatever she told him, he would give her his unwavering loyalty, just as he'd always done.

She whispered, "I was raised to be a Seeker. A real Seeker. One who finds the hidden ways between, finds the *proper* path, and makes things right."

"Tyrants and evildoers beware . . ." Shinobu murmured. That had once been the motto of Seekers, and it had been a mantra for Quin and Shinobu when they were apprentices. "I wanted that to be true," he said.

Quin flipped to the final page of the journal, where Catherine had printed the three laws of Seekers:

A Seeker is forbidden to take another family's athame.
A Seeker is forbidden to kill another Seeker save in self-defense.
A Seeker is forbidden to harm humankind.

They were laws her father hadn't even bothered to teach her; she had learned them only later, from the Young Dread. Yet this was the original code of Seekers. Breaking them had been punishable by death.

"We were true once," she whispered, her fingers tracing the words. She thought of an afternoon by a fire, when the Young Dread—Maud—had spoken to her about history. "There have been many, many good Seekers. Now my father kills who he wants—does it for money. John thinks he's fighting for his family's honor, but he's willing to be a killer like Briac."

"Yes," Shinobu agreed.

"So, when did Seekers become like Briac? And if there were more of us, where have they gone?"

She flipped to the journal's first pages. There the handwriting was ancient, so cramped and full of ink blots that Quin could make out very little—except for the word "Dread," which occurred frequently. These early pages were apparently letters and notes written by others in the distant past, and then pasted into this book by Catherine.

"The first half looks like it's about the Dreads. Closer to the beginning of Seekers. And then there are Catherine's own entries, searching for other Seeker houses, tracing where they might have gone."

"You think the journal will point you to when we went wrong," he said, guessing her thoughts exactly.

"I want to discover where these dishonorable Seekers began."

Shinobu slid a finger down the side of the stone dagger as though measuring it or perhaps contemplating all it stood for. Then he whispered, "So you can make things right?"

"Yes," she said. "If they can be made right."

She could feel Shinobu nod, his head moving against her own, but she sensed that his burst of energy was fading.

"I want that too," he told her.

She closed the journal and laid it on his chest. His hand covered hers where it lay atop the book, his skin almost feverish. Their long conversation was straining him.

"Do you remember where *we* first began?" he murmured close to her ear.

"Yes," she said softly. "It was in the meadow on the estate. You kissed me there when we were nine."

His eyes were half closed, but his face formed itself into a smile, and she felt his sleepy gaze upon her. "I didn't think you remembered that."

"I thought kissing was disgusting then."

"And what do you think now?"

She felt a smile pulling at her own lips. "I could give it another chance."

Shinobu slid his arm beneath her and pulled her to him. Quin's lips met his, and she discovered that she'd been waiting two weeks for this. He turned his body to put his other arm around her, and as he did, he let out a pained cry.

"Shinobu?"

His arms fell limp, and his head rolled back onto the pillow. It took Quin a moment to understand that the reservoir of painkiller in his gut had released a dose when he'd twisted toward her. He lay next to her with his eyes closed, a smile on his lips, one of his arms still caught beneath her.

She leaned her head against his and laughed softly. "I'm sorry."

It was late, and she'd been awake for a very long time. After tucking the journal and athame away, one in her jacket and the other at her waist, she pulled herself closer to him and let her own eyes drift closed.

CHAPTER 2

QUIN

John was there, in Quin's dream. He was so clear, standing across from her—it couldn't really be a dream, could it? She could see every detail of his face and body, outlined in moonlight.

It was cold. They were outside. His breath was clouding the air. And she felt the deep chill herself, sinking into every muscle. Yet somehow she was able to ignore the discomfort, keep the sensation of cold distant, as though it were of so little importance, she could pretend it weren't there. John was disregarding the frigid air as well; he wore only a thin undershirt and shorts, and he wasn't shivering.

He stood a good distance away, yet Quin could discern a small wound near his shoulder, as if her eyes could see much farther in this dream than they did in normal life. *Briac shot him on the airship,* she remembered. *And that's where the bullet went in.* She had a very similar wound of her own—one that John himself had given her, back when he'd attacked the Scottish estate and everyone on it.

She wondered why she felt no hatred as she looked across at John. He'd attacked her, hurt her and those she loved so many times in order to get what he wanted. But in this dream—if it were a dream—she felt neither hatred nor love, merely tolerance.

John began to run, and she was throwing objects at him, her arms moving with a speed almost too fast for her mind to follow. She felt her muscles respond to her own mental commands like lightning, throwing and throwing with a swiftness and force she'd never had in waking life—

"He lied to us," a child's voice said from somewhere nearby. "Our master's not here."

"His athame's here!" a different voice hissed close to Quin's face. "Look! How can that be?"

"Are you going to get it?"

A smell like dead rodents filled Quin's nose.

Her eyes flew open. She was lying on the hospital bed next to Shinobu, and someone was there, leaning over her. Dirty hands were sliding toward the waistband of her trousers.

Quin's arms came up the moment she understood what was happening, and she knocked the intruder away. He staggered back, but quickly lunged for her again. Quin grabbed his shoulders and held him off as his hands ripped at her waist.

"Give it back!" the attacker hissed, his closeness bringing the overpowering smell of dead animals to her nose again.

He was after the athame. She'd tucked it out of view down her waistband as she fell asleep next to Shinobu, but the handle was visible, and the intruder was about to get hold of it.

She pushed harder against his shoulders, keeping him at bay.

"Stop!" he spat.

He was strong. He changed tactics and reached for her throat instead.

He was younger than she'd thought at first, maybe fifteen, with bright, cruel eyes, the color of coal, and matted hair that might have been dark brown but was so dirty it appeared gray. His fingers scrabbled around her neck as she struggled to thrust him off.

Quin scanned the room to take in the full setting of the attack. Someone else was there. A boy—younger than the first, maybe twelve years old—was dancing from foot to foot in the dim nighttime lights, waiting for his chance to help. He looked fair and freckled but just as dirty as his companion.

The older boy leaned his weight against Quin's arms, and his hands slid fully around her throat. He looked down at her with anger and elation, as though choking people were one of his favorite pastimes and he couldn't wait to get started. His lips drew back, revealing filthy, black teeth.

Quin slid sideways, trying not to knock into Shinobu, who was still drugged or asleep. Her feet came off the bed, twisted up, and made contact with the teenaged boy's chest. She kicked him away so violently that he hit the IV stand and crashed with it to the floor. She sprang to her feet.

"Shinobu!" Quin hissed. In one swift motion, she pulled her whipsword from its concealed spot beneath her shirt and cracked it out. She rotated her wrist to force her weapon into the shape of a long, broad sword, and the oily black material flowed into place and solidified.

The younger boy, the freckled one, jumped at her, then away as she slashed her weapon at his face. Neither boy showed any surprise at the appearance of her whipsword.

"What?" Shinobu mumbled, rubbing at the spot on his hand where his IV tube had been sharply tugged when the stand went down.

The smaller boy pulled out a weapon, and Quin saw with shock, a moment too late, that he had his own whipsword. She raised her sword to block him but entirely missed the child's attack. Somehow the boy's sword slid right by her own. She reeled back, her arm cut just beneath the elbow.

"Ha ha," the boy said, tripping backward to get away as Quin came at him again. The older one lurched unsteadily to his feet.

They had whipswords—were they Seekers? Quin had to guess not: Their fighting style was bold but very wild. And they were so dirty and disheveled. Yet what would she know, really, of other Seekers? Her father had hidden their very existence.

Whoever these boys were, their skills were unexpectedly good. In a quick assessment, Quin decided they weren't better than she was; she would best both of them eventually. But Shinobu lay unguarded on the hospital bed, where they could injure him if they took an interest. She had to end this fight quickly.

"Help!" she called as she moved toward the door. "Help!"

Shinobu was up on one elbow, blinking fiercely, trying to understand what was happening. Quin willed the boys not to notice him.

Both attackers came for her as she neared the door. When they lunged simultaneously, she saw why their whipswords had slid by her before—the boys' weapons were half the usual length. Even slender and fully extended, as they were now, their swords were no longer than Quin's forearm, and the tips were not as sharp as they should have been. They were like whipswords that had been inelegantly cut in half.

"So together you have one whipsword?" she asked, swinging wide and fast to block both of them. "Are they two halves of the same sword? Are you each half a person as well?" She was continuing to speak loudly, as though she were a fighter who liked to bait her opponents, when in truth she was trying to rouse Shinobu and also the hospital staff on the other side of the door, and to keep the boys' eyes focused on her. "If you're two halves of the same person, couldn't at least one of you learn how to wash?" Their odor had filled the room.

"Least we're not a thieving girl," the little one said, smiling nastily and displaying his own dirty teeth, which, like the older boy's, appeared to have been smeared with soot. "Give us the athame our master should have!"

The older boy slashed at her with vicious skill, but Quin's larger weapon made quick work of his blows, and she sent him sprawling into his partner.

She turned for the door.

And found her father staring back at her.

Briac Kincaid was hiding in the dark alcove at the room's entrance, barricading the closed door, his own whipsword drawn. A handful of multicolored sparks danced around his head.

Sparks.

Before she could think any of this through, Briac had cracked out his sword and raised it.

Quin wavered.

And then the two boys were on her from behind. Her hesitation had cost her an important moment—

Then a metal tray crashed into the older boy's head, sending him staggering. Shinobu was there, his IV tube trailing off his left arm in a long tangle. He swung the tray a second time, cracking the older boy across the temple and sending him down. The smaller one struck back, and Shinobu used the tray as a shield as the half-sized whipsword clanged off it again and again. Quin could only guess at how much of the narcotic was being pumped into Shinobu's blood with each impact.

She saw her father's sword swing toward her, and turned to parry the blow. Briac was still blocking the door. There were muffled yells from the other side—hospital staff trying to get in.

"Stupid wife! Fiona!" he spat. "Give the athame back."

If it was strange to find her father here, it was stranger still to hear him address her that way.

Shinobu smacked the younger boy directly across the face with the tray, felling him, but Shinobu himself collapsed as well.

Quin made a quick decision. She leapt away from her father, who seemed glued to the door, and grabbed Shinobu by his shirt. Hauling him across the room, she positioned the bed between them and their attackers. The window was directly behind her.

The two boys were struggling up onto their hands and knees, trying to get vertical for another attack, though they had obviously been knocked almost senseless.

"Hold them off!" she said to Shinobu, who was attempting to stay upright. "Do your best."

Hospital staff pounded on the door, but Briac managed to keep it shut.

Quin drew the athame from her waist.

"Don't you dare!" came a yell from the older boy at the sight of the athame. He'd made it up onto his knees, was shaking his head as though trying to clear it. "Don't use his athame! You're not allowed."

"I can't keep standing," Shinobu told her. He'd listed to one side.

"Your implant is drugging you," she breathed. "But adrenaline can overcome it. Think about fighting them!"

The athame's dials were different from what she was used to. She adjusted them as well as she could.

Both boys had made it up onto their feet. Shinobu balanced himself upright, and, swaying, he kicked open the wheel locks at the foot of the bed. Then he rolled the bed directly into the boys.

Quin flicked her whipsword, making it small and thick, turned, and smashed the window. It shattered, allowing cool night air to pour into the room.

She pushed down on one side of the athame's blade with her thumb, and a long, slender piece of stone came free of the blade with a gentle click. This was the athame's lightning rod, its partner and necessary complement, the object that would bring the ancient dagger to life.

She struck the lightning rod against the athame, and a deep, penetrating vibration filled the air. Furniture began to rattle. The pounding on the door stopped as the vibration spread beyond the bounds of the hospital room.

"Stop!" yelled the younger boy, grabbing the bed to drag himself to his feet. "It's not yours! You're a thief!"

Quin reached the trembling athame through the broken window and drew a wide circle in the air below the ledge. Where she traced that circle, the athame cut through the fabric of the world as easily as a fin cuts through ocean water. In its path, tendrils of dark and light were exposed, and these snaked away from each other to create a doorway, an anomaly, humming with energy. Through the doorway was blackness.

"Climb up!"

She pushed Shinobu at the open window, even as she kept her own eyes away from the view. The forty-story drop was making her dizzy.

The door shook behind Briac, beneath renewed assaults from outside. Quin saw her father struggling to keep it closed.

Shinobu climbed up into the window frame with difficulty, Quin steadying him from below.

"Have you got your balance?" she asked. She avoided thoughts of him plummeting all the way to the ground.

"Yes, I'm all right," he breathed. Then he tumbled forward and fell directly into the anomaly. Quin's own stomach dropped as she watched him do it. Then she jumped up into the broken window. The London streets far below appeared to tilt and sway.

I'm scared of heights, she realized. *No, I'm terrified!* It was a new fear, and entirely inconvenient at this moment.

The older boy was reeling across the room toward her, his dark eyes furious.

"I will put you in your place!" he cried.

There was a loud bang, and both boys turned toward the hospital room door. Briac had at last been shoved aside, and uniformed guards were streaming into the room.

Quin turned toward the night, briefly glimpsing the endless lights of London stretched out before and below her. Then the view was swimming, and her stomach was lurching. She was falling through the cold air, falling through the anomaly she had carved from here to *There.*

CHAPTER 3

SHINOBU

The drugs were floating Shinobu away. He'd slid out the window and managed to fall into the right spot, his whole body making it through the anomaly. Now he was *There,* out of the well-lit darkness of the London night and surrounded by this other darkness, blacker and more barren.

He was supposed to say the time chant, to keep himself focused.

"Knowledge of self, knowledge of . . ." he began. What came next? "Quin?" he croaked.

"I'm here," she answered, grasping his shoulder. The feel of her hand helped a little. "Hold on to me," she whispered. "I'm a little dizzy."

Shinobu was more than a little dizzy, but he followed Quin's arms upward to her shoulders and held on to them. That position reminded him of their last moment atop the skyscraper in London, harnessed together, just before they'd jumped and parachuted onto Traveler. He'd left his friend Brian on the building's roof. Shinobu imagined Brian standing alone, with the building swaying gently

— 21 —

beneath his feet, wondering what in the world had happened to Shinobu after he'd jumped.

Now in the blackness, he could almost hear Brian saying, "Where have you gone, Barracuda? I had to find my way back to Hong Kong on my own."

Blinking against the drugs, Shinobu wanted to answer, "I don't know exactly where I am, Sea Bass."

But then he did know. In the blackness, he could see the outline of her face in the faint glow of the athame she held in her hand. This athame, the athame of the Dreads, glowed more brightly than the others he'd seen, and its vibration was much stronger, as though it held and directed more energy than any other.

Say the chant! he told himself. *Before it's too late.*

"Knowledge of self," he managed.

"Knowledge of self," Quin was whispering next to him, *"knowledge of home, a clear picture of where I came from, where I will go, and the speed of things between will see me safely back. Knowledge of self . . ."*

Shinobu hoped those words would focus Quin's mind on the time stream they'd left behind, so she wouldn't lose herself *There*, where time did not really exist, so she might pull them both through—because Shinobu was going to be of no use at all this time.

The air around him sounded wrong, as if he were, at once, in a tiny soundproof room and in an enormous cavern. Quin let go of him, and he'd already lost himself enough to worry that she was gone forever. Then he saw her fingers moving along the athame's dials. She was right next to him.

"Where will we go?" he asked. His voice was thin and stretched out. How long had they been here? Moments? Hours?

"Hong Kong," she whispered. "I hope I'm choosing Hong Kong."

I should breathe, he thought. *Am I breathing?* He inhaled raggedly. He could hear the faint clinks of the athame's dials being moved into place, but the sharp little noises arrived at his ears as distant, slow thuds. Time was slowing down. There was another vibration, low and rumbling.

Her hand was beneath his arm. *Quin, you're touching me,* he thought. That was enough, at the moment, to keep any fear at bay. Her closeness was an anchor in the darkness, drawing him back to himself. Time speeded up as she carved another anomaly. The blackness drew apart, snakes of light and dark coiling into each other, forming the border of a new circular doorway, its energy flowing outward, from the darkness around them into the world beyond.

There were trees and a morning sky out there. All at once, he could see Quin clearly, her dark hair and eyes, her lovely, fair face, and the lips that had kissed him just before he fell asleep.

"Can you walk?" she asked, pulling him across the seething border.

"Of course," Shinobu answered, and he promptly fell down.

CHAPTER 4

JOHN

They had swept some of the debris out of the castle courtyard, and now John stood at one end of the space, facing the Young Dread. She was in the middle of the yard, looking back at him, her body completely still.

It was well past midnight. The moon was low in a partially clouded sky, casting long, dark shadows across the ground and outlining the crumbling remains of the castle.

And it was cold. The temperature was not low enough for ice, but nearly so.

The Young Dread, or Maud, as she now allowed him to call her, had ordered John to strip to his undergarments and remove his shoes. Whenever John began to feel slightly comfortable with his training regimen, Maud found a way to make him uncomfortable again. His breath came out in billowing clouds as he waited for her first command. Yet John didn't shiver. In the past weeks, he'd learned to concentrate well enough that he could stop his body from shaking with the cold—for a while at least.

Against all expectation, the Young Dread had sought him out

after the fight on *Traveler*, and had told him she would complete his Seeker training. When Briac had refused to train him further, John had tried to force Quin to help, but he'd succeeded only in hurting her and others. He was prepared to hurt, or even to kill, if it was absolutely necessary. *You mustn't be scared to act*, his mother had told him, all those years ago, as she was dying in front of him. *Be willing to kill.* And yet it was better, of course, if he didn't have to go after Quin. The Young Dread had offered him an alternative.

She'd asked, in return, for his full dedication to the training. He intended to give it and to prove himself an excellent student. He was eighteen, older than Seeker apprentices usually were. This was his chance, at last, to learn to use an athame and to become the man his mother and grandmother had expected him to be.

The wound beneath his left shoulder, where Briac had shot him on board *Traveler,* throbbed painfully, but it was halfway healed already, thanks to the finest medical treatment his grandfather's fortune could buy. This was good, because Maud didn't accept pain as an excuse for poor performance.

The Young Dread herself was dressed similarly to John, only a loose undershirt and simple short trousers on her slender, wiry frame. Whatever her demands upon John, she was no less demanding of herself. He could see her lean muscles outlined with shadow. She, of course, was not shivering either. She held her body in such tight control, John imagined she would freeze to death before she allowed herself to tremble. He'd come to understand that she preferred discomfort; it kept her sharp.

Maud's hair was tied up behind her head, and the youthful planes of her face looked both terrible and splendid in the moonlight, a statue of a vengeful goddess on the threshold of springing to life.

At her feet was a pile of objects—rocks, rusted metal horseshoes, clods of dirt, broken pieces from old weapons. They had collected these items for days, scouring the estate when his training had begun. And now the Young Dread was using them against him, over and over and over again.

Sitting on the ground near the heap of objects was John's disruptor. Maud had left it in sunlight all day to gather energy. Now its iridescent metal shimmered in the glow of the moon, making it look almost pretty, when in truth it was a weapon designed specifically to instill horror. It resembled a small, wide cannon with a barrel ten inches across that was covered with hundreds of tiny openings. When it was strapped across the user's chest and fired, swarms of electrical sparks rushed from those holes to encircle the head of its victim. And if those sparks caught you, if you failed to get out of their way, they twisted your thoughts and destroyed your mind. You became *disrupted*.

John knew the Young Dread would not fire the disruptor at him tonight. She'd told him that would come only later in his training. Still, she'd brought it here to the castle ward and set it near her where he could see it easily. Terror of the disruptor had been his downfall when training under Briac Kincaid, and so Maud wanted him to become used to its presence. He tried not to look, but his heart beat more quickly whenever his eyes happened upon it. He thought of his mother's words: *Do what has to be done.* Somehow he would overcome this fear.

"Begin!" the Young Dread called.

John kicked his muscles into motion and started running around the perimeter of the courtyard, which was littered with stones, dead branches, and chunks of the ruined castle. He stared ahead, taking in everything before him and everything in his peripheral vision without moving his eyes. Maud had taught him the focus of the steady stare, which he used now. He could see her at the corner of his right eye, her body turning to follow his progress, turning so slowly and smoothly that her feet did not appear to be shifting at all.

"Now!" she said, giving him a warning.

And then she began to throw things. Her arms moved—so fast that he saw only a blur—and a dark object was hurtling toward him.

John pivoted to his left, using his speed to turn full circle, as a rock whistled by his head and crashed into a boulder at the edge of the yard.

"Now!" she said, another warning, and a new black shape flashed toward him.

John leapt atop a piece of rubble and pushed off, carrying himself high into the air. Whatever she'd thrown—a horseshoe maybe?—winged his calf. He landed hard, feeling the shock of the object's impact only when his feet touched the ground. Pain seared up his leg. But still he ran.

Pain is nothing, he told himself, keeping his eyes ahead and his vision still. *Pain is nothing. My mother went through much worse. My grandmother showed me much worse . . .*

Maud wouldn't call out to him again; the following object would come without warning. He was turning the corner at the south end of the yard when he saw the next flash of motion. He threw himself down and rolled, as a large rock soared through the air. Before he was back on his feet, another came. He leapt up, barely pulling his legs out of the way in time. And then another object, and another.

"Very good!" Maud called. "Much improved!"

John knew better than to slow down or look at her. Already a new barrage was coming his way.

"If you'd done this well in your training with Briac," she pointed out, "you wouldn't have had to betray Quin."

The words were said as she said everything—evenly, steadily—and yet they stung as though she'd slapped him. She was trying to distract him, and it was working. *I didn't want to betray her. I loved her. But she wouldn't help me.*

An object caught him in the ribs. It was only a small stone, but Maud had thrown it so hard, it felt for a moment as though he'd been shot. He stumbled to the side but somehow managed to keep moving forward.

"Focus!" called the Young Dread. "Do not look at me."

She was throwing again, using both arms. In his peripheral vision, he thought he saw her bend toward the disruptor as though she would pick it up and aim it at him.

She won't do that.

"Your mother wanted to raise a traitor," she said as he ducked one of her missiles. "She wanted you to be ruthless."

"I'm not a traitor—" John yelled, taking the bait and turning toward her.

A series of rocks hit him in the chest, immediately knocking him from his feet. He landed hard on the gravelly surface. *I'm not a traitor,* he thought angrily. *And she only wanted what was best for me.* He pulled himself up to standing and rubbed his chest, which felt like it had been pounded by a hammer.

The Young Dread was staring at him from the center of the courtyard.

"You let me distract you," she said quietly as she approached him. "My words threw you off. And thoughts of the disruptor?"

John nodded, recovering his composure with difficulty. Why had he reacted to her taunting? "I'm sorry. Let me try again."

"It's enough for tonight. Are you hurt?"

He dropped his hand from his bruised chest. "Pain means little," he told her, echoing the words she always used with him.

She nodded agreement. "It is only pain."

Even so, she examined him carefully from head to foot. She took a moment to inspect the healing bullet wound beneath his shoulder, which was visible through the loose neck hole of his undershirt. Up close, he could see the girlishness in her body and features, attributes that had become obvious as they began training in minimal clothing. Yet as Maud looked him over, he didn't feel as though a girl were studying him, but rather as if he were being x-rayed by a hospital scanner. He looked away.

"You're a good fighter, John," she told him. "When you don't get distracted."

"That's what everyone says—Briac, Alistair, Quin," he muttered, his voice full of the frustration that had hounded him for years during his training on the estate. He was breathing hard from his run, and he worked to calm his lungs. He had been doing so well.

"It's easy to throw you off. A few words, a gesture toward the disruptor, and you're lost."

She was still scrutinizing him, prodding gently at the places where his ribs had been bruised by rocks. It was unnerving when she stood so close.

Abruptly she finished and stepped back. "Pick up the disruptor," she ordered.

John hid his unwillingness. He walked to the center of the courtyard and lifted the weapon from the ground. It was heavy, nearly solid metal, with a thick leather harness that added to its weight.

"Put it on," the Young Dread said. She was still near the edge of the yard and was watching him, her face impassive but her voice commanding.

He slipped the harness over his shoulders, settled the disruptor to his body. Its base covered nearly his whole chest. The holes across the barrel were irregularly spaced and of different sizes, as though they'd been gouged out randomly and viciously by someone disturbed.

When the sparks surround your head, they form a disruptor field. The field distorts your thoughts. You form an idea, but the disruptor field changes it, sends it back to you altered. It had been years since he'd heard those words from Shinobu's father, Alistair MacBain, when Alistair had first explained the disruptor to the apprentices on the estate, but John recalled the words perfectly: *Your mind will tie itself into a knot, fold up, collapse. You will want to kill yourself, but how can you? Even that thought spins out of your control.*

John had last worn the disruptor during the fight on *Traveler,* when he'd fired it at Briac Kincaid. He'd experienced a rush of cruel delight in that moment, but now when he recalled firing the weapon, the memory came with a surge of dread. Before Briac, there had been others John had seen disrupted—Alistair MacBain, and John's own man Fletcher. Those had been accidents, but that didn't take away from the guilt. And before them he'd seen his own mother disrupted, then kept alive for years as a tortured half corpse by Briac. John's experience with the weapon made him more terrified of it, not less; with the weight of the disruptor on his chest, John knew he was cradling another's sanity in his hands.

"Bring it to life," Maud ordered.

"Why?" he asked, coming back to himself.

She kept her unwavering gaze pinned on him and said nothing else; she'd given him a command and expected him to obey.

He slid his hand down the side of the weapon. From within the disruptor came a high-pitched whine, growing in volume. A crackle of static sprang up all around the weapon, and John watched a red fork of electricity climb up his hand, then disappear.

The Young Dread approached him, but stopped halfway across the ward.

"Fire it at me," she said.

"Why?" Nausea was creeping into his stomach. He didn't want to shoot at her.

"Fire it at me."

Her face looked both young and ancient, and it wore an expression of finality: he would do what she asked, or he would not be her student.

John slid his hand farther down the weapon, and the whine spun higher and became more intense. He aimed at her and fired.

A thousand multicolored sparks launched from the disruptor. They came out buzzing angrily and tore across the distance toward the Young Dread. If they reached her, they would swarm her head, and she would never be free of them.

"Move!" he yelled to Maud, panic rising in his throat.

But she'd already whirled to the side, easily removing herself from the path of the sparks before they hit her. They continued on and collided with a large chunk of rock at the edge of the yard. Finding no human target, they disappeared against the stone in bursts of rainbow-colored light.

The Young Dread closed the distance between them, her demeanor as calm as it ever was. "The disruptor scares you, even when you control it."

"Yes," he whispered, ashamed of how true her words were.

"It was meant to do so," she told him. "But it is a weapon like any other. With practice, it can be faced. Anything can be faced."

He nodded, wanting to believe this.

"If we had a focal," she told him thoughtfully, "it would take the terror and distractions away."

"What's a—" he began, but Maud lifted a hand, cutting him off.

She was listening to something, though John could hear nothing but the faint, cold breeze through the trees surrounding the castle ruins.

"What is it?" he asked.

"Something is happening," she said. "Come."

CHAPTER 5

QUIN

Shinobu collapsed against Quin the moment they stepped through the anomaly back into the ordinary world. She grabbed hold of his arms to keep him from falling.

"Are you all right?"

"I think so, I think so," he mumbled as he tried to stand.

Quin had set the athame's symbols as closely as she could to the Hong Kong coordinates she'd memorized years ago, but the difference in this particular athame's dials meant they'd arrived at another location. It was still Hong Kong, though. From the smells in the air and the quality of the light, she knew they were on Hong Kong Island, somewhere near Victoria Peak. The fox athame—the athame with which Quin had trained—had always brought her closer to the Peak itself. Now she and Shinobu stood on spongy soil among thick trees, somewhere farther down the mountain slope.

Over her shoulder, she watched the anomaly lose its shape, the threads of black and white separating from the humming border of the circle and growing across the opening, mending the hole she'd torn in the world. In a moment it had collapsed and disappeared.

"Stop moving, please," Shinobu whispered into her shoulder. "You're making the ground shake."

"I'm standing still, I promise."

"Are you sure?" His eyes were fluttering shut.

"I'm sure. Hold on to me."

His painkiller implants were clearly working in overdrive. She didn't think they would be strong enough to overdose him, but she had to get him to a doctor quickly. His sword wound was barely healed, and he'd twisted his torso like a madman during the fight in the hospital. The bigger question—who were the boys who'd attacked them?—would have to wait until she'd assured his safety.

She felt a trickle at her wrist and saw that she was bleeding onto him from the cut along her right forearm, where the younger attacker had gotten her with his bizarre, chopped-off whipsword. She twisted around so Shinobu was propped against her back and both of her hands were free. Then she ripped a strip of fabric from her shirt and tied up her arm.

"Come on," she said, twisting back and pulling his arm across her shoulder. "We're going to a hospital."

"A different hospital, right?" He laughed sleepily against her. "Don't think we should go to the same one."

Quin smiled. That he was still making jokes was a good sign. "Yes. We're on the other side of the world now."

Some yards away, the trees ended at a narrow, winding path, one of the many that encircled the Peak. Quin moved them both carefully in that direction.

"We could have beaten those boys," Shinobu told her thickly. "We didn't have to run."

"I was worried about you getting injured—more injured—if we kept fighting."

"Who were they, do you think?"

"My father brought them somehow," she said as she maneuvered him between trees. "And maybe they thought the athame was his?"

When she'd last seen her father, he was thrashing about and fighting medical personnel as they tried to load him into an ambulance by *Traveler*'s crash site. In the hospital, she'd seen sparks around his head, and she now understood his wild behavior—he'd been disrupted, at least partially, during the fight on *Traveler*.

"He was disrupted," Shinobu said, echoing her own thoughts. "But he didn't act completely disrupted."

Shinobu had seen his own father disrupted, and he'd described to Quin the unthinking wildness of the state. Briac hadn't been like that, though he'd been strange.

"I—I froze a little when I saw him," Quin admitted.

"Feeling sorry for him?" Shinobu asked her.

She didn't feel sorry for her father, who'd lied to her for years, who'd forced her to do terrible things, and who would dominate her by any means if she let him. She'd been ready to kill Briac Kincaid during the fight on *Traveler*. But in the hospital, she'd wavered—because there had been something helpless about him.

"I don't feel sorry for him," she said, "but I did hesitate."

Shinobu's head lolled against her. He mumbled, "It's all right, because you're touching me again, can't keep your hands off me, can you?" He tried to lace his fingers through hers where they gripped his shoulder. He was losing consciousness. He lurched against her as she moved out of the trees and down the embankment. "You *should* want to touch me," he went on, slurring his words. "I've had many satisfied customers. Believe you, I did."

Quin couldn't help smiling again. "Many satisfied customers? How many, exactly?" she asked, easing him onto the paved path and trying to keep him talking. "Did any of those girls have to carry you to the hospital *twice*—"

She stopped.

She was face to face with her father. Again.

Briac Kincaid was standing in the middle of the path, looking at her, wild-eyed. He opened his mouth.

Quin was momentarily paralyzed. She watched Briac's head swivel in a circular motion, as though he were trying to locate someone. His mouth moved again.

He's going to scream, Quin thought. *He's getting ready to scream.*

She heard a rustling in the branches overhead. Someone was high up in a tree on the other side of the path. And that someone, quite obviously, was there with Briac Kincaid. They'd followed her here—or perhaps they'd gotten here before her.

Careful to keep hold of Shinobu, she grabbed a stone from the edge of the walkway and threw it past Briac's face. Her father turned his head to follow the stone's arc through the air, and Quin seized the moment. She grabbed Shinobu tightly and plowed into the trees on the downhill side of the path. Shinobu was barely conscious and still badly injured—there was no way the two of them could be involved in another fight.

"Ah!" Briac yelled, finally finding his voice. *"Ahhhh! Ahhhhhh!"*

"What?" demanded a young and irritated voice from the tree above.

Half pushing Shinobu, half dragging him, Quin moved deep into the greenery and fell to her knees. Shinobu collapsed in front of her.

"Ow," he mumbled.

Quin pulled him beneath the covering branches of a large, dense bush and eased him down until he was lying on damp soil. Then she slid across Shinobu's chest and glanced upward through the branches. Both boys from the hospital attack were perched in trees, looking north, toward the harbor, which she guessed was clearly visible from their vantage point.

"They must have their own athame," she whispered. "The boys who attacked us are here—with my father." Had she and Shinobu spent more time *There* than she'd thought? It had seemed they'd been gone only moments, but who knew? That was the danger of using an athame. You could separate from the time stream of the world and lose yourself. If you weren't careful, you could lose yourself to the point where you wouldn't come back at all.

"He's making things up again!" This was the younger boy, the freckled one who looked eleven or twelve.

"It's my mother!" Briac yelled. "Come down and find her!"

"Your mother would be ancient," the older boy told him. "And this city is enormous. You've led us on a fool's errand."

"Look at the ships," the little one said, a note of awe in his voice. "There are so many."

"But she was here. I was right," Briac insisted, in a moment of verbal clarity. "And if she's here, the—the athame of the Dreads is here too."

Quin could see her father's legs, still out on the path. He was turning around in circles. "Fiona!" he called. "Fiona MacBain!"

"Shut him up, Nott!" the older boy ordered.

Quin watched the branches shake as the smaller one—Nott—leapt downward. His movements were thoughtlessly graceful, beginning slowly then bursting into explosive action. He was a little bit . . . he was a little bit like the Young Dread, Quin thought.

"Fiona MacBain?" Shinobu muttered, reacting belatedly to what Briac had said. "MacBain" was Quin's mother's maiden name, a name she hadn't used for nearly twenty years.

Quin whispered, "His mind is two steps off. He keeps thinking I'm someone else."

When the boy called Nott reached the ground, Quin saw how beat-up he looked—a huge goose egg on his forehead, a swollen nose and cheek, dozens of other cuts and scrapes from the fight in the hospital, and the marks of many older wounds. The smaller boy pulled Briac off the road, into the greenery and down onto his knees. Then Nott clapped a hand over her father's mouth. Briac wrinkled his nose at this contact, and Quin realized that the boy's odor was so awful, she could smell him even at this distance.

The older one was coming down his tree, his motions even more graceful, as if time were unfolding at an even, easy pace for him. He wore an athame at his waist. When he reached the forest floor, his fist shot out at Briac's neck, and Briac fell, gasping, to the ground. Both boys laughed, revealing the dirty mess of their teeth. They peered around the woods, as if assuring themselves that Briac had not, in fact, seen anyone. Quin flattened herself against Shinobu.

The boys were a bit like the Young Dread in the way they moved, she thought, but they were nothing like her in their glee to cause pain. And her father—he was like their pet. Who were these boys, and how had they gotten hold of Briac? The athame and whipswords indicated they were Seekers, but Quin could not quite believe that. And if they felt entitled to take the athame of the Dreads from her, what was their relationship to the Dreads? Had the Young Dread given Quin the athame, knowing those boys would come after her? She studied their filthy, brutal faces between the overhanging branches. No. She couldn't imagine the Young Dread having anything to do with those boys.

One thing was certain: if she'd thought she and Shinobu would have time and space to explore the mysteries of Seekers on their own, she'd been badly mistaken. Somehow they'd stumbled into a new and dangerous piece of the puzzle.

"How could we possibly find her in this place?" the older boy asked, squatting down to loom over Briac.

"We can—we can find her . . . and the *athame*," Briac stammered.

It appeared to take great effort to keep his thoughts moving in a straight line, but he was making a noble attempt.

"We shouldn't be here at all," the younger boy complained. "We're supposed to get the others, and do our proper search. I thought we were finding *him,* not chasing some girl. He lied to us, Wilkin, to make us help him."

At that, the older boy—Wilkin—cuffed the younger one on the side of the head.

"I say what we do! We've seen the athame, Nott, haven't we? We ought to get it back now that we've seen it. He'll be pleased with us. You know he will."

"Or he'll be furious!" Nott said. "What if we end up in our cave, Wilkin? If it comes to that, I'll blame you."

"And I'll blame you," Wilkin said. "So that's settled."

Who was "he"? Quin wondered. Were they talking about Briac? If so, they were speaking of him as if he weren't present—though, since he was disrupted, that was partially true. Was it Briac who wanted the athame of the Dreads? But the boys were treating him like a possession, not like someone who deserved their respect or fear.

Briac had gotten back up onto his knees, and his face went very still. He was trying desperately to concentrate.

"Quin," Shinobu breathed, "I think you're bleeding . . ."

She was still leaning across his chest. She moved aside and saw that the lower part of Shinobu's shirt was covered in blood. Very carefully she pulled the wet material up off his skin.

"Oh," she breathed. The wound in his abdomen had torn open. Blood was oozing out of it in a thick, dark stream.

"Are you all right?" Shinobu asked her, so softly she could barely hear him. He thought the blood was hers.

"I—I am," she whispered back, gently putting her hand over his mouth. They could not afford to be heard. "Don't speak, all right?"

She'd planned to hide until the boys moved off, but now she couldn't wait. Making as little noise as possible, she moved her hand from Shinobu's mouth and cut off a patch of his sweatpants, folded the material several times, and pressed it firmly against his wound. Then she cut longer strips, to tie the makeshift bandage in place.

As she worked, she glanced through the branches at the boys. The youngest had picked up a small rucksack and from within it had taken out some sort of metal helmet. The older one snatched it away from him.

"If you won't do what we're supposed to do, at least we should use the helm again to figure out where she is," Nott whined. "How else are we going to do it?"

"Don't be an idiot!" Wilkin responded, cuffing Nott again. "We don't know where she is. We never *did* know where she was, or anything about this city. The helmet won't help us!"

"But *he* knows," Nott answered. With one hand he was holding the ear the older boy had struck, and with the other he was pointing at Briac. "I was going to put the helm on *him,* not me. Straighten *his* mind out. Like we did in the madhouse."

The older boy paused, as though the suggestion to use the helmet on Briac were, in fact, clever.

"They have a helmet," Quin whispered. She was reaching beneath Shinobu to pull the strips of fabric around his torso. It wasn't easy, and she hoped her soft words would distract him. "There's a drawing of the same one in Catherine's journal."

She cinched the strips down over the makeshift bandage. The blood was already soaking through. She tore and folded another thick piece of fabric and added it over the wound. It was nowhere near sufficient.

Peeking up again, she saw her father staring at that helmet with shocking intensity. Even in the shade of the trees, the helmet caught the ambient light with glints of changing color. Its metal was irides-cent . . . like the metal of a disruptor.

The two boys put their heads together and whispered, and as they did, Quin watched her father stealthily grab the helmet from the ground and pull it onto his head. Then he reached for the boys' athame . . .

Quin took this moment to make her move.

"I'm going to pull you," she breathed.

She grabbed Shinobu's ankles and dragged him out from beneath the bush. He groaned, his eyes half open and watching her.

When they reached a clear space between trees, she drew out her athame. She hoped she could shift one dial slightly and bring them to a different area within Hong Kong—away from these boys and closer to a hospital. If they could get somewhere safe, even for a few hours, perhaps she could figure out what was happening.

A bloodcurdling screech from deeper in the trees made Quin freeze.

"He took it!" the youngest boy shrieked. "He took it, Wilkin! *And* the athame!"

As quickly as she could, Quin set her athame's dials to bring them *There* and struck it against the lightning rod. A deep vibra-tion followed, and a moment later she heard the competing tremor of another vibration. Her father must have struck the boys' athame. Though Quin could not see him, she guessed he was trying to escape with their helmet and their stone dagger. And the boys were furious.

Quin carved an anomaly, making it as large as she could.

The branches of two nearby trees started shaking—Briac and the boys were grappling with each other just yards away.

"Step through!" Quin whispered urgently, hauling Shinobu to his feet, praying the bandage would hold and she was not killing him by forcing him to move. He managed to stay upright and stumble into the solidifying hole she'd ripped into the world.

"Let me wear it!" Briac gasped within the trees. "My mind will work, we'll find her, we'll find that athame. We'll *have* it."

"Get it off him!" said the older boy.

"He's through!" said the younger one.

"Follow him! Follow him!"

Quin understood: The helmet somehow counteracted the disruptor sparks. *And when Briac's able to think straight, he'll come after me again,* she thought, *in Hong Kong or on the estate or anywhere—to get his hands on the athame of the Dreads.* For years her father had kept the fox athame, which rightly belonged to John. Now John had it back, and Briac must be desperate to find another. Clearly those boys were not going to give him their own—but in some fashion, Briac was allied with them to find the athame of the Dreads.

An object rolled out of the trees and bumped into Quin's foot. As she stepped through the anomaly, she snatched it up, discovering it to be smooth and cool against her skin.

The boys had knocked the metal helmet from Briac's head, and now Quin was holding it in her hands.

CHAPTER 6

MAUD

From high in the oak tree at the edge of the forest, the Young Dread looked through the night air at the commons, the large meadow at the center of the Scottish estate. Around the edge of the commons were dotted what used to be cottages but what were now, mostly, burned piles of rubble, smudges of black in the moonlight. Only a few structures, including the workshop and dairy barn, stood unbroken.

The three visitors to the estate were running between the ruined buildings in a frantic search. Two of these visitors were boys, and they were trailing after the third visitor . . . who was Briac Kincaid.

Maud had last seen Briac being forced into an ambulance in London, fighting wildly against the men trying to help him. Now she understood why. The Young Dread had thrown her sight, sending it out across the distance so she could examine Briac closely as he charged across the top of the meadow, from the abandoned cottages of the Dreads toward the dairy barn. Around his head danced a handful of sparks, flashing in the nighttime air. He'd been hit with a disruptor.

It must have been John's disruptor, used during the fight on *Traveler*, and somehow Briac had avoided all but a few of the sparks. Even so, he was obviously mad.

"Fiona!" she heard him yelling as he reached the dairy and peered inside. "Mother?" Then he shook his head and said, "Quin, for God's sake! Where are you?" He'd done much the same thing at each of the empty or destroyed cottages he'd passed.

Not finding anyone in the dairy, Briac stomped over to the stable, which had burned but still stood partially intact. He disappeared inside, and by throwing her hearing, the Young Dread could follow his motions as he flung things around and called for Fiona and his mother and Quin again—though it seemed to be Quin he really wanted.

It wasn't only Briac's noise that Maud had heard when she'd stood in the castle ruins with John after their training session. She had known he was coming before he'd arrived, because a thought had dropped into her mind: . . . *he'll come after me again—in Hong Kong or on the estate* . . .

She was quite certain that thought had come from Quin. Maud had felt this mental connection off and on for a month. It had begun on the day when Quin had fought John on top of the small barn above the cliff on the edge of the estate. During that fight, the Young Dread had chosen to help Quin by tossing her a lightning rod. It was as though she'd unwittingly created a permanent connection between them in that instant; Quin's thoughts now traveled freely across the link at unexpected moments. The Young Dread could even feel Quin looking through her own eyes from time to time. She was not sure that Quin was aware of the connection, despite its strength.

"She's not here!" the younger of the two boys said. Both stood outside the stable, waiting for Briac to reappear. "He's acting mad again, Wilkin. If we're going to follow him, maybe you *should* let him wear it awhile—"

"He can't wear it now, Nott! He tried to steal it," the other one—Wilkin—said. And then: "Are you crying?"

"I want to wear it!" the younger one, apparently called Nott, replied.

Briac emerged through the burned stable doorway, and immediately headed toward the old barn.

From her perch in the oak tree, the Young Dread heard John approaching below. He'd paused in the castle ruins to put on his cloak and gather up their weapons, and now he was sprinting through the woods toward her, his cloak streaming from his shoulders. The night was dark, but Maud's eyes gathered all available light to allow her to see him easily among the shadows and the trees.

In the short time she'd been training him, John's running gait had changed, become something more fluid, directed and swift. He threw off his hood as he began to climb the tree. To Maud, his motions were loud and clumsy, but he still moved better than most Seekers she'd met. He was learning to focus his mind, and his body was following suit.

Maud was used to perfect clarity in her own thinking. When she'd trained as a girl with her dear master, the Old Dread, he'd instilled in her a certainty of purpose and an ease in decision. A Dread was meant to stand apart from humanity and from Seekers so that her mind was clear to judge. And yet, the years she'd spent with the Middle Dread had eroded her faith in this simple rule. The Middle had interfered in the life of a Seeker—Catherine Renart, John's mother—in a way that was unjust. He had participated in disrupting her. The Middle had committed other injustices long ago, but this one was recent, and he'd forced Maud to participate, which gave her a peculiar responsibility for the results. Was it wrong then, Maud wondered, for her to interfere in the life of Catherine's son, John, in order to make up for what had been done?

Her master had gone *There* after the fight on *Traveler,* to stretch himself out for years and years, decades even. The Old Dread could not answer this question for her. And so the Young had made the choice to train John, to make him a Seeker. A Dread must not take sides, but this was not taking sides; this was bringing an unbalanced scale back to level. She was not sure how honorable John would be, nor how seriously he would take the three laws of Seekers, but surely having a good teacher was the only chance he had.

"Who is it?" John whispered, pulling himself up onto a thick branch next to her. He was breathing hard, but she could see that he was controlling himself, forcing his body to draw in air with an even rhythm. He took his training seriously.

"You'll see in a moment." She nodded toward the old barn in the distance. All three visitors had disappeared inside. "Can you hear them speaking?"

John closed his eyes for a moment, shook his head. "Only faintly."

"Imagine the words are clear," Maud whispered, "coming straight to your ears, with nothing between you and them. Try it."

He stared at the barn, going very still as he concentrated on the distant sounds. Though Maud knew it would take much more than those simple instructions to teach John to throw his hearing, this was the first step. It was not a skill a Seeker required, yet she saw no reason John could not develop it.

The smaller boy, Nott, emerged in the distance, his pale face visible in the dark air. "Why can't we do what we promised?" he was saying. "He doesn't want us to look for this girl or his athame. He wants us to look for *him.* He's the important one. He's going to send us—"

"Stop telling me the same thing over and over, Nott. And stop whining. We *will* do what we promised! We'll find our master, just after we find her," Wilkin said as he appeared.

"Children?" John asked, able to see their size, if nothing else.

"Strange children," Maud answered. There was something Dread-like in these boys' motions, though they were loud in a way that was completely at odds with the behavior of a Dread. They spoke of their master. Who would that be?

Briac stumbled out of the barn, and all three headed for the burned-out training barn, which meant they were walking toward Maud and John and becoming more visible.

"Is that . . . ?" John asked, straining to see details as the figures approached.

"Briac Kincaid," Maud told him evenly. She knew how much John hated the man, how much he longed to fight Briac and punish him for what he'd done to John's mother, and for what he'd done to John himself in denying him his training, but John was her student now and could not be distracted by such an emotion. "We will wait here to see—"

John was already moving, murder written on his face. He leapt from branch to branch as quickly as he could, barely grabbing one before he had dropped to the next. Maud saw him slip dangerously in his haste to reach the ground, but he recovered at the last moment, catching himself heavily on a lower branch.

Unfocused and disobedient! she thought.

She turned to follow, then stopped herself. The older boy, she perceived, had an athame at his waist. The butt of the stone dagger was sticking up from his trousers. The Young Dread held herself perfectly still, gathering her mind so that she might throw her sight farther than she was ordinarily able. She asked her eyes to summon all available light from the night sky. With a thrill of satisfaction, she felt her senses obey. The particulars of that athame became as clear as if she were holding it in her own hands. She saw the detail she sought: at the base of the grip was a small carving of a boar. *A boar,* the Young Dread thought. *How curious.*

Then she moved down the tree, swinging herself effortlessly through the branches. When her feet hit the forest floor, she was already running.

John was sprinting toward the three intruders. *John!* she called with her mind. *Stop!* But John didn't stop, or even slow. During the time she'd been training him, Maud hadn't managed to make any sort of mental connection with him, and she wondered if he were even capable of it.

He was nearly at the edge of the woods.

"Nott, weapons!" she heard the older boy say. They had spotted John, and they looked delighted at the prospect of fighting. Both drew whipswords and cracked them out into solid form.

Even stranger, Maud thought. *They have whipswords and an athame, but are they Seekers?* she wondered. She didn't think so. Something about the boys was off. And then a moment later: *Their swords are not right.*

A memory came to her: she was training with the Middle Dread, long ago. She'd done a poor job fighting him that afternoon. *Improve yourself quickly,* he'd sneered, *or maybe I'll cut your whipsword in half.* It looked as though someone had done just that to these boys' swords. Was it a common punishment among Seekers? She'd never seen it before.

Maud caught up with John and ran beside him.

"Stop!" she said aloud. John must not attack other Seekers, or anyone else, while she trained him. It had been the first promise she'd demanded of him.

Yet he ignored her. His whipsword was in his hand, and his gaze was locked on Briac.

Briac finally noticed the two swift-approaching figures. He stood, frozen, muscles twitching, his mouth working without a sound as sparks gyrated across his face. He found his voice a moment later and yelled, "Strike the athame! Strike it now!"

When the boys did not immediately comply, Briac grabbed the athame from Wilkin's waist. Wilkin snatched it back, and they struggled for control. Briac let go suddenly and instead pulled the lightning rod from its spot on Wilkin's other hip. In one quick motion, Briac swung the rod into the athame that was still clutched tightly in the boy's hands. The athame's vibration spread out from the dagger, reaching Maud through the air and the forest floor.

"Stop, John!" she said again. Of course she could pull him to a halt, but that was not the point. He must learn to focus on her, to push other things aside—especially when he was most distracted. If he could not do that, he would never be a Seeker.

Both boys were yelling at Briac, but Briac was undeterred. He grabbed Wilkin's arm—the arm holding the athame—and with all of his strength he forced that arm into a circle, cutting an anomaly into the air even as the older boy struggled to push him away.

"Go!" Briac yelled again. "Or she'll kill you, she'll kill you. You'll die, I'll die!"

"She's so fast!" the younger boy said, pointing at the Young Dread, who had surged ahead of John and was bearing down on them with all the speed she could muster. "She's like—"

"She's deadly!" Briac spat.

Briac's words had an effect. Wilkin and Briac both grabbed the younger one, Nott, and the three of them stepped quickly through the anomaly.

A knife flew by Maud's head, thrown by John, as she raced toward the gaping doorway. When she reached the threshold of the darkness, she stopped. She didn't intend to jump through, nor to fight Briac or the boys. Now that she'd seen their athame—an athame with a boar upon it—she merely wished to observe them at closer range before they disappeared.

From within the anomaly, the older boy stared out at her. He looked frightened; his mouth was open, revealing blackened teeth. The smaller boy had tears drying on his cheeks and eyes full of amazement. Briac was clutching his back where John's thrown knife had cut him. As the doorway began to lose shape and collapse, she studied their faces, searching her mind for some memory of them.

By the time John arrived at her side, the anomaly had fallen shut. He stood next to her, panting and enraged.

"Why didn't you stop them?" he demanded. "It would have been so easy for you!"

Maud turned, allowing herself to feel anger. She grabbed hold of John's cloak and yanked him toward her, then pushed him firmly up against the stone wall of the training barn.

"He tortured my mother," John said, his breath steaming in the freezing air, his blue eyes clear and furious in the moonlight. "For years. I should be allowed to kill him. He deserves to die."

"Listen closely, John." Her voice was even and slow, but she knew he would have no doubt about the fury beneath it. "If I am to train you, you will heed my orders."

He stared at her, still breathing hard, but he didn't struggle against her grasp.

"It is no concern of mine that Briac Kincaid appears on the estate. You are not in a position to pick a fight. Not while I train you. I do not help you so that you may attack others. I only give you the education Briac did not finish. That is all." She waited until John met her gaze. "You will obey me," she said, "or my help will end."

She kept him pinned to the barn, pressing him hard into the stone, making her point. Finally John nodded.

"I'm sorry," he said. "You're right."

CHAPTER 7

NOTT

They tumbled through the dark doorway into cold, shallow water. Nott landed on his hands and knees, the tiny waves of the lake splashing his face, but even so the first thing he noticed was the smell. Dead animals. He and Wilkin had left a great pile of them outside the entrance to the fort, and there they were still on the shore, rotting in the moonlight.

Nott carried a strip of deer flesh in the pouch around his waist, so some portion of that smell was always with him. But here it was everywhere in the air, identifying this ruined fortress, Dun Tarm, as a place where he and Wilkin and other Watchers belonged. It was where their master had trained each of them and taught them to be so much more than the children they'd been.

Wilkin and Briac were splashing around in the water nearby. Wilkin had Briac in a headlock and was yelling, "Explain yourself!"

Back in the woods of that strange, distant city—*Is it called Kong Kong?*—Briac had almost managed to steal their helm *and* their athame. They'd gotten the helm off his head, but he'd jumped with their athame into the darkness *There,* and they'd been forced to follow. He'd dragged them to that ruined place in Scotland to look for Quin and their master's special athame. But of course she wasn't there and neither was the athame, just as they hadn't been in Hong Kong.

Wilkin pushed Briac into the water, and the man flailed about before eventually finding his feet. It was obvious he'd lost his mind again. He'd gotten it back for a moment when he wore the helm in the Hong Kong woods, just as he'd gotten it back for a while when they put the helm on him in that madhouse where they'd found him—long enough to help them find Quin in the London hospital. But his mind was gone now.

Where was the helm? Was Wilkin wearing it? Nott looked back to Wilkin. The moon was bright enough to show him the older boy's hair, which meant he did *not* have the helm on his head. It must be safely inside Wilkin's rucksack. Nott was relieved.

Wilkin had already said he wouldn't let Briac use the helm ever again. Hopefully this meant they wouldn't be following Briac anymore. They weren't supposed to be looking for the girl, and Wilkin knew that. *But he's an idiot,* Nott thought as he waded through the freezing water to the shore. An example: Nott loved to slap Wilkin at night. The older boy slept like a dead man and often wondered why he woke with bruises on his face. "It's because you thrash about and hit your head on rocks," Nott told him, and Wilkin believed it.

"Leave me be!" Briac roared, struggling out of the lake. "I'll set the dogs on you both. I'll trample you, I'll knife you, I'll impale you . . ."

Nott stepped, dripping, onto the shore. Dun Tarm was crumbling into Loch Tarm. Half of the fortress had been built out over the lake to begin with, and that half was mostly under the lake now. Long ago, water had snuck into what remained and filled all the low-lying places with cold, wet, mossy fingers.

Cradled in a steep valley, the crumbling fort was reflected clearly in the lake, and beyond the water, in the bright light of the moon and stars, Nott could see forested slopes reaching up to crags of bare rock that surged above the tree line, like giants from the ancient times.

"Get inside!" Wilkin ordered, shoving Briac toward the gaping doorway.

Nott passed through the jagged shadows of the remaining fortress walls. He was closer to the animal corpses here, and flies buzzed everywhere, even in the cold of the night. A deer lay on top of the pile, its body intact except for a series of slashes along its stomach. Its glassy eyes stared up at the dark sky. They hadn't killed that deer to eat it; they'd killed it because it was important to kill things. You had to stay sharp. And you had to keep things in their place. Those were the rules their master had taught them.

The helm helped you stay sharp, and it helped you keep things in their place too. It helped with most things. Nott's eyes drifted toward the pack on Wilkin's back. His fingers twitched at the thought of pulling out the helm and putting it on. But Wilkin wouldn't let him use it tonight. He hadn't let Nott use the helm in days.

"Wilkin's a tyrant that way," Nott whispered to the deer as he passed. He imagined the animal winking sympathetically in response.

The smell of decay wasn't as strong inside the fort, where they made their camp and where they'd left most of their gear. Dun Tarm's great room had split. Half had sunken unevenly into the lake, but much of the other half was intact, if you could ignore the streams of water among the stones of the floor. Three of the walls had crumbled, leaving only a small alcove under a roof, but this was large enough that they could sleep in shelter. There were several scrubby trees growing up from the ruined floor, providing protection from the wind that blew down from the distant peaks.

Wilkin pointed to a spot on the ground where Briac should sit. The man was whimpering and trying to hold the wound in his back, which was bleeding all over everything. He'd been hit by a knife as they escaped from the burned estate, a fact Briac only now seemed to notice.

"Sew him up, Nott!" Wilkin commanded. "While he explains himself." Then to Briac: "You tried to steal from us."

"I don't sit!" Briac said, ripping his shoulder away from Nott, and forgetting his wound again. He punched his own leg in an attempt to formulate a coherent thought. "We can't—sit! We must—we must *find* her. Get that athame."

His words sounded more focused than most Nott had heard out of him. The sparks floating about his head were quite visible now that he was in shadow, but they were dancing more slowly than they had been. Maybe Briac's recent few minutes in the helm had done something lasting for him—not that Nott cared.

He found the sewing kit in his own rucksack and pulled out the thick black thread and dull needle they used to stitch themselves up after particularly bad fights.

"You take us to find one girl, then you run away from another," Wilkin said to Briac. "Why?"

"She's, she's, she's . . . she's dangerous, that one. Young Dread . . ."

"What does it mean, 'Young Dread'?" asked Wilkin. "I've heard you call our master 'Middle Dread' before."

When Briac didn't answer, Wilkin slapped him to help him focus. "Yes," the man responded, holding up a hand so he would not be hit again. "She's like him in some ways. Dangerous."

Briac screeched as Nott poked him with the needle and pulled the thread through his skin. The knife wound was producing an unexpectedly large amount of blood, but it was only a shallow slice. Nott had seen worse.

"We're not supposed to be looking for girls, or athames, Wilkin,"

Nott said, for what felt like the hundredth time—but he was trying not to whine. He leaned over Briac and poked the needle in again, doing a terrible job of it. "We're supposed to be following our master's orders, waking the others, and searching—"

"Quiet, Nott. We *will* . . ." Wilkin's face was going through a series of contortions as he considered his options.

The last time their master had come to them, he'd told them to search him out in twenty-four hours if they didn't hear from him again. Twenty-four hours later, they'd made their way to their usual meeting place in London, only to find the entire city swarming around that great crashed ship in the park. And there, in the middle of it, was Briac Kincaid. They recognized Briac because they'd seen him in their master's company several times. They'd used the helm on Briac late at night in the madhouse to which he'd been brought, and eventually he'd started talking some sense—though not much.

If their master—the man Briac called the Middle Dread—was lost, they knew exactly how to search for him. It was their whole purpose as Watchers, to find their master if he was lost. It was the reason they existed and why their master woke them in turns to live out in the world. They were to keep him from disappearing *There,* as his enemies would want him to do. But Briac had said he already knew where their master was, so there was no need to search. And Wilkin— idiot!—loved the idea of finding him quickly and by themselves. *He'll praise us, Nott. He'll know we're the best out of all his Watchers.*

When they'd arrived at the London hospital, it was obvious Briac had taken them to find their master's *athame,* not their master himself. But once Wilkin had seen that athame, he'd been dead set on getting it back. *Our master's going to want this athame back, Nott. If he found out we saw it and didn't retrieve it—well, he'd put us in our caves for that, wouldn't he?*

As Nott sewed, Briac begged, "I can't think straight. Put the helmet on me again . . ."

Nott pulled the thread tight and tied off the final stitch, then whispered to Wilkin, "He wants to get his hands on our master's athame and take it for himself, Wilkin. We should—"

"I know what we should do," Wilkin snapped. "We should do what *I* say we do, because I'm in charge."

Wilkin picked up his own rucksack and began digging through it. Nott realized his partner was going to put the helm back on the crazy man and then continue following his lunatic advice. Without warning, hot tears welled in Nott's eyes and ran down his cheeks. He was aching for the cool touch of the helm as it slid over his head and the buzz of his thoughts as it started to work, but Wilkin wouldn't let him wear it, and Wilkin wasn't listening to sense and Nott would be the one punished. As the smallest, he was usually the one punished.

Wilkin turned to Nott. "We don't keep the helm in your pack, Nott. We keep it in mine."

"I know that. I never said we did. But *you* just said he wasn't allowed to wear it anymore."

"I've changed my mind. He won't be able to help us without it."

"He's not helping us at all!"

"Give me the helm, Nott!"

Nott turned slowly toward Wilkin, finally understanding what his partner meant. The older boy's dark eyes flashed impatiently in the light filtering through the fortress's stunted trees. A twinge of sickness stabbed through Nott.

"*You* have the helm," Nott said slowly. "You took it off him in that city—Kong Kong."

The older boy looked taken aback. "I don't have it. You have it! Where is it?"

He crossed the broken floor and grabbed Nott, examining his

head and roughly feeling his cloak and his small pack, as if Nott had the helm hidden somewhere and was lying about it.

"You've lost it? You've lost our helm?" Nott asked. His nausea transformed into the sensation of outright terror. The helm was the *one thing* their master demanded they keep track of.

"I have not lost it!"

"Then where is it, Wilkin?"

Nott remembered hunting with their master near Dun Tarm years before. They'd gone into the woods and killed a deer—the way their master liked to kill deer, which was very slowly. *It's all right to enjoy it,* he'd explained. *We are meant to enjoy putting creatures in their place.*

The hunting and killing had left their master in a good mood, but when they'd returned to the fortress, one of the older Watchers was waiting nervously by the entrance. That boy, shaking so much he was barely able to speak, had admitted to misplacing his own helm. Their master had flown into such a rage, the very memory of it still caused Nott's heart to beat frantically in his chest. *How can you have any value to me without your helm?* their master had roared.

Eventually all Watchers had been roused and that particular helm had been found. It hadn't mattered. Their master had sent that careless Watcher to his cave anyway, and that had been the end of him.

Wilkin was now tossing around his own things as though he might have overlooked the helm during his first inspection. When it did not magically present itself, he turned back to Nott.

"You left it *There*, didn't you?" Wilkin accused. "In the blackness? Where we'll never find it!"

"*You* had it!"

"I did not—" A different look passed across Wilkin's face. Nott guessed that Wilkin was remembering that he was, in fact, the one who'd had the helm last, when the two of them had been struggling in the trees with Briac, just before jumping into the anomaly.

A moment later, Wilkin looked as sick as Nott felt.

"It's still your fault, Nott," the older boy said weakly. "You were the one who took it out of the pack in Hong Kong."

"But *you* were the one who wanted to follow *him*"—Nott jabbed his finger at Briac—"instead of our orders." They sat glaring at each other. Wilkin was rapidly deflating, and Nott pressed his advantage: "Did you drop it in the woods? Or did you drop it *There,* Wilkin?"

Aside from the prospect of their master's rage and their inability to carry out their orders, the idea of the helm lying somewhere where they might never find it made Nott desperately upset. It had already been such a long time since he'd gotten to wear it.

"I—I think I dropped it in the woods," said Wilkin. "In Hong Kong."

"Well, that's something, at least."

CHAPTER 8

QUIN

Quin walked into the basement, letting the door shut behind her. She ran her hands over the nearest armoire, where mother-of-pearl dragons twined through forests and rivers. The basement was full of chests and cabinets with similar designs: samurai, lakes, villages, eagles.

She turned back to find Mariko MacBain watching her closely from a spot by the basement door, her fine Japanese features full of concern. Mariko was Shinobu's mother, who lived in this small, lovely home tucked into one of the most expensive neighborhoods in Hong Kong. Though Mariko had kicked Shinobu out—when his drug use had gotten unbearable—she still had his whipsword, because Shinobu had left it here, in hopes of forgetting it altogether. That had been nearly two years ago, when he'd tried to erase Seekers from his life, just as Quin herself had done.

Now, lying in Hong Kong, recovering from his injuries, he'd asked Quin to get the whipsword back for him. They had decided they were still Seekers, and now, with Briac and those strange boys looking for them, they needed all of their Seeker tools.

Several days had passed since the fight in London, and though

Quin had been on the lookout for those boys at every moment, she was beginning to hope they didn't know how to find her. Even so, she took only quick trips off the Bridge. She'd arrived at Mariko's house quite suddenly, had given an abbreviated explanation of Shinobu's injuries, and had asked for the whipsword.

Quin had been in this basement once before, but only now did the meaning of all the inlaid designs occur to her. The most common decoration on the furniture was the eagle, which was, of course, the symbol of Alistair MacBain's house, and was the emblem on his athame, which had been destroyed on the estate. But now she noticed the second most common motif: a dragon. The last time she'd been here, Quin had assumed that the dragons were merely a traditional Japanese theme, like rivers and lakes and villages, but now she'd learned from the journal that the dragon, like the eagle, was a symbol belonging to one of the ten Seeker houses. And these dragons looked curiously like the drawings in Catherine's book.

Mariko had lived on the Scottish estate when Quin was young, but Quin had always thought of her as an outsider, a woman who was there only because she'd married Shinobu's father. The dichotomy between them—Mariko, small, delicate, refined; and Alistair, tall, broad, a redheaded Scot—had added to the sense of Mariko's separateness. But what if she hadn't been separate? A series of possibilities opened up before Quin.

"You're from a Seeker house too?" she asked.

Mariko did not respond at first, but eventually she nodded. "House of the dragon. One of the first."

"You . . . you trained to be a Seeker? With Alistair and my parents?" The truth of it came upon Quin all at once. "You were an apprentice with them?"

Mariko nodded again, a short, reluctant motion.

"Did you take your oath?" Quin asked.

She knew her own mother had done some of the Seeker training but had never taken the oath. But this woman . . .

Mariko didn't reply but instead moved deeper into the basement. She stopped at a cabinet up against the farthest wall. Quin followed, watching as Shinobu's mother entered a passcode, then pulled open the cabinet's wooden doors. Inside were several hooded cloaks, a stack of dark-colored exercise clothing, like that worn by apprentice Seekers during training sessions, and three curled whipswords mounted on a rack.

Mariko ran her hands over the hilts of the weapons.

"Shinobu thought he was very clever, hiding his whipsword under the rug in his closet when he came to Hong Kong." Despite her estrangement from her son, Mariko's love was obvious when she spoke of him. "I found it and brought it down here, with the other family whipswords—mine and my father's, which I've saved for Akio, though I don't know if I will ever let him use it."

Shinobu's mother had gotten away from the estate when she was pregnant with Akio, Shinobu's much younger brother. Quin had seen him playing in Mariko's yard just now, before they'd stepped down into the basement. He was eight or nine, with only a tint of the red hair Shinobu had gotten from their father. Probably the little boy knew nothing about these weapons or about Seekers; Mariko had escaped her previous life so thoroughly that even Shinobu had thought she was dead, until he was reunited with her in Hong Kong.

Mariko lifted Shinobu's whipsword off the rack and handed it to Quin. Then she took one of the others, a beautiful weapon with an inlaid mother-of-pearl grip. Quin took a step back, sensing the woman's intention. In a smooth, expert motion, Mariko whipped the sword out into a solid form. Then she sent the weapon through a long series of blade formations, before flicking her wrist and letting it collapse back into a coil.

Quin had been thinking of Shinobu's elegant mother as some sort of rich, pampered businesswoman, with her tailored skirt suit and expensive high heels, but now she saw Mariko for what she was—a trained fighter who had given up that life, but who hadn't entirely forgotten her roots.

Mariko looked down at the curled whipsword in her hand. Her straight black hair was done up in an elaborate bun behind her head that now looked at odds with the hard expression on her face.

"I did take my oath," she said quietly. "I trained with both your father and your mother. And Alistair of course. And others."

"But you . . ."

"I took my oath, I am a sworn Seeker," Mariko said. "But I chose to spend my life as a mother, not . . . something else."

Quin nodded. It was a decision she understood quite well after the life her father had shown her.

"And your athame, the athame with the dragon . . ." She'd looked through the pages of Catherine's journal, studying what had been written about each Seeker house. According to Catherine's records, only the athame with the fox and the athame with the eagle had been seen in the last few decades. But Catherine hadn't known everything; she hadn't described the athame of the Dreads, for example—now in Quin's possession—with its insignia of three interlocking ovals in the shape of an atom.

"Gone," Mariko said, her gaze shifting away from her whipsword to look at Quin. "Our athame has been gone for a hundred years or more. My family still sent children to the estate for training—in hopes that one day we might recover our athame and be a great house again."

"Your athame isn't the only one to disappear."

"No," Mariko agreed. "We were not alone in that."

"Do you know where they've gone and why?"

The woman shook her head. "No. And because I can see the question in your eyes, I will tell you that I don't know the 'why' of many things. My family lived apart from other Seekers for many generations. I do not know why Seekers have become what they've become over the last hundred years. I only know I didn't wish to be one of them."

Quin nodded again. Then she asked, "Mariko . . . did you ever see a strange sort of metal helmet? Something you can wear while training, maybe?"

Mariko continued to look at Quin, but something in her gaze changed, became more cautious.

"I left the estate after my oath, but I went back," she said after a thoughtful moment. "Because I loved Alistair MacBain."

In Quin's recollection, Mariko and Alistair had been happy together, though Quin had to admit that she'd paid very little attention to adults' relationships when she was a child—she'd been blind to the way her own father had treated her mother, for example.

"Maybe I shouldn't have returned," Mariko went on slowly. "Alistair's life and my own would have been easier if I hadn't. But it wouldn't have been much of a life." She sighed and looked away from Quin at last. "Shinobu has always loved you, you know."

"I know," she whispered. "I love him back."

"But perhaps it would be easier for both of you if you didn't love each other . . . or if you didn't wish to be Seekers."

The woman's voice was so heavy with regret, Quin found herself incapable of responding. She thought of Mariko and Alistair MacBain, in love all those years but forced to live apart because of what Seekers had become—and in particular because of what Quin's father, Briac Kincaid, had become.

Eventually she stammered out, "I—I hope we're trying to seek the right things." This sounded weak, but it was the truth.

After a moment of reflection, Mariko nodded, as if coming to a decision within herself. "You asked me a question. The answer is no, I've never seen a metal helmet like the one you described, not in person. But—"

She reached into the cabinet and pushed all the hanging clothing to either side. The cabinet's back wall was white. Over the white, in a deep red, someone had painted a detailed picture of a metal helmet exactly like the one Quin had taken from Briac and those strange boys. Beneath the helmet were several lines of Japanese text—a numbered list.

"It's called a focal. My family had one once, as you can see," Mariko explained, gesturing at the painting. "A helpful ancestor decided to write down instructions for its use."

Quin's eyes scanned the Japanese characters.

"Can you translate it for me?"

"Do you have such a helmet?" Mariko asked her. "I never saw one on the estate."

Quin didn't respond at first. Mariko had left the world of Seekers. Did she really want to know the answer? Wasn't it better if she stayed in the dark, safe in a separate life with her younger son, Akio?

"What if I do?" Quin asked at last.

"Then you should be careful with it," Mariko told her. "Seeker tools are never toys. They are never to be taken lightly."

"I don't take any of this lightly."

"No, I don't think you do," Mariko said meditatively. Her eyes were looking down at the whipsword still coiled in her hand. "But Shinobu might. He's never been as serious as he should be."

"He's saved my life several times," Quin responded. "Those were serious enough to me."

The words came out quietly and sounded far too personal to be sharing.

Mariko smiled unhappily. "Then maybe he's grown up," she said. "In any case, if you have a focal, you should know its proper use."

She opened the lower doors of the cabinet and brought out a small slip of paper that had been folded several times. With a sense of ceremony, she handed it to Quin.

Quin carefully unfolded the delicate sheet to find a list written in a beautiful, foreign hand. It was the translation of the words inside the cabinet:

1. *Be firm in body, in good health.*
2. *Clear your thoughts, begin from neutral mind.*
3. *Focus upon the subject at hand.*
4. *Place the helm upon your head.*
5. *Follow these rules faithfully, lest the focal become a havoc helm.*

"I made the translation for a friend, many years ago, who had also come into possession of a focal," Mariko explained.

"Who?"

"You have your secrets, Quin. Let me have mine. I don't know what she used it for, just as I don't know so many other things. But I can tell you that she was never the same again." Her tone made it clear that the change in her friend hadn't been for the better.

Quin looked back to the translated list. "Was that something to do with the words 'havoc helm'? Do you know what that means?"

Mariko shook her head. "It's been so long since my family had a focal, I wasn't taught anything about it. But it's safe to assume there is danger. My father always reminded me that he was sending me to train on the estate despite the danger."

"Did he mean the danger of training? Or the danger of . . . your Seeker assignments after you took your oath?"

Mariko held up her whipsword, examining the craftsmanship of the inlaid handle, before putting the weapon back in its spot on the rack inside the cabinet.

"Maybe he meant the danger of training—the danger of tools like the whipsword or the focal—or maybe he meant the danger of assignments," she said. She turned back to Quin. "But I think he also meant the other danger." Mariko must have seen the confusion on Quin's face, because she went on, "It's not just athames that have been disappearing. Seekers themselves have been disappearing, Quin, for a long time, and no one could ever tell me why." She was echoing what Catherine had written in the journal. "So . . . if you continue to be a Seeker, and if you choose to use the focal, please take care."

CHAPTER 9

QUIN

The Hong Kong Transit Bridge spanned Victoria Harbor from Kowloon on the mainland to Hong Kong Island, and it was a world of its own. It was ten stories high and topped with a graceful canopy that resembled a mass of ship sails. From far away an observer might think the Bridge was actually a series of enormously tall ships crossing the harbor in a stately procession. To Quin it had always represented a new life, a life away from her father and Scotland, a life she could choose for herself. She and her mother lived in a house on the Bridge's main thoroughfare, where Quin had worked as a healer since arriving almost two years before.

She entered the bridge now with Shinobu's whipsword tucked beneath her jacket. As a resident, she was exempt from searches, and she passed through the security checkpoint with the weapon unnoticed.

It was still bright afternoon in Hong Kong, but the Bridge was always in twilight under its canopy, a condition Quin had come to think of as homey and comfortable. She wove through heavy foot traffic, which was illuminated predominantly by warm, yellow lanterns in the restaurants and outside the healing offices on the Bridge's upper level.

Her own house was near the center of the Bridge, close to the home of her healing mentor, Master Tan. When she reached it, she slipped out of the crowds and through her front door, which closed behind her with a jingling of bells and shut out the noise of the Bridge. Fiona was in the waiting room of Quin's healing office, tidying up with an air of having waited impatiently for some time.

"Hi, Mum. Is Shinobu upstairs?"

"Is he?" Fiona repeated. She set down a canister of herbs and pinned up her long red hair in a gesture of vexation, obviously annoyed about something. "I should say he is."

Her mother's blue eyes were clear, Quin noticed, and her words crisp—both good signs—and she looked as beautiful as ever. Fiona had stayed away from alcohol since the fight on board *Traveler*, and she wasn't working as an escort any longer. Quin and Master Tan were, in fact, instructing her as a novice healer. Sobriety might leave her short tempered, but Fiona looked so much healthier that her moments of anger were, to Quin, like scenes of a film actress pretending to be cross.

"It's a good thing he's up there," her mother continued, "or he'd be driving me mad."

"Is he all right?" Quin asked.

She felt a prick of worry. Shinobu had spent three days in a Hong Kong hospital, followed by days of intense treatment with Master Tan, who was, in addition to being Quin's mentor, one of the most respected healers on the Transit Bridge. The hospital had removed the drug implants and bathed his wounds with Eastern-designed cellular reconstructors, which, the doctors had assured her, were superior to the Western versions. Then Master Tan had worked his ancient herbal magic. Shinobu had healed more in his short time back in Asia than he had in two weeks in London. Still, he was not yet recovered.

"That's difficult to say," her mother responded, slapping the cushions on the couch somewhat viciously. Then, seeing Quin's concern, she held up her hands. "No, no, he's fine. The acupuncturist was here for an hour—until Shinobu chased him out. And he chased me out as well." Fiona pointed up the stairs. "I doubt he'll kick you out, but prepare yourself . . . At least he's up and about, I suppose."

Halfway through this cryptic narrative, Quin began up the stairs to her bedroom. She saw her mother's eyes following, and Fiona's gaze felt freighted with motherly judgment: *I can't stop you from keeping him in your room,* it seemed to say, *but he's a much different creature now from the young boy you grew up with.*

Since these words were only implied, Quin couldn't explain that very little other than sleeping had happened between her and Shinobu. He was the one with all the experience, and he'd been largely unconscious these past weeks, which had left Quin more concerned with keeping him alive than with romance.

She found her bedroom door shut, and she pushed it open, relieved it wasn't locked. Shinobu was perched on top of her bed in a half crouch, staring out the round window at Victoria Harbor. He was wearing only his underwear, and his body bristled with acupuncture needles. There were none in his head, however, because he was wearing, Quin saw with alarm, the iridescent metal focal. She spotted a swath of used needles across the floor. Apparently he'd yanked them out of his scalp himself before pulling on the helmet.

"Hey," she said cautiously.

He turned at the sound of her voice, and his eyes were bright and much more alert than they'd been before she left for Mariko's house, but they also looked a bit wild. He was standing on the bed like a cobra, ready to strike.

"Hey yourself," he said, jumping down to the floor.

She tried to grab him, but he landed fine without help. "You really shouldn't be jumping just yet," she told him.

"No, it's all right. Nothing hurts right now." He stood very close and smiled down at her. "Everything feels good."

The helmet gave off a faint crackling sound, and small red forks of electricity were crawling around its edges, across Shinobu's forehead. Quin touched one gently.

"Sunlight," he said. "I left it sitting in sunlight to charge it. Just like a disruptor."

"When did you put it on?" she asked. Though her real question was *why?*

"I'm not quite sure," he answered, as though nothing could be more natural than his uncertainty. "A few minutes? Or a day?"

"What do you mean you aren't sure?" She grew more alarmed. Had he been wearing it for so long that he'd lost track? Did that mean hours? Her mind went to the focal instructions in her pocket. Shinobu hadn't followed any of them. And yet she didn't think it would be a good idea to yank it off him unexpectedly.

"How long I've been wearing it doesn't feel important," he explained.

He took hold of her shoulders with both hands, as though he would kiss her, or perhaps eat her alive. The needles on the backs of his hands swayed as he moved.

"Quin, you have to try it. It—it—it *does* something. Something amazing. You start to be . . . It lets you *see everything.*"

"I'm going to take it off you now," she told him.

"Already? Why?" He looked upset. His hands went to the sides of the helmet to hold it on.

"You've been wearing it long enough," she said firmly. She took his hands from the focal, thankful when he put up no physical resistance, and pulled it off his head.

Immediately Shinobu groaned and collapsed.

"Wait!" Quin said, grabbing him under the arms to prevent him from crushing acupuncture needles deeper into his skin by sitting on them. "Don't sit. Try to stand."

He clutched his head, as though it were killing him, and moaned again, but he managed to stay on his feet. Quin plucked every needle from his body as quickly as she could, then helped him over to the bed. He sat heavily on the mattress. A hand went to his stomach and he closed his eyes.

"I'm dizzy . . ." he murmured.

"Lie back."

She carefully pushed him flat. What had possessed him to try the focal before she returned? Was it his thrill-seeking nature or simple curiosity? His cheeks were flushed, and his heart rate was fast but slowing down as she felt his neck.

He opened his eyes and looked up at her.

"I'm all right now," he whispered. "I felt sick for a moment . . . but it's gone now." He noticed her hovering over him, and he smiled a lazy smile. "I see you've conveniently gotten me into your bed."

"Idiot!" she said, pushing his shoulder.

"Oof," he answered, and pulled her down onto him. "How can you hit me when everything already aches?"

"Idiot," she said again, more softly. He wrapped his arms around her, but she held him away so he had to look at her. "You can't just put on that helmet. It's not a toy. It can probably hurt you if you don't use it right."

"It did hurt me," he murmured. "I got dizzy, and everything aches again. Kiss me and make it better."

"Shinobu." She didn't feel like flirting or joking. She wasn't sure how many more times she could stand to see him collapse in front of her. "Why did you put it on?"

He looked back at her seriously and finally appeared to have returned to himself. "I was lying in bed all day, bored," he told her. "It was stupid. I'm sorry."

"Your mother gave me instructions for using it."

"Really?"

"Yes, but later. When you're better. When we can be careful about it."

"All right. Of course," he said.

Quin sighed and slowly began to relax.

"I'm no end of trouble and I'm sorry," he murmured to her. She could hear in his voice that the focal's influence—whatever it was—had fully worn off. "Will you forgive me?"

"Probably," she said grudgingly.

He pulled her closer. Now that he wasn't in immediate danger of damaging himself, Quin became aware of their position on the bed, the way his smile pulled up one side of his face slightly more than the other. He was watching her through half-closed eyes.

"Now you're going to kiss me, right?" he asked.

"Maybe," Quin murmured.

And then she did kiss him, because she loved him, even if he was reckless. Half the time, his recklessness saved her life.

The kiss was nice but very one-sided.

"Are you falling asleep while I'm kissing you?" she asked him when she realized that this was exactly what was happening.

Shinobu's eyes opened with difficulty, then shut again. His pain-killer implants had all been removed, so this was real exhaustion. "Of course not," he whispered. "Kiss me more."

But in a few moments he was in a deep sleep, so deep that he didn't respond, even when she shook his shoulder. Quin looked across the room at the focal, which she'd set on her desk. What did that helmet do, precisely, to the person who wore it?

CHAPTER 10

JOHN

John tended to the fire and their dinner while the Young Dread paced. They were in their little camp inside the workshop on the estate, the same place he'd visited Maud once, the year before, the first time she'd agreed to help him. But now he was living here with her, sleeping restlessly each night on a pile of straw in one corner, wrapped in his cloak, while the Young Dread slept, still and deep, across the workshop from him, cocooned in her own cloak like a small, dark angel carved upon a tombstone.

Their hearth was by the open workshop doors, a large circle of stones filled with the ashes of all their cooking fires. A new fire was burning bright orange as John roasted their dinner.

On the wall near the hearth were drying racks where they cured the skins of the animals they hunted together. Several pelts were stretched there, and Maud and John were both wearing vests of fox fur against the cold of the evening.

Along the back wall of the workshop were old shelves and racks of knives and swords that had been rescued from the other destroyed buildings on the estate. They used everything for training.

The Young, who was usually so motionless except when action was required, was pacing back and forth in front of the cooking fire, unable to sit down. He'd never seen her like this, but she hadn't chosen to explain her state of mind, so he was waiting for her to speak. He hoped she wasn't still angry about his earlier disobedience, when he'd chased after Briac Kincaid. If she chose not to teach him anymore, he didn't know what he would do.

John forced himself to look away from her. He had his mother's journal in his lap, which he'd been studying by the light of the fire. He'd done this each night since he'd recovered the journal from a pocket in Quin's cloak, as they all plummeted to the ground on board *Traveler*. Quin had given it back to him. Even if she hadn't meant to, she'd helped him.

Maud stopped at the doorway of the workshop and looked out at the absolute darkness the night had become. It was perhaps three in the morning and very foggy.

"Do you want to speak?" John asked at last.

She turned toward him, her features outlined in the glow of the firelight. Her expression was as calm and clear as it always was; only something in her eyes matched the restlessness of her body. She didn't answer.

John skewered the pieces of rabbit meat and turned them over on the metal grate. The bullet wound near his shoulder was throbbing, though it hurt him much less in recent days. His eyes slid back to the journal.

His mother's notebook was both self-explanatory and very difficult to make out. The first half seemed to be a page-by-page recounting of the Middle's Dread's misdeeds and the justice he'd handed out to unruly Seekers. Those pages were written in ancient hands and were very difficult to read. However, John's grandmother Maggie had often made him read aloud to her from very old books, many of them handwritten, so he'd had practice with archaic English and could decipher much in those early journal pages. He'd asked Maud for help translating what he couldn't understand, but she'd refused. In fact, she'd refused to give the journal anything more than a casual glance.

I have rid the world of the Middle, she'd told him the first time he'd tried to show her the book and explain what he thought it contained. *I have no wish to read an accounting of what he's done. His crimes were many, though most were long ago. I should have killed him sooner.*

John wasn't much interested in the Middle's crimes or justice either, so he hadn't asked for help again. His interest lay in the second half of the book, where his mother—and others—had cataloged the last known appearances of Seekers and athames from the various houses.

According to the journal, there were originally ten Seeker families and each had once possessed an athame. But most of these athames hadn't been seen since twenty years, fifty years, a hundred years before John had been born. Where they were now and why they had disappeared were both mysteries—at least to Catherine and her journal. But she'd been looking for them. Or, perhaps, she'd been looking for *some* of them—the houses that had done harm to her own house.

For generations, other Seeker houses had targeted and killed his family. *Someday you will destroy the houses who have harmed us,* his grandmother Maggie had told him after his mother's death. *You will become what we were in the beginning, powerful but good.* She had been echoing his mother's own words: *Our house will rise again, and the others will fall.*

When he touched the book's pages, he thought of his mother's hands, handling the same leaves, filling them with her clear, feminine writing. And he thought of Quin, though he didn't want to. She'd had this journal in her possession. Her hands had touched it as well. When his eyes ran down a line of text, he could feel her eyes doing the same.

What did she think of this? he wondered. *And what is she thinking now?*

Abruptly Maud turned away from the doorway and took a seat across the fire from John. Her gaze settled upon him. It was always uncomfortable, her direct stare, like being sized up by a leopard. Her long, light brown hair hung down around her shoulders, adding to the impression of wildness.

"I do not know those boys," she said simply. "I am certain I have not seen them before. They are no Seekers I have ever met."

The rabbit was done cooking. Silently John pulled the meat from the grate and handed her a portion on one of the rough boards they used for meals. The Young Dread received the food but held it out in front of her, as though not actually aware of its presence.

"Do you know every Seeker?" he asked her.

"I should be able to place them, by looks, by house. I should have some sense of the family to whom they belong."

"How could you expect to know everyone?" he asked.

Maud couldn't be much older than John. In fact, she looked younger. Even though her lifetime had spanned a great length of years, much of that time, she'd explained, had been spent *There*— hibernating, or sleeping, or "stretched out," as she liked to call it—so the actual duration of her time here in the real world, of her time awake, could not be much more than John's, could it?

She said simply, "If they were Seekers, I would know them, and I do not." Taking notice of the food in front of her, she began to eat. After a few moments, she appeared to come to a decision, and she asked John, "What does your book say about the house of the boar?"

John tried to hide his surprise at this interest in the journal. "The boar? Why that one?"

"Those boys had an athame, and there was a boar carved upon it."

"So . . . couldn't they be Seekers from the house of the boar?" he asked.

"No," Maud responded, "they're not."

When she offered no further explanation, he set his tray aside, wiped his hands carefully, and flipped through the book. In the second half of the journal there was a page with a boar sketched along the top. He held it up for Maud to see.

"She made a record," he explained, "of places where the Seekers in the house of the boar were seen, places where their athame was seen. Like here." He pointed to one of the earliest notes under the drawing of the boar. "1779, Spain, near the city of Valencia."

"What is the last location on that list? The most recent place the boar athame was seen?"

His eyes ran down the next few pages.

"Here. Norway, eighteen years ago, in the possession of Emile Pernet, house of the boar." He showed her the line of text. "No one saw the boar athame after that—until now, I guess."

"Emile," the Young Dread repeated.

"Do you know him?"

"I have heard his name once," she told him. "And what is that, beneath the writing?" She'd moved closer to look at the journal, so they were sitting shoulder to shoulder.

"A sketch of someplace."

Catherine had pasted in a drawing of a barren landscape with sharp rocks strewn across it and a low, dark cave in the distance.

There were several such drawings in the journal. Maud took the book from him and gazed at this picture intently.

"Those are coordinates she's written from an athame," he said. "Do you recognize the location?"

Beneath the drawing were symbols from the dials of an athame—surely they were instructions for finding that cave. The Young Dread had begun teaching him about his athame and its symbols. They'd even used the device a few times, to travel from London to the estate and to other nearby locations, though she didn't let him wield the ancient tool himself, and in fact kept him blindfolded during the process; he wouldn't be able to use it until he'd taken his oath. But when he was a full Seeker, the athame would allow him to follow co-ordinates in the journal, retrace his mother's footsteps to find those houses that had torn down his own.

The Young Dread was still studying the drawing. At length she said, "If that is a cave, I may recognize the location, but it makes little sense. If it is where I suspect it may be, it should have been a safe place for Emile—not the last place his athame would be seen before disappearing." She kept the journal in her hands and tapped her fingers upon it. "May I look at this for a little while?" she asked him.

John experienced an almost physical ache when the journal was out of his own hands—it was such a precious object, and had been missing for so long—but he swallowed his discomfort and said, "Yes, of course."

He took Maud's interest in his mother's notes as a hopeful sign. John had been thinking about his grandmother's cabin on *Traveler*. The airship was still in Hyde Park. The craft's dangerous engines had to be decommissioned on site before it could be safely moved outside London to be repaired. That work was nearly done, and the move would happen in a few days. While *Traveler* was being fixed, the inside of the ship would be stripped, including the contents of Maggie's cabin. There were things in that room John needed, items he didn't want his cousins—the cousins who were already fighting for control of the family fortune—to find.

He hadn't wanted to speak of this to the Young Dread. She didn't like mention of his family or his mother. She wanted him to keep his mind in the present, on his training. But tonight, after seeing those boys, she was different. He watched the careful way she was holding the journal as she looked into the fire. If she was interested in what his mother had written, maybe, he thought, she could be convinced to help him.

"I—I need to go back to *Traveler*," he told her before he lost his nerve. "Just for a short visit. But it will have to be soon."

Maud looked up at him.

"Why?"

"I have my mother's journal, but there are other things of hers in a bedroom on the ship. I don't want someone else to take them."

The Young Dread waited for a better explanation. John tapped a hand nervously against his leg. Maud had been truthful with him, and he'd never lied to her since she'd agreed to train him. He was her student, and he would honor that arrangement as far as he could.

"In her journal my mother was keeping track of the houses that killed our relatives," he explained quietly.

"What you've shown me in the journal says nothing about dead relatives," Maud responded. "I see only lists of locations and dates."

"Maybe enemies weren't the only thing she was writing about, but they're in there," he answered. "When you see what's in my grand-mother's room on *Traveler*, this will make sense. Whatever else my mother was doing, she was tracking those who had done us harm."

"You want to gather evidence for revenge?" Her voice was cutting, despite its slow cadence.

"I've spoken plainly to you about the promises I've made," he told her, forcing himself to hold her gaze. "While you train me, I will take no action without your permission. But I—I must retrieve these things before they're lost."

Maud appeared to weigh his answer in her mind for some time. At last she said, "We can visit the airship." Then her eyes met his. "Your mother didn't only want revenge, you know."

John turned away and said nothing. But his thoughts were clear: *You don't know what my mother wanted.*

CHAPTER 11

MAUD

21 YEARS EARLIER

"What are you doing here?" The girl's voice carried through the woods.

"What do you think I'm doing here?" a male voice asked.

The Young Dread heard an old cottage door being forced shut, and then there were two sets of footsteps moving through the forest undergrowth.

"Stop following me!"

That was the girl's voice again, more clear this time, and Maud paused, one foot raised in the air, listening.

The Young Dread had been in the castle ruins on the Scottish estate, practicing alone, wondering where the Middle Dread was that day. She was now moving south, through the thick woods leading downslope to the river, which was where she often hunted for their meals.

"Go away!" the girl said a moment later.

Something in the sound of her voice bothered Maud. She stood balanced on one foot, then after a quick moment of deliberation, she turned around and moved back uphill.

"I want to be alone!" the girl said. She was out of breath, and judging by her footsteps, she was now running.

The Young recognized the voice as belonging to Catherine Renart, one of the apprentices who was shortly to take her oath and become a Seeker. When Maud reached the top of the hill, she saw Catherine moving swiftly through the trees below. She'd obviously been visiting the small group of abandoned cottages that lay deep in the woods nearby.

Another of the apprentices was chasing the girl. It was a boy called Briac Kincaid, though it was difficult to think of him as a boy. He was only fifteen, like Catherine, but he was already as tall as a man, and his face had a ruthless cast.

Catherine reached a clearer patch of the woods, and here Briac caught up with her. He grabbed her arm and spun her around to face him. Maud saw the flush in Briac's fair skin, which contrasted starkly with his jet-black hair.

"What were you doing in the cottages?" he asked.

"Why are you following me?" Catherine demanded, yanking her arm away.

Briac took hold of her shoulders and smiled. Catherine took a step back and found herself up against a tree.

"You know why I'm following you," he whispered.

Catherine looked more surprised than alarmed.

But why am I here? the Young Dread asked herself. This was some sort of lovers' quarrel. Hardly something that should attract her notice. And yet there were qualities about Catherine that reminded the Young Dread of herself and so held her attention. She'd watched the apprentices training over the last several days, as she and the Middle did each time they came to the estate. While most were entirely absorbed in proving themselves to their instructors, so they might be invited to take their oaths, Catherine's manner was different. It was as though she already saw past her training to her life beyond and wanted to be taught the things that mattered. The Young herself had been like that, asking her master, the Old Dread, a thousand questions about her future, even though he would answer only a select few.

"You wanted me to follow you out here," Briac whispered.

Maud looked down at the two of them from near the crest of the hill. She was concealed among trees, but she didn't think they would have noticed her, even if she'd been standing in the open.

"I did not," Catherine said.

"Come on. Going out alone to the empty cottages?" he asked softly. "Let's go back inside one of them . . ."

"I was looking at Emile's things," she told him. She tugged one of her shoulders out of his grasp.

"Emile?" he responded. "Why would you spend time on him? A failed apprentice who's quit and left."

Catherine tugged free her other shoulder and looked at Briac angrily.

"He was our friend," she said. "He was training with us."

"He was a little boy."

"He was fourteen. Only a few months younger than we are. And I liked the things he wanted to do after he took his oath."

"Like what? Getting rid of corrupt politicians? Helping the poor?" Briac said these things as though they were a naive joke.

"Why do you say it like that?" Catherine asked. "We're supposed to do those sorts of things. It's our purpose."

"Is it, now?"

"My grandfather got rid of an Afghani warlord, we've freed innocent—"

"Bravo, Catherine. You must have a perfect family. But Emile wouldn't have made it to his oath."

"Why do you say that?"

"He picked bad company," Briac said.

"Who do you mean?"

Briac shrugged. "I don't really know, and there's no reason for me to care." His voice dropped back to a harsh whisper: "Forget Emile. That's not why we're out here."

"It's why I'm—" Catherine began, but Briac cut her off by pressing his lips to hers. The girl recoiled, her light hair tangling in the bark of the tree as she pulled her head away. From the short distance between them, she studied Briac, as though analyzing an unexpected natural phenomenon in a laboratory.

"Come on," the boy pressed. "We've been beating each other up in the training barn for three years. Haven't you wanted . . . ?"

A look of suspicion crossed Catherine's face, chased away a moment later by an expression of mild curiosity. She shoved him away from her, then put a hand behind his head and pulled him back. They kissed again.

Maud turned away. There was no reason she should be involved in this moment, and she had dinner to hunt. She had gone a few dozen paces when their voices came to her again. She realized she had extended her hearing to keep watch on them.

"This is . . . too much," Catherine said.

"No, it's good, it's good . . ."

"You're cruel when we train. Half the time I hate you."

"It's only because I want you," he whispered. "Don't you want me?"

A moment later, Maud heard a violent scuffle and without conscious thought found herself turning back. When she regained the crest of the hill, she saw that Briac had managed to pin both of

Catherine's arms behind her. Catherine struggled as he pressed her against the tree, kissing her, one of his hands tugging at her waistband.

"No!" Catherine said, ripping her head away from his at last.

"It's all right," Briac told her, his words barely above a whisper. "I've wanted you all year . . ."

He pushed his lips against hers, and his hand disappeared beneath her waistband. Maud felt her feet speed up as she moved down the hill toward them.

Catherine twisted her head back, then swung it forward. Her forehead cracked into his nose. He cried out and let go.

"Get off me!" she yelled, pushing him.

Briac was stunned by the head butt, but only for a moment. In the next instant, he hit Catherine across the face, his open hand making a loud crack as it connected with her cheek.

Catherine fell to the side, but Maud saw at once that this was a feint. Halfway through the fall, her hands took hold of Briac's shoulders and her knee came up into his groin with enough force that he gasped and stepped backward, clutching himself. Catherine came after him, shoving him down onto the ground and hitting him about his head. Briac raised his arms to fend her off, and she took the opportunity to bring her knee into his groin again.

Maud had stopped walking. Catherine was fighting back ably and did not need help. *Of course not,* she thought. *The girl is almost a full Seeker.*

As Briac rolled over on the ground, Catherine drew a knife from the small of her back and cut the waistband of his trousers. She ripped the material down, exposing his underclothes.

"How do you like it?" she whispered, out of breath.

The boy clutched himself and watched her from the forest floor as she stood and brushed herself off. He didn't try to get up as she jogged away.

After some distance, Catherine caught sight of Maud and came to a stop. The Young Dread realized she was standing completely in the open, and her right arm was cocked back, a knife blade still clutched in her fingers, ready to throw at Briac Kincaid. Catherine looked surprised.

I have surprised myself, the Young thought. *These apprentices can take care of themselves. We Dreads must keep ourselves apart.*

In one fluid motion, Maud tucked the knife back into its place and turned, continuing on her original path south, toward hunting. But Catherine's footsteps were following her now. When the Young Dread did not turn or change her pace, she heard Catherine coming faster, and then the girl was at her side.

"You were going to help me?" she asked, walking along with the Young Dread. "Why?"

Maud glanced at her. Up close, she was struck by the girl's resemblance to one of the other apprentices, a girl named Anna. Of course, that must be Catherine's older sister. They had the same light hair and the same blue eyes. But Anna was more like every other apprentice—she lacked Catherine's inquisitiveness.

Catherine said, "I thought you weren't supposed to interfere in fights between Seekers."

"You're not a Seeker yet," Maud replied evenly.

"I can handle myself."

"I'm sure Briac Kincaid understands that now as well."

"I've never liked him," the girl said, almost conversationally, keeping up with Maud. "We're supposed to put aside family grudges while we're here—you know, the estate's neutral ground. But I shouldn't have let him get so close." Catherine examined her hands. One of her knuckles was bleeding. She put it to her mouth as she glanced around the forest, then let out a small, joyless laugh. "You'd be surprised at the different people you meet in these woods."

"You will be sworn soon, and free to go where you will," Maud told her.

"But how much of a Seeker will I be?"

The Young Dread wondered what the girl meant, but she was not inclined to ask. Already she'd inserted herself too much into this apprentice's life, made herself too accessible. The Dreads must keep separate. That was the oath of the Dreads: to uphold the three laws of Seekers and to stand apart from humanity, so their heads were clear to judge.

"My family's athame has been missing since . . . a hundred years or something," Catherine went on, as though Maud had invited her to elaborate. "The estate is missing tools we're supposed to have for training. So how much of a Seeker will I be when I take my oath? I'll be half of what Seekers used to be. Less than half, since I've got no athame. My sister and I will have to ally with some other family, beg use of their athame, like most apprentices—Briac too. Do you think another family will risk loaning me their athame so I can go off to South America or something, to help get rid of drug lords? They're going to roll their eyes at me like Briac just did."

The words were spilling out of the girl as though she'd been waiting months to tell someone. Perhaps she'd been waiting months to speak to Maud in particular.

"What training tools do you speak of?" the Young Dread was spurred to ask, despite herself. She knew that some athames were no longer in the possession of their original houses and many had disappeared altogether, though she did not know why. But what else was missing?

"I'm not even sure," Catherine said. "I've heard mention of a helmet for training—but other tools as well. You'd know better than I would."

Maud's job with apprentices was only to oversee the administering of their oaths, and she hadn't paid much attention to the specifics of their training for a very long time. Yet now that Catherine mentioned it, she realized she hadn't seen a focal since . . . when? When had she last seen an apprentice using one? At least fifteen wakings ago? And even then, they had been extremely rare, where once they'd been common. There were other implements, not strictly necessary in creating a good Seeker but certainly useful, that she hadn't seen employed on the estate for a few generations at least.

The Young Dread shook her head, to tell Catherine no, but also to dispel her own thoughts in this matter. "You speak of Seeker problems. If Seekers have lost track of their own possessions, it is no concern of the Dreads."

"It's not just our *possessions* that are missing, though, is it?" Catherine asked quietly, looking back toward the abandoned cottages now far behind them. "My friend Emile—Emile Pernet, house of the boar—didn't come back this year. And others haven't come back. Look at all the empty cottages."

"Not everyone finishes the training," the Young Dread told her. "It is hard."

"I've tried to reach Emile lots of times, and he doesn't answer," Catherine said distractedly. "He's gone, and no one seems to care."

"Many apprentices drop out of training," the Young Dread said. "Why concern yourself, or me?"

"You seemed concerned. Earlier." Catherine nodded toward the location where Briac had attacked her. "You're not like the other one. The Middle. He isn't at all concerned about Seekers' lives."

The Young gave her no response. It was not the place of a Seeker, much less an apprentice Seeker, to pass any sort of judgment on a

Dread. If Maud had not just seen this girl attacked, she would have rebuked her. But as it was, the Young Dread simply continued walking and picked up her pace.

"Does it bother you?" Catherine asked, speeding up to match Maud's steps. She was either oblivious to the Young's dislike of this conversation or determined to press on regardless. "Does it bother you—not becoming involved? Always being separate from the rest of us?"

"That is the duty of a Dread."

"Have you ever regretted it . . . what you are?"

Maud's eyes flashed a warning, and Catherine fell back a step. She clarified, more quietly, "I only meant—would it be hard for someone like me? A life like yours?"

"There are already three Dreads, so your question is meaningless."

The girl was quiet for several paces, but still she kept up with Maud. "But—but there's more than one Young Dread."

Maud stopped walking and stared at the girl. "Explain yourself," she said. "There are no other Dreads."

"My great-great-grandfather saw the Middle Dread training others."

Despite her better judgment, the Young Dread asked, "Your great-great-grandfather?"

"He wrote it down. I have his letter."

"No. There are no other Dreads," Maud said again. Of course there were not. "Only the Old Dread himself could create another Dread, and he hasn't done so since he trained me."

"Really? Are you sure?" Catherine looked crestfallen at this news. She cast her gaze down at the forest floor. Then, as though she hardly had the nerve to speak, she blurted, "But if there are only three Dreads . . . do you—do you think the Middle Dread deserves his position?"

On reflex, Maud's right arm flashed up and slapped Catherine's cheek smartly. The girl's hand went to her face. Maud continued walking, this time increasing her pace so that Catherine couldn't keep up without running.

How dare an unsworn apprentice speak to a Dread like this?

The girl was no longer following, and Maud could hear her rubbing her cheek where she'd been struck.

"He's done things he shouldn't have done, and he's not a fair judge," Catherine called after her.

Both of those accusations were, of course, true. The Young Dread had known it for some time. And yet it was not Catherine's place to challenge this.

"A lot of Seekers have written things down about him," the girl said, though she was still not following.

Maud slowed at that, recalling something from a very long time ago. As a child, centuries ago, she'd accidentally spied a fight between the Middle Dread and the previous Young Dread. In his dying words, that Young had told the Middle that he'd written many things down. And then he'd smiled, as though he were the winner of the fight, even though it was clear the Middle Dread was about to kill him. Maud had always wondered what that Dread boy had written. And where he'd written it.

Years afterward, she'd gotten up the courage to tell the Old Dread about that incident. The Old had responded by telling her calmly, "There is little about the Middle Dread that could surprise me, child. He admitted that act to me. And yet he has changed his ways. He is different now. You must leave him to me, for I have him in hand."

Maud increased her pace, until she was in a half run, slipping between the trees with a silent, steady, rhythmic tread. Still, she heard what Catherine said next:

"My parents don't want to know," the girl muttered, "no one on the estate wants to know, and you don't want to know."

The Young Dread drew her hearing back to herself, shutting Catherine out.

Much later, when she was returning to the estate with two wild fowl for supper, she saw the Middle himself. He stood near the cottages of the Dreads, speaking to Briac Kincaid, who had a swollen nose and a blackened eye.

Catherine's strangest comment echoed in the Young Dread's mind: *My great-great-grandfather saw the Middle Dread training others.*

The Dreads often spent time together stretched out *There,* but the Middle had the capability of waking himself, and she did not. This meant that he was often awake when Maud slept. What did he do all those times when he was awake in the world without her?

As the Young Dread watched, the Middle put a hand on Briac Kincaid's shoulder. It was a gesture of camaraderie Maud found unsettling.

CHAPTER 12

QUIN

"Did you ever speak to the Young Dread?" Quin asked her mother.

She and Fiona were sitting on Quin's bedroom floor. Hours ago they'd carefully taken apart their copy of Catherine's journal, and had laid the pages about them so they could study everything more easily. Quin had woken, restless in the middle of the night, and found her mother still awake, and together they'd stayed up through the wee hours and into the next day, transcribing the oldest journal entries into more legible handwriting, and making sense of the difficult words.

Fiona, sitting cross-legged a few feet away, ran her gaze over the pages in front of her before turning to Quin. "I never did," she said. "I stopped my Seeker training when I was fourteen. I saw the Young Dread on the estate a few times, when I was a young girl and she'd come to administer the oath to older apprentices, but our paths never crossed."

"And Catherine? Did you know her?"

Fiona's eyes darkened at the mention of John's mother, but Quin couldn't read the reason for this change. "I knew her slightly," Fiona answered, her manner abrupt and inviting no further questions. "She was a year older than I was. She and her friends probably thought I was weak. I did drop out, so perhaps they were right to think so."

Quin let the topic drop and turned back to the pages on the floor. She was so pleased with Fiona's improved health, she didn't like to bring up subjects that made her upset, for fear she might somehow set back her mother's recovery.

"From the journal, it seems Seekers have been fascinated with the number two hundred," Quin murmured after a while, as she read through the pages. That number occurred several times in the journal, though in each instance Quin was left to wonder two hundred *what*, since this was never made clear. "But Briac and Alistair never said anything about that when I was training. Look—this entry here, from about a hundred and fifty years ago, talks about the 'concentration of two hundred.'"

"I noticed that," Fiona said. "But I've never heard it mentioned before either."

There was a noise like a sigh from Quin's bed. Shinobu was still asleep there, lying in almost exactly the same position he'd been in all night and most of the previous afternoon. She looked up at him, saw him shifting beneath the covers.

"Maybe he's finally going to wake up," she whispered.

Fiona nodded and got to her feet. "I'll go to Master Tan's and fetch his tea for today," she said.

Master Tan had been making Shinobu a medicinal tea every morning, using herbs from his famous collection. The tea was, according to Shinobu, very disgusting, but it was effective in accelerating his recovery.

Fiona squeezed her daughter's shoulder and passed out of the bedroom. Quin thought that squeeze carried more than comfort; it

felt as though her mother were saying, *You brought this one home . . .*
He's yours to look out for now.

When Fiona was gone, Quin got up from the floor and seated
herself on the edge of the bed. At the shifting of the mattress, Shinobu came awake with a start.

"Quin? What . . ."

"You're alive," she said quietly, touching his cheek. "A couple of
times I thought you might be dead." That wasn't quite true, but his
unconsciousness had been so deep she'd been reluctant to leave the
room all night. She was more relieved than she could easily admit, to
see him awake and speaking.

Shinobu glanced at the clock, and she watched him try to make
sense of the numbers. "Have I been asleep since yesterday afternoon?" he asked.

"You have."

He dropped his head back onto the pillow and stared at the ceiling. "How?"

She ran a hand through his hair. "I think the focal made you extra
alert by draining all of your energy."

He blinked a few times, then passed a palm across his forehead
and rubbed his eyes in a gesture that was so boyish and unguarded
Quin had the very strong urge to draw him into her arms.

"It was so interesting when I wore it, Quin. It was like I could
see and understand *everything*. Like the world was so clear. Like my
thoughts were lining up all by themselves."

Hearing his description, she could appreciate why he'd enjoyed it
so much. "It's called a 'focal,' so I imagine its whole purpose is to help
you focus," she told him, "but the first rule for using it is 'Be firm in
body, in good health.' You're not quite there yet."

"You think that's why I fell asleep for so long?"

Quin shrugged. "Maybe."

He sat up, and the covers fell off his bare chest. He was still in only his underwear, just as he'd been when she found him covered in acupuncture needles. She looked at the scar along the right side of his abdomen. It was much, much better than it had ever been, but it was still an ugly purple line seven inches long. And he was too skinny.

"Quin, I want to use it again."

"The focal?" She laughed, then stopped. He wasn't joking. Scoffing a bit, she asked, "You want to use the thing that made you pass out for nearly an entire day?"

"It was doing something for me. My thoughts are still more— more *logical* than they were before. Whatever it did for me has lasted all night. I still feel it, Quin. And I want to let it finish whatever it was doing."

"That's not—"

"So what if I sleep a lot? I could use the rest anyway. I felt all achy yesterday—"

"*Because* of the helmet. You were in pain when I took it off you."

"I just want to use it for a little while."

He'd put a hand on her arm and was staring at her with an intensity that reminded her of how he'd looked while wearing the focal. It was troubling. Quin had treated many drug addicts during her time as a healer—drugs were always a problem on the Transit Bridge—and this was exactly the sort of thing an addict would say when trying to convince you they were making good choices. It was particularly troubling coming from Shinobu, who had only recently stopped using drugs. He was such a good fighter and so tough from years of Seeker training that, she suddenly realized, she hadn't been as alert to his weaknesses as she should have been.

"Shinobu," she told him gently, "let's not think about the focal just now. I've put it away." He looked disappointed at this and glanced restlessly around the room as if planning to immediately search out where she'd put it. She had, in point of fact, set it beneath clothes at the bottom of her closet, but as soon as she had a moment alone, she would find a much better hiding place for it.

She put her hands on either side of his face and said, "Let me work on you. Right now."

His gaze came back to her, but his eyes were cloudy, unfocused. After a few moments, he nodded and his face began to clear—as though he realized how oddly he was behaving. "Yes, please," he whispered.

She settled him back onto the bed and threw the covers off him entirely, so she could see all of his body. The bruises were mostly gone, the broken bones were nearly mended, but there was still something fragile about him.

As she'd trained herself to do under Master Tan's tutelage, she centered her thoughts and let her mind shift. It was like teaching your eyes to go out of focus until something farther away clarified. After a moment, the ordinary world became less crisp and she began to see copper-colored lines of energy surrounding Shinobu's body.

When she'd first trained with Master Tan, he'd been startled by the ease with which Quin achieved this concentration. It was only later, when she'd regained all of her memories, that she grasped how much her Seeker mental training had prepared her to enter this state of heightened observation.

Shinobu's energy flowed in patterns about his body, but the bright lines were broken where there had been trauma. Dark patches hovered above his wounds, particularly the whipsword injury on his right side. And there were dozens of fainter blotches surrounding his head. Shinobu had also added electricity to the equation by wearing the focal.

Quin shut out all other thoughts, calmed her breathing, and

focused more deeply. In a moment she could see her own energy field, bright copper streams running down her arms. She spread her fingers wide, held her hands a few inches above Shinobu's chest, and let the energy flow down from her own arms, over her fingers, spilling off her body and onto Shinobu like a river of lightning.

Methodically she moved her hands across all of the muddy patches above his injuries, breaking them up, washing them away. At last she reached his head, where the copper lines formed whirlpools around a constellation of dark blotches. Slowly these broke up, and the bright streams about his face and head became symmetrical and ran without obstruction.

Shinobu let out a long sigh of relief, and Quin watched him visibly relax. She allowed her vision to settle back into its normal state, and the patterns of energy faded from her view. When he opened his eyes to look up at her, she let her hands fall to the bed.

"Better?" she asked him quietly.

"Better," he whispered back. "You're very good to me."

She smiled. The fragility she'd seen in him was gone, at least for a while. He sat up on the bed next to her, leaned in, and kissed her softly. Then his eyes darted around the room before coming back to hers.

"Did you really hide the focal?" he asked.

She didn't like that he was asking about it again; the metal helmet had certainly gotten under his skin. However, he appeared to be resigning himself to the idea that he couldn't have it.

"I did," she answered. *And I will hide it better.*

He nodded. "Do you mind if we get out of this room? I know I shouldn't wear it. But I need to do something to push it out of my mind. I'd like to fight."

Quin laughed. He'd been asking her about a practice fight for days. Maybe now was the time. As long as they were cautious, it would be good for him to use his muscles.

"I've been up most of the night looking at the journal," she told him. "So there's a very, very small chance you might be able to beat me."

He bumped his shoulder into hers and kissed her again. She was happy to see his mood improving so quickly.

"Should I tie one hand behind my back to help you out?" he asked her. "Or put on a blindfold? Or do you need more help than that?"

"Get yourself out of my bed!" she said.

She pushed him away playfully, then went to the desk against the opposite wall.

"I brought you a better gift from your mother than the focal," she told him.

She retrieved the whipsword from one of the desk's deep drawers and tossed it to him. Shinobu caught it and cradled it in his arms for a moment, like a baby. He looked down at it lovingly.

"I've missed you," he said to the weapon. Then he tossed it back to Quin and began pulling on clothes. "Watch yourself, Quin Kincaid. I'll not go easy on you."

Fiona arrived then, with a soft knock, bearing tea from Master Tan. It was Quin's pleasure to watch him drink down the entire bottle, while plugging his nose and gagging. Then they went up to the roof to spar.

CHAPTER 13

SHINOBU

Shinobu opened his eyes to discover it was nighttime again. He was lying on Quin's bed. Through the round window next to him, a glow came into the room—the distant city lights of Hong Kong reflected off the dark water of Victoria Harbor. A pale oval of this light was slowly making its way across the ceiling. Quin lay next to him in the bed, deeply asleep and breathing softly. Her warm hand was against his arm.

She'd brought him up to the roof of her house in the afternoon, and they'd sparred for nearly an hour. She'd gone easy on him, he knew that much, but he'd been happy to discover that his muscles weren't too out of tone. He was healing well and his strength was coming back quickly.

After the fight, he'd lain on the floor of Quin's bedroom, exhausted. Every part of his body ached, and the wound in his side throbbed with the beat of his heart, but it hadn't mattered. The fight had been exhilarating.

Since Quin had been up most of the night before looking at the journal, the sparring had drained her completely. She'd fallen asleep, and he'd fallen with her. But now he was awake.

His body was aching still, but differently. He rolled onto his side to look at Quin. Her face was relaxed, and locks of her dark hair fell across her closed eyes. Shinobu smiled at how pretty she looked. He thought of the many different girls whose beds he'd found his way into. Usually there was a lot more fooling around and a lot less sleeping next to each other fully clothed, but Quin had watched him almost die twice, and she was being careful. Looking at her now, he couldn't imagine why he'd ever been with anyone else. This was the only girl he wanted.

He pulled her close and put his lips against her shoulder.

"I love you, Quin Kincaid," he whispered.

In her sleep, she turned toward him, and her arms came up around his neck.

"I love you," he said again. He kissed her softly, and he could feel her kiss him back. "I love you," he whispered to her. "I love you. I love you."

She was waking up and pulling him closer and kissing him for real now.

"I want to undress you," he murmured.

She nodded against his cheek.

A noise from downstairs floated up to the bedroom.

Shinobu raised his eyes and discovered that Quin's bedroom door was still open. It was nighttime, but not too late. Fiona must be awake and downstairs.

"I'll be right back," he whispered.

He crawled out of the bed and moved over to the door. Poking his head out into the hall at the top of the stairs, he listened. He could hear Quin's mother in the healing office downstairs, humming to herself.

He began to close the bedroom door, but paused in the middle of the motion. Just outside the bedroom was the open door to the upstairs bathroom. A faint light from downstairs reached into the bathroom, and Shinobu noticed a small ceiling panel that was out of alignment with the others. The panel was only a quarter of an inch out of line, but he'd been trained for most of his life to notice small changes in his environment. He looked at the ceiling and guessed immediately that that was where Quin had put the focal—in a hurry.

He stood in the doorway of her bedroom and stared at the out-of-place panel. The odd ache he'd felt when he'd woken up—now he knew that it was an ache for that metal helmet. He'd woken up wanting it as he used to wake up craving opium. But the focal wasn't a drug. It was only a tool, a tool Seekers had used for hundreds of years, a tool that Quin admitted was to help focus the mind. It was a good thing, and it had made him feel so good the first time he'd worn it. It had given him inklings of something greater than himself, something almost like a *grand design* of which he could be a part. Where was the harm in that?

Quin had taken the helmet off his head before he'd been able to understand everything it had made him feel. She was right, of course—he shouldn't be using it until he was completely healed. She'd shown him the instructions his own mother had written out. And yet she'd stopped his thoughts just as they were becoming clear. When he'd worn the focal, he'd begun—just barely begun—to feel himself connected to the world in a way he hadn't felt since he was a child. He only wanted to finish experiencing that feeling.

He'd told her he wouldn't put it on. And yet . . . he'd stopped all the drugs, and he never wanted to start them again. The focal was something else. He could wear it, just for a short time, right now, while Quin was sleeping. And when he took it off, if he fell unconscious, it would be all right. It was nighttime, and he'd be sleeping next to her.

He looked into the bedroom behind him. Quin had fallen back asleep. He could see the line of her profile in the pale light from the window. She was beautiful, and even if she was dreaming again, she was waiting for him to come back to bed. If he crawled back under the covers, they could finally be together . . .

And they still could be. In a little while. She wouldn't even know he'd been gone.

He stepped from the bedroom and shut the door behind him. In three quick steps he was in the bathroom. He was tall enough to push open the ceiling panel easily. And there was the focal, sitting atop a neighboring panel, glinting even in the low light. With his foot, he pushed the bathroom door shut. Then he took down the helmet, locked the door, and sat on the bathroom floor.

Before he could talk himself out of it, he pulled the focal onto his head.

CHAPTER 14

CATHERINE

20 YEARS EARLIER

"How could anything be in there?" Mariko asked, peering through the metal grating to the dark tunnel beyond. "This place is crawling with tourists. There's probably not one authentic item left anywhere on the island. It's like Disneyland."

"I didn't realize you've been to Disneyland," Catherine said. She was hunched over the edge of the grating, applying the cutting torch—which she was now very pleased with herself for bringing—to the final thick pin holding the grate in place.

"Of course I've never been to Disneyland," Mariko answered indignantly, as though "Disneyland" were synonymous with "strip club" or "prison."

"Ha, catch it!"

The metal pin broke in half with a popping sound, and the grate came loose. Catherine grasped one side, and Mariko took hold of the other, and together they lowered it onto the sandy rocks.

"There isn't anything in here," Catherine explained, answering

Mariko's earlier question. "If I'm right, we'll find an empty space, sort of an underground cave. And we'll learn a little something about my Seeker house."

Mariko and Catherine were both wearing summer dresses, and Catherine was having a hard time getting used to how they looked. After years on the estate together, in drab training clothing, girlish attire seemed like a costume. Now at sixteen, in these clothes, they both looked pretty and, Catherine thought, frivolous. They looked like two of the tourists Mariko so despised.

They'd been waiting all afternoon, wandering steep streets until the tide receded enough that they might look for the tunnel Catherine was sure lay beneath the sea wall. By sunset, they'd nearly circumnavigated the tiny island's beaches, when they'd finally found the tunnel's opening under an old chapel perched high on the island's southwestern edge.

The entry wasn't well concealed. It sat only a few feet above the sand, like the mouth of an ancient dungeon. It wasn't at all inviting, but any curious visitor with the right tools and no fear of arrest could have done what they were doing—removed the grate and entered the dark stone passage behind.

"Now check the beach," Catherine instructed.

They were somewhat concealed behind a large shoulder of rock that stuck out through the sea wall and reached into the tidal flats. Mariko peered around at the rocky beach beyond. In the distance, groups of island visitors milled about, taking pictures in the last of the day's light. Most were moving off the wet sand, up the old stone steps to the streets of Mont Saint-Michel above.

"Everyone's leaving," she said.

"Ready?"

Mariko wiped her hands on her skirt and brushed her long, dark hair out of her face. Then she looked skeptically into the dark passage.

Catherine shone her flashlight inside, but the passage curved and they couldn't see very far.

"It's going to open up eventually," Catherine assured her. She could hear her voice echoing in the tunnel.

"After how long?" Mariko asked. "Does your book tell you that?"

Mariko was referring to Catherine's journal, which was tucked into the small backpack she wore. It hadn't been Catherine's journal originally. It had first belonged to her great-grandfather. Her grandfather had given it to her the year before. He'd decided not to pass it on to Catherine's parents, who, he and Catherine agreed, would care very little about its contents since the journal did not provide an immediate road map to power and wealth. It was instead a record of Seeker history, although a very incomplete one at the moment.

Her great-grandfather had personally written a few entries in the book, but mostly it contained letters and writings from others, which he'd added over many years. Even with all of these, the journal was slender. Catherine intended to fill it up more completely. There were countless letters and diaries to be found in old, abandoned Seeker estates throughout the world, and Catherine had begun to find them.

She had recently discovered two letters, with great difficulty and a significant amount of travel that had been hard to explain to her parents. Both letters were written on ancient vellum, and both concerned the Middle Dread, who was Catherine's particular area of interest, because so many Seekers had seen him misbehaving. She had carefully pasted these treasures into the beginning of the journal.

If she could gather enough evidence of the bad things the Middle had done in the past, and if she could show this evidence to the Old Dread, was it possible he would find someone better than the Middle to judge Seekers?

She had also found, in a storage trunk in her parents' own cellar, a note from her great-grandfather's grandfather, which is what had brought her here, to Mont Saint-Michel. This note described walking down to a beach on a small island, walking over rocks and sand for a long way until one found the entrance to a place—a special cave—that belonged to the house of the fox. He had written out coordinates for getting there, if you had an athame, but since Catherine didn't have an athame, she was following his instructions for traveling by foot. Though information about the Middle Dread was what she chiefly sought, she was happy to learn anything she could of old Seeker knowledge. If she discovered anything interesting here on Mont Saint-Michel, she would add it to her journal.

"I don't know how far the tunnel goes, but I've never known you to shy away from a challenge, Mariko."

Mariko sniffed. "It's lucky for you my summer has been very boring, Cat-chan."

Catherine ducked low and entered the passage. The tunnel was narrow, with rough stones on each side that brushed her shoulders as she passed. Everything was wet and smelled of the ocean. Decaying seaweed lay in clumps on the floor and trailed from stones halfway up the walls, indicating that the tunnel filled with water whenever the tide was particularly high.

"Why did you let me wear sandals?" Mariko complained after a few minutes.

Catherine only laughed—she'd told Mariko at least five times to pick better shoes.

"Even with sandals, isn't this better than listening to my mother lecture us about finding proper husbands?"

"Yes," Mariko agreed, "but anything is better than that. Ow, bumped my head." Then, irritated, she said, "Tell me again why you want to find this cave?"

"Don't you trust me?"

Mariko snorted. Catherine had gotten her friend into trouble on numerous occasions, mostly by encouraging Mariko to ask their instructors lots and lots of questions they'd already refused to answer when Catherine had asked them.

"It was something Briac said, actually," Catherine explained. As she spoke, she noticed that the floor ahead of them was slanting upward, and the only remaining seaweed here was very dry. "He said each house used to have a special place that was only for members of that house. It was sort of a gathering spot, usually a cave, I guess, but secret from everyone else. Does your family have something like that?"

"Not sure," Mariko answered after a moment of reflection. "I think we used to have a sort of mountain retreat in central Japan."

"Well, I think we're going to find the special cave that belongs to the house of the fox. Watch out, the ceiling's getting lower."

"How wonderful," Mariko said. "I was getting so comfortable."

Catherine crouched down farther, so she was walking in an awkward half squat. The air was close, and Catherine was glad Mariko didn't get claustrophobic.

"When Briac told you this, were you clothed?" Mariko asked. "Or had he managed to get you out of your undergarments?"

Only a fellow Seeker would make light of Briac attacking Catherine. Their constant brutal training allowed them to find humor in something that was not at all funny.

"Ha ha," Catherine responded. "No, he told me about the caves before I broke his nose for trying to get at my undergarments."

"I hope he tries again and you disable his manhood permanently with a swift, sharp kick. My father has trained me how to kick a man to ensure you will never have trouble from him again. Perhaps I should have steel-toed boots made for you, so you're ready, Cat?"

"If you hate Briac so much, how can you stand to be around

Alistair? They stick together, those two." Catherine was using her free hand to pull herself along the low tunnel wall now.

"Are we crawling to hell?" Mariko asked.

"We must be nearly to the end. I feel a breeze." She did feel a breeze, but in the beam of her flashlight the tunnel continued. What if there was nothing at the end and they had to back out the whole way? What if she was in the wrong location entirely?

Before Catherine could go too far down that line of thought, Mariko interrupted, picking up the thread of their conversation. "Briac and Alistair have been friends since they were small, and Alistair is loyal, but he's nothing like Briac." Catherine smiled at the fierce devotion she heard in her friend's voice. "Alistair is kind—and so handsome, don't you think?" Mariko added.

Catherine made a noncommittal sound. In her mind, Alistair's friendship with Briac counterbalanced his looks.

"He's a true gentleman," Mariko went on a little dreamily. "Although . . . he's not *always* gentle."

Catherine stopped and turned the flashlight back on Mariko. Her pretty friend blinked at her innocently in the light.

"Have you and he—*already*, Mariko?" she asked.

"Well, not entirely," Mariko answered, looking embarrassed. "My parents would be most displeased if I did that."

"That's one thing you and I have in common," Catherine agreed, turning back and continuing on. Mariko's parents were strict beyond all Western comprehension, but Catherine's parents weren't far behind. Centuries had passed since arranged marriages were popular in England, yet her parents had not quite caught on. "My mother and father seem to think they own me entirely, body and mind. They'll be choosing the boys, and also which questions of mine deserve to be answered. Mostly they choose to answer none."

Mariko sighed. "My parents don't know the answers to any interesting questions. They gave up on Seeker lore generations ago." Mariko was quiet for a moment before she spoke again. "My mother's been introducing me to Japanese boys all summer, so they can settle on a match. Several have been quite attractive, fortunately."

"Boys from Seeker families?"

"No, no. Sending me to the estate for training is only a family tradition. My father wanted me to be trained, he wanted me to take my oath. But he doesn't expect more involvement than that. Our family athame has been gone for so many generations. I suppose he imagines it might magically reappear one day, and I should be prepared just in case."

Catherine and Mariko had both taken their Seeker oaths before the summer. They'd gone on one assignment—to break an old Seeker out of a prison in Africa—and then they'd been called home, Mariko to Hong Kong and Catherine to England. Mariko had come to visit Catherine in London a few days earlier, and it was the first time they'd seen each other since leaving the estate.

"So . . . do you have to marry one of these boys, Mariko-chan?" Catherine asked her.

"Probably." She sounded resigned and less upset than Catherine would have expected. "But . . . Alistair. His *hair*, Cat-chan, his *shoulders*. When he holds me, it's like I'm being embraced by a battle robot."

Catherine laughed at what she could only think of as a very Japanese description. "When you put it that way, I can understand the attraction," she said. But privately she didn't understand. They'd known Alistair for years; it seemed silly to be so smitten by a boy they'd watched grow up.

"Please tell me that's the end," Mariko said. "My neck is killing me and I've scraped everything."

In the beam of the flashlight they could now see the channel opening up, and in a few moments, Catherine was stepping out of the tunnel's confines and down into a large stone chamber. The space was roughly round, about thirty feet in diameter, with a ceiling about ten feet above their heads.

Catherine stretched as her friend came out of the passage and climbed down next to her. Mariko took hold of the flashlight and shone it around the space slowly. The ceiling was of natural rock, as were more than half the walls. Only the side where they'd entered was completely manmade—built from large, uneven stones packed tightly together. The rest of the room had been carved out of the hillside.

There were waterlines on the walls, some of them quite high. In a storm or during a very high tide, the room might fill with seawater. The floor and lower half of the chamber were covered with seaborne debris: bits of driftwood, gritty sand, and ancient seaweed, slowly turning to dust. In a few places, the seaweed was still green, though when Catherine nudged a pile of it with her shoe, it crumbled beneath her foot. Looking up at the ceiling, she discovered small openings. These were letting in the trickle of fresh air that was now brushing past her face.

The strangest feature was a shelf protruding from the wall at about chest height. It nearly circled the room and was wide enough for someone to sit on, but too high to be of practical use. Directly across from the tunnel, above the shelf, a fox's head had been cut into the rock.

Catherine let out a surprised breath when she saw the fox. "I suppose there's no doubt this cave belongs to my family."

"There's something else carved on the wall over here," Mariko said.

They stepped closer and Mariko let the flashlight play over a series of numbers incised into the stone. Before Catherine could study them, something else caught her attention.

"Give me the light," she said urgently. "There." She trained the flashlight's beam on an object that was partially visible on the shelf, directly across the room from them. "Do you see that?"

They waded through debris to the other side of the chamber, and Catherine reached up onto the shelf. Her fingers closed around something made of smooth stone. She pulled the heavy object down into the light, and they both stared at it, speechless.

"That's . . . an athame," Mariko said eventually.

And it was.

Catherine was holding a perfect stone dagger, every inch of it intact. She moved the dials of the handgrip, which spun effortlessly beneath her touch. She turned the dagger's grip upward, to look at the base of the pommel.

She and Mariko both drew in a breath at the same moment.

"It's—it's—" began Mariko.

"My family's athame," Catherine finished.

Carved on the dagger's stone handle was the tiny shape of a fox.

Catherine moved quickly up the stone steps from the beach into the village of Mont Saint-Michel, clutching her backpack to her chest. Inside was the athame, and the lightning rod they'd found next to it. A cold breeze had picked up, blowing in off the water, but there were still lots of people about, photographing each other with the abbey in the background, a full moon hanging behind its spire.

They'd left the underground chamber as quickly as they could. Catherine hadn't wanted to speak—and had hardly dared breathe—until they were out of the tunnel with the athame. It would be too easy to be trapped down there if someone had been following them. But now Mariko caught her arm.

"Why are we going so fast, Cat?" she asked. She pulled Catherine close as they wove through a group of Germans arguing over camera settings. "The athame might have been sitting in that room for years. It's not like someone's looking for it now."

"It wasn't there for years," Catherine said. "It was clean when I picked it up. So was the lightning rod. No dust, not salt from the ocean air. Like they'd only just been placed there."

Mariko thought about this. "That chamber fills with seawater now and then," she mused aloud. Then, coming to the same conclusion Catherine had, she added, "It would be a stupid place to leave an athame for any length of time. It could be washed away. You think it was left there recently for someone to find."

Mariko began to steer them both, and Catherine was grateful for it. Her whole mind was wrapped up in the ancient implement she was carrying. It had been lost for a hundred years, maybe more. And here it was. Her heart beat against her chest. She'd found the athame of the fox. Of all her family in all its generations, *she* was the one to find it. They would be true Seekers again.

It was there in that dark chamber, a chamber that is supposed to belong to my family, waiting for . . . whom?

Mariko led them up more steps, until they were moving along the street in the shadow of the great abbey. Catherine wanted to walk more swiftly. "Whoever put it there might be watching us right now," she whispered to Mariko. "We need to get out of here."

But Mariko held her back with a hand on her arm, forcing them both into the meandering pace of tourists.

"If we're being watched, Cat-chan, we should move slowly and not attract attention," her friend reasoned. "But we *aren't* being watched."

"How do you know?"

"It would be an unbelievable coincidence," Mariko whispered

back. "I agree that someone must have put the athame and lightning rod there *recently*. But not *right now*. Think. You arrive here suddenly on the very day—"

Her friend stopped. She led Catherine to the low stone wall overlooking the village, a view of mainland France beyond.

"Look very carefully," Mariko breathed, "by the steps up to the church doors. Moving down toward the beach stairs."

Catherine looked. There were at least twenty other people between them and the abbey, but she saw immediately whom Mariko meant—a man walking through the shadows of the high, dark building, heading the way they had just come. He wore ordinary clothes and a hat, which left his face in shadow, but there was something about the way he moved, about the tightly controlled motions of his limbs.

"He moves like a Seeker," Catherine said.

"Or an apprentice, at least," Mariko agreed.

"Do you recognize him? Could it be Emile?" Catherine felt hopeful for a moment—how wonderful if she could discover Emile to be alive and well—but the feeling died out quickly. "No, it's not him."

Mariko shook her head. "Definitely not Emile. Too big. I don't know him." She grasped Catherine's shoulder and studied her closely.

"What?" Catherine asked.

"Catherine, how did you figure out where that underground room was?" Mariko asked. "Tell me exactly."

Catherine tried to compose her thoughts as she watched the man disappear down the path she and Mariko had taken. It was as if he were following the same set of instructions Catherine had used.

"I told you. I found that note from my great-grandfather's grandfather . . . or some ancestor, at any rate—I have the family tree back home, which shows—"

"That part's not important," Mariko said.

"Right." Catherine regrouped. "The note described how to find this place, that chamber—"

"Your ancestor's note said the cave was beneath Mont Saint-Michel?"

"No. That was the missing piece. The note spoke about the cave, with instructions to find the tunnel once you were on the island, but he didn't say where the island was. I only figured that out yesterday."

"And how did you figure it out?" her friend pressed.

"There's a picture of a small mountain—a hill, really—in my family crest. My whole life I've wondered where it was. No one in the family is quite sure—like the cave, it's knowledge that's been lost over time. But all at once I realized: the mountain in our crest is the outline of Mont Saint-Michel, minus some of the more modern buildings, and looking at it from the sea side, not the land side. And I wondered if these coordinates he wrote out were meant to bring someone here."

"Catherine, you've stared at your family crest your whole life, and you suddenly realized this yesterday?" Mariko whispered, her Japanese accent surfacing the more quickly she spoke.

"I agree it sounds odd, now that I say it. I don't know how to explain, except that the thought came into my head: *Mont Saint-Michel. Mont Saint-Michel.* The idea was there when I woke up, so strong it was almost frightening." Catherine laughed nervously, recalling the strange mixture of excitement and terror that had overtaken her at that moment of realization. She continued: "I looked it up and found pictures, compared them to my family crest, and it was obvious."

"So you thought we should hurry over to France immediately and look for this cave that belonged to your family hundreds of years ago?"

"The thought was so clear, I was excited to see if I was right,"

Catherine whispered back. "I didn't expect to find anything inside! I didn't even expect to find the cave, not really."

She glanced down the cobbled street again, wondering how long it would take that man to find the tunnel entrance. They'd propped the heavy grate back up in front of it, but that could be moved in moments. When he reached the end of the tunnel and discovered the athame missing, what would happen? What was he prepared to do?

"Catherine—Mont Saint-Michel 'came into' your head. You thought it was important to come here *now*."

"I looked at the crest and figured it out."

"No, you didn't 'figure it out'!" cried Mariko. "Cat-chan, don't you see? You looked inside someone else's mind. You heard someone else's thoughts. Someone else's *urgent* thoughts. You were eavesdropping on the mind of whatever person—whatever *Seeker*—put the athame here. Or whoever is coming to fetch it." She gestured to where the mystery Seeker had walked.

"Come on. Are you being serious?" Catherine scoffed. "You don't believe in that, do you?"

They'd been taught that Seekers often developed, as a by-product of their mental training, the ability to read others' thoughts. But Catherine had always been of the opinion that there were lots of other explanations for what Seekers took to be telepathy.

"You don't have to believe in it to do it," Mariko pointed out. "We got to that hidden chamber moments before someone else came. I was in the middle of telling you that it was an impossible coincidence, when we saw a person following in our precise footsteps. How else can that be explained?"

Reluctantly Catherine saw her point. She recalled again the cold fear that had accompanied her initial vision of Mont Saint-Michel, as though the thought had come from someone dangerous. Perhaps it had come from the very man who had just passed by, and if so, he wasn't someone they wanted to confront without preparation. "Maybe," she admitted.

"And he's about to discover that it's already been taken," Mariko whispered.

Catherine looked at her friend. "We need to go," she said.

"Yes," Mariko agreed. "Quickly."

CHAPTER 15

JOHN

The remains of *Traveler* were a six-story broken mass that had once been a beautiful airship. The ship's reflective metal hide was bent and crushed in places, showing the park's trees and the city's buildings in the warped manner of a carnival mirror. *Traveler* was surrounded by security lights all night, and during the day, emergency crews crawled over every part of it, methodically disconnecting every source of power, in preparation for moving the ship outside the city, where it would be put back together. And one day soon, if John prevailed over the other branches of his family, it would be flown again.

It was nighttime now, and he and the Young Dread were inside *Traveler*. She'd brought them there with the athame, blindfolding John as she always did.

Though the salvage workers were gone at this hour, the blinding exterior lights remained, glaring through every window. All around was the drip and trickle of broken pipes and the smell of burned electrical wiring. Water leaked from the ceilings of the crooked corridors, hissing into steam as it came into contact with surfaces that were still hot. Misshapen shadows lay everywhere.

John's grandfather Gavin, already weak and close to death, had nearly been killed in the crash. He remained unconscious at a London hospital, where John's relatives were gathered day and night, waiting to see if Gavin would live and, regardless of what happened, ready to start a fight over control of his wealth.

That wealth was John's by right. He should be there with those relatives, laying a claim to everything that was his—his because his mother had amassed the fortune for him, so that he might be protected from enemies as she had never been. But legal battles would have to wait. The Young Dread might have agreed to this nighttime visit to *Traveler,* but she would never agree to him returning to London for something so mundane as fighting his cousins in court. Until his training was complete, he must step away from the ordinary world and ignore his relatives as long as he could.

John understood that his absence might be a death sentence to his grandfather. Years ago Catherine had poisoned Gavin as a way to keep him under her control. The poison lived in his body permanently, and he required a daily antidote to stay alive. Now Maggie was gone and John was with Maud. There was no one in London to give Gavin his antidote. Without Maggie, John didn't even know where he might acquire it. He could only hope his grandfather's doctors had figured out a way to counteract the poison and the old man would live. Gavin was, after all, John's only true ally, and no matter how crazy the old man had become, John loved him.

Maud had carved an anomaly directly into *Traveler*'s great room. From there, John led them carefully through the ship to a narrow, half-destroyed passage on one of *Traveler*'s lower levels. In the middle of this passage, they arrived at a metal door that was wedged open against the buckled floor of the hall.

"My grandmother Maggie's room," he told Maud.

Inside was a tiny space—a bed, a small desk, and a closet held shut by the crushed ceiling, everything thrown into disarray. John ducked into the room, clipped a light to the end of the bed, and switched it on, illuminating the cabin.

Everything he needed was on the floor. Maggie's room had been decorated with several framed photographs and pieces of art. These had all fallen violently when *Traveler* crashed, and they now lay broken across the floor amidst shards of glass. He knelt down and began to pick them up.

"What happened to your grandmother?" the Young Dread asked from the doorway.

The question surprised John. When he'd first begun training with Maud, she'd spoken as little as possible and would never have asked a personal question. Her conversation was becoming easier the more time they spent together, as though John and the normal world were rubbing off on her.

"They didn't find her body," he told her. His own voice sounded too even, too detached, but this was a topic he didn't want the Young Dread to take an interest in. Maggie's cold-blooded views would not be to Maud's liking.

"You believe she got out?"

The rescue workers had found everyone on the ship—some dead, most alive—except for Maggie.

"Yes," he answered, "I believe she got off the ship somehow."

The Young nodded at this and took a seat in the corridor. As John watched, she removed Catherine's journal from a pocket of her cloak. He'd allowed her to keep it since the previous night.

When he turned back to the broken frames on the floor, his mind stayed on Maggie—who wasn't really his grandmother but a more distant relative. He'd thought about her often since the crash. He did believe she'd gotten out of the ship, though he couldn't understand how. And where would she have gone? If she were alive and well, why hadn't she contacted him?

Truthfully, he didn't know if he should feel sad or relieved. Maggie had raised him, after his mother was gone. He had loved her, of course, but he'd hated her sometimes as well. She'd made him scared for his entire childhood that someone would be coming to kill him, just as someone had come for his mother and so many others. He should be worried about Maggie, worried that she was injured or lost. But he felt something different—a deep disquiet about where she might be and what she might be doing.

His grandmother had once told him a bedtime story about a woman who lived deep in the forest, away from all of mankind except a chosen few. The story had felt like something more than a fairy tale; Maggie had sounded as though she were describing something she'd actually done. Could she be doing that again, living somewhere remote from London, biding her time?

He stacked the broken picture frames on the bed and picked off the last shards of glass. Each frame held more pictures than one would expect—several were concealed behind whatever had been displayed under the glass. Now John tore the backs off the frames, slid photograph after photograph from their hiding places, and laid them across the bedspread.

The hidden pictures were not pleasant. Each captured a scene of grisly death. The images were of men, women, and children, killed by knife, by sword, by gun, by drowning. The oldest pictures had been taken a hundred years before, or more, but the photographs spanned the last century, in black and white and in color. Maggie had first shown him these pictures when he was eight years old. Each dead person was an ancestor of his, a member of the house of the fox. Here was photographic evidence of all the ways the other Seeker houses had victimized his own. The pictures had convinced John to dedicate his life to revenge, just as his mother had dedicated hers.

They think we're small and weak and helpless. Easy to kill, his mother had told him as she lay dying. *Are we easy to kill, John?*

"No," John murmured aloud now, as he had then to his mother, "we're not."

Looking over the piles of photographs, however, he thought his family *had* been easy to kill. They'd been victims again and again. But no more. The killers would not get away with this carnage.

John thought, *This is my list of who will pay.*

CHAPTER 16

MAUD

While John occupied himself in his grandmother's cabin, the Young Dread sat on the slanted corridor floor within *Traveler*, studying Catherine's journal. She hadn't wanted to look at the journal at first, hadn't wanted to see evidence of the Middle's crimes. She'd been forced to coexist with the Middle Dread since she was a small girl, and that had been possible only by turning a blind eye to the worst parts of his nature. After she'd killed him, it had felt good to imagine that she'd wiped away every trace of him—but the journal told her otherwise. It told her that, while she'd known a few of the Middle's misdeeds, there were countless more of which she'd been completely unaware.

There was an entry near the middle of the book that had drawn her attention the previous evening. She read it again now.

April the Twelfth, 1870

Father,
   The Middle Dread returned not three days past. He did

not announce himself, but Gerald was hunting alone and spied him by the loch and fortress.

Shall I make some acknowledgement of his presence? I do not wish to offend with forwardness, nor with lack of respect.

Further, something new. There are two youths with him, of lowly families by their dress and speech. The Dread instructs them in swordplay. They do a strange arithmetic among them, counting numbers, and always they sum to two hundreds.

What are we to make of this?

My love to you and my brothers.

Thomas

This was written in a fairly modern hand, using modern spellings, and Maud could not make out every word. The earliest pages of the journal were the only ones she could properly read. But she understood "two youths . . . of lowly families," being trained by the Middle Dread.

My great-great-grandfather saw the Middle Dread training others, Catherine had said, years ago, in the forest. This was probably the very letter that Catherine's ancestor had written, Maud realized. And the two strange boys Maud and John had seen on the Scottish estate—was it possible they were the same youths described here? Last night, sitting by the fire, Maud had become quite certain the answer was yes. Catherine had mistaken the boys for additional Young Dreads. Of course they weren't that. They were something else, and they belonged to the Middle.

Maud was convinced he'd taken a whipsword and cut it in half and given it to them, and perhaps he'd given them the boar athame as well. This letter had been written nearly two hundred years before, so those boys were spending time *There,* stretched out, which explained the Dread-like flavor of their physical motions.

The letter was dated 1870. *Was I awake in 1870?* the Young Dread wondered. She knew, in a general way, how long she'd been stretched out, and when, and how long she'd been awake, but she put little emphasis on exact years and so couldn't be sure where she was in 1870. She might well have been *There* while the Middle Dread was out and about in the world training those boys. But what was he using them *for?*

She flipped to the earliest pages of the diary, seeking out, as she had done several times already, one particular entry. Written on parchment was a description of the Middle Dread killing a Young Dread, centuries ago. It was not the murder she'd witnessed but an even earlier one.

This scrap of parchment is proof the Middle killed at least two Young Dreads before me, she thought. *This is surely more than my master knew. If he had known everything, would he have gotten rid of the Middle sooner?* She feared the answer was no. The Old Dread had acknowledged the Middle's old crimes, but he'd been tied to the Middle somehow, unable to bring him to justice, until Maud herself had taken matters into her own hands and killed him.

The Young Dread looked up from the journal and found an unexpected glint of metal in her line of sight. To the right of the cabin doorway, a broken section of wall hung out into the corridor. Through the break was a dark space. Maud pushed the loose piece of corridor wall aside and peered into what must be John's grandmother's closet, which had mostly collapsed in the ship's crash. Its jumbled contents lay in a heap, and among the tangled scarves and shoes, something large and metal caught the light. When the Young Dread wrested this item out through the break in the wall, she recognized its familiar weight and size immediately.

It was a metal shield, such as a sword fighter might wear on his arm. The shield's face was made of several concentric circles that spun independently of each other. She knew what it was at once—*a disruptor shield.* Though they had been common among Seekers in the past, the Young hadn't seen one for at least two hundred years. Her master, the Old Dread, did not put much faith in such tools—he believed one should rely more on swift reflexes—but Maud had occasionally trained with such a shield when the Middle Dread was instructing her.

She ran her hands over the concentric circles on the shield's face and set them spinning. When rotating, the rings created the disorienting illusion that the shield surface was spiraling toward you and away from you at the same time. The shield was designed to withstand the direct onslaught of disruptor sparks, and when used skillfully could do many interesting things with those sparks.

If John gets a bit better, perhaps I will allow him to try this, she thought.

There was something else inside the closet, visible now that she had removed the shield. Maud thought her eyes might be deceiving her, and so she reached in quickly to snatch the object out. It was another tool she hadn't seen in generations: an iridescent metal helmet, a focal.

The Young Dread studied the helmet and the shield, and began to make plans for John's further instruction. When she heard John speaking quietly in the cabin a few minutes later, she set down the objects and moved inside.

The bed was covered in a chaos of images, all of them of death. The warped floor shifted as she moved closer to him. The Young Dread had no desire to participate in John's revenge—or even to acknowledge it—but she found herself picking up a few of the photographs to study. Many were in black and white, which she understood indicated great age. But many others were in full color, with the deep red of blood the most prominent hue. Even in the black-and-white photographs, she could feel the red hidden within the great pools of black: A man, a woman, and four children, cut to pieces, the adults pinned to the wall by long knives, the children crumpled on the floor, their clothing dark with blood. People dead from beatings, from shootings. People killed, with unmistakable exuberance, by whipswords. There were so *many*.

"Were you there?" John asked quietly.

It took Maud a few moments to understand what he meant. He was asking her if she'd participated in killing these people, who were members of his family. It bothered the Young Dread deeply that John thought she would be capable of such evil action, and yet that was how he had been raised—to see threats and killers on every hand.

She looked through more of the photographs. In truth she recognized most of the faces. She had seen these men, these women, even some of their children. She had watched them train, she had given them their oaths. But she had never seen them like this.

The Young Dread shook her head. "No."

Her eyes lit on one of the more recent pictures. A lovely young woman clutched a yawning wound in her abdomen, her blue eyes staring, fixed in death. There was a deep gash across one cheek that, despite its gruesome aspect, took little away from her fine features. *Catherine*, Maud thought. *I was there when Catherine died.*

But on closer inspection, she realized this was not Catherine Renart. This was Catherine's older sister. The girls were very alike, but the one in this photograph had different wounds. Catherine's fatal injury had been to her leg, not her belly. And she hadn't died, of course, not until years later. The Middle and Briac had insisted on disrupting

Catherine and keeping her alive. In that way, Briac could honestly say he hadn't taken her life—though clearly there was nothing honest about Briac's handling of Catherine.

"You knew her?" John asked.

"I gave her her oath on the estate," Maud said. "She and your mother were very alike."

John pointed to the figure drawn on the girl's blouse in blood—a crude ram.

"A ram," the Young said quietly. "Someone drew a ram."

"The killer drew the emblem of his house," John told her in a whisper. "The ram is Quin's house, but she wasn't born yet. This was Briac."

"Possibly," Maud said. *Though anyone might draw anything on a dead body,* she thought.

Now that John had pointed this out, she saw similar figures drawn on many of the victims: the shape of a bear, drawn with a bloody finger on the shirt of a child; in another picture she saw the outline of a boar. The Young Dread tried to imagine Seekers signing their grisly deeds with the insignia of their houses, but she couldn't quite envision it. Why would someone do such a thing? The only result would be to create lasting enmity between Seekers.

John had no such hesitation. He studied the photographs as if he were planning out a battle—which, Maud realized a moment later, he was.

"In my mother's journal, she was recording the locations of different Seeker houses and their athames. But here you can see which houses have gone bad, which need to be stopped," John explained. He pointed to three loose piles of photographs. "Looking at the signs drawn on the bodies, I count seven murders done by the house of the bear, five by the house of the boar, and two by the house of the ram. So the house of the bear . . ."

He trailed off, but Maud knew the words that would complete his sentence: *the house of the bear is first on my list.*

John asked for the journal back, and he leafed through it until he found the page with a bear drawn at the top. Beneath the animal was an illustration much like the one he'd shown Maud back on the estate. It was another drawing of a cave. This one was perched halfway up a hillside. Behind the hill was a line of other hills, with a distinctive pattern. Beneath the drawing was a set of coordinates.

"Here," he said. "My mother last knew of the house of the bear in this location. The journal says the bear athame was last seen in southwest Africa, eighty years ago, in the possession of a Seeker called Delyth Priddy, house of the bear, who possibly had a companion with her. And here are the coordinates. She was gathering coordinates so she could go to these places."

Maud understood his intent. He wanted her to take him to this place so he could retrace his mother's path. The Young Dread recognized the location by the drawing and by the coordinates. It was a cave in Africa that was special to the house of the bear, just as each Seeker house had once had a special location for its own members—though most locations had fallen out of use long ago. It looked as though Catherine had been searching for those caves.

She explained none of this to John, because it suited her, for the moment, to let him draw his own conclusions. She moved back into the hall to retrieve the shield and the helmet.

"What are they?" he asked, looking up at the objects when she returned. "There's a drawing of that one"—he gestured to the helmet—"in the journal."

"This is a focal," she answered, holding it up. "If used properly, it is a great tool. The shield is interesting but less important for training."

"Is the helmet what you were talking about before?" he whispered. "To help me face a disruptor without falling apart?"

"Possibly," she said. In truth, that was exactly what she intended to teach him. How to face the disruptor—and many other things—without falling apart. How to find the proper path.

She looked at the pictures of death strewn across the bed. John wanted to hunt down the house of the bear to avenge his mother and those dead people in the photographs. The fact that no one had seen a member of the house of the bear in about eighty years did not deter him. Nor did the fact that the house of the boar, the next house on John's list, had been missing for a generation—since Emile Pernet had disappeared in Norway. John seemed to think his mother had discovered a secret trail leading to her enemies. The Young Dread was doubtful. If Seekers and athames had been missing for so long, she didn't think they would be easily found.

She made a decision. John could make his search. She would let him look for his revenge on Seeker houses that were long gone. *And along the way I will train your mind out of its petty cruelties and vendettas. I will turn you into something better. And perhaps, following Catherine's journal, I will discover for myself what the Middle Dread has done.*

"It may be I can help you follow what your mother wrote in her journal," she told him. "But I will make you work for the privilege of doing so."

CHAPTER 17

QUIN

"Because Catherine was John's mother, I imagined she was a bit of a lunatic," Quin told Shinobu. "When John talks about what she wanted, there's not room for anything else in his mind. When he was chasing me on the estate—and we fought on the roof of the cliff barn—I thought he was crazy and it was all because of her."

They were in Quin's healing office, and the pages of the journal were lined up along the counters and across the examination table. She'd organized the rows chronologically, just as they'd been in the journal, but seeing the pages out in the open would make it easier, she hoped, to wrap her mind around them.

"You don't think Catherine was crazy?" Shinobu asked her. He was leaning against the wall, his arms crossed over his chest, watching her as she browsed the pages.

"She must have been a bit crazy," Quin answered. "But what I see in her journal is someone who kept track of things that were wrong . . . because she wanted them to be better."

She picked up a few sheets of paper from the examination table. "And she included things that were good, just because they were good. Like this one, about Maud when she was very young and still training to be a Dread. Two Seeker apprentices saw her on the estate, and they wrote to their father, describing how fast she could run: 'like a hawk diving for a field mouse.' Catherine admired the Young Dread."

"And what about the Middle Dread?" Shinobu asked.

Quin glanced up and found that he'd moved closer. He was standing just behind her, reading over her shoulder. He'd been in a funny temper the last few days, quieter than usual, and more serious. His mood ebbed and flowed as he healed. But his interest in the journal was drawing him out.

"I think Catherine hated the Middle Dread," Quin answered. "It seems that any time she found someone with something bad to say about him, she put it in the journal." There were lots of journal entries, particularly early ones, that showed the Middle Dread in a bad light.

"Do you think he's important?" he asked her.

"Important to what we want to know? To why Seekers like my father are so different from how they're supposed to be?" She shrugged. "In the journal, all of the bad things the Middle Dread did were hundreds of years ago. I don't see how we can blame Briac's behavior on that."

He looked dissatisfied with that answer. As she watched, he sorted through several journal pages and picked out one. It was a letter in which one Seeker told the other about seeing the Middle Dread nearby before someone had been found gravely injured. Shinobu held it up for her to see.

"Do *you* think he was important?" she asked.

He took a deep breath and leaned against the counter. "Well . . ." he began, looking uncomfortable. "When I wore the focal—you know, when you found me with all the needles—we'd been looking at the journal just before that, and I . . . felt something."

"You mean, in your mind? In the helmet?"

He nodded and crossed his arms thoughtfully. "I don't think the focal can show you anything you don't already know. But maybe it helps you see what you already know in a different light." He ran a hand across his hair and studied his shoes, almost as if he didn't like what he was going to say. "I might have understood something about the journal. Catherine uses the first half for the Dreads—letters about them, times people saw them, bad things the Middle Dread did or was accused of doing."

"That's right," Quin agreed.

"And most of the rest is a record of where Seekers from the different houses—and their athames—were seen."

He fell silent, and she prompted, "And you saw something about this when you wore the focal?"

Slowly he told her, "I think I saw a connection—between the Middle Dread and what happened to Seeker houses more recently. What if Catherine thought there was a connection?"

Quin's eyes ran over the paper in front of her as she thought about this. "You think the Middle Dread was at the heart of what she was looking for?"

"I think she *thought* he was important. I don't know if he actually was." His gaze had gone back to his shoes, and he was prodding at the floor with the toe of a sneaker.

"She did think he was important," Quin agreed, looking at the early pages of the journal. "But if she figured out a connection, I don't think she wrote it down here."

"Or she did but you can't see it," he said.

He was still looking at his shoes and appeared to be wrestling with a sticky thought. Without looking up, he gently took hold of her elbow and pulled her closer.

"You could . . . you could try the focal, you know," he said quietly.

"You want *me* to wear it?"

"I know *I* shouldn't wear it," he responded, still not looking at her. "But . . . there was something to it, Quin. You'll see things you would otherwise miss." He nodded at the papers surrounding them. "I promise you will. And even if you don't, you can tell me what it feels like for you. Maybe it's different for different people."

She looked around the room and then back to him. He was resisting whatever urge he'd had to use the focal himself, and that was good. She admitted to herself that she was curious to see what the focal did. As long as she followed Mariko's instructions, she would limit the danger. And maybe Shinobu was right and she would learn something.

Quin had Mariko's written instructions in her hands. Shinobu hadn't followed these instructions at all when he'd used the focal, but Quin intended to obey them perfectly. She sat cross-legged on the roof of her house, with Shinobu crouched beside her. The first rule was to be firm in body. She was.

She was now following the second instruction: *clear your thoughts, begin from neutral mind.*

She carefully emptied her mind, just as she did when she worked as a healer. When that was done, she read the next step: *Focus upon the subject at hand.*

What was the subject at hand? *I want to discover where dishonorable Seekers began,* she thought. *And what Catherine might have known about that.* She held these questions firmly in mind.

The next step: *Place the helm upon your head.*

The focal slipped on as though it had been designed especially for Quin. The moment it was in place, she felt a buzzing in her ears and through her skull. It wasn't a noise really, more a vibration, unpleasant and discordant. The one real noise was a faint crackle—the helmet was alive with electricity, and she could feel fingers of it across her forehead and around her ears.

A wave of disorientation hit her, as though she were on the deck of a wildly rocking boat, though she knew quite well she was seated solidly on the roof of her home. She began to tip over, saw the surface of the roof coming toward her, but Shinobu grabbed her shoulders and held her upright.

"It's okay," he said, loud enough so she could hear him despite the crackle around her ears. The weight of his hands was reassuring.

The buzzing in the helmet was getting fainter, but at the same time the sensation through her head was increasing, as though the focal were joining forces with her, becoming almost indistinguishable from her own mind. It no longer felt unpleasant . . . It felt almost good.

And suddenly she didn't need Shinobu's help to stay up. Quin rose to her feet on her own.

The electric vibration of the helmet had fully joined with her mind, and it pushed her into a new mental gear. She gazed down at her body, her hands and arms out at her sides to balance herself, her feet planted wide. Her limbs looked small and far away, and yet they obeyed her commands. Shinobu was right there beside her, poised to take hold of her again if she needed him.

She walked unsteadily to the edge of the roof. From there she gazed up toward the Bridge's high, draping canopy. Then she looked far down the Bridge thoroughfare in both directions. There were swarms of people on the road, hundreds and hundreds of them, and as Quin looked, she discovered she could sense where each person intended to go. The waves of foot traffic were not random; there were lines of flow within the crowds, a logic to each motion. She felt as she felt when healing patients—an expanded awareness—but in the helmet it was ten times, a hundred times, what she experienced on her own.

She turned. At eye level, she could see out to the harbor beneath the outer edge of the Bridge's canopy. The water was gray, flowing away from her toward Hong Kong Island, and it was broken in a thousand places where ships churned it into white wakes. And there was other movement, the trails of speedboats and junks, the tiny ripples around rocks near the shore, the patterns caused by the tide running against the great pillars that held up the Bridge itself.

The water of the harbor was part of a single ocean that circulated in great slow waves and touched every coastline of earth. The people below were pieces of one species, which in turn was a part of all living creatures. She could almost see the entire world . . .

Quin pulled her thoughts back as a fisherman reels in his lines. There was a subject at hand, and it was important. *Catherine's journal. When things changed and why.*

Her mind was larger. She could see those subjects like dark, clear shapes standing out sharply against the rest of the world. She understood, just as Shinobu had said, that the focal couldn't show her something she didn't already know. But there were things she *did* know . . . The journal. The Middle Dread, just as Shinobu had pointed out. There was a logic to what Catherine had written.

Quin let her gaze sweep along the Bridge thoroughfare again, saw the people entering and leaving, sitting, walking, eating, fighting, being healed on the upper level. She could sense as well the hundreds of others below, seeking oblivion in the drug bars on the Bridge's lower levels. She didn't want to sever the connection she felt to all of them, to the ocean outside, to the boats in the harbor, to the gray sky above everything. It felt *right* to see things this way. What if she kept the helmet on forever? Wouldn't that be better? Wasn't *she* better when she was wearing it? She could figure out *anything* with the focal on her head.

She turned to find Shinobu watching her, his face reflecting the strange ecstasy of interconnectedness she was feeling. He had warned her—the focal was something amazing.

Forcing her arms to move was one of the hardest things she'd ever done, but she pulled off the focal in a sudden, violent motion and tossed it aside as though it had burned her.

Immediately the electric buzzing became noticeable again, rough and discordant, as if the helmet and her mind were arguing as they tore apart. Quin felt herself double over, and then Shinobu's hands were on her, easing her down onto the roof. She let herself go farther, until she was lying on the roof's rough surface, staring up at rafters and canopy far above.

"Are you all right?" he asked her. He smoothed her hair away from her face. "You didn't like it?"

"I did," she said automatically, thinking she might never have liked anything more. "I really did." She took a few deep breaths, added, "But it's—it's too much. I can't take it." She was dizzy and disoriented, though she wasn't sure how that was possible when she was lying down. And sick. She was sick to her stomach. Beyond the physical, there was a sense of mental distress pulling at her, a painful low that corresponded to the high she'd felt in the helmet.

Holding on to Shinobu, she pulled herself up to sitting and laid her head against his shoulder. Her temples were pounding.

"Was it incredible?" he murmured into her ear.

She nodded against him. A ripple of exhaustion passed through her, but the buzzing in her ears died out, letting her know that her mind was her own again.

"You were right," she told him. "You put your mind on something you want to understand, and you see it more clearly. So much more clearly. I saw a connection in what Catherine had written."

"Tell me."

She collected her thoughts, and as she did, she began to feel better. Inside the focal they had run through her so quickly and every thought had been connected to every other. But a few had stood out as important. "Those boys we saw," she said slowly. "They kept saying 'our master,' and I thought maybe they meant Briac, but it didn't make sense, because they treated Briac like . . . like an animal or something. But what if their master was the Middle Dread? What if that journal entry about two boys training with the Middle meant *those* two? The same boys?"

"And they're here now, and they're looking for his athame," Shinobu said, building upon her thought.

"If he trained them so long ago, and they're still around . . . then they've been resting *There,* and the Middle was doing things no one understood."

"Yes," Shinobu said, grasping this immediately. He held her gaze with the hyper-alertness she'd seen in him before, the afternoon he wore the focal himself. It was as though Quin using the helmet had almost the same effect on him as using it himself. "How long have they been around, then?" he asked. "And how have they interacted with Seekers all this time?"

He was propping Quin up with one hand, but his other hand was holding the focal, and now he turned it about and looked at it from all angles.

"Don't . . ." she whispered, when it looked as though he was going to put it on. "I know it's given me this idea, but . . . I don't think it's good to wear it, Shinobu. I don't want to wear it again."

He licked his lips nervously, then set the helmet on the ground and moved his hand away from it deliberately. His eyes lingered on it for a few more moments before he turned back to her.

"I won't," he told her. "Don't worry."

Holding on to Shinobu, she got back to her feet, and so did he. He handed Quin the focal, and she noticed he didn't look at it as he passed it to her. She thought he might be scared of it, and now she understood the feeling.

"There are a few pages in the journal I want to look at again," she told him. "I might have an idea."

CHAPTER 18

NOTT

Nott stood guard while Wilkin and Briac used the glowing window to find the girl. Nott was perched on the back of the chair, his feet on the seat. The three of them were somewhere in the city of Hong Kong, in a dark corner of a long, low room filled with dozens of such glowing windows—Briac called them *computers*—each in its own little alcove with a chair in front of it. A handful of young men were scattered about, hunched in front of other computers, doing God knew what. Nott had seen many strange things since his master had taken him from his family, years and years ago. Computers were just one more oddity to add to the list.

There was a small partition separating their desk from the others, so no one was looking their way. *Please be more curious*, he thought, his eyes boring into the backs of the other people in the room. He wanted to beat someone.

The helm hadn't been anywhere in the Hong Kong woods. They'd spent hours looking for it, all the while ignoring Briac's cries of pain from the knife wound in his back. (Well, half the time Briac had cried out in pain, and the other half he'd seemed to forget that he was injured at all.) Eventually they'd given up the search, and Wilkin had had to admit that he might have dropped the helm in the darkness *There*, where they were never likely to find it. They'd both been so distressed by this conclusion that Nott had punched Wilkin directly in the face, and Wilkin hadn't even tried to hit him back.

Losing the helm meant they couldn't properly follow their master's orders without a great deal of luck, so even Nott had agreed they should continue searching for the girl in hopes of recovering their master's athame, while they figured out what to do next.

"Hold still!" Wilkin hissed, thumping Briac's head.

For a while, Briac had been fiddling with a board in front of the computer, pressing letters (Nott could read enough to know they were letters, though he didn't know all the letters in the alphabet. He could learn them, if he wanted to. He was very clever. But Wilkin couldn't read much either, so who cared?) but Briac was whimpering and biting his own fist now, because Wilkin was sewing up the wound on his back again. The stitches Nott had put in the first time had been so sloppy that Briac had never really stopped bleeding.

"Shhh," whispered Nott, watching Wilkin jab Briac with the thick needle, jerk the thread downward, and jab the needle in again. "Can't you make him be quiet, Wilkin? Someone's going to hear."

That was not strictly true. The nearest person was sitting at a desk halfway to the door and wearing something over his ears. But Nott enjoyed making things more difficult for Wilkin. Example: he had once hidden one of Wilkin's boots for three days. Wilkin had hobbled around without it until he found his missing boot half underwater at the edge of Loch Tarm.

Briac cried out as the needle poked him again. Nott shook his head and examined his own arms, where numerous puckered scars decorated his skin. To be alive, to put the world in its place, you needed to fight, and sometimes you got hurt. What did Briac expect?

"Keep looking for her!" Wilkin ordered. He nudged Briac with an elbow until the man forced his eyes to the glowing window again. Nott had no idea how the computer could help find someone, but Briac insisted it could. And back in the madhouse, Briac had used another sort of computer—a *phone* they'd stolen from a nurse—to locate the London hospital where they'd found Quin, though Briac had been wearing the helm then, so he'd been able to think a lot more clearly. Watching him try to hold his mind together now was excruciating, which was one of the reasons Nott kept turning away.

A soft scratching sound alerted Nott to a rat who was crawling through the darkest corner of their little alcove. He slid off the chair and inched closer. The creature was gray and black, with tiny claws skittering across the grime where the floor met the wall.

Nott pulled his smallest knife from his waist and threw it in a slow, practiced arc. The handle struck the rat's head dead on, and he snatched the creature from the floor. When he got back into brighter light, he saw that its eyes were shut, but one of its feet was twitching. Good. Still alive. Nott knew a lot about rats and how much punishment they could take before giving up the ghost, and he'd thrown the knife just right. He stuffed the stunned animal into a pocket in his cloak.

Wilkin was nearly finished sewing up Briac's back. As Nott climbed onto his chair again, the older boy pulled the thread hard one final time and tied it off, leaving a long, jagged row of stitches. He slapped Briac's shoulder and said, "Perfect!"

Briac didn't seem to notice that the doctoring was over. He continued to bite his fist and stare blankly at the computer. At last, he grabbed his head and moaned, "I can't—I can't remember her name! I don't know who she is."

Several people turned to look in their direction.

"Quin!" Wilkin whispered. "We already know her name. Your daughter, Quin Kincaid!"

Briac studied the computer glass for a few moments longer. Then he surged to his feet. Wilkin was thrown backward into Nott, who fell off the chair. The rat squeaked quietly inside his cloak, like a rusty door hinge.

"Without the helmet, I can't do it!" Briac shouted.

Wilkin slapped a hand over Briac's mouth and hissed, "We don't have the helmet!"

Briac twisted away and hissed back, "Then you have nothing!"

He grabbed up the computer, raised it above his head, and before Wilkin could do anything, Briac smashed it onto the floor. With a tremendous noise, the machine shattered into hundreds of pieces, which flew in every direction.

"I don't know how to use it!" Briac screamed, grabbing his head again. The sparks were bouncing around his face. Whatever the helm had done to calm his thoughts was finished. He was completely crazy again. "It's useless! Just like she is—Fiona, Quin, all of them. Pretending loyalty, and then they stab you, they stab you, they stab you!" He punctuated each of his screams by kicking the messy pile of glass that had once been the computer, sending chunks skating across the floor.

Two young men were running toward them across the long room. Everyone else was moving briskly for the door.

"You stop!" one of the approaching men said, his English strangely accented with the language of this city. "I'm calling police!"

Nott wasn't supposed to use his whipsword in front of ordinary people, so he pulled out a knife, his biggest one. He leapt off the chair and landed in front of the approaching men, bringing them to a sudden halt.

"Shall we fight?" Nott asked them gleefully. He crouched down, ready to attack, and his knife glinted in the low light of the room.

Both men recoiled and nearly collided with each other in their haste to get to the door. In a moment they'd followed their customers and disappeared out onto the crowded sidewalk, leaving Nott and Wilkin and Briac alone.

Nott decided it was time for him to take control from the idiot Wilkin. He said, "You know our master's always saying Watchers let their minds run everywhere, Watchers panic, Watchers can't follow the simple plan! We keep going further from what we're supposed to do."

Wilkin nodded. "We should have followed his orders from the beginning and woken the others immediately. And now we can't, because we've lost the helm."

"We *can,* Wilkin. We have the other way, the way our master showed us, if we've no helm."

A spark of hope lit Wilkin's eyes but quickly went out. "But . . . even if we make it to two hundred, the others will tell him we made mistakes—"

"He'll be angry either way—about us not following orders or about us losing the helm. We've already lost the helm, so at least we should try to follow orders."

Wilkin looked frightened, but he was also out of options. He nodded, then took a deep breath. "We're done with you, ye madman!" he said, planting a fist into Briac's gut. Briac sat down heavily atop the pile of shattered glass, where he continued to clutch his head and mutter to himself, as though he hadn't noticed being punched.

Wilkin drew out their athame. Nott bared his teeth, and together they adjusted the dials as they'd practiced so many times. This was what they should have done the moment their master went missing.

When they'd gotten the symbols into the right order, Wilkin hit the athame against the lightning rod. The vibration tickled Nott's bones and shook the desks as Wilkin traced a circle in the air. The threads of the world began to unravel, white and black, light and dark, twisting into each other, creating a gaping doorway.

Nott grabbed Wilkin's arm, and they faced each other.

"Ready?" Wilkin asked.

"Yes," Nott said.

Wilkin slapped Nott sharply across the face.

Nott accepted the blow and slapped Wilkin the same way, his open hand hitting the older boy so hard, the noise of the impact echoed in the empty room.

"Good?" Wilkin asked.

"One more," answered Nott.

Wilkin struck him with the other hand, so forcefully that Nott saw blackness, then stars.

"Another for me as well," Wilkin said, leaning close.

There were black spots floating before Nott's eyes, but he managed to hit Wilkin a second time, just as hard as the first.

Nott shook his head until his vision cleared. He felt what he'd hoped to feel—focus. The pain made his thoughts as sharp as a razor. Their master had taught them this trick, a method of last resort to keep their minds in line.

"Now we count!" Wilkin said, gripping Nott's shoulders.

They grabbed up Briac and dragged him with them like an oversized and dangerous dog as they stepped through the anomaly, walking as the Middle Dread would, copying his strides.

CHAPTER 19

SHINOBU

It took a great force of will for Shinobu to hand the focal back to Quin and let her take it away. When they'd climbed down from the roof back into her house and gone downstairs to the first floor, where the journal was still spread out across the counters, she'd run upstairs with the helmet to hide it from him again. Of course, he knew where she was putting it, so it wasn't really hidden.

She was right; he shouldn't be using the focal. But he'd continued to use it secretly, at night, when Quin was asleep, and sometimes during the day, when she and her mother were at Master Tan's office, helping him with patients. Though he'd never done a good job of following Mariko's instructions for using the helmet, he'd begun to think of his time with it as a ritual—waiting until the house was completely still, going into the upstairs bathroom, folding his long legs tightly against himself on the floor, anticipating the electric hum of his mind, and pulling on the focal.

It was not lost on him that this ritual was a lot like his old rituals of hiding from his mother to smoke Shiva sticks in the pool house, or losing himself in an opium den on the Transit Bridge with his friend

Brian. Brian, who had stopped using drugs, and who must be somewhere nearby in Hong Kong. What would Brian say about Shinobu using the focal as a drug? Surely the helmet was different, though. Like a drug, it took away his physical pain while he used it, but its mental effects were unique. And it was odd, he thought, how the focal's effects were changing over time. He no longer experienced only clarity and focus, as he had the first times he'd worn it. Now it was more like the focal was telling him things.

That was a silly thought. It wasn't as if the focal actually spoke to him. It was more like whispers at the edge of hearing, a voice in a distant room, whose words you can't make out and yet whose emotion and meaning somehow reach you. He couldn't say precisely what ideas the focal had been whispering to him, but he thought they might be, as he'd first glimpsed, hints of a grand plan. Those two boys were part of it. And the Middle Dread . . . he was part of it as well, though Shinobu was at a loss to explain how he knew that. It was a feeling more than a knowing. Such a strong feeling.

He shouldn't wear the focal. And he'd told Quin he wouldn't.

He could hear her upstairs on the landing now. He would admit what he'd done as soon as she came back down. It would be a relief, because then he could explain to her the feelings it had given him. Maybe they were important, maybe he'd glimpsed something they both needed to understand.

Quin's footsteps came lightly down the stairs. He would tell her before he had time to think. And then she would look at him the way his mother used to look at him when she found him passed out by the front door of her house. She would look at him like an addict, because that's what he was, an addict unable to control himself.

"Hey," she said when she came through the door into her examination room.

Shinobu noticed he'd been clenching his fists tightly. He shoved them deep into his pockets to hide them from her.

He steeled himself and said, "Hey, Quin, I—"

He stopped. Quin's face was open and lovely. Her pale skin was still flushed from using the focal up on the roof. And she was preoccupied, he could tell, by the connection she'd made while wearing it.

"What?" she asked, giving him her full attention when he fell silent. "Are you all right?"

"Maybe I shouldn't have made you wear the focal," he told her.

She squeezed his hand, unaware of all the words he'd left unsaid. "I don't have to wear it again," she said lightly. "And now we can use our own minds—without the focal—to look at something it helped me see."

She let go of his hand and began walking slowly past the counter, studying each page of the journal as she went, searching for something in particular.

The moment had passed. Shinobu wouldn't tell her just now. He'd stop using the focal, and eventually—or maybe quite soon—he'd stop *wanting* to use it. It would be easy to tell her then, because it wouldn't matter anymore.

"Look. These are the pages I want us to study," she told him. She pulled several sheets off the counter and knelt on the floor to spread them out in front of her. "If we focus on the Middle Dread—even if we only do it because Catherine focused on him—that will give us a place to start, a beginning in our search for where Seekers went the wrong way." She looked at the pages on the floor. "These three journal entries about the Middle Dread seem . . . related. At least, I thought they were when I was wearing the focal."

Shinobu sat on the floor next to her. Viewing the pages she'd selected side by side, it was easy to see the vast stretches of time spanned by the journal. The earliest entry of the three was written in almost illegibly dense, ancient handwriting. Quin had transcribed this entry with her mother, and she now set the copy next to the original. The other two entries were more recent and so were legible enough on their own.

She picked up her version of the oldest entry and read aloud as Shinobu tried to follow along with the original:

It is the Year of our Lord 1433

The Mydle hath crushed the life from the throt of the Young Dread.

I hid among oaks by the riverbank a good journey from the stronghold and there saw Mydle and Young in full fyte with bare hands.

It were all in play and practice untyl the Mydle bested Young and with hands tyte around throt did say Thou hast seen too much of me. And opened thy mouth to our Master. Now I close it for good and all.

And when the youth expire, from my place among trees I did spy the Mydle binding his corpse, wading to the heart of the river, and disappearing, that he might send his remains into the deep.

"So this entry," Quin said, "describes the Middle Dread killing a Young Dread—obviously a much earlier Young Dread than the one we know now—and pulling his body into the river." She pointed to the series of athame symbols written in the margin by a modern ballpoint pen. "It looks like Catherine figured out where this happened, because she wrote these coordinates next to it."

Questions presented themselves to Shinobu immediately. "Are Dreads allowed to kill each other?" he asked. "Or do they have to have a trial or a vote or something?"

"I don't know, but even if they are allowed, I can't imagine it would be done without the Old Dread present, can you?"

"No."

"I think it's safe to assume the Middle was doing something wrong," she said. "So in the first entry, the Middle kills a Young Dread in a forest by a river, a 'good journey' from a stronghold. Now look at the second one."

He read this one over her shoulder as she read it aloud:

1610?

. . . he did declare justice against my father, Sir Robert, of
the house of the horse, for transgressions against the sacred
three laws of Seekers. He declared Sir Robert had killed
another Seeker and likewise harmed mankind.

He called my father to that place in the forest where he is
often seen. We make it such on our stone device—

Here a series of athame coordinates had been included by the document's author, written in messy quill pen. They examined them for a moment and then continued reading:

Arriving then together, my father commanded me up a
tree to safety. I was to be his witness but not take part. The
Myddle did appear and without argument did he strike my
father dead as punishment for his crimes and removed his
body past the river.

The Myddle come back directly, kicking dirt over my

father's blood on the ground. Hid in the branches of a tree,
I wept but kept silent.

There was a noise of athame, a shaking of the air,
and the eldest Dread Seeker arrived with eyes burning and
whypsword drawn. Fearful argument ensued. The eldest
struck with limbs like lightning, he disarm the Myddle and
cast him to the earth, but the Myddle pled that his actions
were just.

I could not make my limbs move to come down to earth
and say what I knew. There was no crime save my father
witnesseth the Myddle in an untoward act with a woman.
God forgive me in my terror I did not move.

The Myddle left in shame. The eldest Dread remained
and did turn to me and speake thus: He were in the wrong
and ye have my apology. He will not be wrong again, that I
promise. He will be a changed man and a decent Dread.

Within the month my brother too was gone, though
others have sworn to me he was killed by a fellow Seeker, not
the Myddle Dread. I know not what to believe.

When she'd finished reading, Quin looked over the pages for a few moments and tapped a small drawing in the margin that appeared to have been added by Catherine. "What do you think this is?" she asked.

"A hill?" Shinobu suggested. "Or maybe a cavern?"

"In this note," Quin said thoughtfully, "the Middle declares 'justice' against a Seeker and calls him to a particular place in a forest—these coordinates, and maybe there's a hill nearby—where the Middle kills him, as punishment for breaking a Seeker law, while the man's son watches from a tree."

"The son says it wasn't justice," Shinobu pointed out. "And it sounds like the Old Dread agreed and wasn't pleased."

"Yes. It mentions a river as well. And look at the coordinates. Isn't that Scotland? Aren't both entries pointing to Scotland?"

"I think so."

They'd gained a working knowledge of athame coordinates during their training, but unless it was a location they were intimately familiar with, like Hong Kong or Scotland, neither could decipher, based solely on the symbols involved, where a set of coordinates would take them.

"Now the third page," Quin said, and she read out the final entry:

April the Twelfth, 1870

Father,

The Middle Dread returned not three days past. He did not announce himself, but Gerald was hunting alone and spied him by the loch and fortress.

Shall I make some acknowledgement of his presence? I do not wish to offend with forwardness but nor with lack of respect.

Further, something new. There are two youths with him, of lowly families by their dress and speech. The Dread instructs them in swordplay. They do a strange arithmetic among them, counting numbers, and always they sum to two hundreds.

What are we to make of this?

My love to you and my brothers.

Thomas

Again, with a modern pen, Catherine had written athame coordinates into the margin. "Almost the same coordinates," Quin said, "and here's the first mention of him training those boys—if they are the same boys."

"In a forest, and it's by water again, because he mentions the loch," Shinobu added.

"And a fortress. These three incidents must have happened quite near each other. We have the Middle Dread in all of them, and the boys in this last. And Catherine took the trouble to track down the locations of where they took place."

The descriptions of forest, loch, and fortress tugged at Shinobu's thoughts. He experienced a wash of déjà vu, as though he were remembering a half-forgotten conversation or an especially vivid dream. He wanted to see these places—no, he *needed* to see them.

He tried to keep his voice steady as he asked her, "We're going to these coordinates? That's what you're thinking?"

Quin looked up at him. "I can't imagine we'll find anything—the journal entries are so old. But . . . it couldn't hurt to go and look at where these incidents happened, could it?"

"Why not?" he agreed.

It was a tremendous relief that Quin's thoughts were running parallel to his own. Maybe he never had to tell her that some of those thoughts had come to him from the focal. He had spoiled something by lying to her, but he couldn't undo the lie just yet, because he still wanted to use the focal.

But he wouldn't. He wouldn't use it again. And eventually he would tell her.

CHAPTER 20

JOHN

"Prepare yourself," the Young Dread said.

Behind her loomed the decaying hulk of an enormous shipwreck, black against the clear blue sky. Other wrecks were visible in the distance, the remainders of their hulls like jagged rib cages among sand dunes along the coastline. Hordes of seals were barking and basking in the sun close to the water, and beyond the shore, the sand became desert, stretching in every direction.

They had used the coordinates in his mother's journal under the house of the bear—the last location where its athame had been seen—and they were standing on Namibia's Skeleton Coast.

The sand was cool beneath his feet, but the sun was already hot and bright. Behind him was the ocean, pounding against the shore and casting spray high into the air. Before him were steep dunes leading up to a desert with nothing but dry scrub bushes across its face. This wasteland reached from the beach to distant hills in the east and continued on to the south, perhaps forever.

John brought the binoculars to his eyes, focused them again on a sandstone peak beyond the desert. The dark entrance to a cave was just visible, a smudge on the red slope. But even from so far away he recognized the cave, and the line of hills behind it. They matched Catherine's drawing perfectly. He suspected Maud had altered the coordinates slightly, bringing him to a point far from the cave, in order to make him run.

John put the binoculars away. "I'm ready," he told the Young Dread. She had allowed him to come here, but she'd insisted the expedition would be a training session.

"Begin!" she called.

He ran.

Despite the sun, he wore his cloak, just as Maud did. She made him go unclothed when training in the cold, and now she was keeping him covered in the desert heat. *Because she loves discomfort,* he thought. *My grandmother Maggie was like that in her own way. Never leaving me in peace. Keeping me afraid. Have I ever relaxed?* The answer came against his will: *Yes, a few times, with Quin.* But most of his life had been lived under extreme tension.

He charged up the dunes, and was sweating and out of breath by the time he reached the first peak.

"Faster!" Maud called. She had kept up with him easily, despite carrying all of their weapons on her back, including the metal helmet and the circular shield they'd found on *Traveler.* He'd not yet been allowed to use either.

From the crest of the dunes, the sand petered out and became the hard, crumbling earth of the desert. John picked up his pace. *I'm thirsty already. How will I make it to the cave?* And with that, his thoughts ran further away: *That night under the floor in my mother's apartment, I was thirsty like this. I was under there so long . . .*

"Keep your mind here—on the run," Maud admonished, as though reading his straying thoughts. "Only the run."

He did as she said, pointing his head forward, his eyes, with the focus of the steady stare, always on the same spot fifteen feet ahead, watching dusty earth with occasional patches of dry grass or clawlike bushes. One step forward, then the next, over and over. His body was a machine.

Nothing else matters at this moment, just the run, he told himself. *For Catherine, nothing mattered but bringing back our house. It was more important to her than love or death . . .*

His mind continued this way, as it always did, bringing him images of his mother, his grandmother, Quin . . . He shook his head to rid himself of unwanted thoughts. *Run!* he commanded.

After two miles, the cave still didn't appear any closer. He was sweating harder, his clothing sticking to him.

"Come, John!" the Young Dread called. Though she was running slightly ahead and hadn't looked back, somehow she sensed that he'd slowed.

His body hurt. Like a reflex, he was thinking of Quin again. The way he'd pulled her behind the training barn that first time they'd kissed. Her eyes had been bright, her cheeks rosy from the cold. She'd loved him then. The idea that she hated him now gave him a physical ache.

It's nothing, he told himself. *Pain is nothing—in your heart or in your legs. Thirst is nothing. Heat is nothing. Catherine would call them small things. And Maggie showed—*

He stopped his thoughts. He didn't need Catherine or Maggie in his head just now. He needed only to run.

And he did.

An hour had passed before the hill was noticeably closer. By then John was moving across a land of hard-packed dirt and grass, weaving his way through the tiny skeletal bushes that were more numerous here. His feet pounded beneath him like pistons in an engine, tireless now even though he was drenched in sweat. *I might run forever,* he thought. *I love this.*

And then he fell. Before he'd realized it, his head hit the hard earth, dirt firm against his cheekbone.

Run! he told himself. But his body would not. He had used it up.

The Young Dread was there, kneeling next to him. She pulled him to a sitting position, held him against her, and poured water into his mouth from her canteen. John's instinct was to gulp, but he restrained himself and drank slowly for a long time.

"What are you thinking?" she asked him quietly. Her light brown eyes were bright in the sun as she looked down into his face, and her smooth, even voice was comforting.

"I'm thinking . . . I want to run."

"Good," she said. "Your mind is empty."

John handed back the canteen and understood that she was right. His mother's death, his grandmother's warnings, and even Quin were distant. His head, for once, was quiet.

"What do you wish to learn here, in this desert?" Maud asked him. She was holding the metal helmet, the focal, above his head.

"What my mother found in this place," he answered at once. "And how it will lead me to the house of the bear."

"Keep those thoughts in your mind."

With that, she slipped the helmet onto his head and helped him to his feet. John nearly fell as the electric buzz of the focal passed through him. The landscape wheeled. He threw his arms out for balance. Then he steadied.

There was the cave, close enough now to discern details. Waves of heat rose off the desert all around him, and the scrub, for miles in every direction, was moving in a slow breeze. He could feel the pressure of the hot air as it rose up into the vast blue arch of the sky. He was connected to all these things, was part of them, and his thoughts were his own to command.

"Now run!" Maud ordered.

He did.

The sun was beginning to set when they scaled the red earth of the hill and arrived at the cave. The Young Dread reached it before John, and after he'd stooped down to enter beneath an overhang of rock, he found her standing inside the dark space, her cloak blending into the shadows. She looked as though she had not just run ten or fifteen miles, but rather had been waiting in the cool of the cave all day for him to arrive.

She pulled the focal from his head the moment he appeared. When the helmet slid away, there was discord in his ears, a sensation of pushing and pulling, as though it had been holding him tightly and was now struggling to let go. John lost his balance, felt sand and rock beneath his hands, then found himself lying on the rough stone floor of the cave. He lay there, catching his breath, feeling his bullet wound pulsing hotly with the beat of his heart. He stared up at the ceiling as the crackle and tug of the helmet faded. He was, all at once, completely exhausted.

The cave was already in twilight, but there was enough light for him to see the dimensions of the space. It reached inward about twenty yards from the mouth to a back wall, where the red rock blended into shadows. And though the entrance was low, the cave's ceiling was quite high, disappearing above him into hazy dimness.

The Young Dread's cloak fluttered next to his ear as she seated herself nearby. The light was fading quickly, but he could make out her pale face and long hair as she threw her hood back to look down at him. When she handed him the canteen, he lifted himself up onto an elbow to drink.

"Have you discovered anything, during your run?" she asked.

In fact he had. Several things had become clear to him while in the focal. He drank for a while and used the time to put his thoughts in order.

"My mother was interested in all the Seeker houses," he said meditatively. "When I first looked at her journal, I thought it was partly about the Dreads but mostly about revenge, yet she wasn't only following the houses who'd done us harm."

"No," Maud agreed. "Her interests were wider than that."

"Maybe she started keeping the journal before she knew what those houses had done to us," he mused. The Catherine who had written in the journal seemed mostly curious, not angry. "Which is why I needed to look at Maggie's pictures. To focus my search."

The Young Dread said nothing.

John drank again until he felt the life-giving trail of water down his throat, through his stomach, and branching from there to every cell of his body.

"Why did you make me run so long before using the focal?"

There was a pause, and then Maud explained, in her even tone, "It has a second name—havoc helm. A focal bears traces of the people who have used it before, especially if it has been used by one person many times. Thoughts . . . patterns . . . habits . . . may"—she chose her words carefully—"*remain* inside the helmet, like a fog. If you do not fully clear your mind, you will be prey to those foreign thoughts. It can even split one's mind into two parts—one of which begins to look a lot like someone else." She helped him sit up. "A hard run is a good way to empty your mind before using the focal. Now you should feel only your own thoughts, in focus."

John nodded. He was physically spent, but a new mental energy flowed through him. He understood that the focal hadn't taught him anything new; rather it had let him see his own knowledge through a new lens. Catherine had tracked Seekers from the house of the bear here, to this cave. And from here he must discover where to go next.

The Young Dread was using her flint. Bright sparks flew off the stone in the darkness, illuminating her face in bursts of white light. After a few minutes, she'd lit the leaves on a large branch from one of the scrubby desert bushes outside the cave.

She held the torch out for John, and he pulled himself to his feet to take it. The red sandstone of the cave danced around him in the unsteady light. John thought the smoke would quickly fill the space, but as the wood burned, the high ceiling funneled the smoke upward and away. Carved into the striated sandstone of the cave's roof, the lines hewn so deeply they were awash with dancing shadows, was the shape of a bear.

The walls were uneven but bare of any other ornamentation or sign of human presence, until he got to the back of the cave. Here the rock roof sloped down dramatically to meet the floor at a steep, inward angle. Where the wall touched the floor, the two planes made a wedge of space, nearly impenetrable by the light of the torch, as though the ground were being eaten by shadows at the back edge. Above those shadows was a patch of writing.

"Maud."

The Young Dread moved silently across the rough floor into the pool of light. Small figures had been carved on the back wall. No, not carved, John saw, *melted*. The edges of the figures were smooth and rounded, and streams of molten sandstone had dripped from the wall to pool on the floor, where they'd hardened into glassy puddles. The inscription read:

91

30

57

22

PSDS

"What is PSDS?" John asked.

The Young Dread shook her head, telling him she didn't know and also brushing his question aside. "There's something there," she said quietly.

She pointed to the low, dark place where the sloping wall met the ground. Her eyes were much better than his at seeing in the dark, and John could discern nothing in the shadows at first. But when he knelt down and held the flame closer, the light revealed two human figures, wedged as far as they could be wedged against the back wall.

"Oh God," he whispered.

One was a woman, judging by the hair, though she'd been dead so long and was so decayed that she was little more than bones and the dusty remains of dried flesh among dark clothing and cape. His first thought was of his mother. Catherine had been kept alive by machinery in a barn on the estate for years after she'd been disrupted. At the end, with her sunken eyes and transparent skin, she hadn't looked much better than this corpse. The sight of it brought memories of the helplessness he'd felt when he'd seen her that way.

John steadied his mind. He was not helpless now.

He ducked low and crawled closer to study the bodies in the flickering light. There was no smell of death; the corpses were dry. The second figure was smaller, and perhaps had been dead longer, though it was difficult to tell. The clothing on the smaller one was more like a pile of dirty rags.

"Was that one a child, do you think?" John asked when Maud had crawled up beside him.

"It's hard to say," the Young Dread answered.

John didn't want to touch the remains, but Maud had no such qualms. She reached out and picked up the withered left arm of the woman and pushed up the crumbling sleeve of the corpse's shirt.

"Look," she said quietly.

John leaned closer with the torch. There was a discoloration on the leathery skin of the wrist. It was a brand in the shape of an athame. The Young repeated the procedure on the other arm, and John saw a different brand on the woman's right wrist, this one in the shape of a bear.

"Seekers used to brand themselves a second time with the sign of their house," Maud told him. "That tradition seems to have died out in recent years."

John could guess why Seekers like Briac Kincaid hadn't branded themselves with their house insignia. They lived with stolen athames, and it might look strange to have a different emblem on your arm than the one on the athame you were using.

He looked at the female body again.

"The journal said the athame was last known to be here, with a Seeker called Delyth Priddy and possibly a companion. Is this Delyth? And is that her companion?"

They turned their attention to the smaller corpse. The hair had been short and dark, the clothes gray and rough. Maud peeled up shreds of cloth to examine the body's wrists. The skin was more decayed than the other corpse's skin had been, and there were no brands.

"Not a Seeker, then," John said. He was trying not to think too much about the withering skin with the bones poking through, so much like his own mother's collarbone and jaw the last time he'd seen her.

Maud had turned the small body's leathery skull toward the light, revealing dirty, scratched teeth inside a dead grimace.

"Not a Seeker," she agreed, leaning away from the bodies. "This one is . . . more like those boys we saw on the Scottish estate. Their teeth were dirty like this."

This conclusion appeared to affect her deeply. She sat back on her heels and stared at the smaller corpse for some time.

"How long do you think they've been dead?" John asked.

The Young Dread shook her head slowly. "That is hard to say. Dry desert air, away from the elements. They died years ago, but I cannot say how many years. Perhaps the smaller one has been dead much longer than the woman."

She'd gotten back to her feet and was looking at the inscription melted into the wall again.

"The numbers sum to . . ." She fell silent as she added them up.

As John stood, he observed a change come over the Young Dread. Her expression didn't alter as she looked at the carvings, but it was as though a heavy weight of despair settled upon her shoulders. Without looking at John, she turned and walked out of the cave.

He followed, ducking through the low opening and into the desert night. Overhead, despite the bright moon, stars shone in infinite numbers, as though the heavens were larger and richer here than anywhere else in the world. The cave's entrance was halfway up the sandstone peak, and he found Maud sitting on a ledge overlooking the vast stretch of land below.

He seated himself close by, wary of whatever state of mind had overtaken her. She looked as if she were drawing darkness from the night to wrap about herself. As soon as John was sitting, the exhaustion of his long run overtook him again. He was hungry, he was thirsty, and his muscles ached for sleep.

He spoke to her against his better judgment. "It sums to two hundred," he said. "Two hundred is mentioned in the journal several times. Does it mean something to you?"

A long stretch of silence passed before she finally answered, "No. There is a world of things I knew nothing about, a world of events to which I was blind and deaf."

In an unexpected gesture of anger, the Young Dread tossed the burning torch off the ledge. It cartwheeled down the hill, flaring brightly until it came to rest far below. John watched the torch's flames slowly flickering out.

Maud gazed out past the desert to the ocean in the distance, where the moon made a band of white upon the dark blue surface that shifted as waves rolled in to shore. The world was so beautiful here, John wished he could let his eyes, his mind, linger, but he could not. There were two corpses in the cave behind him. Was it possible his mother had already taken her revenge by killing those two, or had she, like John, found only the bodies? Either way, this location was a dead end. He had to try the next, and the next—provided Maud was still willing to help him.

He didn't understand her current mood.

"Why Africa?" he asked, hoping this was a topic she wouldn't find bothersome. "It seems an odd place for a Seeker cave."

"Seekers are most at home in Europe, yes, but they have spread themselves across the world," she answered, her gaze still on the ocean. Her tone was as even as ever, but he sensed frustration beneath it. "There are Seeker outposts in many strange places, John."

"Will you let me go to the next place in the journal?" he asked. "The cave for the house of the boar?"

"Do you think that cave will make more sense?"

"My mother found some of our enemies, and she was looking for the rest. I can find them as well."

"Or maybe what you seek is entirely elsewhere. What if your

mother's notes have nothing to do with your revenge?" She paused, and then said, "I know this cave, John. Each Seeker house had a place like this. A private refuge, meeting place, a place for ceremony and conference, known only to its own members—and sometimes to the Dreads. It should not be a dangerous place for a member of the house to whom it belonged. It should not be a place where they disappear."

The Young Dread lifted her gaze to his face, and he felt his usual discomfort under her steady stare. After a time she turned back to the embers of their torch far below. "I am wondering, John—is it always wise to learn something, simply because it can be learned?"

In the moonlight, he could see emotion creep into her eyes. *She's going to confess something,* he realized. The idea was so strange, he stopped breathing for a moment.

"There are things I would prefer not to know," she told him. Her eyes met his again, and for the first time since he'd known Maud, she looked like a girl instead of a Dread. She looked vulnerable. "If I learn all that the Middle Dread has done," she said, her voice less steady than he'd ever heard it, "if I learn how he has corrupted Dreads and Seekers both, do I share responsibility for his actions? Am I as he was?"

John's breath had come back to him, but it still took a few moments to find his voice. Eventually he said, "Sometimes you remind me of Quin. Too noble to see how things truly are. Too decent to know that nothing in the world is decent."

"Her thoughts often come to my mind," the Young Dread admitted.

"Quin's?" He tried, unsuccessfully, to hide his surprise.

"Sometimes, when you have trained your mind as we have, you can touch another's thoughts directly. Quin's mind and mine cross in this way from time to time. I do think she has a noble heart, or I would never have entrusted her with the athame of the Dreads."

"But—her thoughts come to your mind?" John asked again, trying not to sound foolish.

"At times. Other times I feel her looking out through my eyes. She sees what I see, though maybe she doesn't realize."

He almost didn't want to ask: "What—what is she thinking about when you hear her thoughts?"

She glanced at him. "Why do you ask that? Do her thoughts worry you?"

"No. I—I'm only asking," he said, turning away, embarrassed.

"I try not to listen," the Young Dread told him. "She doesn't mean to reach me."

Her eyes were on John again, and it felt as though she could see his discomfort coming off him in waves. Her voice had returned to the steady tones of an instructor as she asked, "John, do you think of her often?"

"Not on purpose," he answered quietly.

He hadn't wanted to speak to Maud about Quin, but the questions had come anyway. He averted his eyes. "Sometimes you mention her name, when we're training, to throw me off. I know you're just baiting me, but she fills my mind." He wanted to be quiet, but he couldn't. "I think of that look on her face, when she realized I'd betrayed her. When I open the journal, I think of her hands touching it, her eyes reading it. I imagine what she'd say about the things my mother and grandmother ordered me to do. She'd tell me I'm wrong . . . and I want her to know I'm not wrong. I want her to know I'm right. Because I *am* right. She's the one who's wrong."

John managed to stop himself at last, ashamed of how much he'd said. They were thoughts he hardly admitted, even to himself. He wondered if, despite the great lengths to which Maud had gone to help him clear his mind, the focal had made him more talkative.

"I did not understand how much your thoughts were absorbed by another," the Young Dread said after a time. "You are not distracted only by fear of the disruptor or memories of your mother, but by Quin, who is alive in the world now."

"Yes," he whispered after a moment in which he admitted to himself how true this was.

"Others cannot rule your thoughts, John. If you want to be a Seeker, you must learn to rule them yourself. That is half the work of getting to your oath. The focal can help . . . superficially. But a deep habit must be changed by you." John was gripped by the fear that she was about to disavow him as a student. Instead she told him, "I will let you go to the next place you seek in your mother's journal, this cave of the boar Seekers." He was about to thank her, when she held up a hand. "But first," she said, "there is somewhere else I must bring you."

CHAPTER 21

CATHERINE

19 YEARS EARLIER

"He's looking at you," Mariko said.

"What?" Catherine yelled back. She'd seen Mariko's lips moving but couldn't hear anything over the music.

The nightclub pulsed with a beat so heavy, it felt like earthquakes shaking the floor. White laser light cut through clouds of smoke, twisting in designs that strobed in time with the music. Faces and bodies were decorated with glow-in-the-dark paint, highlighting features grotesquely and exaggerating movements.

The club was packed, and Catherine was beginning to understand the pleasure of losing oneself in joyous anonymity. She and Mariko were painted with streaks of silver that sparkled when the lasers played across their faces.

"He's looking at you!" Mariko repeated, screaming to be heard. She touched Catherine's hand and pointed discreetly.

A young man with dark hair was slowly working his way through the crowd, and though he tried to direct his gaze at many things in the club, it was obvious his eyes kept coming back to Catherine. His face was a dark blue that didn't glow, so his features were obscured, almost as though he wore a mask.

They were on the Transit Bridge, which spanned Victoria Harbor from Hong Kong Island to Kowloon. Catherine was staying with Mariko for a few months, and Mariko's parents believed that the girls were, at this moment, taking a night class in traditional dance. It wasn't completely untrue.

"He's quite handsome!" Mariko said privately, by yelling the words into Catherine's ear canal.

"How can you tell?" Catherine screamed.

"I guess I can't! But this could be your lucky night!"

This was the game they played, noticing boys who noticed them and pretending that something might happen. The truth was that Catherine, while enjoying herself immensely, couldn't feel like anything but an observer in a place like this. It was pleasant to pretend she was just one of the vast crowd of revelers here on the second level of the Bridge, but despite the body paint, she was sober, had been trained as a Seeker, and did not actually fit in.

After recovering her family's athame, she'd expected her parents to fall down on their knees in gratitude. They'd been grateful, of course, but when Catherine had told them what she wished to do with the athame, what she wished to become one day, they'd laughed at her. They hadn't meant to be cruel—they'd laughed because they felt sorry for her. Her hopes were so ridiculous and out of reach that she was an object of pity to her own family. They didn't care that the Middle Dread was unworthy of his position. They didn't want Catherine gathering evidence to that effect or fantasizing about who might replace him. Even when she spoke of the immediate things she wanted to do as a Seeker (small acts in parts of the world where a little good would go a long way), they'd treated her like a dreamer.

Her parents saw the athame as a key to family security only. Catherine hadn't shared with them her new conviction that she should find the secret caves belonging to every Seeker house, as a first step to discovering where missing Seekers had gone.

Her older sister, Anna, had been jealous when Catherine brought home the fox athame. Eventually she'd accused Catherine of trying to diminish her older sister's status in their parents' eyes. And so Catherine had left.

She'd done one final act as a Seeker. She'd gone back to the cave under Mont Saint-Michel, alone and hurriedly, and she'd scoured the walls for any clues to the past and the present. She'd found the series of numbers cut into the rock—carvings she hadn't had time to study with Mariko. The numbers added up to two hundred, and beside them were a series of marks almost like arrows. But Catherine was at a loss to understand what the numbers meant. The arrow shapes hinted that they were directions, but beginning where? Were they a measure of distance? Of time?

She'd left France without answers. She'd come to Hong Kong to leave her life as a Seeker behind, for a long while, at least. She would let Anna deal with her parents and their legacy.

Catherine yelped as something poked her near her spine. Enormous, sharp belt buckles were the rage in Hong Kong at the moment, and you had to be careful where you stood in places like this. She took a step to her right.

"May I speak to you?"

Catherine was startled. The young man with the face painted dark blue had worked his way through the crowd and was now next to her at the edge of the dance floor, his head close to her ear. Catherine glanced at Mariko, who was also watching the newcomer. Usually she and Mariko politely declined any such advances. Catherine still found the boys out in the world so different from herself that they seemed almost another species. And Mariko was living under her parents' medieval dating rules. But something about this young man's self-assurance struck a chord.

"All right," she said to him, and Mariko arched an eyebrow so high, it was comical. "Where?"

The young man gestured toward a quieter area at the edge of the main room. Catherine moved with him, weaving through the crowd. She winked back at Mariko, letting her Japanese friend know that nothing had changed; she would talk to this person, and she'd be right back.

"Do I know you?" she asked, turning back to her companion and trying to study his painted face in the changing lights.

"You should know me," he said.

"I should get to know you?" she asked, not sure she'd heard him correctly. He guided her through the lighter crowd at the fringes of the club, with one hand at the small of her back and the other resting lightly on her arm. At first, she'd liked the confidence of this position, but now, with fewer people around, his double touch seemed aggressive.

They were navigating through a series of tall glass columns full of swirling liquid. A few couples were dancing slowly there, but they paid Catherine and her companion no mind at all.

"You should know me," he repeated.

"I should— Ow!" she said.

Something had pinched her back through the light material of her dress.

"Careful." His eyes were camouflaged within the paint on his face. "You caught yourself there."

Catherine saw that the edges of each column were actually designed in jagged patterns. She must have rubbed against one.

"I'm thirsty," she told him, discovering as she said it that she was actually very, very thirsty. The feeling had come upon her all at once.

"Are you?" he asked.

He steered her through the last few columns, and now they were in a darker area, where an open, dim doorway led off toward the washrooms. Catherine stumbled, and he caught her, one hand on her arm and one on her lower back again.

"Ow!" she said.

"Watch yourself, Catherine. You keep bumping into things."

"Briac?" she asked, trying to see through the paint. But he wasn't Briac, even though his hair was dark and he moved like Briac. This was someone else.

"Emile?" she asked. Could it be that Emile had been alive and safe all this time? Had he been hoping to find her like she'd been hoping to find him?

He laughed in a low, unpleasant way that Catherine felt more than heard. "No, I'm not Emile."

She stumbled another time as he guided her through the unlit hallway toward the washrooms. A gaggle of girls ran past without noticing them.

"Wait," said Catherine, suddenly aware of how dizzy she'd become. And so thirsty. What was happening? "Wait."

He grabbed hold of her arms, and she saw a flash of metal between two fingers on his left hand.

"In here," he told her.

He pulled open the door to a single washroom and pushed her. On reflex, Catherine's hands shot out and grabbed both sides of the doorframe, preventing him from thrusting her inside.

In the mirror she could see that his right hand was coming toward her. She understood the motion: he was going to hit her elbow and make her arm collapse. Catherine kicked her left foot backward. Her high heel sank into his shoe with deadly accuracy, which was, she thought, very lucky, considering how dizzy she felt.

With a gasp of pain, he released her, and Catherine turned, striking at his throat. He dodged the blow, lowered his head, and like a mad bull butted her stomach and forced her into the washroom. Catherine fell backward, hitting the floor.

He was in the room with her, locking the door. The light inside was slightly brighter, and she now saw that he wore what looked like plastic rings over two fingers on his left hand. Those two rings were joined, and at the point of connection was a small needle.

"You—you drugged me!" she said. Only now did she grasp how strangely she'd been acting. She'd let him lead her all the way across the club, let him steer her into seclusion.

He was on her then, straddling her on the floor, his knees holding down her arms.

"Where the hell is it?" he demanded.

She looked up at him through half-closed eyes. Some of the paint was rubbing off his face, but she still didn't recognize him.

"What?" she asked.

He slapped her. Catherine felt the pain distantly as her head cracked back against the floor. How many times had she felt the needle's prick? At least three. What sort of drug was it? Something strong. She was close to passing out. Would Mariko be looking for her?

"Where is the *athame*? You took what was mine. It was promised to me."

He raised his hand to hit her again, but held it back, letting her answer.

She tried to make her mind work. This man—or boy, it was hard to tell—was a Seeker, of course. She should have spotted that right away, but his motions had been camouflaged by all the dancers around him. And he wasn't someone she knew.

"Someone promised you . . . my family's athame?" she asked slowly, her words slurring. "Who would do that?"

"You know who."

She didn't know. Had Seekers been trading stolen athames with each other?

"It was you . . . on Mont Saint-Michel?" she asked weakly, recognizing him at last.

"Where is it being kept?" he demanded.

"Where . . . what?"

He shook her, as though that would help her think. Instead the washroom reeled.

"You're attacking me," she said, her own words stupid in her ears.

"Nothing gets by you, does it?" Her eyes were out of alignment with each other, so there appeared to be two of him above her, each ready to strike. "Emile was just as slow," he said, "and things ended just as badly for him."

"You . . . Emile? What happened to Emile?"

He was smiling down at her—two of him were smiling down at her. Her eyes latched on to one item in the room. A glass. It was sitting on the edge of the sink, bobbing in and out of her sight line as he shook her. Someone had brought a glass into the washroom and left it here. Dark lipstick along the rim, dregs of something bright green at the bottom.

Her foot. That was her foot down there, wasn't it? Near the pedestal of the sink.

"My brothers and I will not be bait for someone else," he hissed into her face. "*Our* family isn't going to go away. One of my brothers was in London today."

What did that mean? Was he threatening her family? Catherine tried to think. She'd have to let him hit her again. And she'd have to move quickly. *Can I move quickly?* she wondered.

She worked her lips as though she would answer, then she spit at him.

Kick! Catherine told herself.

He slapped her hard. And she kicked.

Her foot connected with the sink, she twisted her legs to one side, and a moment later she felt the painful thud and wet splash of the glass landing on her ankle bone.

"Where did your family put the athame?" he demanded, shaking her again.

Catherine was writhing beneath him. She managed to roll the glass off her leg and toward her left hand.

"I'll report you . . . to the Dreads," she whispered. "It's my family's rightful athame. They will punish you."

"Will they?"

He smiled in a way that reminded her of her parents and their pity. He didn't fear her going to the Dreads. *Why not?* she wondered. *He should fear them. Even if the Middle Dread is a terrible judge, the Young Dread will have to listen. This person is breaking Seeker laws.*

"The athame's mine . . ." she said. "I'm keeping it . . ."

Her arm was still pinned under his knee, but her fingers were around the wet sticky glass. She felt along its surface, turning the glass so she was gripping it by its heavy base. *I'm drugged,* she thought. *He's relying on that.*

"No," he told her. He leaned close, and as he did, his knee lifted off her arm. "I'm going to kill you and keep it."

Catherine whispered, "I was going to say the same thing to you."

She hit the glass sharply against the floor, then slashed at him with what remained—several long shards attached to a thick glass base. She caught him across the neck, and Catherine could feel the shards going deep into his throat and breaking off.

He cried out, his hands grabbing her hair, pulling it wildly as blood pulsed out of his neck. He was screeching, his air drawn in through the wound at his throat. She still saw two of him as he tumbled forward.

Catherine managed to roll out from beneath him, sliding in his blood. Her own fingers were bleeding around the broken glass, but she continued to grip it tightly as she staggered to her feet. Her right hand scrambled for the lock on the door, but her fingers were wet and slipped off the lever.

The door burst open anyway.

Mariko was standing there, a kitchen knife clutched in her hand, a large security guard with a key standing next to her.

Mariko's eyes swept over Catherine, her pale dress soaked in blood, the washroom behind her.

Mariko took her arm and pulled her away as the guard stared, openmouthed, at the mess within. She bundled Catherine out of the club, and as they left, she said quietly, "Life with you has not been boring, Cat-chan."

Catherine had sobered up by the time she stood, fully clothed, in the shower of Mariko's pool house, as her friend sprayed her off. Despite the warmth of the shower, Catherine was shaking. The water ran in pink rivulets, brightened by the occasional flake of silver paint, as Mariko scrubbed Catherine's hair and arms. She winced as her friend's hands moved over the swollen parts of her skull.

"He was the one on Mont Saint-Michel," Catherine said.

"Are you sure?"

"Yes. He said *his* family wasn't going to disappear . . . as though *mine* would. And as though other families would too. Like maybe Emile's. And the Dreads would do nothing . . ."

"What are we going to tell my father?" Mariko asked, rinsing the soap from Catherine's head and listening to nothing Catherine was saying. "Should we tell him the truth?"

Catherine looked down at her torn dress and the deep gashes in her left hand, where she'd clutched the broken glass.

"I think we'll tell him the truth," Mariko said, answering her own question—almost babbling. "We might have to fight that man now."

"He's dead, Mariko. We won't have to fight him."

"Well, his family, then—"

A phone rang.

Catherine recognized the ring—it was her own phone. Mariko dug through Catherine's handbag, which lay on the floor, still stained with dark patches of blood. Catherine turned off the shower as Mariko held the phone out to her.

"It's your mother," she whispered.

Catherine's mother. Of course. The woman sensed intuitively whenever Catherine was hiding something. But her attacker's words came back to her: *One of my brothers was in London today. Where did your family put the athame?*

Shakily she took the phone from her friend, paused a moment to collect herself, then answered.

"Hello? Mum? Are you safe? Is the athame still safe?"

The voice on the other end of the line was her mother's, but it was incoherent. A series of sobs came through, choked words half audible in between.

"Mum? Are you—"

"Your sister . . ." The words were garbled, and it took Catherine a moment to understand.

"What—Anna?"

"Anna," her mother repeated, still struggling to be understood. "Anna's dead."

CHAPTER 22

QUIN

Quin and Shinobu looked out of the anomaly directly into a wide stream, and this gave Quin the strange sensation of peering across a flowing river of energy into an actual river. They were following the coordinates from the first of their three journal entries—the one that described the Middle Dread killing a Young Dread, back in the 1400s, and sinking his body in the deepest part of the river.

Shinobu jumped down into the water first, then turned to take her hand.

"It's a bit cold," he warned her.

Quin landed in the gentle current next to him, and the anomaly hovered for several moments behind them before it sewed itself closed. The water was knee high and cold but looked much deeper toward the middle of the river, where the flow was strong and unpredictable. It was early morning here—in Scotland, if their reading of the coordinates was correct.

"Come on, my pussy willow," she said, pushing him toward the bank. "What's cold to a Scotsman?"

"The Japanese side of me is very delicate," he told her with mock gravity, looking anything but delicate as he tramped through the water toward shore. He wore a dark sweater and jeans, both of which were a bit too loose on him, but his shoulders were so broad that his backpack looked small on his back.

The river's edge was lush with ferns growing beneath a canopy of oak trees. Shinobu grabbed at the foliage and hoisted himself from the water, then pulled Quin up next to him. They both stood, dripping, on the bank. Quin watched a grimace appear on his face, then disappear just as quickly. He'd insisted on another long practice with whipswords that morning, and she guessed that his injuries were bothering him, however much he tried to pretend they weren't.

Shinobu unfolded their map and laid it across the moss-covered trunk of a fallen tree. Then he drew a positioning device from his jacket pocket. There they were, a dot blinking on the map screen, somewhere in northern Scotland. He zoomed in for a closer view, but there were no nearby landmarks. They were in the middle of nowhere, by a small river, which wasn't much more than they already knew, and was frankly also a good description of almost anywhere in Scotland. He marked their location on the paper map.

"Think we've ever been here before?" he asked.

She shook her head as she studied the map. "Alistair took us so many places in Scotland when we were training, it's hard to say."

"According to the journal, there was once a fortress around here somewhere," Shinobu said. "Though maybe not close enough to walk to. It said 'a good journey from the stronghold.'"

Quin scanned their surroundings again. "The person who wrote the journal entry about this spot was hiding in the trees near the riverbank when the Middle killed that Young Dread. Should we wander a bit?"

"Sure."

He folded up the map and tucked it away in a pocket. Again Quin caught a fleeting glimpse of pain in his face, but he said nothing.

They walked in ever widening arcs away from the riverbank. Quin wasn't sure what they were looking for, except perhaps traces of what had happened with the Middle Dread—traces of what had been written about in the journal. Yet after an hour of pressing through the undergrowth at the side of the river, they had found nothing.

They decided to move on to the second journal entry. After following that new set of coordinates, they emerged from another anomaly into a dense thicket of large bushes within a broader forest clearing. The anomaly let them out slightly higher than Quin had expected, and she landed gracelessly on top of Shinobu.

"Ow."

"Sorry. Was that your bad leg?"

"Yes, but it's nothing," he said as they climbed to their feet and picked their way out of the thicket.

When they got free of the confining branches, Quin saw that Shinobu was looking away from her, as though pain and ill temper had gotten hold of him.

"Hey," she said, nudging him with the toe of her boot. "Are you all right? We can do this another day. I can take you back."

"I'm fine," he told her. He tried to smile, but it didn't come off very well.

Quin brushed twigs from his hair and jacket, refusing to be pushed away by bad humor.

He asked her irritably, "Are you finished sorting my clothes?"

"Yes, I am. You've got a beetle in your hair, but it probably won't hurt you."

Quin, who knew he hated insects, was amused to watch him lean over and rake his hands across his head frantically.

"Is it gone?" he asked, straightening.

"Yes. You look quite beautiful."

His very short hair was standing on end and pointing several directions, but despite this—or perhaps because of it—he did look rather beautiful.

"I hate when you use that word."

His mood was darkening quickly, yet it had begun to remind her so much of times when he'd been cross as a child that she was surprised to find herself enjoying it a little bit.

"You hate the word 'beautiful'?" she asked him.

"You used to call me beautiful," he said, looking away from her to scan the forest around them, more out of vexation than actual interest in their surroundings. But Quin took the opportunity to study the environment herself. The trees and undergrowth were somewhat different here, but the air felt the same as it had in the first location. "And you meant 'untouchable' or 'unlovable'—nothing good."

"'Sullen and bad-tempered,' that's probably what I meant," she suggested, unable to resist teasing him. She'd spent so much time worried, it was a relief to poke fun now that he was out of danger from his injuries.

"You meant I looked like a painting or something— Can we get on with our search?"

"No."

All at once she grasped the source of his bad mood.

"What do you mean 'no'?" he asked.

"You never finished your tea before we left," she told him, feeling like an idiot for not remembering sooner.

She'd gone to Master Tan's that morning and brought back his daily medicinal tea, but Shinobu hadn't drunk much of it. They'd been practicing with whipswords and exploring for hours now, and Master Tan's tea was what made that sort of exertion possible. Shinobu was out of steam.

"I did drink it," he said. "You watched me."

"Give me the backpack."

"I'll check," he told her, turning to keep the pack out of her reach.

He removed it from his back and turned away to search through it, as if he could more easily prove himself right without Quin looking. He turned around sheepishly a moment later with a nearly full bottle of tea in his hand.

"I packed it," she said.

He set the bottle on the ground and looked at it balefully as he tied up the backpack and slung it over his shoulders. Even in the face of proof, he wasn't ready to admit defeat.

"I don't need tea right now," he said. "Do I look like some frail grandmother to you?"

"A little."

"But a 'beautiful' one, right?"

She put the bottle in his hands and kissed his cheek. "Very beautiful. Now drink."

Sullenly, he unscrewed the bottle and drank the whole thing in one go. When he was finished, he coughed and made a face, then bent over as though he might vomit up all of it. This happened every time he drank Master Tan's tea, so Quin merely waited him out.

When he'd gotten over the rotten taste and had wiped his mouth on a sleeve, she asked, "Should we go back?"

He shook his head, and already she could see his good humor returning. Master Tan's remedies worked quickly.

"I don't want to go back. I'm not an invalid. I'm nearly healed." He suppressed a smile, obviously aware of how childish he'd been. Still not quite meeting her eyes, he murmured, "I like it when you order me around."

"I like it when you're in a bad mood."

"Thanks very much," he said, beginning to explore the clearing before them.

"Doesn't it remind you of the fights we used to have when we were little?" she asked, lacing her fingers through his as they walked. "Those were funny."

"Like the time I threw tree sap in your hair and you punched me in the stomach?" Shinobu asked. "That was a barrel of laughs."

Quin felt her own mood slip at the memory. "I'm still cross about that one."

"We were six. You knocked the wind out of me."

"My mother had to cut off a huge chunk of my hair, Shinobu."

She shoved him away playfully, and now he was laughing.

"You sound angry," he told her, suddenly looking very concerned. "Where's *your* tea, Quin? Should we go back and brew up a batch for you?"

She grabbed at his jacket in mock fury, but stopped in the middle of the motion.

"Look," she said, catching his elbow.

They'd been examining the large alder trees along the clearing's border, whose branches nearly joined above them. Beyond one of the grandest trees it was possible to see quite a distance into the woods. Some way off was a fern-covered hillock, and in its side, though obscured from their current position by the forest undergrowth, was an opening that looked very much like the entrance to a cave.

"It's what Catherine drew in the journal, isn't it?" she said.

They approached it carefully, and as they drew closer, the hillock showed itself to be quite large and obviously manmade. It was a nearly perfect circle, domed on top and overgrown by plants. Trees crowded around it, but none grew on top. The opening was low and dark and lined with large stones that had been placed quite expertly. Stone steps covered in moss and wild brambles led down into the dark interior.

"Smells old and rotten," Shinobu said as a trickle of air from inside the hillock brushed past them.

"Did you bring a light?" she asked.

He turned away from her again to rummage in the pack, and turned back with a flashlight. They crouched down, and he shone the light through the doorway.

Inside the hillock was a substantial space, a cave really, lined with stone that had been set in place with rough, sandy mortar. Debris had grown in from the forest and been blown in by the wind as well; old branches, dead leaves, loose rocks, and a large quantity of soil littered a stone floor.

And there were skeletons against the far wall.

Quin and Shinobu both drew back from the opening when they saw the decaying human forms in ragged clothing, remnants of hair and skin around their gaping faces.

"That's not very nice," Shinobu said quietly.

"I guess this explains the smell," she said.

The odor inside the hill was of damp and rot but not of fresh decay. It was the smell of death that had happened in the distant past.

Shinobu swept the flashlight's beam slowly over the cave, but there was no one hiding in the shadows. The space, like the bodies inside it, had been abandoned long ago.

"Shall we?" he asked, gesturing gallantly toward the interior.

Quin nodded, and she ducked beneath the lintel and stepped down into the cave.

The space was large enough to create echoes, but the echoes were short and close, as though the sounds made by her boots were jumping back at her almost before she'd finished making them.

There were four bodies in all. They lay near each other, their jumbled and deteriorating clothing making it appear they were all part of one mass. All of the figures had died with wool cloaks about them, but there was no other similarity in their clothing. The oldest body, little more than bones with a few leathery tatters of flesh, wore a lace-cuffed blouse. It had mostly disintegrated, but the few details that remained placed the blouse's owner somewhere in the 1600s. Another corpse wore blue jeans of a kind that might have been popular a hundred years before present day. Another was quite small, maybe a child, with rotten teeth and coarse attire that was so encrusted with dirt as to be indistinguishable from the remains themselves. The last corpse was a girl, Quin wagered, with golden hoops in her ears and a delicate gold necklace lying across what was left of her shirt and rib cage.

"Look," Shinobu said, his voice a whisper because that felt only appropriate in the presence of death. He picked up a twig from the floor, and with it he moved the necklace from the folds of old clothing. Dangling from the chain was a small golden horse.

"A horse," Quin said. "Could I have the flashlight?"

He handed it to her, and she trained it on the wall behind the bodies, where she'd seen some sort of pattern on the stones. In the beam of light was a horse head chiseled onto the back wall. Off to one side and nearer the ground, a series of letters and numbers had been etched into the stones:

P51
D21
S64
D44
S20

"This cave belonged to the house of the horse, then?" Quin said.

The figures on the wall looked as though they'd been sculpted by something extremely hot. Quin stepped gingerly around the bodies to examine them more closely.

"It's like they were melted into the rock," she told Shinobu as she ran her fingers along the stone.

He came up beside her and touched the lettering. "What could do that?" he asked. "Some sort of modern tool?"

Quin shook her head. "I really don't know."

"The numbers add up to two hundred," he pointed out.

"They do," she agreed. "Like in the journal. But two hundred *what*? What are *P, D,* and *S*?"

Shinobu regarded the wall for a while. "Pounds, dollars, shillings?" he suggested. "Or names? Pippa, Dougal, Sylvia?"

Quin laughed, though it felt blasphemous to make jokes next to the bodies in the cave. She drew a notebook from her pocket and jotted down the numbers and letters. She and Shinobu skirted the space, looking for other carvings on the wall or ceiling, but there were none.

"We should find out exactly where we are," she said.

They retreated from the cave into the open air. Quin was surprised to find the cold gray morning in the forest to be just as they'd left it.

Shinobu unfolded their map against the side of the hillock, drew out the positioning device, and a few moments later had marked their exact location. They were some distance from the first site, still in the north of Scotland, still in the middle of nowhere. Quin's finger traced the distance from their previous location to this, which looked to be about forty miles. According to the map, they were near another section of the same river, just as the journal entry had suggested. Quin held herself very still for a few moments and could faintly hear the river's distant sounds.

"Are the numbers in the cave miles, do you think?" Shinobu asked.

"If they were carved a long time ago, couldn't they be anything? Leagues, furlongs?"

"Feet," Shinobu suggested. "Or something else entirely, like number of blows with a whipsword?"

"Or weight."

"Or how many sandwiches to bring with you."

She laughed at this. Then she said, seriously, "In the journal entry, the Middle Dread kills a member of the house of the horse and drags him out of sight. Did he bring him to this cave? Is the oldest body in there the Seeker who was mentioned in the journal?"

"The Old Dread apologized for what the Middle had done and said he wouldn't do bad things again," Shinobu mused. "So who killed the other dead people in the cave?"

They didn't have an answer. Quin wasn't sure she required an answer at the moment—she was still amazed they'd found anything at all. They spent the next hour walking around the outside of the hillock, then exploring the surrounding woods. But they found nothing else.

"How do you feel?" she asked Shinobu when they were seated back in the clearing, eating the meager lunch they'd brought with them.

He cocked an eyebrow at her. "You want to go to the location of the third journal entry, don't you?"

She looked at him sheepishly; she was almost jittery with a sense of anticipation. They'd found nothing in the first location, something in the second location. What would the third location bring?

"Don't worry about me," he told her. "I feel unstoppable."

Quin nodded. "I feel a little that way myself."

They finished their food. Then Quin drew the athame from her waist. She lined up the dials to take them to the location of the third journal entry, where the Middle Dread had been seen, long ago, training two young boys.

CHAPTER 23

NOTT

It was raining at Dun Tarm, and thick tendrils of mist grew up from the lake, hiding the forest. The distant rocky summits showed themselves as dark shapes peeking through a curtain of gray.

"How many times are you gonna hit me?" Nott demanded from the floor of the fortress, his face in a puddle of stagnant water from Loch Tarm. Raindrops pattered on the back of his head.

"You'll take your beating without complaint," said the brown-skinned Watcher.

His name was Geb. Nott knew this because he'd introduced himself around the time he'd started pummeling Nott. Geb probably wasn't more than eighteen years old, but he seemed to think he was second to no one but their master.

His younger partner, a skinny boy called Balil, was in the process of driving his fist into Wilkin's gut repeatedly. Wilkin made muffled yelps, but Nott was proud to see that his own partner wasn't crying. Why should they give these other Watchers the pleasure?

From that strange room full of computers in Hong Kong, they'd finally followed their master's instructions. After a long walk *There,* they'd found Geb and Balil standing as still as figures in a churchyard, waiting to be brought back into the world. Nott had seen the distant shapes of other Watchers, also waiting in the blackness. In a perfect world, they would have retrieved all of them. But this was not a perfect world, because they didn't have their helm. By the time they'd found Geb and Balil, they'd been in danger of losing themselves in the no-time of that place, and they'd had to settle for bringing back only two.

They'd carved an anomaly back to Dun Tarm and dragged Geb and Balil through with them. The older boys' limbs had been stiff, even though their skin was soft, and it had been heavy work to haul them through the cold water of the lake and dump them in the sheltered area within the fort, to wait for them to wake up.

Geb and Balil both had the sort of dark, dark skin Nott associated with deepest Africa. Nott wondered fleetingly where their master had recruited them, and when. Their master trained all Watchers at Dun Tarm—where he taught them the joys of fighting and killing things, where he taught them the necessity of following his orders, where he punished them, and from where he banished them if they disobeyed him. But of course the training took place over many decades or maybe even longer, and Watchers might have come from anywhere in the world originally, anywhere their master had found likely boys to mold in his own image.

Most Watchers had been purchased from their families, some stolen. Nott himself had been bought, for a few silver coins. He remembered his first glimpse of his master, broad like a bull, with a face not made to smile, his dark cloak hanging about his shoulders as though it were a natural-born part of him. Nott had been terrified as that man took him from his mother, who turned her back on Nott and busied herself with hiding her new coins down one ragged boot. His master had shoved him roughly when he slowed down to look back at his family's cottage, which was, to tell the truth, little more than a pile of stones shored up with earth.

On the floor of Dun Tarm, Nott lifted himself to his elbows. He saw his own reflection in the puddle from which he'd just pulled his head. It was his older brother's face looking back at him: fair skin, lots of freckles, and a mop of brown hair liberally streaked with dirt. *Odger,* he thought. *I've grown, and now I look like Odger.* If Odger had only been at home that morning, he never would have allowed their mother to sell Nott. Odger had been his friend, his protector. He'd taught Nott to fish in the stream behind their home. He'd taught Nott to keep his head down when their father was around.

But Odger hadn't been there the day Nott's master bought him. *Is that a good thing or a bad thing?* Nott wondered. His master had taught him to fight, to put the world in its place. He'd made him better than a boy. But Odger, two years older and as tough as the iron poker their mother kept by the hearth, had made Nott feel . . . what was the word? *Warm,* maybe? That might be it. Odger had made him feel warm—not warm like when you were sitting in front of a fire, warm on the inside.

Was it better to be a Watcher and know you were a cut above everyone else in the world, or was it better to feel warm? Nott wasn't sure.

From where he lay on the floor of Dun Tarm, he could see the dead deer outside the entrance. Its eye seemed to be peering in at him. *You haven't worn the helm in days,* the deer whispered. *You're not thinking straight.* The deer was right—what did he care about Odger anymore?

All of these thoughts had taken only a moment to pass through Nott's mind, but Geb was impatiently prodding Nott's ribs with the toe of his boot.

"Get up, will you?"

Nott struggled back to his feet, his head ringing from the last blow, his legs unsteady on the cracked stone floor. The stunted trees growing through the flagstones were swaying in the cold, wet breeze. Nott shivered.

Geb was grinning as he prepared to wallop him again. The older Watcher's smile displayed the markings on his teeth, which were identical to Nott's. Geb and Balil also had their own helm—though of course they would never let Nott use it.

"May I at least defend myself?" the younger boy asked, trying to stay upright.

"As if you could defend yourself against me!" scoffed the older boy. "You're barely a Watcher, you little runt."

"I'm not a runt!" Nott yelled. "I'm still growing."

"You're a runt who can't follow orders." Geb slapped Nott's face. "This is your punishment for waiting to retrieve us. And for losing your helm besides. Try to learn something from it."

He kicked Nott's chest, sending him back down onto the floor. In a way, the beating felt good, because it distracted Nott from the loss of the helm. He lay there for a moment, enjoying the stillness of the hard stone beneath him.

"How long has our master been missing?" Geb asked.

"Weeks," Nott admitted. Then, from the ground, he explained, "We found his athame. Wilkin thought we should get it back."

"Did our master ever say you should retrieve his athame instead of looking for him? *No.*"

Of course Nott knew this. It was what he'd been trying to tell Wilkin all along.

"What are you supposed to do, Nott?"

"We're supposed to wake every pair of Watchers hidden in that dark place."

"And then?"

"We start from our special point, and we walk and walk through the darkness *There*, spreading out, searching for him inch by inch until he's found."

Nott had once imagined *There* to be as large as the world itself, but his master had set him straight when he taught his Watchers how to find him in that darkness outside of time. *There,* his master had explained, was much smaller and more focused than the space of the world. In fact, if you could keep yourself from getting lost, you could walk a circular path through all of it and end up back where you started—in a single day. That was exactly what the Watchers were supposed to do when they searched for their master.

"That is right," said Geb. "That's what you were supposed to do. Now we have to make up for the time you've lost. He'll be angry with us for something that's your fault."

"You were lying there helpless when we brought you through," Nott muttered, still resting his head on the ground. "It took hours for you to wake up. I protected you. I could have beaten you while you were lying there."

This was not strictly true. Nott and Wilkin had actually left Geb and Balil unattended for quite a while, and had used that time to dump Briac back at the madhouse outside London. But there was no way for Geb to know that.

"Our master would have put you in your cave if you'd hurt us," the older boy said. "He probably still will."

He grabbed Nott by his shirt and yanked him up off the ground. In the middle of this motion, a vibration shook the crumbling walls of the lakeside fortress. All four Watchers turned to look out through Dun Tarm's entrance.

There was a shimmering in the air just outside. As they watched, the threads of the world were being severed and snaking away from each other. Someone was using an athame to arrive at their fortress.

"It's our master!" Geb said eagerly. "He'll sort you out."

In a moment, enough of the circle had been cut that Nott could see who was beyond it. There were two figures in the darkness. Neither was their master. (How could they be, when he didn't have his athame?)

"It's them!" Nott yelled, his eyes sharper than anyone else's. "Wilkin, it's them!"

Quin and her tall, redheaded companion were standing in the darkness, about to invade the privacy of the Watchers' fort.

More than that. The edge of Nott's helm was visible—it was sticking out the top of the pack on the tall one's back. *They* had stolen the helm. Of course. It wasn't lost at all. They were thieves—first their master's athame, then the precious helmet.

"They have our helm, Wilkin!"

With an animal roar, he ripped himself out of Geb's grasp and tripped across the floor to grab up his whipsword. As he ran toward the solidifying anomaly, he heard the others following close behind. He glanced back to see Geb pulling his own helm onto his head. *Good,* Nott thought, *we'll need that.*

All their training, all of their master's plans, were instantly forgotten. They charged from the fortress, weapons drawn, ready to retrieve the athame and Nott's helm besides. And why not? Whoever succeeded in recovering those would surely become their master's favorite, and would never, ever be sent to die in a cave.

CHAPTER 24

SHINOBU

"Knowledge of self
Knowledge of home
A clear picture of
Where I came from
Where I will go
And the speed of things between
Will see me safely back."

Shinobu and Quin were reciting the time chant together. They stood shoulder to shoulder in the darkness *There* as Quin carved an anomaly back into the world.

As the threads of light and dark snaked away from each other, Shinobu saw a gray and rainy landscape—Scotland again, of course. In the distance were forested slopes shrouded in mist, and above loomed dark rock peaks. Close by, just on the other side of the anomaly, was a ruined fortress falling into a lake. The fortress that had been mentioned in the journal, of course.

The place was isolated and in ruins, but not empty. Before the anomaly was even fully open, Shinobu heard voices yelling, then saw four boys running directly toward them, brandishing weapons and looking murderous.

"Quin!" he yelled. "Pick different coordinates! Hit the athame again!"

At the same moment, though, he had the oddest thought: *Here they are. Stay.*

He dragged Quin backward a dozen steps as she turned the dials on the athame to take them somewhere else. But the boys were already at the anomaly. They didn't pause but leapt across its seething border as if it were no more than an ordinary doorway in a house somewhere.

Insanity! Shinobu thought. Jumping *into* an anomaly to fight was madness.

"Your whipsword!" he said to Quin, cracking out his own.

In another moment, the boys were slashing at Shinobu, who'd positioned himself between them and Quin. He was trying to gain her more space to use the athame. If she didn't succeed quickly, they would be trapped. That thought was terrifying . . .

And yet he'd been expecting those two boys. The journal had said this location was where the Middle had trained "two youths . . . of lowly families." All day, somewhere in the back of his mind, Shinobu had been anticipating an encounter. He'd been *hoping* to find them. It was necessary. *But why is it necessary?* he wondered. The answer was as strange as it was simple: the focal had told him it was necessary.

From where he fought, Shinobu could see that Quin was having difficulty reading the athame's dials in the low light. She hadn't been able to strike it yet. She stood at his side now, fighting the oncoming blows of four miniature whipswords. Matching weapons for four mis-matched boys, two dark, two light—though all had the same vicious style of fighting, the same smell of death hanging about them. The anomaly was behind the boys, casting them into shadow and making it difficult to see details in their movements.

He'd expected two boys, but there were four—and the two new ones were older and larger. All four were attacking them murder-ously, suicidally throwing themselves into the dark, unmoored time of *There*. And yet he felt a connection to them.

Stop, he told himself. *There is no connection.*

The small swords were both an advantage and a disadvantage to the boys—a disadvantage because Shinobu's whipsword had a much longer reach, but an advantage because the boys could slip inside his blows and drive him back. Shinobu flicked his wrist, making his own whipsword shorter to match theirs.

He heard Quin muttering her time chant, attempting to keep her focus.

Knowledge of self, Shinobu began in his own mind, *knowledge of home . . .* But the fight took all of his attention.

"Push forward!" Quin yelled. "Out through the anomaly."

"I'm trying!"

He blocked blows and turned his shoulders in an attempt to sepa-rate two of the boys from the others so he might more easily push them back.

He'd already lost track of how long they'd been fighting. Time was lengthening. His muscles were moving differently.

"The anomaly's closing!" Quin said beside him. There was des-peration in her voice, and he heard her making a heroic effort to throw the boys back. "Push forward!"

"We're too late," he told her, his voice disconnected and far away.

The anomaly was out of reach and losing its shape. The light was disappearing. And then it was gone.

In the darkness, he heard Quin strike a vicious blow, and then she clicked on the flashlight she'd taken from Shinobu in the woods. She pointed it into the boys' faces as she slashed at them again.

"Knowledge of self," he heard her chanting, *"knowledge of home, a clear picture of where I came from—* Shinobu, say your chant!"

He was trying.

In the dancing beam of the flashlight, his arms moved automatically to block the two boys fighting him. How was he keeping up with them? His mind slowly turned over this question, and he saw the answer: he wasn't keeping up with them. He was slowing down, and the boys were slowing down as well.

All except one. The largest of the boys was still fighting properly and much too quickly for Shinobu's eyes to follow. Quin's whipsword tore here and there as the flashlight beam bobbed and swung wildly. She was so good at keeping her focus.

"Knowledge of self," Quin was saying, the words so fast that Shinobu could hardly understand them, *"knowledge of home* . . . Shinobu, take him!"

The oldest opponent tumbled into Shinobu. In the moving beam of light, he saw blood across the boy's chest, and something else—the boy was wearing a focal.

A vibration. Daylight. Shinobu was yanked roughly from behind. He fell and landed on grass and soft earth.

He was breathing, he knew that much. He could feel the hilt of his whipsword in his hand. But the air, the breeze, the clouds in the sky, everything was moving too fast.

Quin was standing in the grass nearby, still fighting the boy in the focal.

"Shinobu!" she called as her whipsword crashed into her opponent's. "Please get up!"

Quin . . . Quin . . . With a force of will, Shinobu clawed his way back into the ordinary time stream.

He became aware of the pain all at once. His injuries had sprung back to life in the fight: his ribs, his leg, the sword wound in his side. Everything had been aching for the last few days—since he'd forced himself to stop using the focal. But this fight had turned ache into full-blown pain.

He wouldn't put on the focal. He'd promised himself. He didn't know what might happen to him if he wore it again—

"Shinobu!"

He rolled to the side, ripped his backpack open, and grabbed the helmet. He'd brought it with them on their expedition to Scotland, and he'd hidden it from Quin, though somehow it had ended up at the top of the pack after he'd retrieved the flashlight for Quin. He'd brought the focal with them not because he intended to wear it but because it pained him to think of leaving it in Hong Kong, halfway around the world. But there was no choice now. He was in pain and Quin was in danger.

He lifted the focal to his head—

And something heavy landed on his chest.

"Give it back! Give it back!"

He was being battered by small fists. The littlest of the boys was straddling him, snatching at the focal and striking Shinobu wherever he could.

Shinobu grabbed a fistful of the boy's shirt, saw freckles and blackened teeth, and smelled the rank odor of rotting flesh. He butted the boy's head with his own. His freckled opponent went momentarily limp, allowing Shinobu to get up onto a knee. Then the boy seized at the focal desperately, his nails scratching Shinobu's hands.

No one's taking the helmet, Shinobu thought. *It's mine.*

Planting a foot on the small boy's chest, Shinobu heaved him away and pulled the focal onto his head.

A discordant vibration filled his ears, but he'd come to enjoy that feeling. Even before the focal had settled, Shinobu understood that it would see him through this fight. Already the pain was receding, replaced by a heightened awareness of his surroundings. They were on the Scottish estate, he saw. In the darkness, Quin had chosen the coordinates she knew best.

The youngest boy, the one Shinobu had just booted away, was lurching back to his feet. *Nott. His name is Nott.* He remembered that from their first encounter. Or did that name exist inside the focal? The other three boys were chasing Quin at full speed toward the commons.

They want the focal, but even more they want the athame of the Dreads, Shinobu thought, understanding something the focal had been whispering to him. *They want these things because they belong to their master, the Middle Dread. Without him, they're only nasty children. With him, they have a purpose.*

But the Middle Dread is gone.

Shinobu looked down at his arms and legs. With the focal on his head, his limbs felt farther away, yet more responsive.

He sprinted after Quin.

The grass of the commons had grown unchecked for almost two years and was more than five feet high. The boys and Quin were in the midst of it, only the tops of their heads visible above the tall stalks. One of the boys struck Quin hard with his fist.

"Hey!" Shinobu yelled.

His mind and the focal were humming together, and he saw every move he must make in order to beat these boys. This was his own knowledge and fighting experience, being clarified by the focal; it felt different from the other things he'd felt inside the helmet—things that were new and secret.

As he got closer, he saw that all of the attackers were badly injured. Their faces were ashen, and their initial burst of energy was gone. He plowed into them at full speed, knocking them into each other. One of the older attackers lost his whipsword in the impact. The boy chased after it and kept running.

Another opponent, one Shinobu had seen before—Wilkin—looked desperate. His face was bruised and he was bleeding heavily from his nose. Shinobu lunged menacingly, and that was enough. Wilkin stumbled away through the high grass, and Nott followed at a distance.

The oldest boy, dark-skinned and tall, the one wearing the focal, had Quin pinned to the ground only yards away. He was standing on one of her arms, his whipsword raised to strike.

He's going to kill her, Shinobu thought. *And I'm too far away . . .*

He felt a surge of terror. The helmet screeched in his ears. His own thoughts and the focal were suddenly at odds, as though his panic could not mix properly with the intense awareness brought by the helmet. Immediately his mind began to argue with itself.

Quin.

The boys—I wanted to find them.

Quin. He's going to strike her!

She's not important. The boys are what matters.

She's all that matters. Quin!

The whipsword flashed down at Quin's head. She rolled herself onto the boy's boots, and the sword hit the grass behind her.

Her assailant raised it again. He wouldn't miss a second time.

I was looking for the boys. They can be used.

I don't care. Quin! Quin!

There was a vibration in the focal so high and sharp, it felt like metal picks in his ears. The pain became deeper, overwhelming, as though Shinobu's mind were being torn in half. He cried out as he trampled through the grass.

Maybe I want something different, he thought.

No! I know what I want.

He flicked his wrist, collapsing his own whipsword. Then he cracked it out as a whip. The oily black substance wrapped around the boy's arm, and he yanked him off Quin. Shinobu twisted his wrist hard, drawing the whip back and forming it into a sword. He raised it to strike.

The moment her arm was released, Quin took hold of her own whipsword and was back on her feet. The boy in the focal, bleeding and exhausted, looked at both of them and knew he was beaten. He ran after the other three, who were already at the edge of the forest.

Quin took a few steps after him, then collapsed. Shinobu ran to her.

"Hey," she whispered when she saw him above her. Her dark eyes were unfocused, her hair spread out on the broken stalks of grass.

"Hey," he said, kneeling down.

He gently checked her for wounds, but there was no blood. *Quin,* he thought. Why had he cared anything about those boys? He'd gotten confused. No one mattered but Quin.

"He hit my head," she whispered. "I thought I'd lie here for a minute . . ."

A vibration reached them from the woods. The boys were using an athame.

"Did they take the athame?" he asked.

"No. It's not our athame they're using," she whispered. "It's yours—or your mother's. It had a dragon on the pommel."

"What?"

"They have your family's athame." Her eyes came into focus on him. "You're wearing the focal," she whispered.

"I had to," he told her. "I wouldn't have made it."

She nodded, and her eyes fell closed. He slid his arms beneath her and lifted her easily.

"I'm taking you back."

Her head was heavy against his chest. She was spent. After a moment, she murmured, "I thought he was going to kill me. But you stopped him. You saved me."

CHAPTER 25

QUIN

Shinobu carried her through the anomaly and back to Hong Kong. As soon as they were safely in a taxi, headed for the Transit Bridge, she pulled the focal from his head. He collapsed against her immediately. Quin held him, and he wrapped his arms around his stomach and groaned quietly, as his body came to terms with separation from the helmet.

Her own head was throbbing, and she was dizzy from the blow the largest boy had dealt her. She closed her eyes as she laid her head against the seat, and felt the taxi spinning around her.

When the car had wound its way down steep streets and they were closer to the harbor, she heard Shinobu's breathing evening out. He was lying in her lap by then, and when she opened her eyes, she found him looking up at her.

"You brought the focal with us," she said.

That was why he'd turned away each time he'd opened the backpack. He hadn't wanted her to see it.

He looked ashamed. He closed his eyes. "I've been wearing it, Quin. A lot."

"You have?"

He opened his eyes but didn't look at her. "I don't know why. I—I couldn't stop myself. It was like opium, only much, much better."

She ran a hand through his hair and leaned over, so her face was close to his.

"You saved me with it. You saved both of us."

He nodded, but he didn't look happy about what she'd said. He rubbed his eyes, then took one of her hands in his own. He was gazing up at her with that look that was particularly his, the look that said he would do whatever he must, just as he'd done in this fight, just as he'd done every other time he'd saved her.

"Maybe the focal helped today," he whispered. "But I never want to wear it again. Don't ever let me put it on."

"Was it so bad?"

"It's always strange. But today, during the fight, it *hurt*. I felt it twisting my mind." Such a pained expression had appeared on his face that Quin pulled him closer, as though she could ward off the bad memory.

"I won't let you use it again," she promised him. "I'll find somewhere to lock it up."

"Good," he said. "Good."

Her head fell back against the seat, and she watched the tall buildings rolling by outside.

"We were right about those boys and the Middle Dread," she said after a while. "They were still there, at that fortress where he trained them almost two centuries ago."

"Yes, they were," he agreed. He was holding her hand tightly.

When they reached the Hong Kong Island side of the Transit Bridge, they left the taxi and tottered onto the Bridge thoroughfare. Quin was completely exhausted from the fight, and Shinobu was barely able to keep his eyes open. By leaning against each other, they made it to her house somehow.

Fiona was home. She pushed both of them into Quin's examination room, where she cleaned up their cuts and bruises as Quin tried to explain some of what had happened. Then her mother helped them both upstairs and they collapsed onto Quin's bed.

When Fiona had gone, Shinobu pulled her close, fitting her body into the shape of his own. Quin felt, as Shinobu's father used to say, like a bruised sack of potatoes—and one that had been awake for days.

"I didn't really think we'd find anything, following those journal entries," she whispered. "At least, nothing quite so dramatic."

"The Middle was very busy," Shinobu murmured into her ear. "And whatever he was doing . . . part of it's still happening, with those boys."

She nodded. "Shh now," she said softly. "I can't keep my eyes open another moment."

"You're always trying to sleep with me," he murmured, his voice barely audible, as if he too were almost unconscious.

Quin smiled as she drifted off.

Quin woke to the warmth of sunlight streaming in through the window by her bed. Her body was sore, but her sleep had been so deep and so long that she was restored. With her eyes still closed, she reached out for Shinobu. She found only the rumpled covers, cool and unoccupied.

She opened her eyes. She was alone in bed, still dressed in her dirty clothing from the day before, with splatters of mud on her trousers.

"Shinobu?" she called.

She heard footsteps downstairs, but after a moment of listening, she knew they belonged to her mother, not Shinobu.

When she got to her feet, she saw the note on her bedroom floor.

> Quin—
>> I have to go. Something isn't right in my head. Don't worry. I'm going to make it right again.
>>> —S

She knew at once the focal had harmed him. Had he ever followed Mariko's instructions for using it?

She ran downstairs and looked through all the rooms on the main floor. She found Fiona cataloging herbs in the treatment room, but no Shinobu.

Back upstairs, she pulled open the closet door in her bedroom. She'd thrown the focal in there last night, before they'd collapsed. It had seemed safe enough, just for one night, until she could hide it better.

The focal wasn't in the closet. She searched the entire house for it, just to make sure, but the metal helmet was gone.

So was the athame of the Dreads.

CHAPTER 26

CATHERINE

19 YEARS EARLIER

The train shook as it went around a corner, and the lights flickered off and on. Catherine was in London, gray and rainy London, which seemed so much more severe than Hong Kong had been. Her body swayed as the train straightened out, the dark tunnel flashing by outside the windows. She was riding the Underground to meet her parents.

They'd forbidden her to move around the city on her own, unprotected, but she was ignoring that order. Her parents were probably right. Anna was dead, and she herself could have been killed in the club in Hong Kong. Catherine still bore the bruises of that encounter across the back of her head and on one side of her jaw. But she wasn't unprotected. As the train took another turn, she felt the comforting weight of her whipsword at her back. And she was standing, even though the car was only half full, because standing kept her alert. If another mystery Seeker was planning to attack her, she would not be caught unawares. It felt good to be back, to be ready to fight, to be a Seeker again.

On the same day Catherine had been attacked in Hong Kong, Anna had been attacked—by another person looking for their athame, possibly a brother of the one who'd attacked Catherine. Anna had lived long enough to explain that much. Judging from the amount of blood at the scene, her parents believed Anna had severely wounded her attacker, but she'd died before she reached the hospital. The athame had survived, well hidden in her parents' bank safe.

It was still difficult to believe her sister was gone. Catherine had loved Anna, who'd been only a year older, but they had never been close. They'd fought with each other more often than not, and when Catherine looked back over her childhood, it seemed filled with petty competition and cruelty. Anna had been prettier than Catherine, better at math and science than Catherine, better at languages than Catherine, and she'd made a point of reminding Catherine of this every day since they were small.

But even with all of Anna's talents, she'd been jealous when Catherine grew to be the better fighter. Anna didn't like her little sister beating her at anything. When Catherine, who had beauty in her own right (if slightly less than Anna's), had started to attract interest from boys, Anna had made it clear Catherine would never be anything but a second choice. When Catherine had shown great love for Seeker lore, Anna had mocked her mercilessly for her endless questions. When she'd daydreamed about the good deeds she would do as a Seeker, Anna had ridiculed her for being naive. And when Catherine had returned home from France with their family's athame, recovered after missing for a century, Anna had stopped speaking to her altogether.

Their last conversation had been forced upon them by their mother. Anna had called Catherine in Hong Kong a month before, at their mother's insistence, to brag about how much she loved the boy her parents were forcing her to marry. Archibald Hart. A ridiculous name for what must be a ridiculous boy—he'd have to be if he'd agreed to an arranged marriage in this day. He wasn't a Seeker, but his family was well known, and her parents considered that valuable.

Archie is so handsome. Perfect, really, Anna had said over the phone, in a gushing tone that sounded genuine but probably wasn't. *Tough, a real man, but intelligent.* Each word had seemed chosen by its potential to make Catherine feel less, to make her feel unworthy. *He's head over heels about me, Cat. It's kind of embarrassing. I'm sorry they haven't found a match like that for you. Don't fret, though—there's someone out there for you somewhere.*

As if Catherine had nothing better to do than sit around waiting to see what monstrous boy her parents would try to thrust upon her. She'd gone to Hong Kong to leave all of that behind.

But the joke was on Catherine, of course. Her parents had found someone just like Archie for her. Anna was gone, but the connection to Archie's family was apparently as important as ever, and Catherine was on her way to meet her parents and Archibald Hart right now. They intended that she should marry him in Anna's place. Archie's family name and Catherine's family athame—a perfect partnership.

Hopefully he'll hate me, she thought, not for the first time. *Please let him hate me.*

The train had stopped, and new passengers were pouring on. She spotted Briac Kincaid as soon as the car began moving again. He hadn't come through the glass doors from the platform with everyone else. He'd entered through the door at the end, from another car. And he was obviously looking for her. Had he followed her to the station where she boarded? Maybe she hadn't been as alert as she thought.

Briac stopped when he saw Catherine's eyes on him. He was seventeen now, as Catherine was, and he'd gotten taller since she'd last seen him. He was wearing jeans and a sweater, like any normal person on the Tube, but the clothes looked like a costume on him. She could see him only with a whipsword in his hand, his black cloak hanging from one shoulder, his eyes hard and cruel. Now, however, his eyes looked less cruel. There was something almost pleading in them.

He mouthed: *Speak to me.*

Automatically Catherine's hands brushed over her back, feeling the whipsword hidden there. She flicked her right wrist lightly, and a small, sharp knife dropped into place in her palm.

Of course I'll speak to you, she thought, running her thumb lightly along the blade.

She pushed her way through passengers in the aisle until she was right next to Briac. He reached for her arm, but she slipped away between the final few people in the car. Shoving through the door at the end of the carriage, she stepped into the noisy dark of the connecting platform between train cars. Just over the edge of the platform, the tunnel floor streaked by, illuminated in bursts of brightness by intermittent lighting fixtures.

As soon as Briac stepped out of the carriage behind her, Catherine yanked him away from the door, where he was visible to passengers inside, and pushed him against the metal hide of the train. The knife in her right hand was at his neck.

"Were you part of it?" she asked. "Did you help kill her?"

"Who—Anna? You think I killed your sister?"

Briac held his arms up in a gesture of surrender, letting her know that he wasn't trying to fight.

Liar, Catherine thought. *You're always ready to fight.*

"You hated us, Briac," she said. "Were you part of it?"

She touched the skin of his neck with the knife so he was forced to press himself into the train.

"No, I wasn't part of it, Catherine!"

"Was *he* part of it? The same one who attacked me?"

"Someone attacked you?" Briac looked honestly surprised by this revelation.

"On the same day as Anna. A Seeker . . . looking for something that belongs to *me*."

She moved her hair aside to show him the yellowing bruise that was still visible on her jaw from the attack in Hong Kong, a fading pattern of rough fingers on her face.

"But you got away," he said. His voice held relief and something else. Possibly admiration, though that didn't seem likely. "You're a good fighter, you—"

"I didn't just get away. I killed him."

"Well, that's—that's good." Briac still looked shaken by the news that Catherine had been attacked. It surprised her to see the open worry in his eyes.

"No, it's not good," she snapped, "because I can't beat his name out of him if he's dead." She was proud of herself for saying these words as though beating her attacker had been an option. The truth was, she'd barely gotten away from him. "Who was he? I thought he was you at first."

"I don't know," he told her. He held his hands up as she pressed her knife against his throat again. "I truly don't, Catherine."

She studied him, then relaxed her knife hand slightly. If she had to guess, she'd guess he was telling the truth, he didn't know who'd killed Anna.

Briac sensed her willingness to listen, and went on, "I don't know how many Seekers there are left in the world, or which ones might be after you. Most of us have been hiding from each other for generations."

"How do I find out who attacked us?"

"That's not the important question—"

"Death isn't important to you?" she asked, cutting him off. "I bet your assignments are full of it. You hardly know who you've killed anymore."

She expected him to get angry now, to try to grab her knife, but he didn't. He looked at the blade by his throat, then back up at her.

"It's not the important question, because much bigger things are happening," he told her, lowering his voice, as though someone might be listening out on the noisy platform between cars. "Things could be . . . good, if we're on the right side of them, or very bad if we're not."

"Anna's death could be 'good'? Is that what you think? And what about Emile? My attacker made it sound like Emile could be dead too."

"Really?" Briac asked, looking even more concerned.

"I don't know for sure."

Briac appeared to shake off his worry. "You have to forget about Emile, Catherine. And even forget about Anna."

Catherine reversed the knife, pulled back her arm, then slammed the butt of the weapon into Briac's gut. He doubled over.

She waited warily as he groaned and pulled himself upright against the side of the train. When he was standing again, he looked furious. But he didn't lunge at her. He stayed statue-still as he took a breath in and out.

"A lot of us will be killed or disappear," he said through gritted teeth. "It's been happening for a while. Seeker against Seeker. You know that, don't you? We can be clever about it, or we can be two more victims."

Catherine thought again of the fox cave beneath Mont Saint-Michel. Was it possible it and other caves held the secrets of these disappearances?

"Why don't Seekers go to the Dreads for help?" she asked. "I know the Middle Dread looks the other way when crimes are committed, or blames one Seeker instead of another, but what about the Old Dread and the Young—"

"No one goes to them because the Old has been gone for ages and the Young does nothing apart from the Middle."

"She's in the Middle's shadow, but she's good—"

"Catherine, listen," Briac interrupted, "there are things you don't know." His eyes slid away from her. "Partner with me, and I'll explain what I've learned." He said it as though he were offering her something of great value. "And you'll explain everything you know. You have an athame now—"

"How do you know that?"

"Everyone knows! Partner with me, and there's a chance we could . . . do really well for ourselves. And not end up like Anna did. Because you have your journal, and I can make use of it."

"My journal?" For the first moment in this conversation, she was truly confused. "How do you know about my journal?"

"I saw you with it when we were apprentices, and I wasn't the only one. You told other apprentices about the sort of things you were putting in the journal. You weren't very careful about that, Catherine." He shook his head slightly and said, "It's a better weapon than any other Seeker has. The Middle doesn't want anyone to know of things he's done. If you partner with me, I'll show you how to use it."

She searched his face for some sign that he was being sincere. His hard eyes looked worried and serious, but all she could see in him was the vicious boy who'd tried to force himself on her in the woods. She would never trust him.

"I thought you were engaged to Fiona MacBain. Someone you can push around."

Briac slapped the train behind him angrily.

"I'm not trying to get you to marry me. I'm asking you to be my partner."

"You have Alistair for that."

Briac rolled his eyes. "He's a complete romantic. He wants to be a Seeker like the ones in the old stories."

Catherine laughed and felt a surge of kinship for Alistair. "That's what I want too. Didn't you know?"

"That doesn't exist anymore."

"It doesn't exist because of Seekers like you, Briac. *Killers* like you. When we have a better Dread than the Middle to watch over us—"

"You think someone will *replace* him? Are you mad?"

He slammed his hand into the train behind him again. He looked truly frightened now, and this was deeply disturbing, because Briac didn't scare easily. In a quick motion, he grabbed her shoulders and shook her hard.

"Don't say things like that, Catherine, do you hear me? You don't want to bring the Middle Dread's attention onto yourself. He's already heard of your journal. You want to end up dead for real?"

"The Middle Dread will not kill me. Dreads don't kill Seekers, unless we've broken the law. Even the Middle Dread. It's Seekers who've been killing each other. It was a Seeker who attacked me, a Seeker who killed Anna. If we had a real Middle Dread who was fair and just—"

He shook her again. "Just stop! We can help each other and maybe have a chance. If not, *someone* will kill you, Catherine."

"*You* always seemed the most likely Seeker to do that, Briac."

"I think about killing you all the time," he told her seriously. His fingers dug into her shoulders. "You're maddening."

Catherine swung her arms up through his and brought her elbows down, pinning his arms against his ribs. He struggled as she turned and stepped forward, pushing him to the edge of the platform. They gripped each other's arms as his head swung mere inches from the tunnel wall.

She released him suddenly, and he scrabbled for the railing. Catherine didn't wait to see if he regained his footing. She was already at th   r to the next carriage.

      away from me," she said.

— 214 —

CHAPTER 27

CATHERINE

19 YEARS EARLIER

Catherine had to straighten out her clothing in the washroom of the Tube station after her confrontation with Briac. She felt ridiculous in the boring blouse and skirt her mother had insisted she wear, but at least nothing had been torn or dirtied in the exchange. If she looked anything short of acceptable, she wouldn't hear the end of it.

She left the station and met her parents at the street corner, and her mother maneuvered her into a small alley behind a row of stately mansions to pull Catherine's hair back into a braid. The ugly yellow bruises were still visible on Catherine's jaw, but her mother managed to pull out enough strands of hair to hang loosely over the blemishes. Then they walked to the Harts' front door.

The braid was still so tight a half hour later that Catherine's forehead ached from her eyebrows being lifted up her face, and she imagined she must look extremely surprised. This was confirmed with a glance at herself in the mirror above the fireplace once inside the opulent town house.

Since the train ride, her mind was on her journal, which was locked in a cabinet in her parents' house. The first thing she'd do when she left this awkward meeting would be to find a more secure place to keep it.

"Do you like cars?" Archie asked. He was standing with her at the window while their parents poured tea in the seating area at the center of the room.

The room itself was large and grand, with a fireplace at either end and a high ceiling covered in a mural of the sky. The tall windows gave views of other grand London homes and the park that began at the end of the street. Yet despite its expensive and pedigreed bones, the house had an air of shabbiness. The Harts were not as well off as they'd once been. If they had been, Catherine guessed, there would be no need to marry their son off into a family as odd as the Renarts.

Catherine brought her eyes back to Archie. He was, unfortunately, as handsome as Anna had said. That hadn't been an exaggeration, and Catherine found herself resenting Archie for this. He had reddish-brown hair, slightly too long, in Catherine's opinion, but it framed a face with a fine mix of features, including brown eyes that nearly matched his hair, and lips that, irritatingly, kept drawing her attention. He wore dress trousers and a sweater that seemed tailored expressly to set off the muscles of his shoulders and arms. He was older than she was by a few years, but he was a child.

Arrogant, she thought, *and vain. Perfect for Anna.*

Immediately she regretted that thought. She didn't want to feel contempt for her dead sister.

"Cars?" she repeated.

"I rebuild vintage cars and motorbikes," he said. "I could show them to you sometime. I think you'd like them."

"Why would you think that?" she asked, taking a sip of her tea.

The drink was scalding and burned her entire mouth. It took an enormous effort to act as though nothing had happened.

"Well—they're beautiful," Archie said, his eyes lighting up on this topic. "Some of the cars from last century are works of art."

"I've hardly been in a car for three years," she told him. "There weren't any on the estate."

"So you'd appreciate them even more, don't you think?" he asked, refusing to be discouraged.

"I took the Tube here," she said, as though that put a definitive end to the subject.

She took another sip of tea. It had cooled off slightly, but since her mouth was already burned, it seemed just as hot. She wasn't entirely successful at hiding her discomfort this time. Archie glanced at her tea and at the expression on her face but made no comment. His father had surely ordered him to make friends with her, just as her mother and father had ordered her to be pleasant to him.

Then, with a sudden stab of dread, she worried he might have been looking at the bruises on her jaw. She shook her head inconspicuously, trying to get her hair to cover them up again.

"So you've never been to a proper school, then?" he asked. "Just the estate in Scotland I keep hearing about?"

"A proper school?" Catherine repeated, unable to keep the annoyance out of her voice. "The estate is a proper school, actually. We did learn things there."

"Of course, I didn't mean—"

"We just had . . . a lot more athletics than a typical school."

"Anna told me that," he said. Then he seemed to regret mentioning Catherine's dead sister. He looked trapped, but he recovered gamely. "What—what sort of sports do you do? I'm a bit of a sportsman myself—boxing."

He mimed throwing a couple of punches, in an obvious bid to draw attention to his muscles. She turned her eyes away to watch her mother complimenting Archie's father, Gavin, on the quality of his tea service.

"Fencing mostly," she said in answer to Archie's question. "And running. Some martial arts. Boxing is—well, it seems rather easy when there are so many rules, doesn't it? In a real fight, your opponent would throw his elbow into your throat if it gave him an advantage."

"Boxing—easy?" Archie asked, clearly irked, despite his efforts to put up with her. His teacup landed back in its saucer a little too vigorously. He forced his voice down. "Do you think it's easy, taking a full punch in the face?"

"Isn't the point to avoid getting punched?" she asked. "If you're any good."

"It doesn't always work out that way, does it? Do you always avoid getting hit when you fence?"

"No, not always," she admitted, in a tone calculated to let him know that she hardly ever took a hit. Of course this wasn't true, but then the word "fence" was ridiculous when applied to the kind of fighting they did on the estate.

"Sometimes you have to take a punch in order to deliver another," he told her. "Sometimes that's strategy. And you have to be willing to be hit."

Catherine was thinking of herself on the floor of the washroom in Hong Kong, letting that mystery Seeker hit her so she could get the glass into her hands. Archie was right, of course.

"Is that what you're doing here, with me?" she asked with barely concealed malice. "Taking a hit for your family?"

He smiled at her, a cold smile that showed his patience coming to an end. Very deliberately he set his tea on a side table, balled his hands into fists, and took a boxer's stance.

"Are you going to punch me?" she asked with interest as she took another sip of her tea. Still too hot. Why did she keep drinking it? "Should I put down my cup so it doesn't get broken?"

He took the teacup out of her hands himself and set it aside. He was like a big, stupid child, she thought. He had no idea what it meant to really fight. He'd only ever done play-fighting in his life. He wouldn't last a day on the estate.

"Hit me," he said, resuming his boxing stance.

Catherine didn't have to be asked twice. She struck out at his stomach with her fist, and it connected.

She'd hit him fairly hard, but her hand encountered the taut muscle of someone who'd practiced taking punches from much larger opponents. At once his own fist was coming at her jaw, not to hit her—she could tell by the trajectory that he didn't mean to actually strike—but to illustrate his point.

Catherine couldn't help herself. She twisted to the side so his fist ended up nowhere near her face. Even in play she didn't want him to think she would stand there and be smacked.

She threw another punch at his ribs, intending to hit him a little harder than before. But this time he too twisted out of the way. He was faster than she'd expected. And he was smiling at her, like he was pleased with the speed of her reflexes. That was annoying—he wasn't good enough to pass judgment on her fighting skills.

He threw another punch at her face. She ducked it and aimed an uppercut at his jaw, even harder this time. But he'd ducked away before her blow could land.

He took another swing, fast and sharp, trying to show her that he could beat her when he wanted, but Catherine caught his wrist and pulled, twisting him in front of her. She lifted an elbow to slam it down into his neck as he passed by . . .

All three parents were staring across the room at the two of them. Catherine saw frank horror on her mother's face, embarrassment on her father's. Archie's father seemed amused, but concerned that Catherine might be injured—she read clearly on Gavin Hart's face that he would be very disappointed if something happened to this girl as well.

She grabbed Archie's arm to help him upright. They were clasping each other's forearms for a moment, and she thought he looked pleased again. *What's he so happy about?* she wondered. *I could have beaten him easily.*

She and Archie picked up their teacups and turned their backs on their parents so they would stop staring.

"Of course, it's better to avoid a punch if you can," Archie said quietly as he looked out the window with her. His breath was coming faster. "I imagine it's the same in fencing."

"Imagine all you like," she said, her voice soft but full of venom. She was angry at him, and at herself as well, because she was still looking at his lips. "It's not as though you'd ever be good enough to really fight me."

All the way home, Catherine listened to her mother and her grandmother Maggie, who'd come to pick them up, explain the many benefits of a match between her and Archibald Hart, and the reasons why she should attempt to behave without open savagery the next time they met.

Catherine hated these lectures, but this time it was easy to tune out the cascade of advice and admonitions.

" . . . it's simply more secure, if you're part of a family that attracts attention," Maggie was saying. "They may be past their prime, but the Harts are still a family that newspapers care about. There's safety in that. In case you hadn't noticed, Seekers tend to disappear. If you're married into the Harts, you're not going to disappear without someone noticing."

"Shouldn't we try to fix the *reason* Seekers are attacking each other, instead of accepting that's just the way things are?" Catherine asked her grandmother.

Maggie ignored her. "Catherine," she said, "you want to use your family's athame, don't you?"

"Yes," Catherine said, turning to her grandmother. Defiantly she added, "And not for money, or power, or my personal safety. I want to use it as a real Seeker, to make good things happen."

"All right, you have your dreams," Maggie said, ignoring Catherine's mother, who scoffed under her breath. "Now protect those dreams. Archie's family will help you do that. And you can use the athame to help them."

Catherine nodded and let her gaze wander outside the window of the taxi. It had started to rain. London was gray and wet and ancient.

She saw the view only superficially. She was thinking of that pleased look on Archie's face and wondering what, exactly, it had meant.

CHAPTER 28

NOTT

The four Watchers moved in the darkness with only Nott's lantern to light their way.

"You led us into that fight," Geb said. "You distracted us."

It took Nott a few moments to understand what Geb was saying, because he was speaking so quickly, but anyway it was the same thing Geb had said a dozen times already—that Nott and Wilkin had tricked them into a losing fight with Quin, that Nott and Wilkin had diverted them from their master's orders.

"She had his athame and our helm," Nott responded sluggishly, even though he knew Geb was right.

"Useless, you are," Geb muttered. "I bet you can't even count all the way up to two hundred on your own."

Hearing his own voice as though from far away, Nott said, "We got you, didn't we? Without us, you'd still be sleeping here." Nott didn't feel it was important to mention that he did, in fact, have trouble counting to two hundred all on his own. That was none of Geb's business.

"Shut it, Nott," Wilkin whispered at the speed of a snail. "We're almost there."

Nott fell silent. His hands gripped the lantern's handle tightly, and in the lantern's light, he could see the four of them—himself, Wilkin, Geb, and Balil—moving through the darkness *There*. They were all cut and swollen. Nott had so many bruises on his face, he could feel it puffed into strange shapes; his knuckles and chest were so sore it was hard to move. The others had makeshift bandages over shallow whipsword slashes on their shoulders, and beneath these were ugly seams where they'd sewn each other up.

"Here they are." That was Geb speaking, and he was nudging Nott to hold the lantern higher.

Nott responded after a few moments. His mind was fuzzy and his arms and legs seemed to be swimming through the waters of Loch Tarm. As he raised the lantern, he became aware of two figures standing perfectly still in front of them. More Watchers.

"Let's not stand here and stare," Balil said slowly. "Let's get back. I already feel strange."

"Wait here," Geb ordered. "I'm getting the other things we need."

Geb disappeared farther into the darkness, the lantern's light glinting dully off the helm on his head and licking at hidden forms rising in the black. Geb was now in among those forms, searching for something. But Nott couldn't focus. He was stretching out.

"Should we leave the runts here?" Geb asked. He was back. Nott had lost track of time, and somehow Geb was already back.

"Might as well," Balil said, his words as sluggish as Nott's own breathing.

Were they really planning to leave him here? Nott wondered, though the thought seemed distant and unimportant. No, they were only taunting him; Geb was already hitting the athame and lightning rod together and carving a new anomaly back into the world. The edges solidified, and Nott could see their broken fortress through the hole, illuminated by a waning moon that hung behind its turret.

They didn't let Nott pick up the sleeping Watchers. Wilkin and Geb and Balil did that without him.

"Hold the light steady, runt!" Geb ordered.

Carrying their new comrades, the Watchers stepped across the anomaly and into the shallow waters of the lake. Nott stumbled through after them.

An hour later, the new arrivals were still lying on the floor of Dun Tarm in awkward, stiff poses, staring blindly up at the night sky. It might be hours yet before they began to breathe and move normally again.

Nott hugged his knees to his chest and studied the faces of the two newcomers. They weren't what he'd expected. They were scrawny and spotty, and hardly older than Nott himself. *Is that what I look like when I'm frozen* There? Nott wondered. *Is this what my master sees when he comes to wake us for our turn in the world, our turn to look out for him?*

But these boys did not really look like him. They were dressed, in the way of all Watchers, in gray wool, but their clothes were much newer than Nott's, as though their master had found them somewhere just a few years ago. Their eyes were open and staring, and one of them wore spectacles.

Nott's mind had gotten lost *There,* and it was only now coming back. He asked suddenly, "Why did we get only two Watchers? We were supposed to get all of them."

"Yes," Geb said. "Eventually." His eyes flicked to his partner, Balil, who nodded encouragingly.

"Eventually?" Nott asked. He looked back to the frozen newcomers. "But . . . why did you pick these two? Who are they?"

"I don't know their names," Geb said defensively.

"But—but are they indeed Watchers?" Nott asked.

"They are training to be Watchers. Just as you did once. Just as we all did."

"Training?" Nott asked. "So they're not full Watchers?"

"Not yet."

"But—what about our orders!" He bared his teeth at Geb.

"We will follow them," Geb assured him. "Very soon."

Nott cried, "Soon? That's what Wilkin has been saying all along. 'Soon.'" He got to his feet and tried to look menacing, even though he was the smallest of them. "You beat us for not following the plan."

Geb got to his feet, from which position he towered over Nott's head. He pushed Nott back onto the cold stones of the fortress floor.

"We *will*!" he said angrily. "But you've lost your helm, haven't you? And that girl has our master's athame. And you've already wasted weeks. Even if we obey our master's orders, even if we find him— *when* we find him—he'll be angry."

Balil was nodding. "It's your fault, Nott, but . . . he might see it as our fault too. The lost helm, the delay. We're the oldest. He'll be angriest at us."

Geb gestured at the new, still frozen boys. "These Watchers will help us find the girl. And when we find her, we'll get our master's athame back—*and* your helm. *Then* we'll wake the others, *then* we'll search every inch of the darkness and find our master. He will have no reason to send any of us to our caves. Especially not me. All will be well."

Nott looked from Geb to Balil to Wilkin. All three seemed satisfied with this plan.

"But . . ."

"Sit down," Geb ordered, not meeting Nott's eyes. "That's enough from you."

Nott sat and stared at his feet. Every Watcher was so terrified of being disciplined he was determined to prove he was better than all the others. Their master had been so arbitrary and secretive about his punishment that no Watcher was certain what would draw his anger or what penalty he would exact. The Watchers themselves were one of their master's biggest secrets, but he was full of so many other secrets that Nott sometimes wondered if the man was built of them. *If you removed his cloak and his clothing and boots, would there be anything inside? Or is he filled with the smoke of his own hidden plans? If you pierced him, would those secrets leak out into the world?*

"These are new ones," Balil explained, pointing at the frozen Watchers, "from just a few years ago." He chucked a stone at the frozen boys, and it bounced off one of their faces. Ever so subtly, their bodies were beginning to soften—arms slowly relaxing, legs straightening out against the floor.

"They'll know how to use computers!" Wilkin said in a burst of understanding. "They'll use them to lead us to Quin?"

"Aye," said Geb. "They'll know the modern ways." He gave one of the boys a swift, hard kick. "Hurry up and come awake, will you?"

"And those?" Nott asked.

Behind Balil were two disruptors Geb had retrieved when he'd run off into the darkness *There*. The metal weapons gleamed with faint iridescence in the night's glow.

"When we find her, we've got to scare her, haven't we?" Geb asked. "I don't know about you, Nott, but I don't fancy being cut by her whipsword again if I can avoid it. We'll scare her into giving up the athame and the helm."

"Look!" Wilkin said excitedly.

One of the frozen boys had blinked, very slowly.

CHAPTER 29

SHINOBU

The hospital basement smelled of death and disinfectant. Dark shapes of gurneys and old medical machinery loomed up around Shinobu. The anomaly he'd created had already fallen shut, but its residual tremor was alive in the room, and equipment vibrated around him. It was well past midnight, the heart of the graveyard shift, and except for rattling pipes and the buzz of fluorescent lighting fixtures, the hospital was quiet as he crept into the hallway.

He'd woken in the middle of the night, curled up next to Quin, but all he'd been able to think about was the focal. No, all he'd been able to think about were the secrets the focal had whispered to him while he was wearing it—the boys who'd attacked them, the athame of the Dreads, Catherine's journal. But more than all these things was the Middle Dread himself. It was as if the focal knew the Middle Dread, and the voice Shinobu kept hearing, just out of earshot, belonged to him.

When he'd woken, he remembered that Quin hadn't hidden the helmet yet. She'd only tossed it into the closet before they fell asleep.

He'd shaken her shoulder and whispered, "Quin, wake up, please! I'm going to put it on, and I don't want to put it on."

Quin was so deeply asleep she didn't feel or hear him. He shook her harder, and said, more loudly, "Please, Quin. Wake up! Stop me!"

She came half-awake and turned toward him in the bed. In the pale light through the window he saw her dark eyes flutter open between locks of her hair.

"Are you all right?" she whispered.

He wasn't able to answer her, because something very bad happened. As he looked at Quin's face, still mostly asleep, he didn't see Quin at all. All at once she didn't look like the girl he loved, the girl he'd grown up with, the girl he'd give his life for. He saw her differently: she was a Seeker who thought only of herself and her house, at the expense of anyone else, at the expense of more important plans; she would use Shinobu and then discard him . . . unless he stopped her.

When she put a sleepy hand on his cheek, it was like an enemy touching him, and he recoiled.

He knew straightaway that the focal had changed the way he saw her. It had twisted something in his mind.

I don't think that, he told himself, lying in the bed next to her. *I don't think that. I love Quin. I love her.*

He closed his eyes tight, and when he opened them, the evil vision was gone. Quin had fallen back asleep, her hand tucked comfortably between his jaw and his neck, her hair messy and everywhere, her breathing soft and even. She was Quin again, she was his.

But the memory of that other vision lay upon him like a heavy stone. What if it came back? What if he had no control over it next time? He never wanted to look at Quin that way again.

He got out of bed, grabbed up the athame, and then took the focal from Quin's closet. It required all of his resolve not to pull the helmet onto his head, but he stuffed it into the backpack instead, along with the athame; then he pulled on his boots and quietly left the house.

When he wore the focal, he saw the outlines of something grand and disturbing. Sometimes he thought there was a way to do what Quin hoped to do—understand when and why Seekers had changed—and he also thought, maybe, there was a way to have a measure of control over the future, to stop being victims of others' greedy designs, as he and Quin had been since their earliest childhood.

But the Middle Dread was at the heart of this feeling. The Middle Dread was *in* the focal somehow. Shinobu knew of one person, still alive, who'd been on good terms with the Middle. That was Briac Kincaid. Shinobu had seen their close ties on the estate before he'd taken his oath, and he'd seen them fighting in unison on *Traveler*, before the Young Dread killed the Middle.

It had taken Shinobu some time to locate Briac, but at last he'd tracked him here, to this hospital on the outskirts of London. And now Shinobu had arrived. He was coming to speak to Briac.

He found the stairs at the end of the basement hall and began climbing.

The stairwell was badly lit, and Shinobu was just able to make out the signs posted at each floor. He exited at the third floor and moved cautiously into a brightly lit corridor. He soon discovered there was little need for stealth. With only one exception, the night nurses and orderlies were huddled around a gaming screen, playing an online role-playing game in their messy break room. The exception was a large, unshaven orderly who was sound asleep on a gurney at the end of the hall, wrapped in a fog of beer fumes. Shinobu stepped past the man into the mental ward for adult males.

The smell inside was awful. It took his eyes a few moments to adjust to the interior of the ward. It was a bright night outside, but the only windows here were tiny and high up in the wall, covered with black mesh screens that filtered out most of the city lights. The walls were possibly a shade of gray in daylight, but now they were a ghostly green, fading into shadows in every corner and beneath each of the old metal beds.

There were twelve beds in the room, all of them occupied. Dark shapes lay beneath the government-issued blankets, some turning fitfully, some lying as still as corpses.

A curtain had been drawn around one of the beds to separate it from the others, and beyond it Shinobu glimpsed flashes of multi-colored light. A moment later, he was inside the curtain with a hand over Briac Kincaid's mouth, shaking him awake.

Briac's eyes snapped open. They were wild and unfocused, but when they eventually settled upon Shinobu, a look of pure terror overtook him. Briac whimpered and writhed against the leather restraints that held him to the bed.

Was it Shinobu's imagination, or were the sparks around the man's head brighter than they'd been before? In the dim light, they spun across Briac's face like angry fireflies.

"Shhh! I'm not here to hurt you," Shinobu whispered, but Briac showed no sign of understanding.

Shinobu took the focal out of his pack and held it up for the man to see. Briac's eyes latched on to the helmet immediately, and when Shinobu's intention became clear, Briac stopped whimpering and fell silent. An eager, greedy look came into his eyes.

With the focal in his hands, Shinobu felt an almost irresistible urge to put it on his own head. Its absence had left him with a deep mental ache, as though a piece of himself had been removed and he desperately needed it back to feel whole again. He licked his lips, forced his arms to move, and pushed the focal onto Briac's head. Then he sank into a metal folding chair next to the bed, sat on his hands to stop them from shaking, and waited.

Briac's thoughts had been scrambled by the disruptor sparks, but the focal, Shinobu was certain, would unscramble them—at least for a time. He'd seen it happen in the woods in Hong Kong, when Briac had taken the helmet from the first two boys. And he'd felt it happen in his own mind. The focal had made things clear.

Briac had stopped struggling. His eyes were closed and his body was relaxed beneath the restraints, except for the occasional twitch. He was unwinding himself within the helmet.

As the minutes passed, Shinobu fell into a half doze. He forced his eyes open when he heard motion, a skittering sound beneath a cot on the other side of the room. Small, clawed feet were running across the floor tiles. Was it a rat? The hospital was dirty enough for rats, or mice, or cockroaches. *A rat would be the best.* He could play with it—hurt it even—while he was waiting for Briac to open his eyes. *A really fat one would be good. They squeal the loudest—*

Briac was stirring. The disruptor sparks orbited his head now in lazy sweeps, much calmer than they'd been when Shinobu arrived; the focal had brought them into some kind of order.

"Electricity," Briac said at length, his eyes coming open to stare at the dark ceiling. His voice was raspy, as though he'd spent days in silence.

"What?" Shinobu asked.

"Doctors. Sparks. They . . . can't figure them out." He nodded weakly toward the medical equipment arrayed around the head of his bed.

Shinobu noticed a device with foam-padded electrodes sitting on the other side of Briac's cot. With an unpleasant start, he understood that this apparatus was designed to deliver an electric shock to a patient's brain. The doctors in this dirty, state-funded hospital had seen the sparks around Briac's head and had dug up an ancient electrical contraption to see what would happen. That explained why the sparks looked brighter. As much as he disliked Briac Kincaid, the thought made Shinobu shudder.

"Couldn't put two thoughts together," Briac muttered. "Or even one thought. I want to kill them, kill them, kill—"

"And can you put two thoughts together now?" Shinobu asked, cutting him off before he could begin to rant. The rainbow flashes gyrated more violently the moment Briac's thoughts strayed.

"Yes," Briac whispered. "You always come through for me, Alistair."

"I have questions," Shinobu said. He turned the man's head to face him. "I am a sworn Seeker. You must answer my questions. Or I could be justified in getting rid of you."

That was a bond, a law, between Seekers—whatever Seeker knowledge one had been taught must be shared with any other sworn Seeker who asked. Shinobu hoped Briac would honor this, if only out of fear for his life.

Briac laughed harshly. "I've never hidden anything from you, Alistair."

"I'm not Alistair. I'm Shinobu."

"Alistair, Shinobu, Fiona. Redheaded fools. Born to follow. I can say anything, anything at all, and you swallow it."

Maybe the focal was working too well—bringing Briac's true self to the surface, unvarnished. Shinobu wasn't prepared for his own reaction; he imagined his hands sliding up to Briac's neck and choking the life out of him. It would be easy—Briac was strapped to the bed—and more satisfying than hurting a rat.

Shinobu stopped the twitching of his hands toward Briac's throat and said, "I want to talk about the Middle Dread."

Briac's dark eyes came into focus. "That's not a question about Seeker knowledge. My oaths don't bind me to answer that."

"All right." Shinobu reached for the focal as if to pull it off.

"No!" the man said quickly, twisting as far away as he could, which was not very far owing to his restraints. "No, please. I will answer. I knew the Middle Dread . . . maybe better than other Seekers knew him."

"Tell me about those boys of his. I've seen them twice now."

Briac said, "They found me here. Took me away and hit me, in Hong Kong and on the estate. They hit me, they hit me! Disgusting boys, disgusting—"

"Stop," Shinobu said, putting a hand heavily on the man's shoulder to settle him.

Briac made an attempt to control himself. "And then they put me back here," he went on, "and the doctors were angry I'd escaped—"

"What did the Middle use them for?" Shinobu asked, cutting Briac off with another firm press on his shoulder.

"He called them his Watchers. What do they watch? Him? Us? Us?" Briac was losing the thread of coherence again.

"How many of them are there?" Shinobu asked.

Briac shook his head. "Lots, maybe. Lots! I don't know, don't know, don't—"

"But you know about the focal?" Shinobu asked, trying a different topic, hoping the man would calm down.

Briac collected himself. "I used it as a boy," he said. "My father stole one and had it for a time. And *he* let me use another one. Briefly. He handed out favors like that. For a moment, and then you never knew what would happen. A knife in your back, a reward, a sudden fight with someone who'd been your friend, torture. Anything, anything at all. I had him under control only because I stole Catherine's journal and hid it from him. Blackmail. He was desperate to get it back, and treated me well. He was worried the Old Dread would read it, learn what he'd done . . ."

Briac's eyes had drifted away, and the sparks swirled more

vigorously around his face. Shinobu took hold of the man's chin and forced him to make eye contact.

"The Middle Dread. *He* let you use a focal. *He* handed out favors. *He* was scared of the journal. *He* was planning . . . big things."

Briac nodded carefully. "When he let me wear the focal, he was wrong, wrong—" his voice rose, but when he noticed the look on Shinobu's face, he reined himself in and whispered conspiratorially, "It was a mistake, letting me use it. Because he's *in* the focal. I *saw* things he was planning."

"I might see them too."

"And he told me things . . ."

"Tell me what he told you and what you saw," Shinobu ordered.

Briac's eyes snapped back to his. He pressed his lips together as though to seal them, and shook his head.

Shinobu reached for the helmet, and the man's dark eyes locked fearfully onto Shinobu's hovering hands. He began to mutter curses and threats, but these seemed to fall from his mouth automatically, with no real thought behind them. The disruptor sparks were dancing wildly.

"It's all I have left," Briac whispered. His eyes were pleading as he watched Shinobu's hands get closer to the focal. "It's all I have—Stop! If I tell you, maybe you and I can follow what we saw in the focal together? Help each other."

"Like you and my father helped each other?" Shinobu asked coldly.

"We've always looked out for one another, Alistair," Briac said.

"How did you keep him loyal to you all those years?"

"You'd broken so many laws already, Alistair," Briac said. "What other Seeker would partner with you?"

"You tricked him into killing."

"You liked killing," Briac said, something of his old nature coming back into his voice. "You were so good at it."

"He never liked it." The thought of his father enjoying a kill enraged Shinobu, and again he imagined his own hands around Briac's throat. It would take only a minute or two, a minor struggle, a few muffled cries. "You made him a killer, you told him he could never be anything else, you took him from Mariko."

"Yes," agreed Briac, his expression brightening, "all of those things."

"The Middle Dread," Shinobu prompted. "If you want to keep wearing the focal."

The expression on Briac's face became awful, as though telling Shinobu any more would kill him, but the promise of keeping the focal on his head, even for a few minutes, won out in the end. He started to speak in a low whisper, as though the words were too precious to scatter about loudly:

"The Watchers are his . . . bodyguards. No, no, no, wrong word, wrong word—" Shinobu gripped Briac's shoulder, hoping to help him focus. Briac gathered himself and continued, "They watch for him. One pair is always awake in the world, waiting for his signals, checking on him. But there are more, hidden *There*. If something happens to the Middle, the Watchers look for him here in the world, and they also know how to look for him *There*. If Quin hadn't found the Middle and me, lost in the blackness after the attack on the estate, his Watchers would have come for him eventually. So he can never be lost or trapped *There* for long."

The words flowed from him smoothly, as if he had, perhaps, committed this explanation to memory years ago and was now reeling it off by rote.

"But he's dead," Shinobu said. "The Young Dread killed the Middle on the airship. If they're looking for him now, they'll never find him."

Briac looked tormented, as if he were waging, and losing, a fierce internal battle not to speak. "I promise you they don't know that!" he said at last, the words tearing from him. "They have no idea he's dead. They're waiting for him to use them for their real purpose."

"What's their real purpose?"

Through gritted teeth, Briac answered, "Getting rid . . . of us."

"Getting rid of Seekers?" Shinobu repeated.

"He's been whittling down our numbers decade by decade," Briac whispered. His face was red with the effort of speaking against his will. This information, Shinobu understood, was a treasure Briac had been hoarding to himself for a very long time.

"The Middle Dread has been getting rid of Seekers? Recently?" Shinobu repeated again, trying to grasp why and how this would be.

"He's been getting rid of us for a long time."

"That can't be right," Shinobu responded, almost to himself. The Dreads weren't meant to interact with Seekers unless meting out justice or giving them their oaths. "There are entries in the journal that mention him killing Seekers—but that was centuries ago, and anyway the Old Dread stopped him—"

"Stupid!" Briac cried suddenly. "You deserve to be slapped, kicked, hit, hit, hit—"

"Stop!" Shinobu dug his fingers into the man's arm.

Briac closed his eyes for a time. When he opened them again, he took a breath and said, so quietly Shinobu could scarcely make out the words, "He wants us gone."

"He—"

"He turns us against one another. We kill each other *for* him. Sometimes we sign our killings with the emblems of other houses, to make Seekers take revenge on each other—to confuse them, to misdirect them. Maybe he gives us something in return. And the Seekers who help him think they're the only ones, his favorites, safe. Until someone comes after them."

Shinobu was silent as he tried to digest this statement. If the Middle Dread had been turning Seekers against each other . . . all at once a host of things made sense—the isolation and emptiness of the estate; the vacant apprentice cabins that had once been full; Briac's and Alistair's silence about other Seeker houses; Briac's possession of the fox athame, even though it rightly belonged to John's family; even the cruel, murderous use to which Briac had been putting that fox athame.

"Why would he do that?" Shinobu said at last. "Why would he want Seekers to kill each other?"

He watched the strained workings of Briac's facial muscles. At last the man said, "When there are so few of us left that we'll be easily disposed of, the Middle and his Watchers will put a final end to us."

"He wants to put an end to us . . . because Seekers have been breaking the Seeker laws?" Shinobu asked at last.

Briac laughed, an unpleasant chuckle that quickly turned into something high and frightening. "He doesn't care about the laws. He wants what Seekers have—our artifacts, our athames, our tools. He wants to control them . . ."

"*Why?*" Shinobu asked. "He's already a Dread. He already has every—"

"Why? *Why?* If *he* has control, no one else does . . ." Briac was panting as the sparks circulated riotously around his head, accelerating.

"Explain that," Shinobu said.

Briac took several shuddering breaths, attempting to quiet his thoughts. "He has his reasons, reasons, good reasons or bad reasons . . . How can I know them? It's between him and the Old Dread. Those two . . . He *hates* the Old, always eavesdropping on his mind, seeing what the Middle does, punishing him when he does wrong. This is how he gets out from under the Old Dread's control . . ."

Briac's mind had scattered again, and the sparks were not settling down. He was closing his eyes tight, trying to hold on to the threads of thought. It was a long time before he spoke again: "I don't know his reasons, but the Middle wants to tear down everything the old man built."

"You mean—it's *us* he's going to tear down? Seekers?"

"It's us," Briac agreed. "Unless"—the words were coming, though he tried to stop them—"unless we are clever enough to change our own fate."

"But his plan failed," Shinobu said quietly.

"Did it?"

"The Middle Dread is dead."

"Yes," Briac whispered, "and the Watchers don't know it yet. They are waiting for someone to command them."

He took several slow breaths. Then he began to speak again, this time without any prompting, as though, despite the cherished value of his hidden knowledge, it was an immense relief to share it with someone else at last.

"While the Middle was getting rid of Seekers, he was hoarding things, keeping them *There* . . ." Briac began, and as he spoke, Shinobu cradled his own head in his hands, letting Briac's words—some coherent, some not—flow over him.

Shinobu tried to catch hold of what made sense, such as when Briac explained about two hundred and about the real use of the focal and about a stone medallion, and he tried to ignore what sounded insane, such as Seekers justifiably killing each other's families, and an Old Dread who was simply a flawed, aging man, too trusting and often wrong.

In the end, he'd heard enough to form a sort of plan.

CHAPTER 30

SHINOBU

The hospital storage room stank of dirty clothing, mildewed paper, and something sweet and sour, like apples that had been left to rot. And rats. He could smell them, and he could hear them scurrying across shelves and inside the walls. If there had been one rat back in the ward, this room was their home base.

Shinobu had put the focal back into the backpack. It hadn't been easy getting it off Briac; the man had started crying and thrashing. Once the helmet was off, however, the disruptor sparks surrounding Briac's head had immediately spun out of control, his thoughts had scattered, and his cries had quickly dwindled to incoherent mumbles as Shinobu slipped out.

It hadn't been easy to keep the focal off his own head either. Shinobu had crept down the hall and into the storage room, but all the while he kept imagining the cool touch of the helmet between his hands and the electric joining of it with his mind.

But he did not put it on.

He had the answer Quin was looking for. He knew why Seekers had changed. They'd changed because the Middle Dread had turned them against each other. They'd changed because the Middle was trying to destroy all of them, while cleverly covering his tracks.

Now the Middle was dead, but those boys—the Watchers—were still out there. And the Middle had had other tools as well. One of the Middle's tools was right here in this storage room.

Quin wanted to make things right, to figure out what Seekers should be. And Shinobu wanted to protect Quin. So, what if . . . what if he took control of all the Middle's tools, including the Watchers?

Shinobu assessed the shelves before him. Patients' belongings had been thrown into cardboard boxes that had been stacked haphazardly. It looked like the shelves had been ransacked repeatedly by hospital staff looking for valuables. The newer boxes were mostly intact, though—maybe the staff waited awhile before robbing their patients.

Something brushed against Shinobu's fingers as he searched for the right box. Instead of drawing back in disgust, in a strange surge of curiosity, he thrust his hand forward and caught something warm and furry—a small black-and-white rat with a long tail and tiny eyes that gleamed wetly. It twisted frantically in his grasp to try to bite him, and without thinking, Shinobu smacked it against the metal shelf. The animal went limp, but he could still feel its heart beating rapidly, see its small chest moving. *It will be good for a while,* he thought, stuffing the creature into a loose pocket of his jacket.

When he finally located Briac's box, he pulled it down and opened it to find only a few items inside: a long dark cloak, boots, and a coiled whipsword. He was amazed the sword hadn't been stolen, but then it wouldn't work for anyone but Briac, so it would have appeared to be a fairly useless object—a coiled whip that refused to uncoil.

He tucked the whipsword into his largest jacket pocket, then set about searching Briac's cloak, methodically turning each pocket inside out. But all were empty. Had Briac lied to him? Shinobu was about to stuff the cloak back into the box, when a trailing edge of the garment hit the floor with a muted thump.

A small, hard object had been sewn inside a fold of wool at the edge of the cloak. Shinobu could feel it by sticking a finger through the stitching. He tore the seam open, and the object fell out into his hand. It was a finely shaped stone medallion. It fit easily into his palm. In fact it seemed meant to do so.

Shinobu held it up to look at it carefully. Even in the low light he recognized the carving on its face immediately—three interlocking ovals, a simple representation of an atom. It was the same design on the pommel of the athame tucked into his waistband. It was the symbol of the Dreads. The back of the medallion, at first glance, was flat and smooth, but as he tilted it, he saw dozens of faint scars in the stone.

According to Briac, he'd stolen this medallion from the Middle during the fight on *Traveler*. It was an object all Watchers would recognize as belonging to their master. And since their master was dead, the possessor of this medallion could *become* their master. That had been Briac's plan, though he was far too crazy now to see it through.

Shinobu slipped the stone disk into a pocket and carefully buttoned the pocket shut.

The rat had awakened. It was turning itself in circles inside Shinobu's coat, looking for the exit. *I don't want Quin to see it,* he thought. *She wouldn't understand.* She would already be upset by him leaving in the night. He didn't want to upset her further with rats. He pulled the animal out by its tail and held it in front of his face, watching it twist and turn as it tried to bite him. Suddenly the idea of having a rat in his possession seemed odd. He threw the creature onto the floor and let it scurry off.

"That was strange," he whispered aloud.

Shinobu drew out his athame and set the dials. He was going back to Quin to apologize and to make new plans. Now that he understood what the Middle had intended, he and Quin could take control.

CHAPTER 31

CATHERINE

19 YEARS EARLIER

The courtyard adjacent to the large house was narrow and dimly lit by lanterns that cast a flickering glow like the dance of real flames. A tangle of flowering vines climbed one of the brick walls, providing plenty of places for someone to hide.

The motorbike was parked on the cobblestones in a shadowed corner of the yard, the rider's helmet sitting proprietarily between the handlebars, waiting for its owner to return.

Catherine stood with her back against the brick wall, concealed in the shadows of the overgrown vines. She looked across the court-yard at the house, which rose four stories, tall and expensive and old. There was the window where she and Archie had stood together drinking tea. God, he'd annoyed her.

It was hard to say exactly why she was here now, and yet here she was. She'd dressed herself differently this time, in a leather jacket over close-fitting dark clothing, like a Seeker who had joined a motor-cycle gang.

After a long while, Archie came out of the house. He looked irritated in the way Catherine guessed she must also look irritated after spending time with her parents. Archie had only his father, but Catherine guessed that Gavin Hart was as difficult as two or three parents.

The night was cold, but he was in shirtsleeves as he jogged down the steps from the side door. Only when he approached his bike did he pull on his jacket. It bothered Catherine immensely that she noticed a host of physical details about him without trying: the way his hair flopped down loosely after he ran his hands through it, the flex of his shoulders and arms as he slipped into his jacket.

For God's sake, Catherine, she thought, *pull yourself together.*

Archie turned back to the house as he zipped up his jacket, and she used that moment to step from the shadows. She silently walked over and was leaning against the seat of his motorcycle when he turned around.

Archie jumped when he saw her, but he recovered quickly. His expression became unreadable as he studied her.

"You look different," he said cautiously.

"My mother dressed me last time," she told him.

"And who dressed you this time? Satan?"

"Is it bad?" she asked. "My friend Mariko isn't here to help, and I don't know anything about styles."

"No, it's not bad," he said, in a tone of voice that told her she looked anything but bad. Then, in a friendly way, he asked, "Are you here to beat me up?"

"That would be too easy," she responded immediately. The words flowed from her naturally, as though she were practiced at flirting, when in fact this was the first time she'd ever heard that particular tone in her own voice. "Not worth the trip."

He laughed and Catherine was vexed by how much she enjoyed the sound of his laughter. He leaned against the other side of the bike seat so his shoulder was almost touching hers, though they were facing in opposite directions.

"You know, I'm actually a good fighter," he said seriously. "I'm not as foolish as you think I am, Catherine Renart."

"I know you're not." She did know it. She'd even known it the first time they met.

She was looking away from him, at the lanterns and their real-seeming flames. The question she wanted to ask was hard to bring to the surface. Archie sensed she was about to speak and stayed silent, waiting.

"Why did you look at me that way?" she asked at last.

"You mean the way I looked when you nearly knocked me out in front of my father?" He said it as though the moment had been frozen in his mind just as it had been frozen in hers.

Catherine nodded.

He said, "I was thinking, *She handles herself better than any girl I've ever met. It's too bad she despises me, because this is the luckiest I've felt in ages.*"

Catherine had convinced herself she had no idea how he would answer her question, but when she heard his words, she realized she'd known all along. She'd seen those thoughts written clearly on his face when they'd met in his father's grand living room. She looked down at the sleeves of her jacket, so like the sleeves of Archie's jacket, now that she was paying attention. She'd found the jacket and put it on for him. That was the truth, if she were willing to admit it.

"I didn't want to like you," she whispered.

"I didn't want to like you either," he said quietly.

"You were meant for my sister," she said. "You're my parents' choice."

He let his shoulder brush against hers. "Yes. I hate that too." They were quiet for a little while. Then he told her, "I want you to know

— 245 —

that your sister didn't care for me at all. Marrying me was only another duty she expected herself to carry out. And when she died . . . the idea that my father would replace her with another one just like her, as if my future life partners were all interchangeable—"

"I'm nothing like Anna," Catherine said, the words coming out more sharply than she'd meant.

"I knew that as soon as we met."

Somehow the inches between them were gone and his shoulder was pressing against hers, solid and reassuring. Archie was there, next to her, and he was listening. He was the sort of person who *would* listen, she thought. Even to the crazy theories that were chasing themselves around inside her head. Even though he was not a Seeker, and knew nothing of her life, he might even care, the way she cared, about finding the truth of things and making them better. When she forced herself to look at him, he turned his head and met her gaze.

"You're not what I expected," she whispered.

"A frivolous boxer who likes to play with old cars?"

She shook her head. Her gaze dropped to his hand on the motorcycle seat between them.

"And you're not some strange girl my father is forcing me to marry," he told her. He lifted his hand from the seat and very carefully pulled one of her hands from its position at her waist. "You're just Catherine."

The way he said her name made her feel she'd never properly heard it before. His hand was warm on hers, and its pressure made her feel queasy in a strangely pleasant way.

"Why is he forcing you to marry me?" Catherine asked.

Archie thought for a minute before he spoke. "He's . . . a bit strange, my father. He's convinced that your family is how my family will recover itself. Financially, I guess, though I don't know how—and

I don't care about that. He tells me I'm someone important in disguise. That the disguise has saved me, but now I need you."

"What does that mean?"

Archie shrugged. "I have no idea. If I'm in disguise, it's a terrible one. My family's social activities are in the papers all the time."

"Maybe that sort of fame *is* the disguise. It makes you less disposable," Catherine said thoughtfully. "My parents seem to want that fame for me." *Though I doubt it will save me, if I can't stop Seekers from killing each other,* she thought.

"So your parents are as strange as mine," he said.

"Oh, I think they're much stranger."

They both laughed. Then Catherine asked, "Is this a trick, Archie? Is this how you get me to trust you so I drop my guard?"

"Yes," he whispered, pulling her closer, "because I definitely knew you'd be hiding out here waiting for me. I've been rehearsing this meeting all day."

She smiled. She was the one who'd come to him, snuck in, waited for him.

"The way you're dressed," he said, "I should be asking if *you're* trying to trap *me*."

His face was near hers. He had the faintest growth of stubble on his jawline, but his lips looked soft and warm. Catherine knew what she wanted now, and it no longer mattered if it was what her parents wanted also. They had become irrelevant.

"Maybe I *was* trying to trap you," she whispered. "I was worried you'd never want to see me again after the way I behaved last time."

"You shouldn't have worried."

He leaned closer, and Catherine thought he was going to kiss her. Instead he glanced over at his house, his eyes traveling up all four stories of it. He pulled away.

"I don't want to be here," he said abruptly.

Without waiting for her response, he picked up his helmet and slid it onto Catherine's head.

"Come on," he told her, throwing a leg over the motorcycle seat. "I'll take you somewhere else—away from my father and this house."

A few moments later, she was perched on the back of his bike, holding him tightly as London streets flew by. As soon as they'd left the courtyard and the house had disappeared behind them, Archie felt different beneath her arms. He wasn't Gavin Hart's son, and she wasn't her parents' daughter. Not at this moment.

They began kissing each other in the dark stairwell leading up to his flat. After putting her arms around him on the motorcycle, it had seemed only natural to keep them around him when they got off.

"Have you done this before?" he whispered.

"Kissed someone? Once. It didn't go well."

"Good," he whispered, half lifting her into his arms as they felt their way.

They tripped on their way up the stairs, fell against each other, and it was an excuse to kiss again. Why had she never suspected that kissing could be like this?

At the landing, Archie fumbled for his keys, still holding her. Then they were inside his flat. Catherine's eyes took in a few rooms lit by the streetlamps outside. The furniture was fine, as though it had come from one of his family's old houses, but the space was somehow spare and masculine, like Archie. She pulled off his jacket.

Catherine looked at him in the light that trickled in through the living room window. Somehow, through a miracle she didn't understand, here was someone who made sense to her.

"You should know that there are many things wrong with me," she whispered. "Anna died, and that sort of thing might run in my family."

"Early death?" He was laughing, but he stopped when Catherine looked back at him seriously. "Impossible," he whispered. "I know how to punch things, remember?"

Catherine allowed herself to smile then. "I think I can . . . be with you, Archie. In my life. Maybe you'll even help me figure everything out."

"I don't know what you mean, but yes. Absolutely yes," he whispered back. "I wasn't sure what I was going to do with myself if you hated me."

"I don't hate you."

She took one of his hands from her waist and tugged it, so he would follow her. She led him through the living room, finding her way in the unfamiliar space, until they had reached his bedroom. Her fingers laced through his, she pulled him inside and closed the door.

CHAPTER 32

CATHERINE

19 YEARS EARLIER

"Archie, you're not sleeping, are you?"

"Mmm?" Archie mumbled. A warm, lazy hand came up and covered her mouth. "Shhh," he whispered.

Catherine bit his finger softly.

"Ow." He shifted in the bed, tugging her closer.

Archie had pulled the curtains shut, but moonlight shone through the sheer material, coloring everything it touched in cool blues and greens, especially an old-fashioned secretary's desk near the window. Carved on the side of that desk was an elegant stag, its antlers branching widely. From the bed, Catherine had been studying the design for ten minutes. Similar stags adorned nearly every piece of furniture in the room.

She threw the covers off, crossed the room, and opened the curtains.

"What is it?" Archie asked. He was awake now, watching her from the bed.

She pulled over a chair and stood upon it to more closely study the carving on an ancient armoire against the far wall.

"It's a stag," she told him. She was tracing the design with a finger. The deer on the armoire was simplified and more angular than the others in the room—and it happened to look identical to a stag drawn in one of the old letters safely pasted into her journal, which she now kept in a locked safe in her parents' basement.

"Yeah," Archie said, running a hand through his messy hair, which didn't seem too long to Catherine anymore. "Some ancestor loved stags. They're on everything in our houses—cupboards, footstools, chamber pots. I'm surprised you didn't notice in my father's house."

"I was distracted by hating you."

Archie smiled. "Our last name is Hart. A hart is a male deer. So stag, Hart, Hart, stag."

"Hmm," she said. "Like 'Renart,' my name, is a fox, and we have foxes on everything. Where is this armoire from?"

"Country house, I think? We have piles of old furniture. At this point most of our remaining wealth is in furniture," he said, flopping back onto his pillow. "You look very pretty. Please come back to bed immediately."

She cast him a flirtatious look but stayed where she was and pulled open the armoire's doors, letting light from the streetlamps spill into its interior. Archie's clothes were hanging inside.

"You have a funny look on your face," he told her, sitting up more attentively, "like you're about to rip my clothes out and throw them all over the floor."

That was exactly what Catherine did. Twenty minutes later, Archie's clothes were strewn everywhere, and together they'd pulled out the drawers in the bottom of the armoire. They discovered a false back behind one of the bottom drawers—a space Archie had never suspected was there—and Archie's arm was now shoved deep inside, feeling around a hidden gap within.

"There's—something in here," he told her. "Something hard and sort of round."

"Can you get hold of it?" Chances were she and Archie had discovered something completely useless—a tin of old coins or someone's lucky horseshoe collection from hundreds of years ago. But Catherine felt unaccountably excited.

"I've got it," he said.

There was a scraping sound as he brought his arm back out. Clutched in his hand was a dusty helmet. Catherine inhaled sharply as she took hold of it. Though she'd never seen one in person, she recognized it immediately. It was a focal, the metal helmet Seekers had once used to train their minds.

"A motorcycle helmet?" Archie asked. "From a hundred years ago? It looks ancient."

She wiped off the dust, revealing silver metal that flashed iridescent colors when light fell upon it. Unaccountably she thought of the Young Dread and imagined speaking to her about it. Perhaps she would one day. But she brought her mind back to Archie.

"It's not a motorcycle helmet," she told him.

"What is it, then?"

"It's . . ."

She turned the helmet over in her hands. The interior was lined with canvas, which was torn and fraying in several places. Tucked beneath the canvas lining, visible through a small tear, was a slip of paper. Catherine slid it out carefully. She'd collected enough Seeker memorabilia from attics and basements and abandoned barns to guess what it would be, even before she saw the writing.

It was a letter, scrawled hastily, by the look of it:

Edward,

> *We've made an arrangement and hope it might be honored. What we've promised will not be pleasant, but the alternative is even less pleasant.*
>
> *If lucky, we'll be back with you soon. If unlucky . . . I shan't finish that thought.*
>
> *At least this helm remains with you. It is ours, it is yours. Keep it safe, Son. It might see you through a long walk, or a desperate fight.*
>
> *Do not forget what you are.*
>
> *Your Loving Parents*

Archie read the letter over her shoulder, then took it from her hands and read it again. Catherine watched him, understanding more about him now than he did himself. He was from a Seeker family, probably on his mother's side, since his father hadn't appeared to have any knowledge of Seekers. Archie's mother had been dead since he was a child, and Catherine guessed she had taught him nothing of his heritage, or perhaps she'd decided it was safer not to be a Seeker at all.

"Edward was my grandfather," Archie said thoughtfully. "Or, no, great-grandfather."

"On your mother's side?"

"Yes. The Harts are all from my mother's side. It's her name. My father changed his when they met, though he was a distant cousin of hers."

"What happened to Edward, your great-grandfather?"

He studied the letter again. "I think he's the one who died in a traffic accident before I was born. I have no idea what sort of arrangement his parents are talking about."

Catherine's mind was putting pieces together. Seekers had been attacking Seekers, probably for a very long time, and yet this was not a letter written by a willing killer, but rather a reluctant participant . . . in what?

She said, "It sounds as though they were forced into doing something they didn't wish to do. Maybe something violent . . . and then they disappeared?" *Is that what happened to Emile?* she wondered.

"You seem very knowledgeable about my distant ancestors, for a girl I just met."

He was taking this lightly, but Catherine was not. "Archie, I'm afraid our families might have certain things in common."

"What do you mean?" he asked. "Disappearing relatives?"

"Maybe," she said soberly.

"You sound so serious." He glanced at her, then back to the helmet. "What is this thing?"

"It's called a focal," she told him, "and as far as I can tell, no one's seen one for about a hundred years."

"What do you mean 'no one's seen one'? Were people looking for this thing?"

"Yes."

Archie started to pull the helmet onto his head. She caught his hands quickly.

"Don't," she said. "It's not . . . well, it's not frivolous. We need instructions."

"Catherine, will you please explain what the hell you're talking about?"

"This helmet, this focal, is a tool for Seekers," she told him. "But the focals have been missing. Like the ancestor who wrote this note perhaps went missing as well. Lots of things, and lots of people, have gone missing—maybe they've been killing each other, or maybe missing some other way."

"Am I supposed to know what a Seeker is?" he asked.

"It's why our parents want us married, I suspect. My parents must have known yours was a Seeker family that might still have . . . well, things like this helmet. Actually, I suppose it was my grandmother Maggie who thought this through. She seems to know everything about everyone."

This focal, Catherine now understood, was all that remained of a once great Seeker house, the house of the stag. Archie's mother had been a Seeker, and his father had perhaps known something about it.

Archie looked like he was running out of patience. "Catherine, are you going to tell me what a Seeker is—and how you know this—or do I have to beat it out of you with the shoes you've thrown all over the floor?"

She drew herself into his lap.

"*I'm* a Seeker," she told him. She held both sides of his face and kissed him lightly. "And you, it seems, were supposed to be one too."

CHAPTER 33

MAUD

The Young Dread stood with John on the thoroughfare of the Transit Bridge in Hong Kong. He glanced at her, nodded to tell her he understood his assignment, and then turned and joined the foot traffic. Maud watched for a few minutes as he disappeared down the roadway, and then she herself turned and walked off the Bridge and into the streets of Kowloon.

She'd brought him here to see Quin. The Young Dread did not much understand romantic love, but John obviously loved Quin—or at least couldn't stop thinking of her. And because his wishes and Quin's wishes were at odds, John lived in a state of deep distraction. He was distracted by many other sources besides Quin—particularly his mother and his grandmother—but Quin was different; she was alive in the world right now, capturing his attention by her very existence.

He was welcome to his love, but it was not possible to train him further unless he could rule his own thoughts. The Young Dread had brought him to the Transit Bridge to find Quin and discover if he was capable of doing so.

She moved through the side streets of Kowloon until she found a secluded spot at the end of a foul-smelling alley. There, with John's athame, she brought herself to the top of a very high building. It was windy on the roof. Not far away, the bulk of the Transit Bridge was visible where it crossed the harbor, and beyond that were even higher buildings climbing up Hong Kong Island toward Victoria Peak.

The sky was full of towering clouds, but the sun appeared in bursts from time to time, illuminating the ends of her hair and the nap of her old wool sweater, and changing the look of the world. She would not allow herself to worry about John while he was on the Bridge; his decisions were his own—no matter what she might wish for him. She turned her thoughts away, took a seat in the open air, and spread her thick, gray cloak out before her.

This cloak had become as familiar to her as her own skin, but it was not originally hers. It had belonged to her dear master, the Old Dread. During the fight aboard *Traveler*, he had settled it onto her shoulders before stepping *There* and leaving her to be the Young, the Middle, and the Old Dread all by herself.

The cloak had brushed the ground when she'd first worn it, too long for her. Now it hovered just above the ground when she stood— she'd grown in this month awake. She suspected she was growing more slowly, aging more slowly, than a typical fifteen-year-old, but she was growing and aging nonetheless.

The cloak held a number of items that belonged to the Old Dread. As she had done once or twice in secret over the past weeks, she pulled objects from the cloak's many pockets and set them before her. She'd gazed at her master's cloak when she was a little girl and wondered at the mysteries it contained. Now some of those mysteries were in her own possession, yet they were as mysterious as ever.

Among the items in the pockets were a few small metal tools. Only one of them was familiar—she'd seen her master use it in the secret chamber that lay far beneath the ruined castle on the Scottish estate. He had used that tool to tap a wall of rock in a hidden cavern, setting off a tremor so deep Maud had thought it might bring the roof down. The other implements, however, meant nothing to her.

The cloak also contained items made of stone. One or two were carved from the same translucent white stone from which athames came, but others were different, darker and muddier. There were weapons also, mostly knives, but only a few that had come from her master; the rest were hers.

A vibration drew her attention. A burst of sunlight was playing over one of the strangest items from the cloak, and it was shaking against the gravelly surface of the roof. Maud picked it up, making sure to keep it in the sun. It was made of stone but also of metal, and it had a face of glass set into it. The glass was dark and thick, as though many layers had been stacked on top of one another. It was no bigger than her outstretched hand, and it was now vibrating against her skin. A moment later, the sun went behind clouds and the stone object fell still. Yet it had come to life with the touch of sunlight, as disruptors and focals did. Perhaps many of these items would wake up if she left them in the sun long enough.

Her master had worn two faces—one ancient and one almost modern. These objects were like him. Some looked as old as the natural rock beneath the ruined castle in Scotland, but others might belong to the strange world of the present day.

Perhaps John, as a modern person, could identify these things, but she could never allow one who was not a sworn Dread to see the contents of her master's cloak. And yet, she'd seen a change in John that had begun to alter her view of him. After his run across the desert in the focal, she'd seen him question, for a moment, his purpose in chasing after the other Seeker houses. She'd begun to turn him toward better things.

CHAPTER 34

JOHN

John kept his gaze pointed straight ahead, examining the crowds on the Transit Bridge through his peripheral vision as the Young Dread had taught him, taking in the motions around him with clear and steady eyes. He'd begun to see his old weaknesses plainly—his scattered mind, his temper—as he carefully shed each one. Maud was turning him into the Seeker he had always wanted to be. If he could learn to control his mind, perhaps his training would be almost complete.

The Young Dread had brought them to Hong Kong and used the athame to get them onto the Bridge surreptitiously, but John was on his own now. She'd made it clear that this was his task to carry out by himself, and that if he succeeded, she would continue his training and also allow him to go to the next place in the journal.

He'd thought it might be difficult to find Quin, but as he neared the middle of the Bridge, he saw her immediately. She was out in the open near her own front door, saying goodbye to a very old Chinese man in a healer's smock. She looked the same, dark hair falling past her shoulders, dark eyes large against her fair skin. The ties of her blue healer's smock pulled the material tight at her slender waist, calling to mind countless times he'd placed a hand there and drawn her closer.

John's breath came a little faster, and he could hear the thumping of his own heart. Of course she looked the same, he reminded himself, it had been only a few weeks since he'd last seen her on *Traveler*. She looked almost as worried now as she had then.

The other people on the Bridge faded from John's sight as he maneuvered through foot traffic. He moved the way Maud would move, and the focus of the steady stare came automatically. He was pleased to notice how much he was coming to be like her.

Then his hands were on Quin's arms, and he was pulling her into the narrow alley between her house and the next. Only when he had her cornered near her back stairs did he realize how fast he'd been going. He hadn't wanted to give her time to tell him no, and so he'd come at her with a sudden, near-impossible burst of speed, like a Dread.

Quin had her whipsword drawn before she had time to see his face clearly. John could see the change in her eyes when she realized it was him. She froze, for the space of a breath, when her gaze locked on his; then she jerked herself out of his grasp.

"Quin, I only want to talk to you." He had slowed himself down so he could speak properly, and he kept his voice calm. He had his own whipsword with him, but he had no intention of drawing it.

"You say that a lot before we fight, John." Her voice held anger and something else, a sense of exhaustion, as though being near him drained the life out of her.

"Truly, I mean it." And he did mean it; he wanted her attention for only a little while.

"Weren't you satisfied with the concussion you gave me last time we saw each other?" she asked sharply. "Did you want to try harder now?"

Her whipsword was still coiled in her hand, yet her dark eyes flashed a warning at him. She would have no problem using it.

"I'm sorry for what happened on *Traveler*. It didn't go the way I'd planned. And I didn't want to hit you."

"Your hands just moved on their own, did they?"

He thought of Quin on *Traveler*, leaning over Shinobu, who'd been lying injured on the floor. The way she'd spoken to him, her tone of voice . . . John had been so jealous that he'd lost control completely. He'd hit Quin as hard, as viciously, as he could. Maud was right—he had no control over his heart and his thoughts when it came to Quin.

He closed his eyes for a moment. "I . . . I wanted to see you," he said at last. The words sounded so childish, though they were the unfortunate truth; he looked away in embarrassment. *I think about you so much it's getting in the way of my training,* is what he should have said.

"Well, you've seen me," she said coldly. "Now you can go."

She pushed him aside and headed out of the narrow alley toward the busy thoroughfare they'd just left. John caught her arm.

"Wait, Quin, please." He kept his voice soft and his grip on her wrist light. He didn't want to seem rough.

She yanked her arm from his grasp but stood there looking at him, waiting for him to speak.

"I—I try to keep you from my mind," he stammered. "But I can't quite—"

"We're not friends, John," Quin interrupted. "You don't have to confess anything to me."

She was turning again, not even giving him a chance to explain, when he was desperate for her to listen. He tugged her back gently and was relieved when she didn't pull her arm away this time.

"I don't think of you as a friend," he said, in little more than a whisper. "I think about us in the woods together. I think about the plans we made."

She said nothing for a moment, as though words had failed her. Then her eyes softened, and John thought, perhaps, he'd actually reached her. The softness was gone as soon as it came, however. She told him, "It's just habit."

"What do you mean?" he asked.

"Thinking about me. It's just habit." She didn't meet his eyes. She bit her bottom lip, and her voice dropped to a whisper as she said, "Eventually you'll stop thinking about me. And I'll stop thinking about you."

John's chest constricted. Was it a habit she had too? "Do you—"

"I was going to marry you, John. Of course I think about you." Her voice was so low he could hardly hear her as she added, "I see you in my dreams sometimes, running and fighting. I feel you there, nearby, like you used to be when we were together, training on the estate. And I wish I didn't."

It took a moment for John to connect Quin's words with similar words he'd heard from the Young Dread, but as soon as he did, a deep sense of disappointment engulfed him. He tried not to let it show on his face. *She hasn't been thinking of me at all. Not at all.*

"Those aren't your thoughts," he muttered, the words feeling poisonous in his throat. Her eyes turned up to meet his, and he forced himself to explain, "You're seeing into the Young Dread's mind. She . . . she agreed to finish my training, since Briac wouldn't. You're seeing what she sees, feeling what she feels. She feels your thoughts too sometimes."

He watched understanding slowly dawn on her face, and the look that came over her nearly crushed him. She was relieved—no, *grateful*—that the thoughts weren't hers.

"We're not enemies, Quin," he whispered. "I don't want you to think of me that way. You gave me everything I needed when you helped me on *Traveler*."

It was the wrong thing to say. The momentary truce between them was shattered, and he watched her face fill with anger.

"I didn't *help* you, John. You kidnapped my mother, you tried to kill me. Have you forgotten? Don't you remember the things you've done?"

"I never tried to kill you," John swore. "Think back. I never did."

"Just beatings, then?" she asked, acid in her voice. "The last time you were here on the Bridge, you brought five men and had them beat me! And you struck me yourself."

Her face had closed off from him entirely, like they were strangers. She took a step back and cracked out her whipsword into a long, sharp blade.

"Quin . . ."

"Please go, John."

"Why?"

"Because I don't want you in my life."

She raised her whipsword so the point was at his chest. She held the weapon perfectly steady, ready to thrust forward and kill him. John wrapped his hand around the end of the sword, holding it to his breastbone and staring into Quin's eyes.

"Do you love him?" he asked. "Do you love him like you loved me?"

"I love Shinobu differently. He's *pure*. He is what he says he is." Slowly she shook her head. "I didn't know you, John. I loved something that wasn't real."

The sword was still in his hand, barely touching his shirt, and yet John felt as though she'd stabbed him through.

"It was real," he whispered.

"My father was raising me to be a killer. And you *want* to be a killer, so you can chase someone else's revenge."

"It's not someone else's revenge!" he cried, losing his temper at last. Urging his muscles to Dread-like speed, he batted her whip-sword away and grabbed her wrists. "It was my mother's life. All of their lives. Why don't you care about that, Quin?"

She didn't bother to push him away. In fact, she pulled her wrists toward her chest, bringing him closer. Her face was twisted in hate. "Why did you come here? Did you think I'd tell you it was all a mistake, and I still wanted to be with you?"

He shook his head. The Young Dread had brought him to Hong Kong to face her. Maud had told him that he must choose what occupied his thoughts. That was why he was here. So now he must choose.

And he did.

"No," he told her. "I know you'll never be with me." He felt the weight and the truth of the words. "I think I came to apol—"

Midsentence John lunged forward and grabbed her shoulders, and with all the force he could muster, he pulled Quin to the ground behind the rubbish bins lined up in the alley. With a vicious twang, a knife planted itself in the wall and stood quivering with the force of its impact—exactly where Quin had been standing a moment before.

Three teenaged boys stood at the alley's entrance, more knives in their hands, ready to throw.

"Oh God, not now," breathed Quin. And then, almost like a prayer, she whispered, "Shinobu, where are you?"

CHAPTER 35

QUIN

Quin rolled out from beneath John and was back on her feet in a moment, crouched behind the bins, her whipsword in one hand, a knife in the other. She ripped off her smock, which was getting in the way.

"I don't have anything you want!" she called at the boys—the Middle Dread's boys. Trained by him, kept by him for . . . what? To chase after his athame, after he was dead?

Of course, Quin realized. *They don't know he's dead. All this time, they've been talking about him as though he's still alive.*

"Liar!" said the smallest one, Nott. He and the other two were moving down the long, narrow alley.

"You've seen them before?" John asked, huddled beside her.

Quin nodded. "You too?"

"Yes. They run if you challenge them."

"They don't run from *me* without a huge fight first," Quin told him grimly. "I don't have anything you want!" she called again.

It was true enough. Shinobu had taken the focal and the athame of the Dreads, which also meant she had no easy way to escape the boys. Where had Shinobu gone? Her body still ached painfully from the last fight. Facing a new one without him was an unpleasant idea.

Mentally she made a quick inventory: she had her whipsword and a few knives. She had been walking around armed since their last fight with the boys, in case they showed up suddenly again. But she hadn't expected them to find her on the Bridge, not really. And she wished, for once, that she'd chosen to wear a gun, though they were hard to come by in Hong Kong and against the Bridge's rules.

"Then let us search you!" one of the older boys called back. This was a dark-skinned one. She'd fought him on the estate.

"Your master is dead!" she called out to them. "If you had let me get a word in before you attacked us yesterday, I could have told you. You have no one to retrieve the athame for."

"Shut your mouth!" the dark one snapped.

"You're a liar!" yelled Nott.

"Who's their master?" John whispered.

"The Middle Dread," Quin whispered back.

The third boy stepped out from behind the others. He was in his late teens, with dark, dark skin, and he'd been their worst opponent on the estate. He was wearing a focal on his head . . .

And he had a disruptor strapped across his chest.

"Lying girl!" he spat.

Quin realized she'd been hearing the disruptor's high whine for some time, but the sound had been obscured by the noises of the Bridge. Before she could react, he fired the weapon.

"Oh God," she and John said in unison, dropping to the ground. The disruptor sparks hit the metal bins and ricocheted off in a hissing, flashing mess.

"I don't have what you want!" she yelled. "Your master is gone. I watched him die!"

"Stop saying that!" yelled the boy in the focal.

He fired the disruptor again.

She and John pressed themselves low against the bins as a new swarm of sparks collided. A handful bounced through a gap, soared past Quin's face, and smashed into the metal stairs behind her.

She could smell the boys. Death hung about them like an invisible cloak.

"Come out and *show us* what you have or haven't got!" the oldest one ordered, and he fired the disruptor again.

"How is he firing it so fast?" she asked. Unlike the disruptor she'd trained with on the estate, this weapon took almost no time to recharge.

"He sounds like he *wants* to disrupt you," John whispered, "like he's dying to do it whether you come out or not."

"Shinobu and I injured them pretty badly. They'd probably rather not fight." Indeed all three boys looked wounded, with dirty, blood-caked bandages in various locations. "And they think I have an athame. They don't want to give me a chance to use it."

"And they really don't like what you said about their master," John said.

He was right. The boys were arguing as they got closer. Quin heard Nott say, "He *can't* die. She's a liar!"

"Course he's not dead!" said the oldest one. "And we'll put her in her place."

The disruptor was whining higher, preparing to fire again.

"We charge them and get out onto the thoroughfare?" John proposed.

"No. The narrow alley, the fast disruptor. They'll hit us easily."

"You're right."

She nodded toward the back of the alley. "We should go up and over," she said.

Behind them, the alley ended in the outdoor staircase of her house, which led to the bedrooms on the second floor. Beyond the stairs was the steel latticework of the Bridge itself, the barrier between its upper level and the open air beyond.

The boys' voices were coming to them in a furious jumble as they argued with each other. The disruptor fired from much closer this time, and the sparks rattled among the bins in angry flashes. She and John took that moment, the brief pause before the disruptor would be able to fire again, and ran in a crouch straight up the stairs toward her second floor.

Someone was there. Three figures had been crouched down on the balcony, and they now stood. One was the older boy who'd attacked her in the hospital, Wilkin. And he too was wearing a disruptor. Behind him were two more boys she'd never seen before.

"They're multiplying," John breathed.

He and Quin were caught halfway up the staircase. The disruptor above was emitting a high squeal, ready to fire, echoing the sounds of the first disruptor below them.

The boys below had moved in and were standing at the bottom of the stairs. The dual whine of the disruptors was like a physical object piercing Quin's ears.

"Stop your lies about our master," the largest boy below said. "If you put your hands up and get on the ground, we might not disrupt you." But his expression said he would gladly disrupt her if it meant shutting her up and avoiding a fight. A bright red splotch had appeared in the center of the dirty bandage on his shoulder. An earlier wound had opened up—probably when he'd thrown that first knife. He was wounded and angry.

Quin wasn't about to submit. A glance at John told her that he understood and agreed. They began to lift their hands in surrender . . .

Then Quin leapt onto the stair railing and leapt again, with John right behind her.

Both disruptors fired. Quin caught herself on the steel lattice behind the stairs. Through its slats, she glimpsed Victoria Harbor, waves, ships, Hong Kong Island beyond.

John landed next to her. Above them, the lattice stretched almost endlessly to meet the Bridge canopy.

"Climb!" Quin yelled.

She began hauling herself up the grid work as the disruptors fired again.

CHAPTER 36

NOTT

Could their master really be dead? Nott wondered. He didn't think so. But even if he were dead, Nott supposed they would still have to retrieve his athame from Quin—no thieving girl should have it. And also she had Nott's helm.

The helm.

Nott had been without the helm long enough to realize that it clouded his judgment. He still loved it, he still needed it, he still planned to kill another of the Watchers if necessary to get his hands upon a helm. But even so, he could now see the device's limitations. And he understood that the helm was clouding *everyone's* judgment.

If their master wasn't dead—and it was doubtful, in Nott's mind, that the man could actually die—he might as well sack this whole lot of Watchers and start over with new boys, because Nott and the others were idiots. But of course, it was their master who'd made them use the helm. He was the one who'd taught them to trust it. So he'd made them into idiots.

The two half-trained Watchers—*the babies,* as Nott liked to think of them—had used the magic of computers to point them to the

Bridge in Hong Kong, where Quin lived. Now Geb wanted to use the disruptors to take away Quin's fighting skills so it would be easy to grab the athame back. Geb was also furious that she kept telling them their master was dead—and Nott understood this, because he was furious too. But what if she *didn't* have the athame just now? She was yelling that she didn't have it. If that was true, how would they ever find it if she were disrupted?

They should concentrate on capturing her, even if it meant getting wounded again. What were a few more injuries at this point?

They had climbed the steel latticework after Quin, and they were now all up among high metal rafters. She'd probably been trying to get across one of the large beams that spanned the Bridge and down onto the main thoroughfare, but the Watchers had blocked her and she'd been forced to go up higher instead.

The rafters up here were a maze of steel limbs, crisscrossing and intersecting each other beneath the Bridge's canopy, so that he and the others were crawling between and around beams as they tried to keep her in sight. She and her companion (who was, oddly enough, the same fellow who'd thrown a knife at Briac Kincaid) were above the Watchers, right up against the great sloping canopy that was the Bridge's roof. The babies, Jacob and Matthew, looked scared and exhilarated by the chase, which showed how truly idiotic they were, since Quin could make mincemeat of them if it came to a real fight.

Nott wondered how his brother, Odger, would have gotten the others to act sensibly. He imagined asking: *Odger, what should I do now?* But Odger, too amazed by the modern world to be of any use, would only answer: *What about some of them comfortable shoes I see on everyone's feet, Nott? Could you get me a pair of those?*

I could not, Odger, Nott replied, *'cause you were dead and buried ages ago.*

Why, after all this time, was he thinking of Odger? He'd left brothers and families and all of that in the past.

Geb wiggled between two beams (having a hard time of it with the heavy disruptor strapped across his chest), saw an opening, and fired. Half the disruptor sparks collided with a rafter a few yards away and bounced wildly off the metal, nearly rebounding into Geb's own face. He ducked quickly. The rest of the sparks died out long before they reached Quin. Geb was proving himself to be as idiotic as Wilkin. Example: everything he'd done since they'd woken him up.

"Stop using the disruptor!" Nott yelled.

"Shut it, Nott!" hissed Wilkin, who was right behind him, a huge bruise on his left cheek visible even in the dim light among the rafters. He too was struggling to climb with a disruptor on his chest. At least Wilkin was clever enough not to fire it.

"Geb almost disrupted himself!" Nott whispered defiantly. "We shouldn't fire it unless we're in the open!"

"Then go faster!" Balil said, roughly pushing Nott through a tight spot.

There was a blinding flash of light up ahead. Quin had cut or ripped a piece of the Bridge's canopy, and she was pulling the material back, exposing the sky beyond. And then she and her companion disappeared though that flap of canvas and out onto the canopy itself.

CHAPTER 37

QUIN

Quin stepped through the hole she'd cut, out of the darkness of the rafters and onto the exterior of the Bridge's great canopy. She was hit with a gust of wind and, even though the day was cloudy, nearly blinded by the light of the open air. She almost lost herself in a rush of dizziness. It was so very *high*. The canopy itself swept out and down, a great sail spreading below her and then rising again at its far edge, where it overhung the Bridge like the eaves of a roof. Beyond the edge and far, far below was the gray water of Victoria Harbor, and beyond that was Hong Kong Island.

She clutched the rough canvas material behind her. She was as high up now as she'd been with Shinobu on that night they parachuted onto *Traveler*. Her stomach felt as though it had become disconnected from the rest of her body and was sliding down toward her feet. Her hair flapped crazily about her face in the strong gusts, adding to her dizziness. Her new fear of heights made it hard to breathe. John grabbed her arm to keep her from tumbling forward.

"Maud, please!" she heard him mutter beside her.

"What?" she asked.

"Where can we go from here?" he asked, gesturing to the steep sail below them.

He looked tense and serious but not panicked, and Quin had a fleeting thought that whatever the Young Dread was teaching him was having an effect.

She turned from the panoramic view and concentrated on the canopy itself. From a distance it gave the impression of enormous ships' sails moving across the harbor. Up close, it was a series of steep mountains plunging into valleys. They had come out about midway up the height of the canopy. The steepest peaks rose far above them, and below, the sail upon which they stood dropped away quickly, until it bellied out into a valley, then rose again at the edge of the Bridge.

"We go down," she said, "and at the bottom we find a place where we can cut back inside—away from them." She jerked her head toward the flap they'd just crawled through. "Then we climb down to the thoroughfare and get help."

The sails were supported by cables and a hidden framework of rafters, but out here, only the canvas was visible, stretched taut in some places, rippling in others in the ocean breeze.

There was a whine and a buzzing behind them, audible over the wind. Quin turned as a mass of disruptor sparks hit the canvas, lighting it from inside in a kaleidoscope of color. A handful of sparks burst through the cut she'd made, missing her and John by luck only and dispersing in the air.

Her eyes swept down to the distant ocean, and she felt desperation rising, threatening to blot out all rational thought. The idea of plunging down the face of the sail was terrifying, but there was little choice, and she couldn't imagine her pursuers following her with live disruptors on their chests. That would be madness.

"I'm going!" she said.

Without waiting for John's response, or for her courage to fail her, she plunged forward, down the steep curve of the sail. In a moment, she was sprinting headlong, her feet sinking into the canvas and sliding as she went. It was more like skating than running, and she was moving much too fast. At every moment it felt as though she would pitch forward over her feet and roll wildly out of control.

She did lose control at last, her forward motion overtaking the pace of her feet. She sprawled onto the sail, then careened downward, end over end, the canvas absorbing each fall and sending her onward.

"They're coming!" John yelled from above as she at last pitched to a stop in the belly of the sail.

He was right behind her, still on his feet, but moving so fast she wasn't sure he'd be able to stop. He threw himself forward and rolled the rest of the way, fetching up a few yards from her, the sail rippling beneath him.

High above, all six boys were coming down the steep incline, like the Mongol hordes galloping across the steppes of Russia.

The wind carried the whine of the disruptors straight to Quin's ears.

CHAPTER 38

MAUD

Atop the high roof in Kowloon, the Young Dread had examined every item from within her cloak and had returned them to their pockets.

Had John found Quin? Had he brought his thoughts of Quin under his own control? Would he continue to be her student?

If the answer was no, what would Maud herself do? Every day the Young Dread spent awake in the world, in this time and place, was a day lost from her life as a whole. And yet she couldn't return to sleep now, not while she was the only active Dread. She did not even know how to wake herself.

John was an apprentice Seeker, but in recent days Maud had caught glimpses in him of a potential to be more than that—if he could commit himself.

Maud, please!

She heard the call in her mind and knew at once that it was John. Their minds had never touched before, but his thoughts came to her clearly, urgently. He was in a panic, running for his life. *Maud, I need your help . . .*

In a single practiced motion, the Young Dread stood and wrapped her cloak about her shoulders. Her athame and lightning rod were in her hand as she stared across the dense buildings of Kowloon toward the Transit Bridge.

CHAPTER 39

NOTT

Nott's frustration at his fellow Watchers was obliterated in a rush of fear when he burst through the flap in the Bridge canopy. They hadn't even paused to come up with a plan. Geb had herded all of them after Quin at a run, yelling that they mustn't let her get away.

At once, the cloudy Hong Kong sky was above them, the endless drop of the sail was below, and the six Watchers were careening down the canvas faster than Nott had ever run in his life. After only a few steps, they were moving too fast to stop. All twelve of their feet made divots in the sail with each step, and each divot created ripples, so the canvas was moving in fiercer and fiercer waves under him as they ran.

Nott didn't want to look anywhere but directly in front of his own feet, yet he had to know if he was going to run right off the edge of the Bridge. He glanced up and was relieved to see that it would be impossible to do so. The sail swooped down and down to create a valley at the bottom; then it rose again, up to the edge. Quin and the other one were in that valley now, doing their best to run away.

Just in front of Nott, Geb was flailing his arms to keep his balance.

One of his hands knocked against the disruptor on his chest, and the weapon fired. The sparks buzzed and hissed in a swarm, hit the surface of the sail, and bounced in all directions. They were stepping on remnant sparks as they hurtled downward. It was lucky disruptors didn't damage you unless they got to your head.

One of Nott's feet hit the sail wrong as he tried to avoid the sparks, and then his legs were behind him and he was rolling instead of running. He crashed into Geb and Balil, taking both of them down. The impact of all three with the sail was enough to topple everyone else. A moment later, all six Watchers were rolling, bouncing, flailing down the slope in a maelstrom of arms and legs and knives and heavy metal disruptors. Nott heard both disruptors fire in the middle of the turmoil.

The six boys ended up in separate heaps in the valley at the bottom of the sail. The canvas was still rippling and shifting, adding to the dizziness of the long roll. When he could finally see straight, Nott spied Quin fifty yards away, running for the neighboring sail.

"She's getting away!" yelled Wilkin.

Geb rose up, the disruptor hanging crookedly across his chest. He looked furious.

Someone was screaming. It was Jacob, the skinny half-trained Watcher who wore glasses. He convulsed on the canvas, a storm of disruptor sparks about his head and chest. Sounds of animal agony came out as he beat his own head, then scratched helplessly at the sail beneath him. Nearby, his baby partner, Matthew, was staring with an open mouth.

"Everybody up!" ordered Geb. "Go!"

The Watchers—all except Jacob, of course—scrambled after Quin. Geb paused long enough to plunge a knife into Jacob's chest.

That's what you get when you're a Watcher, even a baby Watcher,

Nott thought. *You live with madmen, and then one of them stabs you to death.*

Nott was grabbed by the collar, and Geb hissed into his ear, "You made us fall, Nott. *You* killed Jacob." The older boy pulled a rope from his cloak and said, "You're going first."

CHAPTER 40

QUIN

Quin and John climbed out of the valley of the sail to its edge, where it overlapped the next sail. One of the boys had been disrupted in their mad fall, but the other five were in the valley behind them and heading their way, the wine of the disruptors preceding them.

"Come on!" she yelled.

They leapt from the edge of the sail down onto the neighboring one.

"Do we cut through here?" John asked.

"Yes!"

They both dropped to their knees and, making their whipswords short and sharp, began sawing violently through the canvas. When they'd made a large cut, they grabbed hold together and pulled, tearing a large flap free. The loose material blew toward them in a gust of wind, and Quin found herself looking through the gap straight down hundreds of feet to Victoria Harbor below.

"Dammit!" cursed John as he stared at the water.

They weren't over the Bridge itself at this spot on the canopy; they were standing on an overhang, and they couldn't climb down.

The piece of the canvas they'd cut was flapping wildly, striking Quin's feet and revealing the distant harbor again and again. The view spun until she forced her eyes away. Over the lip of the sail she saw the boys coming straight at them.

She turned to look the other way. The valley of the new sail was spread out before her, and to her right, it swept upward to a new peak.

"Should we keep running," she asked, "onto the next sail and the next?"

John shook his head. "I don't think we can beat them on foot."

He was right. In the open, the disruptors could catch them, and the slanted surface of the sail would work against them, deflecting disruptor sparks into their faces as they ran.

"We have to climb quickly, then—just until we're over the Bridge itself," she told him. "Then we cut through again and get down inside."

John nodded.

Behind them were the bobbing heads of their pursuers, rapidly climbing up out of the valley of the first sail. She and John moved diagonally, traversing the sail as they climbed. But even so, the canvas quickly became so steep that they slid backward with each step.

"Knives!" John yelled, panting as he pulled two from his waist.

Quin drew her own knives, and they used them like pitons, digging into the canvas and dragging themselves higher.

The wind was stronger with every inch they moved upward. She glanced down beneath her right arm—to avoid looking directly over her shoulder, where she might catch a terrifying view of the drop to the harbor—and saw a shape fly over the lip of the sail. It was Nott, with a rope trailing from his chest, soaring spread-eagle through the air. He hit the canvas and was brought up short when the rope jerked tight around him. The boy gasped for breath, and the sounds of choking were carried on the wind.

"You can jump!" Nott yelled when he was able to speak. "She's right here!"

It was so steep now that Quin was nearly hanging off her knives.

"There's a girder," she called to John.

John called back, against the wind, "I feel it."

"Let's cut here!" Quin leaned into her left arm and with her right pulled her whipsword from its spot at her waist. She cracked it out and twisted her wrist, sending the oily black substance flowing around itself. The whipsword transformed into a long, wide knife. She put her wrist through another complicated series of motions, and sharp teeth bloomed along each side of the blade. "Make your sword short and jagged," she told John.

He was already copying her with his own whipsword. Then they attacked the canvas, sawing with abandon.

Don't look down, Quin thought, keeping her body tight against the surface of the sail. If she lost her balance, it would be a quick slide to the bottom, and the boys would be on her with their disruptors in a matter of seconds. They were already on the new sail, climbing toward her and John. In twenty or thirty more yards, they would be within range to fire at them.

She and John sawed until they'd created a man-sized flap, but their cutting job had been uneven, and the canvas was still sticking in a few places.

"We can tear the rest!" John said, his voice at a yell in the wind.

Quin nodded, stowed her sword; then together they ripped the last threads of canvas away from the girder. A large flap snapped up from the sail, and a gust of warm air hit Quin from under the canopy. She slid beneath the canvas flap, John at her back.

It took her eyes a moment to adjust, but when they did, she saw a network of crisscrossed trusses stretching up and away from the girder on which they were perched. Somewhere below was the top level of the Bridge, but the trusses in front of her here were so densely packed, there was no way to climb through them.

She and John were trapped.

Outside the flap of canvas, she could hear the disruptors. With rising distress, Quin peeked out to find the boys only twenty yards below them. She was looking directly into the barrel of a disruptor, and sparks were launching from its hundreds of holes.

"Move back!" she yelled, shoving John.

She pressed herself sideways beneath the canvas, into the tiny void between the steel truss work and the canopy.

Light burst all around the flap's edges, hissing and crackling. A dozen sparks found their way through the jagged cut and ricocheted violently between the trusses, just inches from her face, before dissipating in rainbow-colored explosions of light.

Quin didn't wait to see if she'd been disrupted. She gripped the blade of her knife, lifted the flap. All five attackers were spread out below. Without hesitating she chose her target and threw. Her knife planted itself in the arm of the one with the focal and the disruptor. He cried out but didn't fall. These boys were hard to stop.

Next to her, John threw two knives in quick succession. One grazed a boy's shoulder, and the second one would have taken out an eye, but the boy ducked at the last moment.

Nott swung himself toward Quin, a blade flashing in his hand.

"Give me my helm, you stupid, thieving girl!" he yelled.

She gripped the trusses behind her, pulled her legs up, and kicked the boy's chest, knocking him back.

The other disruptor fired. She and John pressed themselves sideways as a new barrage of sparks hit the canvas.

"I don't have any more knives," John said.

"I've got one!" Quin responded. "I'll try to make it count!"

The desperate fury of the fight was upon her, and she would not let herself think about the fact that they were cornered and nearly out of weapons.

They ripped open the canvas flap. Quin threw her last knife and watched in horror as one of the dark-skinned attackers lifted his disruptor like a shield and the knife clanged off harmlessly.

Both disruptors whined again with piercing intensity. But before they could be fired, all eyes turned. There was movement below on the sail. There was a blur of dark against the gray of the canopy. A figure was running so swiftly up the incline, it seemed to be half carried by the wind. It was the Young Dread, so light and quick she didn't need knives to help her climb.

She was throwing something. A round, flat object spun out from her hands, skimmed up across the surface of the sail in a black streak.

John caught it beneath a boot. It was a shield, a metal shield, with an edge so sharp, it had carved a line in the canvas as it whirled toward them. He flipped it over, grabbed Quin, and they ducked beneath it as sparks rained onto them.

They crouched low on the girder, the flap of canvas snapping in the wind as a new fusillade of sparks sizzled and hissed against the shield.

A handful of sparks bounced under the shield's edge and knocked against the girder frantically, encircling Quin's ankle. She swept her leg along the beam to brush them off her, and dearly hoped none had gotten to her head. Before she could take stock of herself, the disruptors were firing again.

And then, all at once, the disruptors stopped, and all Quin could hear was wind and the noise of distant aircars.

CHAPTER 41

SHINOBU

Shinobu returned to the Transit Bridge to discover the main road-way in turmoil. Pedestrians were running off the Bridge or milling about in nervous crowds, looking up at the canopy, which was shaking overhead in rolling waves.

He knew at once that Quin was up there somewhere. He'd left her, and while he was gone, something bad had happened. He stared at the Bridge canopy and cursed. Then he ducked into a shadowed space between two buildings on the thoroughfare and drew out the athame. He studied the stone dagger for a long while, his fingers nervously adjusting the dials based on his limited knowledge of coordinates—hoping to figure out how to cut an anomaly to the top of the canopy. It should be possible with the athame of the Dreads.

He glanced up as a particularly large wave passed through the Bridge roof; out on the thoroughfare, crowds gasped.

Shinobu looked back at the athame dials desperately. *Dammit, I don't know enough to do this!*

He yanked his backpack around, drew out the focal, and shoved it onto his head. His mind joined with it almost immediately, vaulting him into its higher state of awareness. He turned the athame over and over in his hands, and as he did, he let his mind relax, he let the focal sink deeper into his thoughts. After only a few moments, he understood how the dials might be adjusted for a minute maneuver like the one he wanted to make. His fingers moved along the dials; then he turned them one after another, clicking them into place for the first jump *There.*

He hit the athame against the slender lightning rod.

In the darkness *between,* he adjusted the dials again, then cut a new anomaly. Through the seething doorway was the top of the canopy. He'd done it—or the focal had. He was looking out at a vertical steel rod that stuck up like a mast from the summit of one of the great sails.

Shinobu leapt through the anomaly and grasped the steel. The wind was fierce up here, taking hold of his cloak and snapping it out behind him. The anomaly fell closed, and he surveyed the canvas beneath him.

His heart sank. He'd chosen the wrong sail. He could see five Watchers far below on a different section of the canopy, racing madly upward. Quin wasn't visible from this angle, but she must be just beyond his view, about to be trapped by those boys. Knives were glinting in the Watchers' hands as they climbed.

Aircars circled, their loudspeakers ordering the combatants to climb down immediately.

"Dammit, dammit!"

He was terrified for Quin. Somehow he made his thoughts relax again, let the focal do his thinking for him as he studied the athame. Almost at once he understood which coordinates to use.

He set the dials, hit the athame against the lightning rod. Another jump *There,* another set of coordinates, and he'd done it. He emerged onto the pinnacle of Quin's sail, one foot on either side of the peak.

Below him, a flap of canvas waved in the wind. Quin was trapped there, beneath some sort of shield. The boys were firing disruptors at her over and over, and the sparks bounced off in nearly constant flashes.

They're going to disrupt her, or kill her, he thought, fighting off full-scale panic. How could he have left her alone so long?

The other half of his mind gave him a very different thought: *Why do you care?*

I care because it's Quin!

And what is Quin? Only another Seeker. She isn't valuable except as a tool against others.

That's not what I believe.

In the future we have planned, we don't need her, the new half of his mind said.

"We" haven't planned anything, Shinobu thought angrily. These thoughts weren't his. They lived inside the focal and pretended to speak with his own voice. *I know who you are. You're a killer. Of Seekers and of rats. I'm not listening to you.*

You are me, half of his mind insisted, *and she isn't important.*

Shinobu screamed as loudly as he could to drive the second voice out of his head.

Everything the focal had shown him, everything he'd learned from Briac—all of that was to help Quin. He channeled all of his thoughts toward her.

She's what matters.

He could only hope that Briac had told him the truth, and he would be able to command those boys' attention and send them away, leaving Quin unharmed. He reached into the pocket of the cloak and fingered the smooth oval stone that fit so perfectly into his own palm. Then half sliding, half running, he plummeted down the sail toward the melee below.

CHAPTER 42

MAUD

The Young Dread released the shield and watched it spin far up the canvas into John's hands. The moment he and Quin were safely behind it, she drew her bow from her pack and let an arrow fly.

Her bolt pierced the shoulder of the dark-skinned young man wearing a disruptor, throwing him forward into the sail. He slid downward with arms and legs scrambling for purchase.

She was aware that she was involving herself in order to save John and Quin. While a Dread must stand apart from humanity, and from Seekers, John was her student now, in a fight that was not of his own making. He and Quin were being attacked by those boys, creatures of the Middle Dread who had, it seemed, been wreaking havoc in his name. A Dread must stand apart so that her mind was clear to judge, but the Young Dread's mind *was* clear. A Dread had created those boys, and she felt no qualms about stopping them.

She nocked another arrow at once, but the boys had stopped. They were gazing upward at something higher on the canopy. Someone was there, sliding down from the peak of the sail toward the attackers.

Maud threw her sight and saw that it was Shinobu, using the point of his whipsword as a brake against the canvas to keep himself from careening out of control. A Seeker's cloak billowed about his shoulders in the wind that buffeted up from the harbor below.

He was yelling something at the boys. She threw her hearing and caught two words: "Watchers! Away!"

The attacking boys moved toward him, turning their remaining disruptor in his direction.

Maud lifted her bow again, but the attackers stopped moving, and so did Shinobu. She couldn't see him now, because the boys—*Watchers?*—were standing in her line of sight. As she traversed across the sail to get a better view, she heard Shinobu say to them, "I don't want you here. Go. Go!"

When she could see him again, he was pointing down the sail and away.

And the Watchers were leaving. Even the one with Maud's arrow through his shoulder had staggered to his feet and was following the others in a painful retreat.

Why would they suddenly retreat at the sight of Shinobu? she wondered.

John and Quin had lifted the shield and were watching their attackers flee. The Young Dread found herself relieved when John's eyes immediately sought hers. Then he and Quin shared a brief look between them, an unspoken goodbye, before Quin moved toward Shinobu and John ran toward Maud.

"You heard me," John said as he arrived at her side. He looked shaken, and he was massaging the wound beneath his shoulder, which must be aching after the fight, but he also looked triumphant. "You heard me in your mind," he said.

"I did," she answered.

The Young Dread observed something different in John's gaze.

He was not looking over his shoulder to see where Quin would go or what the Middle's servant boys were doing. He'd returned to the Young Dread, and she had his full attention.

"I've made my choice," he told her. There was no need for him to say more; it was entirely clear that he had chosen to master himself and train with her.

She rested a hand on John's shoulder and said, "Good. We will go to the next cave from your mother's journal now."

He was still out of breath from the fight and his run down the canopy. "No rest first?" he asked, with half a smile crossing his face.

"Rest?" she repeated. "Now, after the heat of a fight, is the best time to train your mind."

QUIN

Quin leaned against the face of the sail and edged her way toward Shinobu across the narrow lip of the girder protruding beneath the canvas. He was carefully making his way to her as well. He was wearing the focal, and his eyes were bright with something like terror. When they were close enough to each other, he grabbed Quin's arms.

"Quin, I'm sorry. I left you. When I saw the disruptors firing, I—I . . ."

He looked completely shaken, and Quin guessed she must look exactly the same. The bombardment by disruptors had pushed her past her limit of endurance. He was holding her up, and she was grateful for it. Her legs weren't quite able to hold her anymore.

"How did you get rid of them?" she asked.

"Oh God . . . I have so much to tell you." He looked down to where the boys were now leaping back onto the first sail in a full-speed exit. Aircars were circling above the Bridge, loudspeakers ordering everyone off the canopy. "We should get out of sight."

They edged their way back to the flap she'd cut and ducked beneath it together.

"I've got to take off the focal," he told her.

Shinobu put his hands to the sides of the helmet, and with what appeared to be an immense amount of difficulty, he slowly pulled it off. As if it were too hot to touch, he dropped it onto the girder and used his foot to keep it from falling. Then, grabbing his head with both hands, he collapsed against the crisscrossed steel trusses.

"I see two of everything when I wear it," he muttered. "Two sides to everything, and one side is so bad . . ."

Quin's leg muscles were shaking. She sank to her knees and pulled him down with her, holding him against her tightly. The jangle of aftershock from the fight ran through her body. She caught a glimpse through the rip in the canvas: far below, John and Maud were disappearing into the shadow of a neighboring sail, moving in the opposite direction from the retreating boys. She averted her eyes from the steep drop.

"Quin," Shinobu breathed, beginning to recover. He took her face between his hands and looked at her as though amazed to find her unharmed. She was shivering, the adrenaline still coursing through her, yet the intensity of his gaze made her feel warm all over. He kissed her softly again and again on her lips and cheeks and neck. "I'm so sorry I left you. I shouldn't have left. How could I leave?"

"You scared me," she whispered, holding on to his arms so he wouldn't let go of her. "I thought I hadn't been careful enough about hiding the focal and maybe it had done something irreversible to you."

"I'm all right. I understand it now. Are you all right?"

Quin nodded. She was all right, though she was trembling uncontrollably. Now the canopy was trembling as well—a faint vibration from an athame was reaching up to them through the sail. The boys were leaving—or perhaps it was John and Maud. Shinobu's gaze turned from her to look out through the tear in the canvas, as if he'd had the same thought.

"John was here," he said. "Why? Did he hurt you?"

She shook her head. The confrontation with John felt as though it had happened days ago, though probably not more than an hour had passed.

"No. It was like he thought I might go off and help him. As if there were something still between us," she whispered. "But he did help me, Shinobu. They would have gotten me if he hadn't been here."

Her muscles were starting to shake more violently. Shinobu pulled her closer to him.

"I learned a lot," he told her. "We were right about the Middle Dread. He was doing so much . . . You have to help me think everything through." He drew the athame of the Dreads from his waist and began to adjust its dials. "But first I'm taking you home."

CHAPTER 44

CATHERINE

18 YEARS EARLIER

It was late at night, or perhaps very early in the morning, depending on one's perspective. Catherine sat cross-legged in the middle of the living room floor of Archie's flat, which had become her flat as well. He'd fallen asleep hours ago, but she wasn't tired.

Before her on the floor was a small piece of paper that bore writing in a tidy, foreign hand:

1. *Be firm in body, in good health.*
2. *Clear your thoughts, begin from neutral mind.*
3. *Focus upon the subject at hand.*
4. *Place the helm upon your head.*
5. *Follow these rules faithfully, lest the focal become a havoc helm.*

Mariko had written out those instructions and sent them to her. The five steps were directions for using the other object in front of Catherine—the focal she'd found inside Archie's wardrobe.

She picked up the helmet and felt its cool metal between her hands. She'd let it sit in the sun for days, soaking up energy, just as one did with a disruptor when charging it. Now it crackled faintly when she moved it, hinting at the power within.

Resting the focal lightly atop her six-months-pregnant belly, Catherine studied its details for the hundredth time. Or perhaps for the thousandth time. She had never worn it, however, never pulled it fully onto her head, even though she'd had Mariko's instructions for months.

The baby moved, and Catherine put a hand to her belly. There was always fresh amazement to feel him and to think: *There really is a child in there.*

She'd never given any thought to being a mother. There were so many things she wanted to do as a Seeker, and beyond that, there was the other idea, what she'd dreamed of becoming one day if the Old could be turned against the Middle Dread . . . and motherhood didn't fit into that plan.

But Archie had changed the landscape. He'd surprised her entirely by being overjoyed at the news that she was pregnant. When she'd suggested the timing wasn't great, considering that she was seventeen years old and they weren't married yet, he'd teased her for being old-fashioned. "We'll get married when we feel like it, anytime," he'd said calmly. "That's a ceremony for our parents, not for us."

She had slowly embraced the change in her life. Though she was only eighteen now, she would have a child, she would have Archie, and together they would search for truth in the history of Seekers.

Now, sitting on the living room floor, she read the first line of Mariko's instructions again:

Be firm in body, in good health.

There was the catch, the reason she hadn't used the focal. The reason she'd done nothing, as a Seeker, in a long while.

She felt perfectly healthy, and yet things were not so certain. Catherine had started to bleed at three months, and the doctors hadn't been hopeful that she would keep the child. She'd gotten into bed, and she'd scarcely gotten out since—and her bleeding had stopped months ago. Surely there was no more danger?

The weeks and weeks of rest had been torture. She'd made Archie clear out the living room furniture and rig up a practice dummy, and she'd spent vast amounts of time lying on a sofa shoved against a wall, instructing him in the use of whipswords and many other weapons. (She'd even adjusted the whipsword to work for Archie as it worked for her, which she'd promised him was the most romantic gesture a Seeker could make.) The dummy was badly battered but still looked better than the walls of their living room, which were covered in slashes and divots and outright holes.

And she'd taught Archie a good deal about Seekers. Though she hadn't told him everything, he understood that Catherine had an unusual way of getting from place to place, and that this method of travel was dangerous—you could lose yourself as you went, if you weren't careful with your mind. She'd immediately regretted her honesty when Archie made her promise that she'd do no such thing while she was pregnant, that she would take no risks until their baby was safe in their arms.

The next direction on Mariko's paper was:

Clear your thoughts, begin from neutral mind.

Catherine did. She emptied her mind of everything but an awareness of sitting on the living room floor, the metal helmet in her hands.

Focus upon the subject at hand.

For a long time she'd thought she understood what was happening to Seekers. They had run wild, because the Middle Dread was lax and cared very little about his duties as a Dread. There was a saying that within a house an athame ended up with whom it belonged. But because the Middle was not handing out proper justice, Seekers had begun to attack other houses, to steal athames to which they were clearly not entitled.

Now, however, Catherine was not sure things were this simple. The letter she'd found, tucked away in this very focal, had sent her thoughts off in a new direction. What if Seekers were not simply disappearing because of other Seekers' greed and because of a lack of Dread justice?

She'd always hoped she would find Emile, but it had been a quest in the back of her mind, not her prime focus. Now she felt that discovering what had happened to him might lead her to the heart of things. Perhaps he was dead, as her attacker in Hong Kong had implied. But if so, she wanted to know how it had happened, and why, and where.

She read the next instruction again: *Focus upon the subject at hand.*

Emile Pernet, house of the boar, she thought.

Place the helm upon your head.

She lifted up the focal and held it just above her hair, letting it hover there, inches from her scalp. She'd gotten this far dozens of times before, but she'd never actually put the helmet on. *I promised Archie I wouldn't do anything risky,* she thought. *But the baby is out of danger, and it's not as though I'm injured, and shouldn't I take this time to teach myself, so I'm ready after the baby comes?*

She felt the pull of the focal, as though it were willing her to slip it all the way onto her head. She inched it closer, and her eyes swept over the last line of Mariko's instructions:

Follow these rules faithfully, lest the focal become a havoc helm.

What did that mean?

"I know you don't put much importance on your own life," Archie had told her after she tried to get up and go for a walk during that first week of confinement to bed. "But I need you to put our child and yourself first now."

"But—" Catherine had started.

"But nothing," Archie had told her firmly. He'd given her a wicked look and said, "I'm your husband and you have to obey me."

"You're not my husband!" she'd said indignantly from the bed as he pulled the covers up to her chin.

"I'm better than a husband," he'd answered, kissing her forehead. "I'm the boy who got you pregnant and hasn't bothered to marry you yet."

She'd laughed at that, and so had Archie, but then he'd turned serious, taking her face in both his hands and leaning his head against hers. His voice had been husky as he said, "You will take care of yourself, and protect our baby. Promise me, Catherine."

Tears had sprung into Catherine's eyes at his tenderness. She wasn't used to having someone look out for her. Even her parents, for all their concern about her safety, her behavior—they thought of her as a valuable tool for their own ends, not as someone they wished to keep from harm for her own sake. She'd nodded against Archie's head.

"I promise," she'd told him.

Still, sitting now on the living room floor, she lowered her hands until the sides of the focal were brushing her temples. She felt a thrill of electricity where her skin touched the metal edges. *Can it really hurt to try?* she wondered.

Before she knew what she'd done, she'd pulled the helmet onto her head.

Catherine lay on the couch, curled around her journal, her small night-light illuminating the well-worn pages covered in rich and varied ink, including her own. The focal hummed on her head, expanding her mind so that it felt as though her awareness filled their whole flat and spilled out into nighttime London beyond. She was studying the entries under the illustration of a boar, Emile's house. There were pages and pages for that family, all the times when, and places where, members of the house of the boar or their athame had been spotted. The list ended a few years ago. Catherine herself had written the final entry:

Emile Pernet, seen on the Scottish estate.

She'd included the date of the last day she'd seen him. No one had admitted to encountering Emile or his parents since.

But Emile's mother was from a different house. She'd been born into the house of the horse, a fact Catherine had never thought about much. Yet now, wearing the focal, the connection was obvious. She flipped back and forth between the pages of the boar and the pages of the horse, comparing both. Between them, there was a repeating location. *Yes.*

She removed the focal. An unpleasant sensation washed over her, as though the helmet and her mind were stretching each other thin as they pulled apart. When it was off, she felt a rush of dizziness and had to lie back on the couch cushions with her eyes closed. Nausea came next, scaring her for several minutes, but eventually all of the sensations passed. After a time, when she was able to get to her feet, she returned the helmet and the journal to the safe they'd installed under a cabinet in the bathroom. Then she carefully crawled into bed.

Archie was sound asleep after a particularly grueling practice session that afternoon.

"Archie," she whispered. She shook his shoulder lightly.

Instantly he woke. His hand came out to touch her belly, and his eyes searched hers. "What is it? Are you all right? Did something happen?" he asked.

She shook her head. "I'm fine."

"You sure?"

As if on cue, the baby moved beneath Archie's warm hand. He lay back on his pillow, looking relieved, and she settled next to him.

"I might know where Emile's parents are," she said.

"Who?" he was already drifting back to sleep.

"Emile, the apprentice who disappeared from the estate."

He struggled to get his eyes open. "Right, him. From the estate."

"His parents disappeared too, but maybe they're just hiding." She moved her chin onto his shoulder and whispered, "Maybe there are still a lot of Seekers around, hiding, waiting for the right person to find them. I think there's somewhere we can check." She was aware that her excitement on this topic was strangely intense, as though her natural reaction was being magnified by her use of the focal.

"We can't go anywhere until after the baby comes . . ." he murmured.

"There hasn't been any bleeding for two months, Archie. The baby's all right. I'm all right."

"Catherine . . ."

"It's not too far. We shouldn't wait. What if I'm right but they don't stay in this place for much longer? I might not find them again."

She heard Archie sigh beside her, obviously exhausted. He slid his hand across her belly and moved closer.

"Suppose you find them," he murmured. "How do you imagine this search of yours will end?"

"I'll know what happened to Emile. And that might tell me what's happened to everyone else."

"What would you do if you knew that?"

Catherine took a slow breath. She didn't want to say her most private thoughts out loud—it felt as though the mere sound of them in the air could somehow call attention to what she was doing or jinx her search. Or more precisely, it felt as though whatever murderous Seeker mind she had unwittingly connected with, back when she'd found the athame hidden on Mont Saint-Michel, would be drawn directly to her if she formulated her deepest wishes into words. The memory of that strange connection always made her shiver. Whose mind had that been, with its cold, unpleasant, and ruthless thoughts?

But this was Archie, and she wanted to tell him, even if the telling felt dangerous. "Seekers are the ones killing each other, but the Middle Dread has allowed it to happen," she explained quietly. "And a long time ago he did many bad things. He even killed a Young Dread."

"So at the end of your search, you want to kill him?"

"No." Strangely, she realized, that idea had never even occurred to her. The Middle Dread, regardless of his faults, was a Dread, and she was a Seeker. The idea of murdering him went against her basic principles.

"Then what?" Archie pressed. He still sounded half-asleep, but she could tell she had his full attention.

"I don't want to say," she whispered.

"Why not?"

"It's private."

He laughed against her shoulder. "All right, then."

"You'll make fun of me, like my parents did."

"Do I ever make fun of you?"

She pulled his arm more tightly around her, and they lay that way for a while, both drifting off toward sleep. When she was in that state between awake and unconscious, her mind floating freely, Catherine murmured, "I've always felt I was meant to be a traveler through our past as Seekers and into our future. I imagined I would find the Old Dread. Somehow I'd find him. I'd tell him what the Middle Dread did to that Young Dread centuries ago. I'd tell him the other things the Middle Dread has done and failed to do . . . And then . . . the Old would get rid of the Middle and he would make *me* a Dread. He would train *me*. I would be the new Young Dread. And the Young Dread would become the Middle—because I think she's good. And we'd put things back the way they should be."

It took some time for Archie to answer, "You want to become a strange creature that lives for hundreds of years and hands down justice?"

"They're not strange creatures, Archie. They're people. They don't live for hundreds of years. They spend long stretches *There,* so they *seem* to live for hundreds of years. Their actual time awake in the world is just a normal lifetime's worth, or close enough."

"Hmm."

"You *are* making fun of me."

"I'm sorry," he whispered, "but wouldn't you rather just be Catherine?"

Catherine's eyes were still closed. She could feel Archie breathing evenly. His brow was against the back of her head and his warm hand on her belly.

"Being the Young Dread was what I used to want," she murmured. "But now I have you, and we'll have our son. He'll grow up in time, though, and someday, maybe a long time from now . . . what if we both trained with the Old Dread? What if we both became Dreads together? Maybe we could be with each other, travelers going forward through time, being just, being fair, helping. For centuries. What could be a better use of our lives . . . ?"

She was falling asleep even as she spoke, as though the focal had taken all of her energy. She was already dreaming, seeing herself and Archie walking into that strange future together. Before she lost consciousness entirely, Archie whispered, "You're such a romantic, Catherine. Most girls just want jewelry . . ."

CHAPTER 45

NOTT

Nott got his blindfold off by rubbing his face against the rock wall. He scraped his left cheek in the process, but that hardly warranted his notice. He was too busy staring furiously about his frozen surroundings and cursing his fellow Watchers.

They left me in my cave! Even saying the words in his head made his heart beat wildly with fear. It was what their master had always threatened them with—and many times he'd carried through on that threat. Nott knew this because sometimes their master woke a bunch of his Watchers at once and made them train together, and that didn't always end well for the Watchers. Now it was Nott's turn to be abandoned to die in his cave, the worst fate that could befall him.

It wasn't a cave exactly (and he was not entirely certain why it was *his* cave); it was more like a tunnel through rock and ice. Most of the ice was overhead, so thick in places that it was as dark as earth, but in others it let light through, like a great, irregular sheet of glass. There was sunlight somewhere above that ice, but too far away to bring him any heat.

The floor of the cave was rock that had never been warm. It radiated waves of cold that penetrated his muscles and sank into his bones. He was relieved to see that his feet were not tied, but this probably also meant there was nowhere for him to go.

He looked up and down the tunnel. The weak light from the distant sky made it impossible to tell which direction was the way out. Wilkin and the others had brought him here blindfolded, and they'd dragged him along for quite a while. Eventually they'd turned him around and around, then shoved him against the wall and pelted him with pebbles as they ran off. The pebbles had ricocheted everywhere, creating echoes that obscured which way the other Watchers had gone.

Nott chose a direction at random and stumbled into motion, his hands still tied behind his back. His fingers were numb—they'd gone numb even before the others had left. He'd have to cut through the ropes on his wrists soon to keep his hands from freezing altogether, but he hadn't seen anything sharp enough yet.

Something moved in the big pocket of his shirt. *My rat,* he thought. He'd caught this one near the deer carcasses at Dun Tarm. Knowing the animal was near made him feel a little better, and not quite so alone. If he managed to get his hands free before they froze, he'd have something to keep him occupied. It might take an hour to kill a healthy rat. The thought cheered him.

Nott didn't seem to be moving downhill, but even so, he began to wonder if he were headed deeper into the cave rather than toward its opening. He stopped and turned in a slow circle, but there were no clues pointing to the direction out.

"Stupid Wilkin, stupid Watchers," he said aloud as he forced himself into a jog. "Blaming me for losing the helm, blaming me for disrupting that baby Jacob."

It was good to hear his voice. It echoed slightly, coming back to him a fraction of a second later. It was almost like speaking to another person, or like speaking to the rat in his pocket.

In the confusion after the fight on the Bridge canopy, all the Watchers had returned to Dun Tarm, exhausted and still badly injured, and they'd started yelling at each other. They'd been scared by the appearance of that tall redheaded fighter—Shinobu, he was called—on the canopy, with their master's medallion clutched in his hand. The medallion would seem to be proof that their master was indeed dead, and it also might mean that Shinobu himself was their new master. All the Watchers were in a panic, wondering what would happen to them.

Everyone had been angry with everyone else, but Geb had been particularly furious about Nott tripping the others on the Bridge canopy. And then Wilkin had stood up and blamed Nott for losing the helm in the first place and for jumping into that anomaly during the earlier fight with Quin and Shinobu, which had been bad for all of them.

The other Watchers had all agreed that almost everything was Nott's fault and they had best get rid of him while they figured out what to do about Shinobu and their master's medallion.

"So they put me in my cave," Nott said aloud to the rat. "As if *they've* never done anything wrong."

The rat was still for a moment, and Nott imagined it had stopped fidgeting to listen. Like any prisoner, the rodent would be eager to keep his jailer talking.

It's not fair, he imagined the rat saying.

"It's not fair!" Nott agreed. "I jumped into the anomaly to get back the helm. Anyone would have done it. They followed me willingly."

You're small, said the rat. *They don't like to think you're equal to them.*

"I s'pose you know what that's like, being small," he observed.

"Everyone looking down on you all the time," the rat concurred, out loud this time. His voice sounded just like Nott's, but Nott didn't mind. Maybe he and the rat were from the same part of England.

"I'm smarter than they are," he told the rat. "I suppose I should be happy I won't have to follow those fools. Do you know—"

He stopped speaking and jogging. He'd come around a bend in the tunnel and was faced with a pile of rubble filling half the space. To pass it, he'd have to climb over. Since he hadn't been forced to climb over anything when he'd been brought into the cave, Nott reasoned that he'd been heading in the wrong direction all this time. The light from outside was getting dimmer; the sun was setting and he'd be in darkness soon.

"I chose the wrong way."

"Are you crying?" demanded the rat.

"Course not," Nott said, though his eyes had in fact started to fill with tears. "I'm not a baby."

At least some of the piled rocks had sharp edges. He stumbled over and went down heavily on his knees.

"Ouch," said the rat.

"Sorry," Nott told him. That word had come to him suddenly from distant memory. *Sorry.* His mother used to say it to him and Odger: *Say you're sorry. Sorry, are you? I'll make the two of ye sorry!* What did it mean exactly?

He twisted around so the ropes were up against a sharp edge of stone. It was difficult to find the right place to rub since his fingers were numb, but eventually he managed it. The friction produced heat, which felt so good that Nott momentarily forgot everything else. When the rope suddenly ripped apart, he was completely surprised.

"Look, hands," he said, bringing them in front of him and wiggling his fingers. They felt twice their normal size.

"I'd love some hands," the rat told him. "All I've got is feet."

"But you've got four of them," Nott pointed out. Then upon reflection he added, "Though maybe not for long."

He rubbed his hands together until they began to prickle and then burn as blood flowed into them. It felt like Wilkin and the others were poking hot needles into his flesh over and over and over.

"He probably *would* stick you with needles, if he thought of it," the rat mused.

"I poked him with a needle once while he was sleeping," Nott admitted. "All over his leg. I told him in the morning that a spider had bitten him."

"Did he believe that?" The creature sounded amused.

"He did. That and lots of other stories. He'll believe anything, Wilkin will."

When his fingers finally felt close to normal, Nott got stiffly to his feet. He turned back the way he'd come—and nearly jumped out of his skin.

Someone was lying on the tunnel floor up against the opposite wall, only a few yards away.

"Look," he whispered to the rat.

It was a dead someone, he saw on closer inspection, a teenaged boy, maybe Wilkin's age. He was dressed in warm clothing and a thick cloak, but he was frozen solid. He had probably been lying there for a very long while. By his clothes and by his cleanliness and by the sparkling white teeth Nott discovered when he pried up the boy's lip, Nott concluded he was not a Watcher.

A flash of metal caught Nott's eyes, and he drew a silver necklace out from beneath the boy's shirt. In the fading light he could make out the shape of a small silver boar.

There was blood on the necklace, and Nott soon found a fatal wound near the boy's heart. Blood had soaked through his clothing and then frozen, leaving a stain of dark ice on his shirt. There were stains on the boy's hands as well. In fact, it looked as if he'd dipped his right finger into his own life's blood and, with it, written something in the palm of his left hand:

EMILE

"Em-i-ly. Emily?" Nott sounded out. The boy seemed to have written a name.

"That's a girl's name," said the rat.

"So it is," said Nott. He'd had a cousin named Emily, long ago. She'd known how to write her name. That was why Nott could read it. "What's that?"

Something had been carved into a flat area on the cave wall, just above where the body lay. In the dimness, Nott could make out a series of numbers, so smoothly etched they seemed to have been melted into the rock. There were letters also.

He knew his numbers, mostly, but only some of his letters. He concentrated on the numbers, which he determined, after some scrutiny, to be 63, 48, 89.

"What do they add up to?" he asked the rat. "And why are they on the wall?"

The creature squirmed in his pocket but didn't answer.

"Course you don't know," Nott said. "You don't have to be embarrassed. Must be hard to learn to count if you haven't got hands. I think I might be able to sum them, though."

He stared at the numbers and tried to add them together. After several minutes he was forced to admit that the task was beyond him.

Soon it grew so dark that he couldn't see the ground properly and the carvings had all blurred into shadow. He'd been standing so long his legs felt like blocks of ice, but he couldn't walk anymore to get the blood flowing—he wasn't going to wander in pitch blackness.

He lowered himself to his knees. With a great deal of effort, he stripped the cloak and clothes from the stiff body of the boy named

Emily. He pulled the clothes over his own, then wrapped himself in his cloak and the boy's. Huddled on the cave floor, he tugged his hood over his head as far as it would go, and compressed his body into a tight little ball to trap his own warmth around him. It helped a bit.

Suddenly he had a thought.

"I bet it sums to two hundreds!" Nott whispered.

"I think you're right," the rat whispered back.

"So . . . this is a different two hundred than the one we Watchers use. But why is it here in my cave?" Nott ran his tongue across his teeth, feeling the grooves that had been carved there and the oily soot that was packed into them. "The two hundred I know is how we find the other sleeping Watchers in the dark place," he explained to the rat. "Our master had us all learn it by heart. We use the athame to go *There*—to our special spot—then fifty-three steps forward, fifty-nine to the right, fifty-four to the left, thirty-four to the right. That's how we found Geb and Balil and the babies."

"Waking them up might have been a mistake," the rat pointed out.

"True," said Nott. "Do you think these carvings, this other two hundred, are instructions for this dead boy?"

The dead boy had a boar around his neck, and Wilkin and Nott's athame had a boar on its pommel. Perhaps this cave was connected to boars in general.

"I don't know half the words you're using," the rat said.

"You're just a rat," Nott whispered. Then, with a flash of understanding, he said, "I think I'm supposed to freeze to death here, right here. Maybe that's why we get left in our caves—so my head and the numbers on the wall are kept together. Wonder what I'd find if I could follow what's on the wall."

The rat was struggling in his pocket. Nott's new position was pulling his shirt too tight for the creature's comfort. He slipped the rat out and held it in his hand. It didn't try to bite him. It was still too dazed for that.

He thought about setting it on the ground and hacking its feet off one after the other with pieces of stone. Rats really screamed when you did that. And they always tried to run away, even though they didn't have feet anymore.

But there wasn't enough light to see the rat or the stones. And there was something nice about holding the creature. Even the small amount of warmth it was generating made Nott feel like he had company.

He tucked the rat under his cloak and against his chest, and he let his eyes close as he clasped the creature to him in the dark.

CHAPTER 46

QUIN

Quin had expected Shinobu to take her back to her house on the Bridge. Instead they emerged onto the Scottish estate, not far from the small stone barn that was perched on a cliff above the river. Behind them, the anomaly Shinobu had cut lost its rhythm, began to vibrate more harshly, and then collapsed.

When it had disappeared, they were alone in the quiet of the forest. The only sounds were from the river far below and the birds in the trees behind them.

"You brought us . . . to our real home," she said.

Her muscles were still shaking from the fight on the Bridge canopy. She felt as though she might collapse at any moment. Shinobu didn't look much better, but he gently took hold of her and steered her toward the cliff barn.

"It seemed safer than going back to your house," he explained, his breath warm in her hair as she leaned against him. "The Bridge was in chaos, and now those boys know how to find you there."

"Are you wearing my father's cloak?" she asked. There was something about the look of it that reminded her of Briac.

He nodded against her head. "I saw your father when I was away from you. That's where I went. I made him answer my questions."

"He talked to you?"

"I used the focal to force him to talk to me. But here—you're shaking. I want to let you sit down. And I need to sit down too." He was guiding her toward the open doorway into the barn.

"You brought us right to the barn. How did you know these co-ordinates?"

"Honestly? The time I've spent in the focal helps with that. Wearing it's a bad thing, mostly, but it has its uses, and we're going to need it."

They stepped into the barn. Quin breathed in the smells of old straw, damp, and dust. The last time she'd been here was with John. They'd talked and they'd fought each other on the barn's roof, and she had finally seen John for what he was—a boy who'd been hope-lessly twisted by his mother. Not a Seeker after all, not really, because he wasn't seeking the better way, the proper path. For a moment, back on the Bridge, she'd experienced a twinge of what she used to feel for him. But she'd chased that treacherous feeling away. The John she'd once loved had never truly existed. He'd played a role to get what he wanted.

They walked past empty stalls that had once held animals, then came to the base of the ladder leading up into the barn's loft.

"Can you climb?" he asked softly. "I want us to be up where we can see outside. In case anyone comes."

"Do you think those boys will come here?"

"I don't know. I hope not," he said. "I ordered them to go back to their fortress."

"You *ordered* them?"

"I'll explain, but I have to get off my feet. I've been awake since I left you."

She was shaking so much that it was difficult to move up the ladder, but he kept a hand at her waist to steady her.

They emerged out of shadow when they reached the loft. There were large, glassless circular windows at each end of the barn, one above the loft and the other on the opposite wall of the building. It had been midafternoon in Hong Kong when they left. It was early morning here in Scotland, the pale disc of the rising sun visible through a layer of clouds. It painted the loft and the rafters beneath the slate roof with a ghostly light.

The windows gave a view up and down the river and to the hills beyond the estate. Shinobu leaned out to look back toward the forest.

"We're still alone," he murmured. He let out his breath in relief, as though only now would he allow himself to relax.

A wooden platform was wedged up against one wall, with a bedding of straw atop it. Quin had slept here once, after her first assignment—when she had, against her will, helped her father commit murder. She'd brought the straw to the barn herself and had slept here alone while dreaming of getting away. Now Shinobu settled her onto the makeshift bed, and she was grateful to be still. He lay next to her and pulled her into his arms, keeping her warm. Eventually she stopped shaking.

"I have so much to tell you," he whispered. "I think I understand the focal now . . . but it still makes me strange. Don't let me wear it again unless you're with me, all right? You have to tell me if I'm behaving oddly. I put a rat in my pocket . . ."

"A rat?" She tried to imagine why in the world he might do that.

He laughed, sounding exhausted. "I let it go."

She felt Shinobu sit up and opened her eyes just enough to see him removing his cloak. He spread it out over both of them, then lay back down and pulled her to him.

Her heart was steadying. The intensity of the fight and the terror she'd felt when those disruptors had fired, over and over, were gradually releasing their grip on her. Shinobu's arms were around her, his hands warm across her center. They were safe for the moment, in a quiet place, out of danger.

Feeling Shinobu's heartbeat against her back, Quin drifted off.

They must have slept for a long time. When Quin was next aware of herself, the light in the barn was different. Darker clouds had moved in, and rain was falling in heavy drops against the roof. She didn't want to open her eyes all the way. Instead she turned and tucked her head into Shinobu's warm neck, pulled his arms back around her.

The rain fell steadily, drowning out the noise of the river and the forest, isolating them from the world. Quin moved just enough to find Shinobu's lips and kiss him. He stirred and kissed her back. And then they were both awake enough. Somehow he was pulling her clothes off as if they were nothing more than gauze he was brushing away, and he was kissing her lips, her neck, the soft hollow at the base of her neck, and she was whispering to him, "I'm . . . I've never . . ." And he stopped for a moment and looked down at her, a slow smile spreading across his handsome, sleepy face, and he whispered back, "I'm so glad you've never."

And then they were warm and together, at last, and neither one of them fell unconscious, not for a long while.

CHAPTER 47

CATHERINE

18 YEARS EARLIER

Though the china cup in Catherine's hand was so delicate that sunlight shone through it, its fragile body was decorated with a savage pig, drops of painted blood dripping from its tusks and casting spots of red across the murky tea within. The tea itself was good—rich, creamy, and just the right temperature. Catherine took another sip as she watched Monsieur Pernet's back.

The man stood at the kitchen sink, refusing to look at her. He was staring out the window instead, a teacup clutched in his large hand, and Catherine guessed he was keeping a close eye on Archie, whom she'd last seen kicking pebbles around by the front door. Archie hadn't wanted her to come to this secluded French village, and he hadn't been happy about the long uphill walk to the Pernets' hidden cottage, which stood nearly concealed among the ruins of a fifteenth-century monastery.

Catherine had gained entrance only by showing the Pernets the athame-shaped scar on the inside of her left wrist. They'd responded by, somewhat unwillingly, showing her their own identical scars. Archie didn't have such a mark yet—though Catherine would finish his training soon enough, and one day she'd get the Young Dread to make him official—and so he was waiting outside.

Catherine had been nursing a hope that she would find Emile in the house with his parents, that he had been alive and safe all this time. But no, only his mother and father were living in the cottage. Madame Pernet sat in an armchair across from Catherine, darting looks at Catherine's pregnant belly. Sunlight came in through the kitchen window, lighting the old stone walls in warm tones.

"I always liked Emile," Catherine ventured. "He was very good in training. We apprentices were surprised when he didn't come back to the estate. Our instructors told us he quit."

Monsieur Pernet's wide back shifted, and his wife coughed nervously.

"You thought we were keeping him from the estate," the wife said, "and we thought the estate was keeping him from us. But in reality he'd gone off without telling us where."

The husband shifted again.

"Sit down, darling, please," the woman said to her husband in French.

The man lowered himself into the other armchair. He glanced at Catherine from beneath heavy brows, then looked away.

"I'm sorry to show up unannounced," Catherine told them. She turned her wrist so the athame brand was clearly visible again, to remind them both of the obligation that came with their Seeker oaths. "I only hope you will honor the code among Seekers and answer my questions. They're asked in the spirit of fellowship with all Seekers."

The man made a gruff sound of agreement. The woman pulled an ancient cigarette from a box on the side table, lit it with a tarnished metal lighter, and took a long pull from it as she glanced out the kitchen window. She seemed to be watching Archie's shadow, which stretched, long and thin, down the path toward the village.

"My husband and I both trained on the estate when we were younger," the woman said, her eyes flicking to Catherine, then away. Her French accent was light. "We were never the most active Seekers, but we did our part in a small way. We spent years finding and destroying the camps of men who created child soldiers. And smaller acts, closer to home as well . . . though for a long time we have kept to ourselves.

"When Emile was old enough to train on the estate, he went. He was happy there for a while. But in that last year, he became . . . quieter. Perhaps he began to question the value of being a Seeker. I thought it was natural. The training gets harder, life is less like play and more like work. He had few friends there. He preferred the company of his cousins, who trained at home and not in Scotland.

"My husband caught him at Christmas, that last year. Emile had found our family's athame, even though it was very well hidden in our attic. He was"—the woman motioned with her hands, miming adjusting an athame's dials—"preparing to use it."

The husband nodded slightly but still said nothing.

"But . . . wasn't he too young to know what the athame was then?" Catherine asked. She'd last seen Emile when he was fourteen, months before he would have been trained to use an athame.

"Of course, yes," his mother said. "But still he acted as though he knew how to use it. I assumed they had accelerated his training on the estate." She inhaled deeply from her cigarette, her eyes still restlessly roving the room and the view outside. "They had a fight, my husband and my son. When Emile disappeared—with our athame—we thought he'd gone back to the estate to get away from his father and taken the athame. But of course he wasn't there. We couldn't find him anywhere."

"And on the estate, our instructors told us that you'd kept him from coming back."

"Perhaps they didn't want to frighten you."

The woman had finished her cigarette. She crushed it out in an ashtray with a boar emblem stamped into it. Emile's mother was not very old, Catherine realized, and once must have been very fit, but she seemed used up and frail, as though fear and the loss of her son had taken decades from her.

Catherine asked, "Do you have some idea where he—"

The woman shook her head emphatically, cutting Catherine off. She got to her feet and took a framed photograph from the mantel.

"Emile is our only son, but my cousin has sons, Emile's closest friends."

She took a seat again and handed the picture to Catherine. Catherine stopped breathing when she saw it. It was a photograph of Emile and four other boys. On Emile's left was a young man with dark brown hair and an easy smile playing across his lips. She had seen that smile. His face had been covered in dark blue paint, but she'd seen those lips sneering at her. *Where is the athame?* he'd demanded, straddling her on the floor of the club bathroom in Hong Kong. *Emile was just as slow, and things ended just as badly for him.*

Catherine tapped the boy's face. "This . . . is Emile's cousin?"

The woman nodded. "Second cousin. There are four brothers. I would have told you to ask his oldest cousin, Anthony, where Emile went. But Anthony is missing now as well."

He's not exactly missing, Catherine thought. She'd crawled out from under him as he bled to death in Hong Kong. She swallowed, attempting to push the memory from her mind.

"He . . . Anthony was never on the estate," Catherine said softly, trying to keep her voice even. "But he trained as a Seeker?"

The woman nodded distractedly. "His father trained him and his brothers himself—though, why, I don't know. They'd lost their family athame—house of the horse—three generations ago. And yet still Anthony has disappeared, like Emile disappeared, like many Seekers disappear. And one of his brothers was recently attacked and left injured."

That must have been Anna's attacker, Catherine thought.

Monsieur Pernet looked uncomfortable. He was shifting in his chair and staring at the floor.

Hesitantly Catherine asked, "It's only— Do you think it's possible the cousin had something to do with Emile's disappearance? If his family didn't have an athame anymore . . . isn't it possible he was after Emile's?"

"They were family," the woman said in a harsh whisper, as though the very thought of what Catherine suggested was overwhelming. "Of course that's not possible. They were the best of friends."

Emile's father raised his eyes to watch Catherine closely. His face was red with some suppressed emotion, and Catherine wasn't sure if he was on the verge of throwing her out of his house or if he was about to cry. At last the man drove one of his fists into the open palm of his other hand. "He can't kill Seekers himself," he said.

The wife looked up at her husband quickly, her expression frightened.

"Who can't?" Catherine asked.

"You must know who by now."

At once she understood. This man was trying to tell her something very like what Briac had hinted at. "You're talking about the Middle Dread," she said evenly.

The man nodded his head once slowly.

Catherine said, "But—of course a Dread wouldn't kill a Seeker . . . unless a crime had been commit—"

"You misunderstand me," the man told her, cutting her off. Then, his voice rough with the weight of the subject, he said, "He *wants* them dead. He *desires* to kill them himself. But he can't."

"Why would . . . A Dread has his oaths. He would never—"

She was interrupted by a rumbling sound from the man's barrel chest, which she recognized after a moment as a disgusted laugh. He said, "Oaths? No. You can't think of him as a Dread. He is . . . his own creature. With his own plans. He desires to kill Seekers but he can't do it himself."

Catherine stopped herself from speaking as she wrapped her mind around what Monsieur Pernet was telling her.

At last she asked, "*Why* can't he kill Seekers?"

"That is a bit of a mystery," the man answered gravely. "It is something between the Middle Dread and the Old Dread. I have my theory. Are you able to read another's thoughts, Catherine?"

Catherine was startled by the sudden question. "Not—not on purpose," she answered him. She recalled the cold mind that had touched hers before she went to Mont Saint-Michel. "But it's happened a few times."

"So you know it is possible."

She nodded a bit reluctantly; it was a part of being a Seeker that she didn't much care for.

"I believe the Old Dread sees into the Middle Dread's thoughts," Emile's father told her gravely. "He will know and come after the Middle if he kills Seekers himself, because the old man is just and would not tolerate such evil acts. But if the Middle gets others to do the deeds for him, perhaps the Old Dread doesn't know."

"Stop!" his wife hissed, reaching to cover his mouth, like a small child shushing a larger one.

He held her away and went on, "So he does not kill them himself. He gets them to kill each other instead."

"Be quiet!" His wife was frantic. "He will *know*."

"How will he know?" Monsieur Pernet asked her, raising his voice. "He doesn't see into *my* mind."

In a low, terrified undertone, she said, "He will hear from someone what we've done—"

"We've lost our athame. We've lost our son. We're not Seekers anymore. He doesn't care about us."

"We agreed we would say nothing," she pleaded in a whisper.

"I will tell her what we know," Monsieur Pernet said. His wife was struggling in his grasp, but he continued to hold her patiently, like a lion holding an unruly cub. More gently he said, "If we cannot tell a good Seeker the truth, we serve no purpose at all."

Madame Pernet turned her head away, and Catherine suspected the woman would have cried if she'd had the energy for it.

"He can't kill Seekers himself, or the Old Dread will know what he's done. So he gets Seekers to kill each other for him," Catherine repeated.

In a way, this was what Briac had been trying to tell her on the Tube. For a long while she sat still, thinking through the ramifications of this new information. How stupid and naive she'd been! All this time, she'd thought only that the Middle was a terrible Dread, failing to keep Seekers honest. But this made much, much more sense. The Middle was the one *causing* Seekers to do terrible things. That was why so very many terrible things had been done. She asked, "How does he get them to kill each other?" But she realized she already knew. "He . . . he promises them the athames of other houses?"

"Sometimes, yes," the man told her. "And other times he encourages them to take revenge on another family for past wrongs done."

"How did you learn this about him?" she asked.

"The Middle hides his tracks well. Most Seekers who have been his victims have suspected nothing of his greater plan," he said.

"But the Middle does not hide his tracks perfectly. A friend, in my training days, he confided to me that he'd made a pact with the Middle Dread. He made me swear an oath that I would never tell another person. But this agreement with the Middle—my friend said it would secure an athame for his family, an athame belonging to another house. If you come from a family that is desperate enough to get their hands on an athame, you might be willing to make such a pact."

"And did he get an athame?"

The man slowly shook his head. "I never saw him again. He disappeared, but not, I think, before killing someone else." The man paused, and Catherine perceived how long the man had been holding his silence, how strange it was for him to speak now but what relief it brought. In a moment, he continued, "You see, the next year, on the estate, another friend of mine had become obsessed with taking revenge against the first friend's family. Enemies had been made."

"But why?" Catherine asked. "Why does he want us dead?"

The man shrugged, a heavy, exhausted motion. "He is his own creature, with his own plans. That is how you must think of him. One of his plans—maybe his only plan—is to get rid of Seekers."

"And you think that's what happened to Emile?" she asked him. "The Middle Dread convinced someone to come after him for his athame?"

After a moment's careful thought, Emile's father answered, "I believe someone came to Emile and made him doubt. Someone close to him"—Monsieur Pernet *knew* it had been Emile's cousin Anthony, Catherine understood all at once, but he hadn't shared that unpleasant truth with his wife—"offered to show him things about Seekers that he wouldn't learn on the estate, things that were more true than what his instructors were teaching him. This person convinced

Emile to come away with him. And then, yes, he killed Emile for his athame."

But why did Anthony need my athame, then? Catherine wondered. *Wouldn't this mean he'd had Emile's already by that time?*

Emile's mother leaned into Catherine and whispered, "Do you want all of our family to disappear?" She gestured at Catherine's pregnant belly. "And yours as well?"

Catherine was still holding the man's gaze. "Do you know where Emile was going at the end? Where his killer took him?" she asked, sensing the answer would be different now.

The man released his wife, who curled into herself, as though she could shrink away from their conversation.

"I believe he went to a cave—a place that belongs to our family, to the house of the boar," he said.

Catherine's breath caught in her throat. She was coming full circle, back to the hidden caves, which she'd been certain must hold traces of where the missing Seekers had gone.

He took up a pen and a piece of paper and carefully wrote out a series of symbols. Beneath these, with a sure, quick hand, he sketched a landscape with a cave at its center.

"Have you ever been to Norway?" Catherine asked when she'd left the house and joined Archie outside.

The day was fine and warm, and the slight breeze carried the scent of flowers and the distant ocean. From the Pernets' house, they looked down a steep cobbled lane to the village spread out below them, and to vineyards and fields beyond that.

"Why do I get the feeling it doesn't matter how I answer that question?" Archie asked as they began to walk.

"Look at this."

She held up the slip of paper with the coordinates Emile's father had written out for her, and the drawing of the cave.

"You know I can't read those made-up hieroglyphics," Archie said. He was teasing her, because he could read them, a bit; she was teaching him.

"We have to go to Norway," Catherine told him. She tucked the paper into her pocket and slipped a hand into Archie's.

"You can't go to Norway now," he said.

"It will be all right, Archie. I came here, didn't I? I'm fine."

He fell silent without agreeing, and Catherine was already thinking about ice fields and warm boots. If she could get proof of the Middle causing Seekers' deaths, the Old Dread and the Young Dread would have to listen to her.

When they reached the bottom of the lane and emerged into the open square of the medieval village, Catherine tumbled forward onto her knees and cried out.

"What is it?" Archie asked, catching her and pulling her gently upright.

She didn't know how to answer him. She'd felt a warm wetness down her leg, which she knew immediately meant she'd started to bleed again. But there was something else that was harder to explain: The moment they'd emerged into the square, she'd had the strangest vision. She'd seen herself and Archie from afar, as though watching herself from the other side of the square. Along with that vision, she'd experienced such a surge of hatred and fury, her knees had given out.

"Catherine?" he said urgently.

"I'm seeing . . . He's here . . ."

She was peering inside the mind of another person. It was the same mind she'd touched once before, that morning when the words

Saint-Michel" had fallen into her thoughts. The connection had disturbed her then, but now—now she grasped whose mind it was, and she was terrified.

Archie held her up. "There's a man looking at us," he said. His eyes were on the other side of the square.

"Where?" She tried to follow the line of his gaze. It was summer, and great numbers of locals and tourists milled about the sidewalks. "Where?" she asked again.

"That way, but he's gone."

"Archie, what did he look like? Was he wearing a cloak? Was he tall?"

"A cloak? Like something from the olden days? Of course not. He was wearing a T-shirt."

"Was he tall?"

Archie shrugged. "Big, at any rate. Like a bull."

She didn't need more description. This time, when their minds had touched, she'd recognized him. She hadn't, as she'd thought before, heard the thoughts of a Seeker who was willing to kill; she'd stumbled into the mind of the Middle Dread himself.

Though Catherine had been looking for proof against the Middle for a long time, she'd always felt protected by his role as a Dread. She'd believed he was a terrible judge of Seekers, but a judge nonetheless—a Dread and not someone who would target her. After her conversation with Monsieur Pernet, she had no such illusions.

Past incidents appeared to her in new light. When Anthony had attacked her in Hong Kong, he hadn't been acting of his own volition. The Middle Dread had spurred him to do it. She must have ruined the Middle's plans by taking the fox athame from the chamber beneath Mont Saint-Michel. The Middle had sent Anthony to Hong Kong to find her athame and maybe also to get rid of her, and she'd obstructed his plans even further.

And now the Middle Dread had followed her here. If she'd seen inside his head, was he seeing inside hers? Had her years of searching out his misdeeds made a connection between them?

"We have to go," she said.

"You want to go to Norway *right now*?"

"No—take me home. Please." She was leaning over, clutching her belly. "I need to see the doctor . . ."

Archie's face fell. With no further words, he slipped an arm around Catherine's back and walked briskly with her away from the village square.

CHAPTER 48

JOHN

John could barely keep his eyes open in the glare of the sun. Like the Young Dread, he wore deer pelts over his clothing, against the frozen air, and their weight and warmth felt natural to him. The ice field stretched out around them on all sides, its flat white surface broken by tall columns of black rock. The footing was treacherous, deep fissures revealing themselves suddenly, just as John was about to set his foot down. Even so, he was running, using a hopping, leaping gait across the upward-sloping field. The focal helped, urging his thoughts into an expansive state that allowed him to see a dozen things where once he might have seen only one.

"Faster!" the Young Dread called.

In the distance, difficult to see because it meant looking directly into the sun, was the snow-covered slope of a high peak. Low on its flank was another cave, this one belonging to the house of the boar.

The Young Dread had been right to bring him to confront Quin on the Bridge. Now Quin, Catherine, Maggie—all had receded in his thoughts to shadowy, distant figures. He was again running with the focal, sensing the ice, the sky, the cave ahead, and the distant ocean beating against the frozen shore miles away. He fixed his thoughts on what he wished to know: *If my mother came to this cave, what did she find? And if she didn't make it here, what had she hoped to discover?*

Maud ran parallel to him, her strides fast and light. She'd warned him this run across the ice would not be easy; she was going to push him to the edge of his capabilities.

"Ready yourself!" she called. She was wearing the disruptor, and she'd given John the metal disruptor shield.

A narrow crevasse showed itself, almost invisible in the shadow of a pillar of rock. John leapt the fissure as the disruptor began to whine. That sound filled him with trepidation, but for the first time ever, his fear of the disruptor didn't change his focus.

A few moments later, the Young Dread fired the weapon. Sparks came out of the barrel in a swarm, buzzing in the cold air as they raced toward him. John pivoted, swinging the shield to give him momentum. Then he held it in front of him and let the sparks burst into nothingness against it in a shower of rainbow light.

Almost immediately, Maud fired again.

John leapt forward and twisted behind another icy pillar, and when the swarm had passed, he continued to run.

The sparks will come, John thought. *Let them come. I will be ready.*

Before the Young Dread could fire the disruptor a third time, he drew the focal from his head and tossed it to her.

"Take it!" he called.

He nearly stumbled in a wave of disorientation, but in another few steps, the feeling was gone. *My focus is mine,* he thought. *The helmet is only a crutch.*

Without the focal, the bullet wound near his shoulder began to throb, but the pain didn't linger in his thoughts. *It is only pain.*

The Young Dread fired the disruptor again. John turned to the side, nimbly jockeying around a series of deep, interconnected crevices. Almost as an afterthought, he raised the shield and warded off the sparks.

"Careful, Apprentice," Maud said in her slow and steady way— she was not even out of breath. "When you think too much of your own skills, that's when they will fail you. Your mother's mind was unsound, and she still thought well of herself. And that was when she was attacked and disrupted, John. Deservedly."

She was taunting him cruelly, but—

They are only words. Sounds in the air. My focus is stronger.

He glanced down at the shield on his left arm and comprehended its true purpose. His fingers found a lever on the underside. When he twisted it, the shield sprang to life. It hummed on his arm, and its interlocking rings began to spin, some clockwise, some counterclockwise, in a dizzying array.

The Young Dread fired the disruptor. John turned the shield, and the sparks streamed into it, buzzing and crackling. And then the sound changed. The rings of the shield were spinning faster, and the crackle of electricity became louder. The shield strained against his arm, moving with gyroscopic force. The disruptor's sparks were thrown from the shield like fireworks from a Catherine wheel, spraying back at the Young Dread. She dove for the ice and rolled as the swarm flew over her. John felt a glow of satisfaction—for once he had surprised Maud, not the other way around.

The cave was close enough now to see it in detail, despite the sun's glare. When the Young Dread had gracefully regained her feet, John tossed her the shield. It was a fascinating device, but it too was a crutch.

She caught the shield with one hand and fired the disruptor at him again with the other. She wasn't going to be easy with him just because he'd decided to give up his protection.

Without focal or shield, John was completely exposed as the

sparks rushed toward him. He let the fear come, without changing his concentration. He leapt onto a mound of broken ice and jumped from slab to slab, carrying himself upward. The sparks hit well below his feet, dispersing harmlessly against the ice. Then he leapt down and sprinted for the cave.

He reached it before the Young Dread, the first time he'd ever beaten her in a footrace. He stood in the frozen interior, waiting for her and feeling a small sense of triumph. When she arrived a few moments later, there was something different in her presence. Maud did not smile at him, or pat him on the back or make any move out of the ordinary. But when she spoke, it was as though he were receiving the highest praise one person could offer another.

"John," she said, "that was very good."

CHAPTER 49

MAUD

The frozen cave was like something from a fairy story, a place Maud's nurse would have described to her at bedtime, back in the long-ago past, when the Young Dread had still been an ordinary child. The cavern had a high roof of rock, with seams of ice branching through it, and from these seams hung vast, intricate icicles like handblown chandeliers or tiny enchanted cities. At the back of the cave was a smaller tunnel leading deeper into the mountain, but the sun had already set, and exploration would have to wait for morning.

There was no wood here, but the Young Dread built them a fire with the charcoal from John's pack. It was John's duty to make their fires and cook their food, but she was content tonight to let him wander the cavern in the twilight for a few more minutes.

Maud felt an upwelling of satisfaction as she watched him staring at the hanging icicles. When she'd first begun his training, she gauged his progress by the intensity of her own irritation—if she'd felt slightly less vexed after a training session, she'd counted that as success. But pride was an entirely new sensation. John's run across the ice field had been impressive, and the Young Dread could see the elation of that run still surrounding him like an airy mantle.

When he came to sit by the fire, however, his manner had entirely changed and the elation had all bled away. By then, the fire was burning red, and John stared into it pensively as he began to heat the dried strips of rabbit that would be their dinner.

"Have you been here before?" he asked her at last. His quiet voice echoed in the enormous space.

"Yes," Maud replied. "I came once, when the Seekers from the house of the boar held a ceremony welcoming two new children to their family. That was a very long time ago, when these caves were still in use."

John nodded, but he didn't appear to be listening very attentively. His mind was elsewhere as he handed her the food.

They ate, and guessing at the source of his current mood, the Young Dread told him, "I taunt you when we train, John. I try to break your focus. But I don't believe the things I say about your mother."

He glanced up at her, and she was reminded of how he'd looked as a child, on that night in Catherine's apartment, small and lost.

"That's just it," he said. "What if she *was* mad?" He was wrestling with something. Maud remained quiet as he looked back into the heart of the fire, as though an answer might be waiting there for him. "I don't feel it," he told her after a long while, and his voice was pained. "Before we came here, I was *certain*. My mother was hunting down the houses who had harmed us. She came here—or she intended to come here—to find the boar Seekers and make them pay. And I was doing the same. But . . . I don't feel it."

His eyes sought hers, and there was dismay in his countenance. He whispered, "On the ice, you were firing the disruptor at me, and I

— 333 —

was running for my life. I was scared of the disruptor, but fear wasn't what I felt, not really. I felt something else. And I still feel it. I feel my mother's hope. I feel her curiosity." He paused, then said, "I know she hated the other houses. I was with her until I was seven years old, and she was full of hate. But . . . that's not the Catherine I see in her journal. And now it's not the Catherine I see in my mind. I feel the other Catherine. The real one."

A strong emotion came over Maud, one she didn't quite know how to categorize, though it was, perhaps, *camaraderie.* She'd experienced the very same thoughts about Catherine as they ran across the ice; perhaps she and John had shared those thoughts between them. The Young Dread had seen who Catherine really was and what she'd intended—before Catherine changed, before she'd become cruel and violent and fixed on revenge.

"I feel her too," Maud told him. "She wasn't mad, not at first. Not for a long while." She thought of Catherine on the estate as an apprentice, and she thought of Catherine later. Of all the Seekers the Young Dread had known in recent times, Catherine had been perhaps the *least* mad, the most aware—in the beginning, at any rate. *If you put all this effort to other use,* Catherine had said on that night, her last true night alive, *imagine how different things could be.* "Your mother was a Seeker in the noble sense of the word," she told him.

"I think she was," he whispered.

Then John's head dropped into his hands, and his shoulders began to tremble. This was so unexpected that it took Maud some time to understand that he was crying. Then the grief came like a storm and he sobbed helplessly.

Eventually, when the squall blew itself out, he spoke with his face still in his hands. "I've done so many terrible things . . . to Alistair, to Shinobu . . . but mostly to Quin." He lifted his head and looked across the fire at the Young Dread, his face vulnerable. "She *should* hate me, Maud. I deserve her hate. My mind's been so narrow and so wrong . . ."

The Young Dread let silence fall between them. Then she said, "We have all done things we regret, John. The question is how to change."

"*Can* I change?" he asked her.

The Young Dread studied the coals for a while, watching the pulse and dance of the heat. Their sprint to the cave had changed not only John's mind, it had changed her own. When she spoke, it was in her steady way, but she felt the words more deeply than most she'd uttered.

"I have realized something about your mother today," she told him. "She asked me, many years ago, about the Dreads, about the Middle Dread. She wanted to be rid of him—to help other Seekers and to help me, though I brushed her off and ordered her away. She wanted to be rid of him, and she wanted to become a Dread."

John's tears had stopped, and he was watching her closely. "To *become* a Dread?"

She considered her words before she spoke again. She said, "I do not wish to be called the Middle Dread. That name has been ruined. And yet I cannot be the only Dread in the world. We Dreads must take turns moving through time, often one stretched out while the other is awake. To make this possible, I must train another, just as I was trained. And with that other, I must learn the purpose and use of all of my master's tools. Whoever I train must help me learn everything I must know."

He was looking at her almost as if in a trance.

"John," she said, "I can train you enough to be sworn as a Seeker. You will make it to your oath, I am certain. But I believe you could be more than a Seeker."

His voice was scarcely a whisper as he asked, "Do you mean *me*? Train me to be a Dread?"

"I cannot say that you would succeed. But it is possible."

She watched him absorb her words. After some time, he asked, "My mother . . . wanted this?"

"I believe she did."

He was quiet, and Maud watched the dance of orange light across his face. John didn't look sad anymore; he looked as though he stood at the edge of a cliff and was deciding whether or not he would jump.

At last, he asked, "Do you feel . . . human? After spending so much time *There*? Or do you lose your humanity?"

It was nearly the same question Catherine had asked her years ago, in the woods on the estate: *Would it be hard for someone like me? A life like yours?* Catherine's question had stayed with her, and Maud knew she had no answer for it. Had she lost her humanity? If you became different from every other person who had ever lived on the earth, were you still one of them? Or did you become something else?

Eventually she said, "I've felt happiness and hatred. And compassion, John—I have felt compassion for you and for your mother, and others. But Dreads must stand apart."

"Would I . . . would I ever be able to love a girl? Or become a father?"

"We Dreads do not . . . become intimate," she answered. She heard the steadiness of her voice and wondered if that very steadiness was arguing to him against becoming a Dread. From what she'd glimpsed of men and women, or boys and girls, they didn't want perfect steadiness from each other. They wanted passion. She had a sense of what that word meant, but no experience of it.

"But who is 'we'?" he asked. "If you are the only active Dread, can't you decide what it means to be a Dread?"

For a fraction of a second, Maud took offense at the insolence of his question. But why shouldn't he ask? She was suggesting he do far more than be her student. She was suggesting he change himself in a fundamental manner.

In a flash of clarity, the Young Dread saw him differently, and herself differently as well, as though she were seeing through John's eyes. She looked down at her hands and extended them in front of her, marveling at the very ordinariness of them, their similarity to the hands of every other person alive.

"Is that sort of feeling . . . that sort of love . . . is it so very important?" she asked him. She could almost hear herself saying, *It is only love,* in the way she often said *It is only pain.*

"I don't know," John whispered. "Maybe. I—"

But she rose to her feet, cutting him off. There was noise in the dark tunnel at the back of the cave. "Extend your hearing," she told him quietly.

John was still very much a novice, but he was getting better at this skill. "Someone's coming through the tunnel," he said after a moment.

The Young Dread nodded. It was what she'd heard as well.

They waited a long while as the dragging gait got closer and closer, pausing frequently and moving in irregular bursts. They were hearing the footsteps of someone forcing himself on when his body didn't wish to comply. And it was someone small, Maud thought, judging by the lightness of the tread. She let her hands rest on the weapons at her waist.

At last the footsteps were only yards away, and then a figure shuffled around the final bend of the icy tunnel and stood bathed in the weak glow of their coal fire. The apparition raised an arm against the light as though it were so bright as to be blinding. The figure wore two cloaks and so many clothes that its body disappeared inside them, and yet it managed to convey the impression of being half frozen.

Maud recognized the visitor. It was the youngest Watcher, the one who looked perhaps twelve years old. He lowered his arm as his eyes became accustomed to the light in the cavern, revealing a dirty, swollen, freckled face. He looked from Maud to John and then back again. If he knew them from their earlier encounters, he gave them no indication.

After he'd stood in the mouth of the tunnel for a long while, he suddenly plunged a hand inside his layers of clothing. He drew out a small dark shape and hurled it viciously onto the ground at Maud's feet.

It was a rat, frozen solid.

"What's the point!" the boy yelled. "It died in the cold! *I* was supposed to die here in my cave with it."

His eyes swept the chamber and grew wide when he spotted something behind the Young Dread. Without warning, the boy threw himself across the cave at a run, knocking past her as he went. He seized upon their pile of supplies like a jackal onto a freshly killed carcass.

In two quick leaps, the Young Dread got hold of him. She grabbed fistfuls of his clothing and pulled him well off the ground. His dirty fingers were groping for the focal, but she nudged it away with her foot.

"I need it!" he cried. "I need the helm! Please! Please!"

And then, suspended in Maud's grasp, the focal out of reach on the floor, he burst into tears.

CHAPTER 50

SHINOBU

When Shinobu woke up again, it was nearly evening. The rain had stopped, and the setting sunlight lit the heavy clouds from below, dividing the world into a gray heavens and a radiant underworld of pink and orange and blue. Quin lay wrapped in his arms, and the two of them lay wrapped in his cloak on a bed of straw, and Shinobu thought he would be happy to never sleep any other way ever again.

"Quin," he whispered.

He felt her hand tighten around his arm, but otherwise she didn't move. She was really rather small, when he held her like this. And yet Quin wanted to change the course of all Seekers. Shinobu wanted that also, but he knew that, if left to his own devices, he would probably choose less noble ways to spend his time. It was Quin who inspired him to be better. It had always been that way.

He propped himself up on an elbow and looked at her, asleep and using his sweater for a pillow. The otherworldly light from the sky touched her skin, and he thought it was fitting. There was something so determined and unafraid about this small girl, Quin Kincaid, that she was otherworldly to him. He made a vow to himself: *I will live up to her. And I will protect her.*

It bothered him that even in this moment he was still thinking about the focal. He was aware of its exact physical distance from him (under the pallet on which they were lying, about a foot from the edge), and if he let his mind linger on it, he began to feel a visceral urge to pick it up and put it on.

He wouldn't do that, not unless Quin was there to help. They needed the focal, he knew that now, but they would use it together, and only together, because that was the safe way. When he'd used it alone, it had broken off a piece of his mind, and it required constant work to ignore the thoughts from that piece, and channel all of himself into protecting Quin.

He pulled her closer to him and kissed her cheek. When her eyes came open, she smiled at him sleepily, then stretched.

"You're very nice-looking, do you know that?" she murmured.

"Am I?" It secretly delighted him to hear her say it. He tucked a lock of her hair behind her ear. "I want to tell you what happened with your father. And everything else."

"Tell me," she said.

She sat up on the straw-covered pallet and pulled her jacket tightly about her in the chilly air.

"I found him in a hospital outside London," he told her, propping himself up on his elbows. "It was an awful place, Quin. But I used the focal on him, and he started to make sense."

He told her everything Briac had said, about the Middle Dread, and his Watchers, about turning Seekers against each other and getting rid of Seekers altogether, about Briac himself trying to take over for the Middle Dread now that he was gone, but being too crazy to follow through.

He watched the effect of his narration on Quin. She didn't interrupt him, but when he'd paused, she said thoughtfully, "That explains why there have been fewer Seekers with each generation. And why my father tried to stick close to the Middle Dread, to win his favor."

"Besides what he's gotten Seekers to do to each other, the Middle Dread was doing something else," Shinobu told her. "The most important thing Briac told me was this: the Middle has been using different locations *There* to—to keep valuable things."

"What do you mean different locations *There*?"

Shinobu understood her confusion; he'd felt it himself when Briac had explained. Though there was plenty of room in the dimensions *There,* Briac and Alistair had taught Quin and Shinobu to use the exact same coordinates each time they jumped from the world to the dark space *between.* It was so easy to lose yourself in that blackness that Seekers were not supposed to linger—ever—and there had been no reason to think much about other possible locations *There.*

He told her, "We have one place *There* we use with the athame. We use that same spot over and over. That's why you were able to find your father when he was lost *There*—he had lost himself in the same spot we always go to. But the Middle was using other points *There* to store . . . things, I guess, that he wanted to keep secret. Like his Watchers. He kept them hidden in places none of us use."

Quin's eyebrows shot up in surprise. "He stored *people There*?" Clearly the possibility had never occurred to her.

Shinobu nodded.

"What else did he keep? And where—where are these hiding places?"

"I don't know what else he kept *There,* and Briac didn't know where the hiding places were," he answered. "He knew they existed *somewhere* in the darkness. But, Quin, listen . . ." Shinobu felt his eagerness returning. "I think I know how to find them."

"How?" she asked. When he didn't immediately answer, she

grabbed his hands as though he were torturing her by dragging out the explanation. "Shinobu! How?"

He allowed himself a dramatic pause, then said, "You have the clue."

"*I* have the clue?"

He dug through the pockets of his cloak and pulled out the athame of the Dreads. Holding it in front of her, he slid his fingers along the dull blade, then across the dials of the handgrip.

"Can you remember what coordinates were on this athame when the Young Dread came back for us on *Traveler*?" he asked her.

It took her a moment to understand what he was asking.

"After the fight on the airship? After we crashed?"

Shinobu nodded. "Yes, exactly."

"Why those coordinates?" she asked. "Wouldn't they be the coordinates of the ship itself?"

He shook his head. "No, I don't think so. Remember what happened? The Young Dread killed the Middle, and then she and the Old Dread dragged him out of the fight in the big room on *Traveler*. She came back alone—a short while later."

"We know she took the Old *There*," Quin said. "She took him *There*, and then she came back to help us."

"Yes," Shinobu agreed. "But she was gone for only, what—one or two minutes? I don't think the Young went *There* with him. I think she carved an anomaly, the Old Dread stepped through, and she stayed on the ship."

"So the coordinates on her athame would take us to where the Old Dread is?" she asked, following his logic. "But—why do we want to find the Old Dread just now?"

"We don't."

He saw understanding dawn in her eyes. "You think the Middle Dread's body is with him."

"Yes."

Quin closed her eyes, concentrating, but after a minute, she shook her head. "I saw the athame in the Young Dread's hands, but only for a moment."

"We're going to use the focal," he told her. "I know you don't like it—I don't like it either—but it's going to help you remember."

CHAPTER 51

QUIN

The barn loft appeared to glow in the light of Quin's expanded awareness. She'd cleared her mind, then slipped the focal on. The disorientation passed more quickly this time, and she was vaulted into that peculiar state of concentration the focal made possible. She became aware of ten thousand motes of dust suspended in a weak beam of fading sunlight, the small gusts of air moving past the barn window, even the multitude of varied currents in the river far, far below. And there was more. She saw all the times she'd been in this barn before, all the steps her feet had taken on those previous visits.

Shinobu's hands were on her shoulders as the focal buzzed and entwined around her own thoughts. The pressure of his touch steadied her.

"The coordinates," he said. "Can you remember?"

She threw her mind into that past moment when she was lying inside the crashed airship. The Young Dread had lifted a great sheet of glass off Shinobu and Quin. When Quin had crawled free, she'd looked up to see the Young holding the athame in her hands.

There. The coordinates were lined up along the dials between the

Young Dread's hands. They were suspended, perfectly still in Quin's memory.

Her mind came back to the present. She took the athame from Shinobu and quickly turned each dial until they matched what she'd seen in that past moment.

"Here," she said, handing the ancient dagger back to him. "This is where the Young Dread took the Old Dread, before she came back for us."

She removed the focal then, and gritted her teeth through the noise in her ears and the headache and nausea that came on immediately. She sat heavily on the platform and closed her eyes.

Shinobu sat with her, put an arm around her. "Sorry. I know it feels bad when it comes off. It gets worse the more you wear it."

"I'll be all right in a moment."

She breathed in slowly until she felt steady. When she'd recovered, she looked up to find that Shinobu had put the focal on the floor and pushed it some distance away.

"Show me," she said, gesturing at the athame.

Shinobu nodded. He slid his thumb down the athame's blade, dislodging the lightning rod. When he struck athame and rod together, the whole of the stone barn began to shake. Shinobu carved an anomaly into the air. Long threads came loose of their surroundings to twist away and form the humming border.

The threshold pulsed with flowing energy, and in the darkness beyond they saw a hunched figure, outlined in the light coming in through the barn window.

Shinobu took Quin's arm. "Follow me," he said. They stepped over the seething border, and in only a few steps had reached the figure.

"It's him," she whispered.

They were looking at the Old Dread. He stood perfectly still, his shoulders stooped, where the Young Dread had parted from him during the fight on *Traveler*.

His face had been shaved recently—Quin remembered that from the last time she'd seen him—and his cheeks and chin were covered with only the faintest white stubble, which made him look, somehow, quite modern. His eyes were closed and his hands were clasped before him. His robe hung about his frame oddly; it seemed the wrong size and didn't reach past his ankles. He'd given the Young Dread his cloak, Quin realized. *What else did he give her?* she wondered.

"Get his legs, Quin," Shinobu said.

"His legs?"

She looked up and realized Shinobu wasn't talking about the Old. He was leaning over another figure that lay at the man's feet. Feeling her way, Quin stooped down and grabbed on to two legs. They felt as stiff as a marble statue in her grasp, though they were still soft to the touch. Together Quin and Shinobu hefted the body upward, dead weight in their arms. They backed out through the anomaly, the body threatening to overbalance and topple to the side. When they were firmly on the loft floor again, they set it down with a dull thud.

Quin knew whom they were carrying, but the man's eyes—open and gray and staring—gave her an unpleasant shock. In the dimming light, lying inflexible and motionless, a great wash of blood across his chest where the Young Dread had stabbed him through the heart, was the Middle Dread.

Shinobu looked down at the Middle with an equal measure of distaste and fascination.

"Now," he told her, "let's find out where he put things."

CHAPTER 52

QUIN

"I know he's dead, but I could swear he could start moving," Quin muttered.

She and Shinobu were kneeling on the floor of the barn loft, removing the cloak from the frozen form of the Middle Dread. If he'd been alive, he might have been waking up by now, reentering the normal time stream. But he was, indeed, very dead. Only the blood on his chest had come back to life, trickling thickly from his fatal wound, filling the air with its metallic tang. The rest of him was gray and still.

"Check every pocket," Shinobu said.

"What are we looking for?"

They'd gotten the cloak off the Middle's stiff form and were rifling through it, pulling out knives and small tools and weapons. Shinobu examined what looked like a stone chisel, then threw it aside.

"If he was keeping people and things *There,* he must have some clue on him that helps him remember exactly where they are."

"What if he simply memorized the locations?" Quin asked.

"That's possible," Shinobu admitted. "But the Dreads spend years, decades even, stretched out *There*. Doesn't that do something to your mind? Make it foggy? I think he'd have a more permanent record than his memories."

This made sense to Quin. Their search of his cloak, however, turned up nothing helpful. Shinobu sighed and gave the Middle a look of distaste. Then he reached, unenthusiastically, for the pockets of the Middle's trousers.

"We have to check his body," he explained.

Quin wasn't disturbed by being near a dead body, but this particular body turned her stomach. The Middle had been an unpleasant presence while alive. Death had improved his company, but not by much. Nevertheless, she felt gingerly along the Middle's trouser legs, then pulled off his strange leather shoes. There was nothing inside.

When Shinobu's search of the man's trouser pockets found nothing, he slit the man's shirt with a knife, running the blade up from the waist to the neck. He ripped aside the two sections of the garment, revealing small, black tattoos on the man's abdomen.

Quin let out a breath, surprised.

"Come over here and look from this angle," Shinobu said, sounding excited.

She joined him near the Middle's head. From there, it was obvious the tattoos had been drawn so the Middle himself could read them easily. Symbols and letters and numbers were inked into his skin, oriented for his own eyes. Perhaps he had drawn them himself.

One group of symbols stood out, a set of coordinates—but not for a place in the world; they were for a location *There*.

Looking at the line of coordinates, Quin had the distinct feeling that she'd seen them several times recently, though she couldn't remember quite where.

"And look," she said, gesturing to the words inked beneath the symbols in ornate printing:

Protenus 53
Dextrorsum 59
Sinistrorsum 54
Dextrorsum 34

"*Protenus*—it's Latin for 'forward,'" Quin said, thankful for all her mother's language lessons when she'd been a Seeker apprentice. "And *dextrorsum* means 'to the right'; *sinistrorsum* means 'to the left.'"

Shinobu's eyes lit up with understanding. "It's our *P, S,* and *D* from the cave we found in the woods."

Quin quickly added up the digits next to the words. "The numbers sum to two hundred—like the numbers in the cave we found, and in the journal. But two hundred *what*? We still don't know."

"Maybe we do," Shinobu told her. He got to his feet and paced across the loft, both hands running over his head as though he were juggling a maelstrom of thoughts and needed his hands to keep them inside his skull. He stopped in front of the round window, then turned back to her. "There's that journal entry about the Middle Dread instructing two boys, counting numbers—"

"To two hundred," Quin agreed, "but—"

"It's *steps,* Quin." He walked back with a look of discovery transforming his countenance. "Your father explained—but it was so confusing I didn't understand until just now. It's how many *steps* to get somewhere *between.* We follow the coordinates, they'll take us to a certain point *There,* and from that point we walk in exactly those directions."

Quin furrowed her brow. "How could Briac know that?"

"Your father admitted that he'd spent years trying to understand the Middle Dread—to try to keep himself alive. He once hid near the Watchers' fortress and *saw* the Middle training his boys. He saw them as they practiced 'counting their steps,' over and over. They were practicing for this." He pointed at the tattoo on the Middle's skin. "But Briac didn't know about these coordinates. He didn't know where to start from."

Quin thought about this, but when she considered the practicalities, she shook her head. "Two hundred steps *There*? You would never make it. You'd lose yourself."

"Don't you see? That's the point. Anyone would lose themselves." His expression spoke of many pieces falling into place very quickly. "Two hundred steps guarantees that no one could follow these clues unless the Middle taught them how to do it. They'd get lost and stuck *There*." Unconsciously, a fever of realization now upon him, he grabbed his hair and made it stand out from his head. "That was the real secret, Quin, the most important thing Briac told me. It's why the Middle Dread was hoarding all the focals." He retrieved the metal helmet from the floor and held it up for her. "You don't lose yourself *There* if you're wearing a focal."

Quin stared back at Shinobu. "You don't lose yourself *There* if you're wearing a focal," she repeated, letting the words sink in. *Of course.* Now that he'd said it, this fact seemed both logical and obvious. "That's why one of the Watchers was always wearing a helmet each time we saw them," she reflected, with growing excitement, "to keep himself from getting lost *There*."

"To get whatever the Middle was hiding, you needed the coordinates, the directions—two hundred paces—and you needed a focal."

Quin felt parts of the mystery resolving for her as well. "That's why my father so badly wanted to get his hands on the Watchers' focal."

"Briac wanted to find whatever the Middle had hidden, and he wanted to take over where the Middle left off."

"But what does that mean? What will we find if we follow these instructions? And there were different instructions in that cave in Scotland—still two hundred, but a different pattern of steps. Why?"

Shinobu picked up a small knife from among the Middle's scattered possessions. With it he scratched a circle into the floor of the loft.

"What if this circle is all of the space *There*," he said, "and this"—he stuck the knife straight down, making a dot within the circle—"is where you go if you follow those coordinates on his skin? And from that point you can walk different ways to find different things."

Quin's mind was catching up with his now. She took the knife and scratched a steplike path with the blade to represent the paces inked on the Middle's body. She said, "These paces, from his tattoos, get you here." She made an X at the end of the line she'd drawn. Then she drew another path, going a different way from the original starting point. "The paces written in the cave in Scotland might get you here." She made an X at the end of the second line. The two X's were quite far apart, despite having the same point of origin.

"Exactly," he agreed. "They're all little pirate maps, pointing to something hidden *There*."

"So which set of paces should we follow?"

"Every set we can find—eventually," he answered. "But this one . . . he tattooed this set on his body. It must be the most important."

"But . . . what could be there?" she whispered, feeling jittery at the thought of following in the Middle's footsteps. So far, his footsteps had led them into all sorts of trouble.

"I—I don't know," Shinobu answered seriously. "We might find whatever he was going to use to get rid of Seekers."

Quin bit her lip and stared at the Middle's tattoos and his tools and weapons. Her mind was reeling. The Middle had been planning so much and causing so much harm.

"Do you not want to go look?" he asked softly, nodding at the inked instructions on the Middle's body.

She pulled her thoughts together. There was still so much they didn't know; the Middle had left an intentionally complicated trail. But they were, it seemed, on the cusp of understanding. Quin felt an excitement that was close to terror.

"No, of course I do," she told him, embracing the feeling. "We have to look."

He put a hand to her cheek and smiled at her. "If we're going to go, one of us will have to wear the focal to make it through the two hundred paces," he told her softly.

Quin watched a strange expression pass across his face. "You don't want to wear it?" she asked.

"No." He hesitated. "But I also don't want you to wear it." He picked up the helmet and turned it around and around, regarding it much as a soldier might regard an unexploded grenade. "It did something to my thoughts—and I—I don't want it to do that to you. I made you wear it earlier, but that was for a short time. This would be much longer."

"I might be better at clearing my mind first than you are," she pointed out, moved by his worry. "Maybe it won't be so bad for me."

"You *are* better. That's part of what I mean. You keep your mind so clear, Quin, without the focal. When we were fighting the Watchers *There,* you didn't slow down. You held your focus. And when you work as a healer, I can see how intense your concentration is. That's why I don't think you should use the focal. I don't want to risk it damaging your mind."

She thought about that. It was true, she'd managed not to lose herself when they'd fought those boys inside the anomaly, though she considered she'd been more lucky than skilled in that instance.

Still, there might be some truth to what Shinobu was saying. Eventually she nodded.

He looked relieved.

"Good," he said. "I'll wear the helmet for the two hundred steps, and you'll keep your eyes on me. You'll make sure I don't do something strange."

CHAPTER 53

MAUD

The tears had dried on the youngest Watcher's cheeks, leaving clear pink trails through the layers of grime. He sat on the cave floor with the focal over his head, his hands clamped onto the sides of the helmet to prevent anyone from removing it.

They'd confirmed that his name was Nott but hadn't gotten much else out of him. The Young Dread and John crouched nearby, watching him closely. Maud had tried to help the boy clear his mind before putting on the focal, but he'd been so desperate for it, he hadn't listened to her at all. It probably didn't matter much; whatever damage the helmet was capable of inflicting had already happened to this boy.

Nott was rocking back and forth, moaning. His tears began again, welling in his eyes, then spilling down his cheeks. Without warning, he tore the helmet from his head and threw it viciously. John, with his newly sharp reflexes, caught it before it hit the cave floor. Nott looked from him to Maud, his face twisting into an expression of absolute distress. A deep sob came out, and as it did, he struck at Maud with both fists.

"It doesn't work right!" he yelled. "It's not like mine!"

She easily blocked his blows, caught his wrist, and twisted his arm behind him. The boy yelped, and his young eyes stared at her, full of resentment.

"It doesn't feel right on my head," he told her, almost spitting the words out. "It doesn't feel good!"

He struck at her with his free hand, but Maud caught that one as well and squeezed it tightly.

"Stop!" Nott pleaded.

She released him, and he regarded her hostilely but didn't try to hit her again.

"It's not the same focal you've used before," the Young Dread explained patiently. "This one has had different owners."

"I'm becoming a boy again," he told her, as though this were the worst fate he could imagine. "I was a Watcher. I put the world in its place. Now I'm a child. I miss Odger and our stinking cottage."

"You were always a boy," she said. "The focal has fooled you."

He shook his head, sending several droplets into the air. The Young watched them patter across the cave's rough floor.

"No," he said, "I was different."

He picked up the frozen rat, which was lying on the rocks near his feet. Cradling it gently in one hand, the boy held it out toward her as his thumb stroked its belly.

"I wanted to cut it up. It's *good* to hurt things. But now . . ." He shrugged, then wiped at his eyes with his other hand.

"You can't use a focal without proper help," she said. "It changes you."

"It makes you better!" he yelled.

"No." She said the word firmly. "If it's been used often by someone else, the focal keeps that person's thoughts, Nott. If you don't set your mind right to begin with, you won't be able to tell those thoughts from your own."

"They were *my* thoughts," the boy insisted. "I saw how much better I was than everyone else."

The Young Dread responded calmly, "They weren't your thoughts. I can guess to whom those thoughts belonged." There was a flicker of interest in his eyes, even if he didn't want to listen. "Your master is someone I knew well," she told him. "You've been wearing one of his focals. I've seen him with many different helms throughout many years. He used to wear one often when our own master was not around. I have seen the Middle Dread do terrible things to small animals. He loved that. And the helmet has passed on that love to you."

She'd watched the Middle slowly disembowel live squirrels and rats around the campfire, taking obscene pleasure in the animals' agony. He had once bragged to her, when the Old was out of earshot, that he could keep a rat alive for hours while he tortured it.

The boy glanced down at the rat and moved it gently with his fingers, apparently considering what Maud had said.

"If I'm not like him—if all those thoughts were his—what good am I?" he asked. His fingers closed gently and drew the rodent to his chest. He stared down at the tiny body and pressed his own back into the cave wall, as though he hoped to disappear inside it. "They were right to leave me to die here in my cave. I'm useless."

"I've heard you call this your cave twice now," John said. "What makes it yours?"

"My cave. *My* cave," the boy said defiantly, as though John were questioning his claim on the place.

"But why?" John's voice was soft, but there was something urgent in his tone.

"Because I—I belong to it some way. I have a boar on my athame. Well, I don't have the athame anymore, Wilkin has it. But I used to have it. And it had a boar. And there's a dead boy named Emily with a boar around his neck back there. He's got a boar, I've got a boar—it's my cave."

John and Maud looked at each other.

"There's a dead boy in the tunnel?" asked John.

"Yes," said Nott. "I'm wearing his clothes."

CHAPTER 54

JOHN

They found the body deep in the frozen tunnel the next morning. Sunlight came through the ceiling of ice in a blue glow, making the corpse's skin look bruised. The body wore only underclothes; the fatal wound to its chest was dark and ugly against the frozen skin.

Nott had accompanied them and was standing near John, shivering in his two cloaks and double clothing.

"Look there," Nott said, pointing. "I didn't see that last night."

High up on the tunnel wall, partially obscured by ice, was a deep engraving. John pried up a sheet of ice from the rock and tossed it to the ground. Where it had been, the full carving was now exposed. It was a boar with great tusks and angry eyes.

"I told him this cave was for boars," Nott muttered.

"Told who?" John asked.

"No one," Nott said immediately, throwing John a suspicious look. Then one of his hands disappeared into a deep pocket in his outer cloak, and clutched, John thought, at the dead rat that he'd insisted on carrying with him.

John knelt on the cold rock floor next to the body. He pulled up its left hand and found the boy's name drawn in blood on the palm. *Emile.*

"Emile Pernet, house of the boar," he whispered. "My mother wanted to find him." He'd thought she'd been searching for revenge, but now he saw things differently. Emile had never been an enemy. He was a boy who'd been misused, who'd been given no justice, just as John and Catherine had been given no justice. "Were Emile and my mother friends?" he asked the Young Dread.

"They were," she said.

Low on the wall, near Emile's body, small figures were sculpted into the rock:

PRO 63
SIN 48
DEX 89

"There are more letters in this cave," John noted. "Fewer numbers. Though"—a quick calculation—"they still make two hundred."

"These letters make sense," the Young Dread told him, "if they indicate the Latin words for 'forward,' 'leftward,' and 'rightward.' They are directions of some sort."

Nott curled his lips back into a smile that bared his teeth, and he murmured knowingly, "Latin, of course."

Maud's thought entered John's mind: *His teeth!*

The Young Dread moved forward smoothly, and before the boy could react, she'd grabbed him and lifted his upper lip. Nott's teeth looked rotten at first glance, but John saw that they had, in fact, been carved with fine designs, then smeared over with a thick, black grease.

"Look closely," Maud told him.

He leaned over the boy with her, and then he understood. The patterns on Nott's teeth were not random. They were, in fact, symbols from an athame. All together they made a set of coordinates.

"These will take us somewhere *There*," Maud said, contemplatively. Then, to Nott: "What do you find when you follow the carvings on your teeth?"

A shifty look came over the boy, as if he would never trust them enough to answer any of their questions. But in the next instant, perhaps thinking of the focal and the potential for John and Maud to feed him, his face became friendlier.

"The symbols on my teeth—and Wilkin's!—are how we find the other Watchers who are sleeping *There*. We go to this place"—he tapped his teeth—"and then we walk."

The Young Dread asked, "What do you mean, 'walk'?"

"He'd kill me for telling you, but he's dead, and I'm supposed to be dead, so I reckon it doesn't matter." Nott had drawn the frozen rat out of his pocket and was stroking it again. "When I say 'walk,' I mean 'walk.' Two hundred steps, and the other Watchers are there, bang at the end of it."

Maud gestured at the numbers on the wall. "These two hundred steps?" she asked.

The boy looked indignant. "No. We have our own."

"So what are these?" John asked.

Nott shrugged and kicked at the floor. "I don't know everything about everything."

Maud was very still for some time, though John saw her eyes flick between the boy's teeth and the numbers sculpted into the rock wall.

"These caves," she said at last, speaking to herself as much as to them. "Each house had one. I have been to some of them—invited by the Seekers to whom they belonged. This cave belonged to the boar, the one in Africa to the bear. But they've fallen out of use . . . perhaps because the Middle Dread has been using them for his own ends." John heard her feeling her way toward certainty as she spoke. "Whatever is done here in this cave, whatever is left here—it looks as though it was done by the boar Seekers themselves, since this is their place. Do you see? Because Emile is here, it appears he was killed by his own family. And a Watcher left frozen here will look like a member of that family as well. It is another way the Middle hid his tracks."

Maud's thoughts had begun to mingle with John's own as she spoke, and suddenly he understood something else. "There's more—Nott's teeth," he told her. It almost felt, in this intense moment, as if he and Maud were one mind speaking with two voices. "If he freezes to death here, his teeth—with their coordinates—are safely kept nearby these walking instructions. A full set of clues."

The Young Dread began to line up the symbols on their athame to match the coordinates on Nott's teeth.

"If the two hundred paces Nott uses bring him to other Watchers . . . What if this two hundred paces will bring us to something else?" She indicated the boar hewn proprietarily into the tunnel wall, and a new rush of thoughts leapt from her mind into John's.

"The house of the boar?" he whispered. "The Seekers who've gone missing . . ."

"What if they are missing, but not entirely gone?" the Young Dread asked him.

"You think we might find whatever is left of them," John said, giving voice to her thoughts.

Maud held up the athame's hilt, showing him the dials, which had been arranged in the pattern on Nott's teeth.

"I think we must look for ourselves and discover what the Middle has done."

She reached for the lightning rod at her waist.

CHAPTER 55

CATHERINE

18 YEARS EARLIER

Catherine had locked the bathroom door, but she wasn't in the bathroom. She was sitting on the floor of the tiny room—little more than an alcove, really—which was to be the nursery. This small space adjoined the bathroom and their bedroom and was tucked into the farthest corner of the flat.

She didn't want Archie to worry if he noticed the locked bathroom door, but she also wanted warning if he came close. She was wearing the focal again, an activity she'd continued to keep secret from him.

She sat cross-legged between the half-assembled crib and the stack of baby things her mother had been sending. Her mother's gifts had ended abruptly the week before, and Catherine hadn't been able to reach either of her parents since. Now that she knew the Middle Dread had followed her in France, she was worried that he might be after her family. She was still confined to bed—even more strictly than before—so she couldn't go looking for her parents, and she didn't want to send Archie into danger on his own. She was trying not to let hysteria take hold.

Gradually she became aware of a repeated thumping noise that was coming from the living room. Archie had been practicing with weapons every waking moment since their return from France, three weeks before, after he'd fortified their flat with all sorts of door and window locks. (As if locks would keep out a Seeker or a Dread.) *He must be punishing the training dummy severely right now,* she thought.

Catherine's mind hummed with the focal as she studied the journal, trying to make new mental connections from the old entries—to understand who had been manipulated, and when. She'd added to the journal the coordinates for the cave in Norway where Emile had been heading, and his father's drawing. She would go there as soon as she could—she would try to find all the caves as soon as she could—but what else could she learn while she waited for her child to be born?

After an unknown amount of time had passed—it was hard to keep track of time in the focal—she noticed a change in the noise from the living room. It was no longer the sound of Archie striking the dummy but of something else, something heavier—it was the sound of a body hitting a wall. That happened occasionally when he practiced, but a moment later she heard the sound again. And then again. There was a new noise on the heels of the last thud—a shatter of glass against the floor.

Catherine got to her feet and slipped into the bedroom. She grabbed her whipsword from its hiding place in the wardrobe, then tucked a knife into the pocket of her loose dress.

The crashing in the living room continued, and now she heard voices, three male voices. She could not make out what they were saying, but they were angry and demanding, and not one of them belonged to Archie. She ran into the bathroom, and from there through connecting doors to the apartment's tiny pantry and then kitchen. A gun went off, once, deafening, and then the weapon clattered to the floor.

She saw the attackers through the open kitchen doorway. Archie had an ordinary sword in his left hand, and his right hand—which had clearly just fired the gun—was now empty. He drew a long training knife from his belt.

The three intruders circling him were young. They moved like trained Seekers, and Catherine recognized them at once. They were the three younger cousins in the picture she'd seen in Emile's house, brothers of Anthony, who'd been Emile's best friend—and probably his murderer—and who'd attacked her in Hong Kong.

He can't kill Seekers himself, Emile's father had said. *He gets them to kill each other instead.* And here they were to finish what Anthony had failed to do in Hong Kong. What would their reward be? Her athame? Her focal? Or something else?

"Where is the girl and her book?" one of them demanded.

Ah, the book, her journal. Maybe that was the real reason the Middle was after her. Briac too had wanted her book. *You have your journal,* he'd told her. *It's a better weapon than any other Seeker has . . . I'll show you how to use it.*

In a flash of understanding—aided by the focal—she finally grasped the journal's full danger. It was, in large part, a record of bad things the Middle Dread had done or had allowed to happen or had asked others to do. While Catherine had imagined using it so that the Old Dread would cast the Middle out of the brotherhood of Dreads, the Middle Dread must have seen it as an even more serious threat—a threat to his survival, if the book was shown to the Old Dread. Briac had tried to tell her this, she now realized, but Catherine had held on to her stubborn notion that a Dread, at heart, would be honorable, and she hadn't understood the kind of danger the Middle would see in her keeping a record of his actions. The Middle didn't know precisely what was written in it, of course. He could only guess—and likely he'd guessed she knew more than she actually did. He saw it as a bigger threat than it actually was. A threat worth killing for.

And Briac—he must have thought that by controlling her journal he would have leverage over the Middle, something to keep himself alive.

These thoughts ran through her head in the space of a single breath. Then her mind was back in the flat, in the kitchen, as she looked in at the attackers.

"Where is she?" the attacker closest to Archie asked again. He cracked his whipsword out toward Archie's wrist, trying to disarm him, but Archie moved aside and, in a flash of steel, cut the attacker's arm with his knife.

"She's not here!" Archie said. "She hasn't been here in weeks."

None of the attackers had seen Catherine yet. Standing in the doorway, she silently flicked out her own whipsword. It felt good in her hand after so long unused.

"You're lying," the lead attacker said.

"She's gone!" yelled Archie.

Catherine gripped her whipsword tightly. She'd spent most of the last three months lying in bed, and her muscles had been neglected, but she'd had years of training. When she was fit, she was a great fighter. Even now, she would be a good fighter. She was at the point of leaping through the open doorway into the living room to join the fight, when she felt the warm trickle down her thigh. She brushed a hand across her leg, and her palm came away smeared with bright red blood.

How could she be bleeding? All she'd done was run from the bedroom to the kitchen. But the doctors had told her, after that day in France, that her pregnancy was balanced precariously.

"Dammit!" she breathed.

Archie was grappling with one of the attackers, when he caught sight of Catherine and the blood on her hand. His eyes were wild, but their meaning was perfectly clear.

Go! he mouthed to her. *Now!*

She retreated back through the pantry and into the dining area, trying to decide what to do. Archie was a good fighter, but he would need her help. Catherine gripped the pommel of her whipsword tightly. She could feel the motions it would take to jump into the fray.

A gush of blood ran down her leg.

At that moment, one of Archie's attackers flew through the living room doorway and crashed into the dining table, blood pulsing from his throat—a fatal wound.

One down. Was it possible that Archie could beat all three of them? It was possible, she granted, but by no means certain.

If she helped him, would the baby survive? Would she? *Promise me, Catherine,* Archie had said. And she'd promised.

"Dammit!" she whispered again.

Her whipsword still clutched in one hand, Catherine grabbed the journal from the nursery and the athame and lightning rod from the safe, then moved back into the pantry.

"Where is she?" one of the attackers said again.

"I told you, she left!" Archie spat. The pain in his voice made Catherine pause. "Only a fool would stay here with me." The words were directed at her; he was begging her to go. Catherine heard him cry out angrily, the way he did when he thrust his sword in practice. There was a thump of a body against the living room floor.

"Are you going to dance around, or are you going to fight?" Archie said, baiting one of his attackers. Catherine's hopes rose. He was still standing? He was still winning?

She lifted the door in the pantry floor. It opened onto a set of narrow, steep stairs. The building was an old one, owned by Archie's family, who had believed firmly in alternate routes of escape.

Catherine moved down the tiny set of stairs in almost complete darkness. The passage was so narrow, she had to descend half-turned to the side, navigating her pregnant body carefully.

The stairs ended in a sort of hall. Dark and narrow and low, it reminded her of the tunnel beneath Mont Saint-Michel. She could hear her own breathing like the rhythm of a steam train. She was not used to moving. She was already tired. Her belly brushed the opposite wall as she moved along beneath the living room. A chink of light hovered above her, a crack between two of the living room floorboards. The sounds of the fight came down to her clearly.

She heard something else also. There was noise behind her, from the pantry stairs. Boots approaching. One of the attackers was following her.

"Where did your friend go?"

That was Archie, speaking almost directly above her.

"My brother's gone to find her," another voice said. "He'll find her! But you'll be dead by then."

Archie bellowed in rage, and there was a sound of bodies colliding with each other, and then with the floor.

Catherine struggled to turn herself, so her right arm, her sword arm, was toward the back, between her and her pursuer.

"I hear you," said a soft voice, only yards away. "Stop. He wants us to kill you. But I don't have to. Give me the journal and your athame, and you can go."

She could see the glint of a weapon in the sliver of light through the living room floor. Catherine dropped the journal, and her athame and lightning rod. She cracked out her whipsword and swept it upward. It collided with her pursuer's own whipsword.

A shadow blocked the light, and she saw Archie's face above. He was pressed into the floor, struggling.

"Archie!" she yelled.

He opened his eyes and found her in the darkness below. He was gritting his teeth.

"Go!" he hissed. "Go!"

Her own pursuer struck out with his sword again. Catherine struck back, but her arm faltered under the blow. She was weak. Blood was still running down her leg. She would die, her child would die, Archie would die.

She felt a crackle of electricity around her ears and noticed the high humming in her mind. The focal. She'd forgotten she was wearing it. She had to give herself over to it, let it help her, or this would be the end.

Immediately she felt her mind expand. Her attacker was striking again. She blocked him more easily this time, shoving his weapon into the wall. Archie was above her, grappling with his opponent, groaning. All she could see, through the crack in the floorboards, was a portion of his hair. She was aware of each individual hair, reddish brown, the odor of sweat and fear, the position of her arms and legs, the weight of the weapon in her hand.

Her pursuer struck down at her. She took three quick steps backward, allowing his whipsword to crash into the floor between them. Then she moved forward, her whipsword straight in front of her, long and thin and deadly. He turned at the last moment, realizing her intent, and her sword pierced his side, sliding between ribs.

He gasped.

There was blood now, on her arms, but it wasn't hers and it wasn't his. It was dripping onto her skin from above.

Archie's face was at the crack in the floor, looking down at her, and he was no longer struggling.

"Archie!" Catherine cried. "I'm coming. Wait for me!"

Her attacker was grievously wounded, but he was still coming after her, bellowing like a cornered animal. He'd turned himself around and was using his other arm to wield his whipsword frantically, viciously.

"Archie . . ." Catherine said.

His blood continued to patter down around her. She could see individual drops, highlighted from above.

The focal was buzzing discordantly through Catherine's head. The electricity was painful now, piercing. Her thoughts were tumbling against each other, as though her mind had divided itself into two camps and they were arguing.

I can save him. I will save him.

He's already dead.

This is my fault. I tried to learn things I shouldn't know.

I will know everything. No one can stop me.

They're going to kill me.

No one will kill me. I will kill them first. I will make them pay. They will all pay.

Her attacker was within reach again. When he struck, she moved inside the blow. His fist crashed into the focal on her head, and the force of the impact sent his whipsword flying from his hand.

Catherine collapsed her own sword into something short and thick and deadly sharp, then plunged it forward into the boy's heart.

He folded onto himself on the floor of the narrow space. Catherine leaned against the wall, her breath coming hard. When the boy's body settled, his face became visible in the light through the ceiling. He was younger than she'd thought. He looked about fourteen.

I don't kill children. I believe in justice.

I kill them if I have to. I kill anyone if I have to.

You must do anything to protect your family. Anything.

Above her was motion. The last attacker was still alive. It sounded as though he were pulling himself across the floor, moaning as he went. Catherine crawled over the body of the boy—probably the youngest brother—and made her way back down the narrow passage, then up the stairs.

She emerged into the kitchen and saw her own trail of blood, which had led the boy straight to her down the escape passage. The second dead brother was lying on the dining room floor.

Archie was in the living room, his head against the floorboards, a pool of blood growing around him and trickling through the crack in the floor.

"Archie . . ."

She knelt and carefully turned him over. His face was hollow and gray. His skin was already cooling, and there was no heartbeat at his neck. An hour before, he had lain next to her on the bed and showered her belly with kisses. She had brushed the hair away from his handsome face, and had been foolish enough to feel happy.

She pushed the bloody hair from his face and held his head in her hands. The spark of life was gone from his eyes.

She sat that way for some time, until a noise roused her. She looked up to see the third attacker in the entryway, pulling himself toward the front door, a smeared trail of blood behind him.

Catherine crawled over to him on all fours. When he saw her coming, he rolled onto his back and held up his last weapon, one of their kitchen knives. He'd been grievously wounded in his lower abdomen, and the blood there was dark and thick and pulsing. He did not have long to live.

He might have been twenty years old, or younger, but the pain written on his face made him look ancient. He wore heavy boots, and these added to a resemblance to Briac Kincaid, a resemblance his brother Anthony had shared. Did the Middle think all of these boys were interchangeable pawns? She batted the knife out of his hand, and he put up almost no resistance—he knew he was finished. Catherine brought her whipsword to his throat.

"Did you kill Anna?" she asked him. "Did you murder my sister?"

He closed his eyes and slowly nodded, the skin of his neck pulling against the edge of her sword.

"Why?" she asked. "What did the Middle Dread promise you?"

"He said . . . he said there were not many Seeker families left. We were nearing the end . . . He told Anthony, we could keep two athames . . . if we got rid of the families to whom they belonged . . ."

"Don't you think he . . . he would have killed you when it was all done?" she asked. "Or gotten someone else to kill you?"

"No. We'd helped him," the boy whispered. "And we were going to run. Two athames between four brothers . . . we could hide, outsmart anyone who came after us."

"Outsmart *him*?" she asked softly. This boy had known nothing of all the others the Middle had tricked. She felt something almost like pity for him.

"Anthony thought it was . . . worth the risk. Two athames . . . we'd be the most powerful Seeker house in history . . ." He licked his lips, his eyes locked on hers. His breaths were shallow but coming fast. "It sounds stupid now . . . now that you've taken care of us . . ."

"You killed my family out of greed," she told him. Tears were running down her cheeks. "And Emile."

"I was looking out for my own," he told her, licking his lips again.

Catherine felt a thought form in her mind, almost as though it had fallen whole from within the focal itself, as though the thought had been living inside the helmet, waiting for her: *I won't trust any-one. I will kill them all before they get to me or my son. I'll kill anyone who gets in my way.*

"Are you ready for your end?" she whispered.

He nodded and shut his eyes.

She killed the wounded boy, the last of the four brothers of the house of the horse, with a quick cut of her whipsword.

Then she stumbled back to the secret passage, gathered up the athame and lightning rod and her journal. She made her way out to the street, covered in blood. She ripped the focal from her head, only because she thought it might raise questions, might make her appear something other than a pregnant victim of a crime. She stuffed the journal into the helmet and gripped it and her belly. The athame and lightning rod, which she'd shoved through the lining of her dress pocket, banged against her legs as she staggered away into London, calling for help.

CHAPTER 56

SHINOBU

The sun had gone down, but the clouds had broken and the sky was still bright with afterglow. Shinobu had used the coordinates from the Middle Dread's body, and now an open, humming anomaly hung before them above the barn loft. Quin stood at his side, a hand on his shoulder. They'd lit the old gas lantern from the corner of the loft, and Shinobu held it up to cast its light into the darkness beyond the borders of the anomaly.

"You keep up with your chant," he told her, "and keep your eyes on me."

"I will."

She squeezed his shoulder, and together they stepped across the threshold into the darkness. Shinobu had written the numbers and directions on his arm, and he looked at them in the lantern light.

"Fifty-three steps straight ahead," he said.

He began to walk, counting off each pace in his head. Behind him, Quin recited the time chant:

"Knowledge of self, knowledge of home, a clear picture of where I came

from, where I will go, and the speed of things between will see me safely back. Knowledge of self . . ."

He focused on the steps he took and on the pressure of Quin's hand. She was here with him.

He reached fifty-three paces and turned sharply to the right. He glanced at the instructions on his arm. Fifty-nine paces now. With the focal on, it was remarkably easy to keep his focus and count. But the helmet was whispering things to him, at the edges of his awareness: *Why are you with her? She's using you . . . She'll never let you succeed . . .*

He ignored those thoughts entirely. He knew they didn't belong to him.

He looked back at Quin. Her eyes were fixed on him as she continued the time chant:

"Knowledge of self, knowledge of home . . ."

Here and there, in the darkness around them, were shapes, huddled mounds off to one side or the other that could be human forms—perhaps the bodies of others who had tried to follow this path and hadn't made it. Shinobu wanted to look at them more closely, but he didn't let his eyes nor his mind deviate from their path. He must count and walk properly. He reached the fifty-ninth step and turned to the left. Quin was still gripping his shoulder, her hand warm and reassuring. He paused to listen to her chant and discovered it was slowing down.

"A clear picture . . . of where I came from . . . where I . . ."

He couldn't waste time. She was good at keeping her focus, but she wouldn't be able to do it indefinitely. Fifty-four steps now, then turn right.

Who cares if she loses her focus? the focal whispered to him. *What if she doesn't matter as much as you think she does . . .*

Shut up!

He came to the end of fifty-four steps and turned to the right. Thirty-four steps for the last leg. He began to walk. They were almost there.

"... the ... speed ... of things ... between ... will ... see me ..."

Quin was still chanting, but her words were slow.

All this while, the light from Shinobu's lantern had hung before him like a perfect yellow sphere in the blackness. But now, when he reached the final twenty steps, the lantern's rays met something up ahead, directly in his path. After a few more paces, he could see the outline of standing figures, their blinking eyes reflecting the lantern's glow. This was both frightening and exhilarating; they had discovered the Middle Dread's secret place.

The focal murmured more insistently: *My Watchers, waiting for me; all of this, waiting for me.* Shinobu pushed these ghostly thoughts away and concentrated on the weight of Quin's hand.

Four figures were now clearly visible, two on the right and two on the left. He could see, in the flickering reach of the lantern, wool clothing and cloaks and young faces.

They're waiting for me ...

They walked between the two sets of Watchers, the smell of death hanging heavy around them. Shinobu had no need to count anymore. The lantern illuminated a great pile of objects ahead. As he pulled Quin onward, these became recognizable. There were disruptors, a great row of them, there were whipswords, there were athames ... and there were countless other objects that looked dangerous and valuable.

All of this is for you. Quin is slowing down ... Let her slow down ... No!

He walked with Quin to the very center of this collection and held up the lantern. Faintly, at the edge of its reach, he could make out other pairs of Watchers, forming a circle around the treasure.

He shut his mind to the focal, held its whispers at bay. Yet he could feel them trying to seep back in. One thought came to him, so gently and irresistibly that he was not sure if it was his own or not: *What if she's safer here?*

What would happen if he and Quin woke these Watchers and tried to use them for their own ends? The stone medallion should give them authority over the boys, but even if it did, Shinobu didn't believe that gaining control of them would happen easily or smoothly. All on its own, his mind ran through every time he'd seen Quin's life in danger: John galloping after her on the estate; John and his men beating her on the Bridge; Briac attacking her on *Traveler;* the Watchers in the hospital room, and jumping through the anomaly, and on the estate, and on the Bridge canopy. Each time had felt like death to him, but worse than his own death would be.

Anyone who'd followed the Middle—the Watchers, Briac, Seekers who were willing to kill each other—was a danger to Quin, whether she had the Middle's stone medallion on her side or not. Yet here she was, with Shinobu, walking in the Middle's very footsteps. They were surrounded by Watchers, sleeping in the darkness, waiting to wake up. What else might be hidden here, *between,* ready to attack?

Is she safer here? came the thought again, stronger now, almost like a physical blow.

Without any awareness that he was doing so, he had slipped a hand into a pocket of his cloak, and he was gripping the stone medallion there. He felt the cool disk in his palm, and his thumb and the tips of his fingers clutched its smooth edges.

If Shinobu could take the Middle Dread's place, if he could gather to himself whatever tools the Middle had found, whatever schemes the Middle had begun, if he could understand them and use them for his own purposes—for *Quin's* purposes—he could protect both of them. He could make up for the bad things that had been done in the name of Seekers; he could change their future. He and Quin would never be victims again.

But until he had control, how many more times would he have to see Quin attacked? And what if, one time, he wasn't able to save her?

The medallion had begun to vibrate in his pocket, but he'd already taken his hand away and only perceived a tickle against his leg. He was looking at Quin.

The thought came again: *She's safer here.*

Was this a true thought? Was it his own thought, from his own mind? Or was it a trick? What if there was no way to tell? Shinobu turned toward Quin.

"Quin, Quin!" he said, taking hold of her shoulders, as the medallion shook inside the cloak.

Her eyes drifted slowly to meet his as the next few words fell from her lips: *"safely . . . back . . ."*

"Take the focal off me," he said urgently. "Pull it off!"

He took her hands and put them on the sides of the helmet.

"Take it off!" he said again.

He couldn't do it himself. He couldn't remove it with his own two hands. The idea was too painful.

Quin had heard him, but she was shaking her head slowly.

"Not here . . ." she whispered. "As soon as . . . we . . . get back . . ."

"Now! It has to be now!"

Her hands fell from the helmet to hang limply at her sides.

He put his own hands to the focal.

Take it off! he ordered himself. *Just pull it off!*

He couldn't do it. His heartbeat sped up in a panic.

Is she safer here? I want her to be safe.

CHAPTER 57

QUIN

It seemed they'd walked for years. Quin was still chanting, but time was floating, its fingers cool on her body, her head, a dark lake taking her in.

She'd seen shapes loom up out of the blackness. And then she'd heard Shinobu's plea to remove the focal from his head. But how could she? If she did, they would both be lost here forever.

They weren't walking now. One of his hands was on her arm, solid and warm. He was real. But time itself had shifted, and she lost the chant.

How long have I been standing here looking?

"Knowledge of self," she began again, forcing the words out, though her throat felt endlessly distant, *"knowledge of home, a clear picture . . ."*

The last word came on a long exhale, and then she did not breathe in again. It didn't seem necessary.

"I want you to be safe," she heard Shinobu say.

His words came so quickly—she herself must have been slowing down almost to the point of stopping. She moved both hands to

Shinobu's cloak and clutched him, attempting to pull herself back into the now.

"I'm losing time . . ." she murmured, forcing out the words as though her lungs were filled with sap. "Help me say the chant."

He put a hand on her face. In the glow of the lantern his eyes were bright and focused. Just looking at him brought her back to herself a bit.

"You don't need the chant, Quin," he whispered. Fingers of electricity crawled about his forehead beneath the lip of the focal.

She was breathing again, but it seemed a year passed as her breath went in and out one time. She felt Shinobu's face against hers, his arms around her, and she could hear the buzzing of the focal on his head as it pressed up against her own.

"I'm losing myself," she whispered in a final effort to stay aware. "Take me out. Carve an anomaly."

CHAPTER 58

SHINOBU

Shinobu held Quin in his arms, feeling the warmth of her body against his. The stone disk in his cloak had fallen still.

"I love you, Quin," he whispered. It was something he was absolutely sure was true.

"Wha . . . ?" Quin said, but the word faded out before it was completely formed, became a perpetual *What?* that she was sending into the blackness of this place. She was slowing down in earnest. He could feel her chest letting out air so faintly, hardly moving at all.

Her fingers shifted, ever so slightly, against his chest, as though she were trying to grab on to him, to wake herself up. But she was already falling into a single moment that would last, to her, an eternity.

"I love you," he said again, knowing there was no need to tell her, knowing she could no longer hear him, and yet unable to go without saying it.

"I'm going to make it safe for you. Then I'll be back." The words nearly choked him.

How can you leave her here in the darkness? he asked himself.

I'm protecting her, he answered.

Don't leave her! his mind cried out. *How can you leave her? She's all that matters. This doesn't make sense.*

I'm not leaving her. I'm keeping her safe.

He forced himself to release her. Stepping back, he looked at Quin in the warm light of the lantern. Her dark hair hung around her lovely face, her dark eyes looked out at him without seeing.

"I'll come back for you, Quin," he whispered. "As soon as I can."

He meant it, didn't he? Didn't he? He couldn't imagine life without her.

He turned away from her and surveyed the piles of Seeker weapons all around him and the many pairs of Watchers lined up so neatly in a huge circle, barely visible at the edge of the lantern's light but there nevertheless, real and solid and ready to wake up.

All of this had been the Middle Dread's once.

Not anymore.

Who will survive?

Find out in the epic conclusion to the Seeker series. . . .

DISRUPTOR

Spring 2017

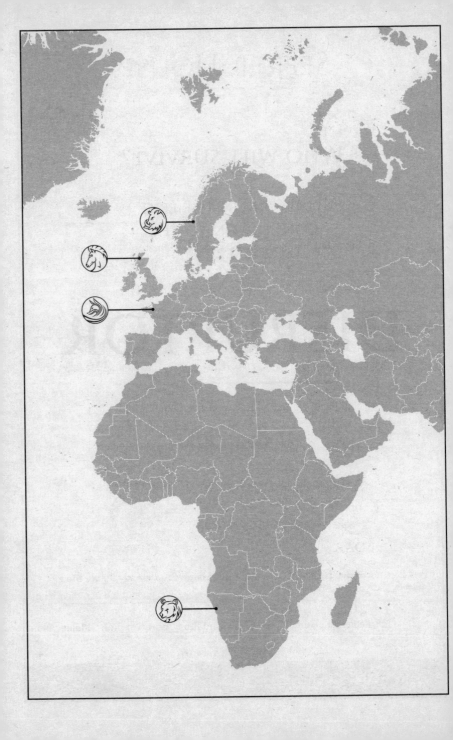

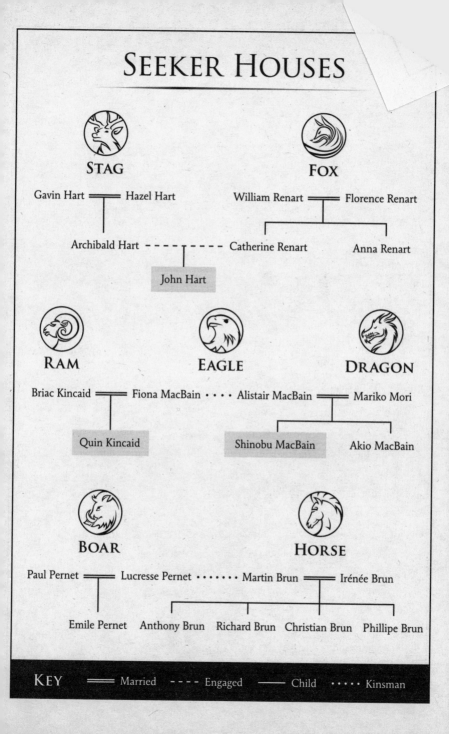

SEEKER HOUSES

STAG

Gavin Hart ═══ Hazel Hart

Archibald Hart - - - - - - - Catherine Renart

John Hart

FOX

William Renart ═══ Florence Renart

Anna Renart

RAM

EAGLE

DRAGON

Briac Kincaid ═══ Fiona MacBain • • • • Alistair MacBain ═══ Mariko Mori

Quin Kincaid

Shinobu MacBain   Akio MacBain

BOAR

HORSE

Paul Pernet ═══ Lucresse Pernet • • • • • • • Martin Brun ═══ Irénée Brun

Emile Pernet   Anthony Brun   Richard Brun   Christian Brun   Phillipe Brun

KEY ═══ Married - - - Engaged ─── Child • • • • Kinsman

ACKNOWLEDGMENTS

Krista Marino! Thank you for your love of this world and for throwing your heart into it alongside mine. I couldn't ask for a better editor. <3<3<3

Jodi Reamer! Thank you for being the most honest reader I've ever met, as well as the best agent in the universe (I checked). You call it gut instinct, I call it gut genius. Potato, potato. (Apparently this potato reference is a lot less effective in writing.)

Barbara Marcus, you inspire me. If I ever grow up, I'd like to be you, though I realize that may create some confusion. We can sort out the details later.

Beverly Horowitz, lioness, editor extraordinaire. Thank you for your encouragement and support for *Seeker* and *Traveler*.

Judith Haut, thank you for steering this series!

Also thanks to Alison Impey for the *stunning* cover, and to Stephanie Moss for the lovely interior design.

Thanks to Kathy Dunn and Dominique Cimina for shepherding *Seeker* and *Traveler* (and me) out into the land of readers.

Thank you, Felicia Frazier, for your huge vision and heart and rallying spirit.

Thank you to John Adamo, Kim Lauber, Stephanie O'Cain, and Rachel Feld for bringing *Seeker* and *Traveler* to the world cleverly and with so much care.

Tamar Schwartz, thank you for managing everything so ably, and thank you, Monica Jean, for all the big and small things you do every day.

Thank you to my copy editors, Bara MacNeill and Colleen Fellingham, for all the careful thought and for making everything clear.

Thanks to Sam Im for bringing this futuristic book series into the future.

Thanks to Sky Morfopoulos for being a great beta reader and an even better friend.

Thank you to my children, for occasionally visiting me from Mudgistan, Emerica, and Finn-Land.

And of course, thank you to Mrb. You know who you are.

ABOUT THE AUTHOR

Arwen Elys Dayton is the author of *Seeker* and *Traveler,* the first two books in the Seeker series, and the e-novella *The Young Dread.* She spends months doing research for her stories. Her explorations have taken her around the world to places like Egypt, Hong Kong, Scotland, and Iceland.

Arwen lives with her husband and their three children on the West Coast of the United States. You can visit her and learn more about the Seeker series at arwendayton.com and follow @arwenelysdatyon on Twitter and Instagram.

THE TRUTH WILL END THEM ALL

SEEKER

ARWEN ELYS DAYTON